EMBRACE INVERSE VIBRATIONS

A novel by Adam James Chouinard

For inquiries about ordering, licensing, publicity, or permissions please contact Proavia Press: PO Box 50663, Eugene, OR 97405

Paperback ISBN: 978-1-7351679-1-6 (ISBN-10: 1-7351679-1-6)

Hardback (978-1-7351679-4-7) | e-book (978-1-7351679-6-1)

Library of Congress Control Number: 2020910980

www.embrace-inverse-vibrations.com

www.proaviapress.com

Printed in the USA

For the Flora and Fauna...

...from Here to Nirvana

May We Give, as We've Been Given...

...and Embrace Inverse Vibrations

PROLOGUE / APOGEE

The light of the breaking day beamed through the cracks of an old and rustic cabin. It fell upon the unsuspecting eyes of a man trapped in slumber, the only part of him longing to see what the new day may bring. The sound of waves crashing on the shore filled his ears, beating the darkness like a drum. As he stuttered into awareness, a stranger awoke yet again into the morning, in his abode at the utmost edge of the world.

His feet touched down on the floorboards, which croaked beneath the weight of his body as he made his way to the door. With each rigid step, his soles fell into worn and faded grooves in the wood, carved by the relentless force of the same steps he took at the dawn of each passing day. The room itself was mundane, offering little more than the barest need: a shelter from an unknown storm. He stepped through the threshold into crisp morning air and took in what should have been reminiscent surroundings, if such a thought were even possible.

He looked first to the east to see the rising sun. There he beheld a bright and diverse array of colors too seldom considered, for he found not the beauty inherent within. With these unsung splendors came a warmth that struck his face, but even this brought little comfort.

There were no dwellings in this direction for as far as he could see, only rising hills capped by a dense thicket that shrouded and guarded the eastern horizon. Below the hills stretched vast fields of purple flowers, his only companions. He lived in total solitude, though he felt no longing for the company of other living things. In fact, he felt little of anything at all.

He cast his eyes next to the west, to the undulating waves of the Infinite Sea. A cool breeze washed over his body as it poured onto the land, stirring a vague impression which he had almost let vanish entirely. It felt as though a great pressure had been bearing down on him in the night – the suffocating sensation of something tremendously important, but which could not be remembered upon waking. The wind in this direction seemed to whisper hints his way, but he could not be drawn to inquire any further.

Stepping fully through the doorway, his feet fell again into the ruts of footsteps past. They led him down, toward the shore of the neighboring bay, and to a large rock that loomed over the water. Directly below it was a small, circular pool, isolated by a barrier of land. The outcropping stones reached just high enough to contain the water, and sever all ties with the ocean in which it long had resided.

The man stood upon the overhanging rock and looked out far across the sea. The sunrise behind him cast a long and lanky shadow below. This absence of light stretched as far as it could toward the glow of the western horizon, though it would never quite be able to reach. The surface of the water reflected the calm, cooling blue of a welcoming sky. Taken together, the beauty of the morning offered prospects and promise for the momentous change that even a single day may bear.

His attention turned, as it did each day at this time, to the contents of the pool itself. Within it swam a large fish, ensnared somehow against its will, sundered from its kindred spirits in the sea. How it had ended up all alone in so small a pool was yet another question the man could not think to consider; he felt only his own necessity at the sight of it. The fish moved slowly, as the building of a wave before breaking at the crest, circling in the motion of an endless figure-eight.

The fish turned gracefully in increasingly larger repeats of the same principal pattern, leaving a series of ripples in its wake. Each oscillated first upward, then downward, forming impermanent peaks and valleys. The individual waves would eventually reach the edges of the pool and fade into obscurity, but the pattern itself emanated ever outward from a single central point.

The cyclic motion of the fish enticed the man, lulling him into an unbreakable trance. In his daze, the sky slowly faded – from the hopeful blues of but a moment before, to a monochrome gray, bleak and impartial. In stark contrast, the fish below still shone with iridescent colors, a sole refuge for those of the sun in a world grown dull. And yet sadly, as before, there was little beauty of the sort that the man could comprehend.

When he stumbled somehow back into his wits, the sun was now far away in the west, beginning its steady descent to the edge of the sea. He shook off his muddled thoughts, turned to the side of the rock, and grasped a wooden spear left to rest there, like so many days before. With a brisk downward thrust and not a shred of hesitation, the spear pierced through the water and impaled the fish in its side. He pulled upward to lift his prey from the pool, slid it off the deadly point, and the world slipped into darkness. Whereas the sky before had merely dimmed, it sank now into a dreadful, blackened red, as the rusting of blood that's exposed to the air.

Jumping from the rock, the man hardly seemed to notice, and he carried on dispassionately in his invariable routine. His feet sank into another set of footsteps in the cold sand below; they led away from the rock, back up the gentle slope, and toward the patterns yet to come. The trail wound upward along the shore to the north, eventually arriving at an old fire pit on a high bank. There he again looked out over the waves toward the setting sun.

The fire in this pit burned so hot, and for so long, that the coals at its base never expired. The stones lining its edges were scarred with soot from an untold age of use. In the center was a single flat rock, as if it were a funeral pyre, surrounded by eternal flames. As the man laid the fish on the stone, bright flashes of flame exploded all around it. Grave shades of red and green danced with one another in an epic battle, until eventually only one shade remained, and the fire matched the tone of the sky.

As the man began to eat the fish, there were no savory sensations, nor any other pleasures he could notice. The only satisfaction it brought him was the satiation of a primal compulsion that awoke with him each dawn.

After the meal, he collected all that remained of the carcass and walked inland with his back to the sun. He made his way through the fields of purple flowers, whose petals bore the only other color amidst the red that engulfed all aspects of his world.

It took a long walk before he found the edge of a field where no flowers yet grew. He set his knees upon the ground and dug a small hole in the soil. He placed the remains of the fish in the bottom and poured the dirt back over top of the carcass. When the wound had been appeased, and the last grain of soil had come to a rest, the man rose from the ground and watched patiently. He knew of little else to do.

After a moment, a small shoot emerged from the mound at the edge of the fields. It reached up through the air and blossomed before his very eyes into an elegant purple flower, alike in every way to the innumerable others that shared its fate. This was but the latest testament to yet another passing day – the newest member of a seemingly ceaseless sea of petals behind him.

Turning back to the west, he followed the trail through the flowers and returned to his high seat by the fire. By now the sunset was well underway, and its lowest edge had just begun to touch the surface of the sea. The sun was not alone, for its reflection could be seen in the water, as bright as the star itself. After so long a time apart, both parties finally met, and the two hazy shapes began the inevitable process of melting into one.

For the moment, the two circles sat perfectly on top of one another. As the man rested, his pupils couldn't help but trace their edges in the same melodious pattern as the ever-encircling fish. They followed along the top of the sun's perimeter, and upon contact with its reflection, crossed over to trace the edges of the other side, only to come back around, cross over again, and arrive in the end at the beginning.

Before long, the sun had fallen lower still, and together with its reflection, it formed a perfect circle around the horizon. The clouds churned violently in the sky, ever-changing as they broke apart and formed anew. With each bit further that the sun sank beyond the edge of the sea, the squalls doubled in strength, until it was almost impossible for the man to stay firmly in one place. He fought with every effort to hang on to his ledge, diligently watching this drama unfold at the closing of the day. Still, the wind knows no mercy, and only continued to blow the clouds about more fiercely – forming, breaking, and forming anew – as if the movements from an entire age of the world had been condensed into the span of a single day.

So too did the fire beside him thrash more wildly as the sun continued to sink, growing bolder in response to the vicious winds. Though he could not turn away, the colors were blinding and agonizing, frightfully different from those which had struck his face that very morning. It would have seemed like a lifetime ago if he were only able to reflect upon it. As the rays burned sidelong through the atmosphere, they further strengthened its crimson hues – as if the colors were no longer of the sunset, but had been set loose to consume all of creation.

The earth began to quake; the sea began to boil. Soon, the very ground he stood upon was in peril of corroding, blowing away into dust, leaving behind only a memory for the peoples of another time and place to recall somehow if they could. Far away in the distance, beyond forest, canyon, and desert, over miles of ashen wasteland, the Great Volcano erupted, and the whole world was cast into flames.

Eventually, all that remained of the two sources of light was a single small circle surrounding the horizon, at the edge of the Endless Ocean. The tempest had built over the course of a long and exponential crescendo, but at last there was a momentary silence. As quickly as it began, the silence was shattered by a sweeping implosion. The fiery rays of the sky reeled backwards into the last meager remnants of the sun; and in an instant, they were gone. All that he saw vanished into the darkness of an all-encompassing black, and he knew nothing more.

Although his own pattern was longer and less symmetrical, his existence was equivalent to the cyclic motion of the fish he would hunt in the same place each day. While he moved forever onward, he never thought to ask why his footprints lay before him at every step along the way. In truth, he was not capable.

There, by the edge of a timeless sea, sat a man with no name, thoughts, or memories. His mind was a void, but for the most basal of instincts. He knew no notion of joy or sorrow, warm reminiscence or the cold grip of regret; he knew nothing of love, laughter, or wonder. For how many days he rose in the morning, he could not say, though rise he would. He would walk down to the sea, spear the ever-encircling fish, place it on the fire, and wane with the setting sun. So it was on this day, as every day before, he had lived to see the ending of a world he barely knew.

ONE

1.1 / Rude Awakenings

The light of the breaking day beamed through the cracks of an old and rustic cabin. It fell upon the unsuspecting eyes of a man trapped in slumber, the only part of him longing to see what the new day may bring. The sound of waves crashing on the shore filled his ears, beating the darkness like a drum. As he stuttered into awareness, a stranger awoke yet again into the morning, in his abode at the utmost edge of the world.

He placed his feet upon the floor and traversed the trail of faded footsteps to the door. His head turned first to the east to see the light of the newly born sun and feel its warmth upon his face. He cast his eyes next to the west, to the undulating waves of the Endless Ocean, and basked in the cool breeze pouring over the land. He walked down to the shore, climbed upon the overhanging rock, and peered into the pool below to find a radiant fish swimming the circles of an enthralling pattern. The fish moved slowly, as the building of a wave before breaking at the crest.

But on this day, like no other day before, the crest broke.

The fish turned about gracefully, in increasingly larger repeats of the same principal pattern. The circles grew grander with every pass the fish would make, its ripples emanating ever outward from a single central point. The man was caught in an inexplicable enchantment, and he stared deep into the heart of the pattern, astutely aware of every detail, while focusing on none in particular. The shape had always been enrapturing, but this time he couldn't break free of it. The sky lit up, like the simultaneous explosion of ten thousand distant suns, but his focus did not falter.

The pattern below continually grew, always expanding yet staying perfectly in place. His will to stand tall was rapidly diminishing. Soon he lost sight of the fish altogether, and his eyes remained fixed on the central point of the concentric rings. The shape now encapsulated his entire field of vision; everything else had been blinded by an incomprehensible light, and the man could see nothing but the outwardly streaming waves – an infinite repetition of an infinite symbol. His will failed him completely: he fell forward off the rock and plunged into the abyss.

The next thing he knew, the man awoke on the shore, soaking wet at the edge of a vast field of purple flowers, far away from any footprints he had ever left before. The noonday sun shone high overhead, directly above where he lay on his back in the gentle blanket of shoots and petals. In his pocket was a rolled piece of paper, perfectly dry.

He curled open the edges and read it as follows.

My dear friend,

I know it seems strange to awaken so strangely
I myself must admit, I was taken aback
I'm rather surprised to have found you so quickly
But found you I have in the waters so black

You wake in the morn like the birth of the sun
You act so alone, but it's all in your mind
You live and you breathe and you carry out cycles
You live on your own; is that all you can find?

You sleep dreamless eves in the darkness of night
You wake dreamless days in the darkness of light
I know who you are, though you think it arcane
I know where you've been and where our ending lies

Godspeed,

The Sentient Sage

For the first time in recollection, a spark of awareness was piqued by the odd and entirely novel notion of curiosity. It came like the germination of a seed that he didn't know had been planted. Neither was he aware of the meaning of these peculiar words, or the change they would bring to the monotony of his existence. All he knew was that, like the fish on the spear must be placed into the fire, so too must he follow these words to fulfill an unyielding need for something which he dare not question of yet.

With no direction leading home and no signs to guide his way, the first destination to which he arrived was a state of utter confusion. In defiance of habit, he looked first to the west. The sprawling field of petals rolled like the waves of the Endless Ocean beyond them, and he could not tell where one ended and the other began. The breeze carried tidings of change, and in its midst, he drew in a deep breath of cool air. With little effort on his part, the man felt a flicker of insight as he scoured the fluttering petals before him.

Each flower was a witness to insentient routine – each shoot, the fruit of a day's worth of need. Below him were the proofs of one life taken so another could live, as they sprouted anew from a fresh death each day. In seeing them there on this new morning's christening, he wondered how many days he had slept in a dark cloud of process and pattern. Like the dew from the flowers in the warmth of daylight, so too was the fog of oblivion burning off in the sun on the first day of growth.

The man turned from the scene slowly, for there was little more that the west could offer him as of now. After all, he had no boat; and even if he did, he dared not brave the Infinite Sea on his own. For now, his newfound curiosity drove his attention to the east. Whoever had left that note was presumably out there waiting, taunting him with answers to the myriad questions that were suddenly flooding his mind. As he turned to face the dense woodland growing high on the hills above him, a strange urge he had never encountered implored him to walk in that direction, to explore deep into the shadows that lay beneath the trees.

Making his way ever slowly upward through the rolling fields, he picked berries as he passed them and savored every flavor. *Delicious,* he thought. And only then did he notice that everything he experienced was recently bringing him so much enjoyment: the bright blue of the sky; the warmth all around him; the air in his lungs; the ground underfoot; the dull smell of grass. His senses were bombarded by a whirlwind of pleasures that he'd never have noticed on previous days. His thoughts flitted about from one joy to the next. *I've never known a more beautiful day.*

Just as he was about to be ensnared forever by the appeal of hedonistic delights, he felt the warmth on his skin start to dissipate. The breeze had now dithered; the ground had gone dark. He lifted his eyes to assess the cause of this change and saw that he'd arrived at the edge of the woods. The sunlight beamed over the dense evergreen canopy, illuminating the valley below, leaving a halo of gold above the tops of the ancient trees.

Where he currently stood, however, was immersed entirely in shadow. As he stared into an immeasurable black through the branches before him, he felt the first wave of yet another new emotion: Fear. His recent elation had fled like a flock of frightened birds, as he learned so early on that every emotion has its counterpart.

As his confidence wavered, he inspected the surroundings for any clues as to the ease of his passage, should he dare undertake it. And as he sought, so was an answer provided. Nearby he found a small opening in the brush to his right. The indications were subtle, but there was something unnatural about it, as if someone had cleared away the brush as an entrance. This forced him to deliberate on the concept of others inhabiting his realm for the first time in earnest. He had read the note, surely, but its implications were far from understood. Only now were they coming to the forefront, and the idea baffled him. *I am not alone,* he realized slowly. *I am not alone?*

From where he stood, however, on the brighter side of the trees, he saw the opening as a sign that at least someone had entered this uncharted land before him. Perhaps this was the path of the other whom he sought. Turning his head ever so slightly, he made one last westward glance from the corner of his eye. Far away in the distance was a tiny cabin on the shore by the bay, and he knew that somewhere down there were deep footprints engraved in the sand by long ages of toil.

It's either now or never. He turned back to the shadow and walked in through the gap, footprints be damned.

1.2 / The Branching Path

Under the canopy, the trees were even thicker than he'd anticipated. Little light made it down to the forest floor, but what little there was made it clear that it wouldn't be an easy journey. A small trail extended inward from the opening, but it was faint, winding, and otherwise difficult to follow. It meandered to and fro, and sometimes he despaired that he had lost it altogether. Far worse yet, the path diverged incessantly.

At first, the man stumbled blindly along, barely questioning the consequences of his decisions. When eventually he did consider them, every occasion to turn led him only to perplexity. Without even knowing the destination he desired, the endless possibilities unsettled him. He didn't know where both turns led, but it was safe to say someplace different. Finally, he succumbed to frustration, slowed his pace, and debated which path to pursue. So soon on his journey, he was tired of making choices — one of the many burdens of the role he now embodied.

If each path leads me to a different end, how do I know which one is best to follow? He didn't have an answer. To make matters worse, he knew that each branch in the path only led him to more branches, each of which led to branches of their own. *Choices upon choices: it goes on and on and on.* He put his hands on his head to subdue the growing ache. *If I can't see the end, how am I supposed to know which paths to take?*

His mind was engaged in a heated self-debate, pondering the unseen consequences of a will he barely knew. Countless voices lobbied him to take one or another of the many possible combinations. And yet, another part of him, somewhere deep beneath the din, didn't force itself to commit. Rather, it waited patiently in silence, staring at the fork in the road in an effortless contemplation. It was this part of him, the calm under the chaos, which first noticed the tree at the far side of the crossroads.

As he stood bewildered by his dualistic decisions, the limbs of the tree began to glow with a soft, but vibrant light. It traveled in pulses up the stem, from the base of the trunk to the tips of the leaves, illuminating the flow of transpiring water as it rose from the soil and returned to the atmosphere. At each node between branches, the lights broke apart, each eventually arriving to differing positions in their very own leaves.

But these all arrive at the same type of end, he protested. *I'm not so sure my own road will be so forgiving.* The shadows all around him were not far from his thoughts, and his mind raced away in panic at the sudden epiphany that his future was entirely uncertain. Cutting through the sounds of the forest, the voices grew louder. They shouted, chanted, taunted him, each refusing to let go of their compulsive observations.

One road leads to the saddest fate I could uncover
One road leads to the greatest dreams I could discover
How am I supposed to see beyond the branch in front of me?
How am I supposed to know which paths lead where I want to go?
How am I supposed to be the master of these countless voices?
I can't take them back, so what's the use in making choices?

Other troubling thoughts of the sort filled him with doubt, and he watched as the lights of the tree before him slowly started to fade. The voices, however, grew ever more adamant, convinced of their convictions, committed to seeing their desires actualized. They pushed and pulled on him, so many from so many directions that he could barely distinguish them. But every so often, one broke through.

"If I'd only turned left at the twenty-first curve!" shouted someone from over his right shoulder.

Circling nervously, he found that there was no one there. *I must have imagined it.* He wondered what his own voice might sound like, should he prove to ever have one.

"Try all you want, but you cannot rewind. Could all these decisions be breaking his mind?" The voice teased him again, this time from his left.

I'm exhausted, he confessed silently. *I need to rest and recover my sanity.* Still unsure of lefts and rights, he sat anxiously in the middle of the trail, his legs folded under him. He closed his eyes for a moment of peace, to drown the din with silence. But his mind would not be stilled so easily; the impression of his worldly surroundings receded, but the vision of the illuminated tree played over again in his memory.

When relaxing his eyes, the tree simply shimmered; but as he focused, he could trace the individual pulses, following branch after branch, until they sizzled away at the tips of the leaves. In replaying it again in reflection, he saw the process in a wholly new light.

The ends that they find might be final, and they certainly got there by picking a path; but they never had any choice in the matter of whether they would continue to rise. *So too for me*, he decided. There was no longer any sense in questioning whether or not he would carry on. He rose to his feet and followed the trail to the right.

His chosen path eventually descended into a deep ravine, where the little light that was present before would now have been a luxury. *And to think I found the dark foreboding when I first entered this place.* As if the gloom weren't enough, the underbrush had grown far thicker in this direction, which made it difficult to persist. More than once he considered turning around, but whether driven by pride or doubt, he could never quite concede to do so. Instead, he struggled onward, getting scraped, stung, and stabbed by the various obstacles in his way, the most imposing of which were a cruel breed of vines armed with long, sharp thorns. After a hard-fought distance on the trail, he noticed a most unexpected sight.

Pinned to a trunk at the side of the path was a small scrap of paper of a memorable hue. He plucked the paper from the tree. *That's called Instinct,* it read, *though you knew not you had it.* The note was composed in the very same script as the one he was currently carrying in his breast pocket.

Instinct alright! he protested. *I've barely begun and already picked the worst possible path.* He threw his hands down, despondent; the paper floated to the forest floor.

"Not the very worst," spoke the voice from behind.

He turned quickly and shouted aloud.

"Who's there?!"

To speak was a feeling he'd never yet felt, and his voice was not entirely as he expected – a little too similar to the one that had been haunting him.

His echo scattered off the surrounding vegetation and reverberated. It sounded like a chorus of terrified people, all slightly out of sync, alarmingly asking: "who's there?" Unlike most echoes, however, this one grew louder as it lingered, its tone more uneasy with each repetition. Now that the question had been spun back around on himself, much to his dismay, he could find no reply. He turned every which way in paranoia, his eyes jolting from one direction to the next. The darkness made panic a deadly endeavor. As he circled in this manic state, he stumbled backwards over a root but found no ground there to catch him.

From what little he could see in the darkness, the world was now spinning, tumbling downward. In one false step, he had entirely lost the control he so desperately desired. Release came only in a swift and painful crash into level ground at last. His arms and feet kept reeling, scrambling, not quite sure if he had stopped.

When the ground around him finally did stop spinning, he slowly climbed to his feet and swept away the dust from his clothes. The accusatory echo could still be heard faintly in the distance far above. Squinting his eyes at the soil below him, he surveyed for signs of the trail but found no such reprieve.

"All that fuss about which path to follow and now I've lost it altogether," he said softly, for fear of repeating such unfortunate luck.

Unsure why he'd never yet spoken, he supposed the thought had never entered his mind. Once it had, he found his own reassurances an odd comfort in such a dark and lonely place. Loneliness was another feeling of which he hadn't been formerly aware. But now that it sat like a weight in his chest, he was quite convinced that to live life without it wasn't such a bad thing.

Having reestablished equilibrium, he scanned his surroundings to decide yet again where he should turn. There was but one small clearing, barely visible through the brush, so he made his way there and sat upon a decaying log to regain his composure. The lingering tension slowly left his body with each passing breath, and at last a cool sense of calm replaced the warm ache of anxiety.

Though settling back toward normalcy, the weight in his chest that had so recently arrived was still stifling his hopes for complete peace of mind. As he contemplated this unexpected desire for companionship, he heard in the distance a dim crackle of fire. Upon further inspection, there appeared a soft glow through the foliage. Having mostly gathered his thoughts, and with no good ideas of what to do next, he had no choice but to investigate.

Parting the thick undergrowth, he made his way slowly toward the crackling in the distance. The sounds grew louder and clearer as he went, and so too did the soft glow become a bright beacon of light in the otherwise intimidating forest. Before long, the scrub began to thin, until it finally dissipated as the route cleared away into nothing but the trunks of tall trees.

Walking easily for the first time since he embarked on this path, he came to the edge of the tree line and looked out over a small sunken grove. There were woods on all sides of it, presumably for at least as many miles as he'd traveled so far. Looking up, however, there was a circle of dark sky overhead, full of bright little flickering lights, the likes of which he'd never observed. In the center of the grove burned a fire, though there was no one there to have started it.

The lonely man wandered down to the fire and took a seat on one of two boulders by its side. Though he'd sat by a fire every day, never until that very moment had he truly appreciated it in the profound manner he was now experiencing. He stared at it, mesmerized by its form: shapes within shapes, ever-changing though always the same.

While he sat looking intently at the flames, he reflected on what a tremendously different day this was, as compared to his customary routine.

What could have possibly caused all this to occur? he wondered.

Then he remembered at least part of the answer: the note. He pulled it from his pocket, uncurled the edges, and read through the cryptic message a second time.

"Nothing but a bunch of nonsense," he said, and tossed the paper into the fire.

To his great surprise, the lettering began to glow, shooting sharp beams of light up into the night sky. As the flames moved inward from the edges, soon there was nothing left but ashes and memories.

"I see you got my note," said a strange voice from the edge of the trees.

1.3 / The Sentient Sage

Such a surprise may have hitherto proven shocking to the man, but after all he'd experienced in these woods, he simply turned to address the stranger who had spoken. The figure moved slowly as it emerged from the shadows. When the chance finally came for a good inspection, the man was surprised to find that his visitor was no more than a small child. The boy continued down to the grove and sat by the man's side at the fire.

"You're the one who wrote the note?" said the man.

"Indeed I am," replied the stranger.

"So, you're the one who started me down this path?"

"Oh, no, don't be foolish," he laughed. "I couldn't take credit for that."

"But you wrote the note, I followed, and here I am."

"That's right..." said the boy with an air of insinuation. "You followed."

"Right: you wrote the note, and I followed it here."

"But who are You?" asked the boy.

"Who am I?" repeated the man, dodging the question.

"Who _are_ you? Yes."

"Well, I'm..." said the man, reaching for the words to respond.

"I – I'm..." He stuttered until it forced him to pause. _I don't know!_

The boy just looked at him patiently with a large and innocent smile, but the implication embarrassed and annoyed the man.

"Well who are _you_?" he asked in defense.

"Why, I am the one who wrote the note. I thought we made that clear."

"Yes, but who _are_ you?"

The boy raised his head to view the night sky.

"I am the Sentient Sage. I have thousands of names in as many languages, over as many ages of Time. Still, very few do me any more justice than that."

"The Sentient Sage? I was expecting someone a little ... older."

"I am as old as the stars that shine above us. In this form, I have walked these shores for an untold number of epochs."

These shores, thought the man to himself, grasping at the idea of space for the first time.

"Where are we?" he asked. "I've lived by the sea for as long as I can remember, but I've never thought to ask that until now."

"Well," said the boy, "I have to admit, my young lad, that despite all the eons I have spent in this place, I don't fully know the answer to that question. I suppose you'll need to be patient for that one. Perhaps we can find out together."

The man, now slightly dejected, was tempted to simply let it go at that and enjoy the rest of a lovely fire, even if under unusual circumstances.

Turning his head away from the conversation, he again began to stare intently into the rearranging flames, affording time for his mind to catch up. As of now, the fire was the only sense of normality he possessed. There had been quite enough commotion for one day, especially considering he was used to having none at all. He might have been content that his wishes were so quickly granted; after all, he was enjoying the company of another.

This is not quite the company I was hoping for.

Detecting a bit of his disappointment, the Sage attempted to lift the poor man's spirits and picked up with hardly a moment's hesitation.

"I can't say exactly where we are; all I know is that we <u>are</u>."

"We are?" repeated the man, obviously seeking clarification on this ambiguous use of a familiar word.

"Well of course we are!" scoffed the Sage innocently, as if it were a silly thing to even question.

"No, but I mean..." started the man. He paused for a minute, acclimating to this atypical conversation. "What do you mean: we <u>are</u>?"

"Well, of course, by that I mean: we're not not-being."

"We're not not-being?" asked the man, just as confused.

"Well of course we're not!"

"I don't understand," he said defiantly. "And to be perfectly honest, I don't think you do either. You're nothing but a mad child, probably just as lost and confused in these woods as I am."

The Sage responded in a patient tone.

"I may be lost, but I'm certainly not confused. You don't understand because you haven't realized that you are."

"Haven't realized that I am what? Confused?"

"Well you're certainly that!" laughed the Sage. "But no: you haven't realized that you <u>are</u>."

The man gave no reply, just a blank stare of bafflement and apathy. He was on the verge of giving up again. The Sage, however, was insistent.

"When I asked you who you are, you didn't have an answer. You are Someone after all, aren't you?"

"Well..." he stalled. *I've never really thought of it that way before.* The man paused to do so longer. "I'm not not-someone, I suppose."

"Then it sounds to me like you've got it all figured out," said the Sage.

"All figured out? I've never been so confused in my life!"

As a matter of fact, he'd never been much of anything as of yet.

"Let me try again," said the boy. "Do you see that frog over there by the edge of the grove?"

He pointed over his left shoulder as he inquired. The man hadn't seen it, but now that his attention was drawn to it, he wondered how the boy had without ever moving his head.

"If I were to take this stone in my hand, and throw it at that frog, do you suppose it would move from its path?"

"Yes?" he hesitated, as if knowing the answer but expecting a trick.

"Well, perhaps," cautioned the Sage. "Sometimes we can't always see these things coming. But suppose it did see it coming. In that case, you're absolutely right. The frog would simply extend its legs, leap through the air, and be safe from the blow. Now, do you think that you are like the frog, or like the rock that I flung through the air?"

"I don't tend to think I'm very much like either one," he answered.

One might have suspected the man was perhaps trying his hand for the first time at humor. After all, he should have inferred that he'd been the brunt of it a few times himself in this very conversation. The truth of the matter, however, is that he truly did not think himself at all like a frog, in any sense whatsoever.

"You couldn't possibly be more wrong," said the boy. "If I threw a rock at you, I am sure you would move." He paused, peering closer at the man. "Though, from the looks of the scrapes covering your face and arms, perhaps my assumption is not as warranted as I might have hoped."

As ever, he meant a great deal more than mere words might imply.

"Why are you asking me if I'm like a frog?" asked the man. His frustration ticked up another notch. "What's the point in all of this?"

"At the end of the day, when you would sit to look out at the sea, what did you see?" said the Sage. The man kept playing.

"A wide flat surface that reached as far as my sight."

"And would you say that it was singular or plural?"

"The sea? It's singular." *What a ridiculous question.* "You don't say: I looked out at the seas."

"I am not speaking of syntax, my friend," said the Sage. "It would not be so absurd if you knew what made the sea. If it was so unquestionably singular, why are you able to reach into it?" He patted the boulder where he sat. "Why isn't it firm like this?"

"I guess I've never really wondered that."

"But you do wonder now, don't you?" asked the Sage.

"I suppose," he answered meekly.

"Well then there you have it: you are."

"I am what? Wondering?"

"Well you're certainly that!" laughed the Sage again. "But no: you <u>are</u>."

Though progress had been slow, a concept which he still hadn't fully grasped was beginning to take hold in his thoughts. He turned away from the Sage and looked into the flames again.

It looks like I could reach into that as well. It must be plural. He hadn't realized it, but the boy had stood up beside him from his seat at the fire.

"You never did tell me your name," said the boy.

The man was again caught off guard by this inquisition and struggled to find the words to reply. The Sage hardly gave him a chance to respond.

"It's Davis," he said firmly.

Immediately following these words, the fire exploded from its center in a fierce outburst. The grove was engulfed in a circle of flames, and the young boy was nowhere to be found. Like before in the forest, the last words he heard echoed everywhere, growing louder each time.

"It's Davis," they said — over, and over again — in dozens of different, yet eerily recognizable voices. "Davis."

The voices brought with them yet more that he hadn't experienced, and which he could hardly describe if he tried. Out of the onslaught of surrounding flames leapt life-like images that consumed his whole view. At first, he tried to hide from them, but soon he found that he could not avert his attention. They lashed out at him quickly, one after another in a constant barrage on his every sense.

The frames changed rapidly, like the very flames that bore them, but contained within these moving snapshots were what must have been years' worth of love and hope, grief and despair. He spun ceaselessly, reaching out to grab them, but each time the flames shifted at the closing of his hand, and the images vanished.

First there came a motherly face, looking down from above, surrounded by the sides of a cradle. Her expression was joyful, so full of limitless love. Amid all this chaos, he somehow felt safe and serene in the strength of her presence, short-lived though it was.

The next thing he knew, he was riding on horseback, rolling over the grass of a freshly grazed meadow. He could feel the wind in his hair and trust in the reins. They spoke not the same language, but he knew somehow that they communicated deeply, in ways that escaped all rationality.

Then came the scene of two children at play. They frolicked peacefully on the grass of a large yard. A tall fence formed an edge in the distance, its whole length lined with lush fruit trees. A young boy was chasing a girl a few years his elder, though there was no sign of menace, just two children enjoying the freedom of youth. They both turned to look back at the man, bright smiles shining like the warm summer sun.

He was sobbing by now, though he didn't know why.

The scene quickly changed to the rolling of ceiling tiles, interrupted only by light fixtures flashing overhead as he passed down a hallway. He thought he could barely hear some of those same familiar voices. They cried out in anguish as they ran along behind, trying to follow him wherever he was going. They wanted only to be at his side as he passed down the length of the corridor, but they were silenced by solid white doors that slammed shut.

Last of all came the face of a beautiful woman. He knew her somehow, though he couldn't say why. Her eyes were full of patience and giving — unrelenting commitment. He wanted to stay in that image forever, but her face turned to ashes and fell to the earth.

As the last bit of ash landed gently on the dirt below, the enormous wall of fire enveloping him shrank downward, disappearing just as quickly as it formed. His legs gave out from under him, as though all the blood had been drained from his body. He sprawled on the ground in immeasurable pain, though he couldn't explain where these overwhelming feelings had come from. *I don't even know those people.*

Sobbing and hyperventilating at first, his breath very slowly returned, until he was subject to only the occasional stutter. Staring up from the ground, he could see the bright glow of the stars. He'd quite forgotten they existed beyond the far-reaching columns of flame. Completely exhausted, he raised his hands to wipe his eyes and then placed them on his chest. In doing so, he felt a bulge in the pocket on his breast.

He reached inside and pulled out a small piece of paper with the edges curled in. Unfurling the note, he witnessed a familiar script, spelling out two meager words.

You Are.

1.4 / The Lord of the Land

Confused, upset, and frightfully alone, he tried to make sense of all that had happened. The fire next to where he lay had extinguished completely at the close of the turmoil, leaving him basking only in starlight. As he bathed in their presence, he wondered what the Sage meant when he spoke of them. *As old as the stars.* He wondered what he meant about most things.

Though he couldn't understand him completely, somehow deep inside he believed that the boy spoke the truth. Why was he able to reach through the sea? Why couldn't he grasp the ever-changing flames? What was all that drivel about being or not? The unsettling conversation played relentlessly in his mind, but none of his deliberations brought him any further clarity. As he considered these and other questions, he drifted to sleep beside the smoldering bed of cinders, clutching to whatever warmth was left.

The morning sun was vivid and brought a new sense of life to the man who had not yet awoken. His awareness blossomed slowly into a startling vision: the snout of a frog rested no more than an inch from his nose as he opened his eyes. It inspected this unusual giant lying face down in the grass, and let out a skeptical croak. Before the strength to sit up had arrived, he reached out his hand to shoo the frog from his face, still insulted that the Sage should compare him to so primitive a creature. It hopped away to the edge of the grove and entered into the shadows cast by the towering trees.

As he followed the creature scurrying clumsily away, his focus thus fell on the woods once again. He'd almost forgotten they were out there, but he now unfortunately had no choice but to deal with them. The sun produced plenty of daylight in the clearing, but little broke through the impassable canopy. The dark of the woods was a force to be reckoned with – one he wished he could avoid.

Sitting up fully, he was bothered again by the strange end of the night. The Sage was nowhere to be found, but even more startling was the observation of a single stone at the edge of the fire ring. *Did I imagine the whole conversation?* That would certainly help to explain its outlandishness. He considered this option for several minutes but ultimately felt sure he wouldn't have hallucinated so long and involved an experience. Though unsure why, or whether to trust it completely, something in his gut was telling him that it happened.

Still, there were few other explanations. The boy was far too small to walk off with so large a stone, nor was there any plausible motive to do so. *Why would he come back to the grove just to move it?* Erring on the side of reason, he decided that he must have misremembered an extra stone being present. It was by far the most parsimonious explanation.

The Sage was no doubt the cause of great cognitive dissonance, and still the man couldn't help but feel a lingering affection for him through the shroud of annoyance. The boy surprised him with exciting new prospects, and while he didn't fully comprehend them, he knew somehow that they were important. Stumped once again with no obvious direction, he began to wonder what advice the all-knowing Sage would provide in his situation.

Probably something enigmatic and unintelligible. But what? *Trust your Instinct, he would probably say.* And at that, the man laughed aloud. *As if Instinct had gotten me anywhere useful so far.*

"Well what does my Instinct say to do next then?" He shouted aloud this time, finally attempting his first shot at humor. He raised his voice higher still, a defiant challenge to anything that could hear him. "Let's call on its ever-infallible judgement!"

As the words left his lips, the ground began to tremble, and the wind began to howl. With it came a chill that ran down the length of his spine. The trees creaked under duress, the growing storm attempting to blow them away. *Evidently this place doesn't appreciate sarcasm.* The treacherous vines encircling the grove began to encroach, reaching ever inward, rustling with spite as they closed in on top of him. The moaning of the trees grew; the sky was getting darker. The last pale gleams of light soon disappeared completely, and he felt himself moving, though he moved not a limb.

When at last he could see again, he was being thrust forward powerfully, spit out by the tangled mob. He sprawled out on the ground, face down, covered in wounds from the unforgiving thorns. As he lay on his chest, he saw before him the shape of two enormous feet, covered in thick black fur. He lifted his eyes slowly to see what kind of creature would wear such strange boots; when they had given him his answer, he shot back like a whip and clambered to his feet.

Before him was the form of a gigantic ape, sitting kinglike upon an enormous golden throne. Even from its seat, the ape towered over the man standing at full stature. Its arms were the size of his whole body, its chest like a wall that would yield to no man. Its teeth were like daggers, its eyes as dark as the depths of the abyss.

Though he dared not lose sight of the monster too long, he scanned the scene quickly for a means of escape. In the distance he saw the shape of another, perched in the shadows on the broken limb of a tree. From what little the man could decipher, it seemed like a bird. His best guess was some form of an eagle, though in the moment he supposed it didn't matter too greatly. He certainly didn't want to have to outpace it.

While the bird was a good distance away, the man could still tell that it was terribly large; it must have been at least as big as himself. There was very little detail which the man could discern in the quick glance he afforded himself, and its body was shrouded in darkness but for two glowing eyes. They scrutinized him intently, never breaking their stare.

The ape was gnawing on a bone, the femur of an unfortunate soul who came before him. Behind the throne was a pile of older bones, as high off the ground as the great brute itself. The ape now fixed its interest on this newfound intruder. The man braced for a flight. As its focus shifted, it tossed the large bone irreverently over its shoulder. It landed in the pile with a crash that shook the nerves of its guest.

"Who are you, I charge thee," interrogated the ape. "How dare you enter my domain?"

"I'm..." started the man. He'd been through this before. For some reason, he had the ephemeral thought that he might have a name. "I'm nothing but a lost soul, a stranger in this land. I meant no offense, your eminence."

The ape immediately saw through his pitiful attempt at flattery. There was no social game that one could employ to outsmart or out-savvy the Lord of the Land.

"I..." said the ape in a long, drawn-out manner as only the truly important can manage, "...am Regulus, the Great Ape. This is my kingdom and you are now my thrall, by way of my verdict. All of the land that you see is my birthright. All the many assets it bears are for me. The land is my servant and I am its Master. For your misdeeds in my realm, you will be justly rebuked; but not without due process."

The man was alarmed by its eloquence and dignity. For being so large and imposing as to never have to convince anyone of anything, it spoke with a tone of soothsaying persuasion. Here was an ape that fed poisonous lies through the guise of sweet medicine.

Without much in the way of a warning, the ape broke out into verse.

I pity you, stranger, for your stark lack of grace
Your wandering ways are the peak of disgrace
You have no real value, no pride in your face
The only real honor is in owning a place

I challenge ye: appeal for your own liberty
I would have you slaughter the mightiest tree
Or perhaps kill the beast that's a sad mockery
To my glorious fiefdom, the land of the free

It seemed to the man that the ape intended to continue in this vein, but the thought that arose within it was far too intriguing to mislay. The ape trailed off into a world of its own deliberations, before regaining its poise and engaging again in the conversation.

"Precisely," it said abruptly, as if confirming a thought that was not spoken aloud. "For your injustices, I condemn thee to perform an important service for the good of my land."

23

The man still wasn't exactly sure what his offenses were, though he didn't think that raising this point was going to get him anywhere worth going. He glanced at the pile of bones.

"The land of late has been plagued by the foulest of beasts. Its despicable ways are in opposition to everything that my good nation stands for. It must be stopped, and I would have you be the one to do it, as penance for your recent offenses.

"Travel due north until you come to a shining white rock that grows from the ground. There you will find the scourge of all things sacred, the blight upon my kingdom. You must slaughter it, and return to me with its heart. Then, and only then, will you be pardoned of your treason."

As problematic as this adventure already seemed, the man was still waiting for the catch. The ape continued.

"Before you embark on your righteous mission of redemption, you should know that strength alone cannot overpower this foe. No being can best it by force; you will need to use all of your wits and wile to succeed."

The ape rose and lumbered over to a large golden chest by the side of the throne. From behind the opened cover, it lifted out a dagger. The ape pulled the knife out from its sheath, rotated it slightly so that the blade glistened in the light, and thrust it back harshly into its cover.

"Take this," said Regulus. "It is the Blade of Entitlement. Use it to claim me my trophy when your deed has been done. If you can do this, your transgressions will be forgiven, and I will set you free upon the trail that you seek. If you fail, however, then your doom is full wrought, by the beast's hand or mine."

The man took the dagger into his grasp. He felt the cold touch of the handle in his palm, and could not help but think briefly of other options he might pursue. *No,* he thought, looking up again at the colossal ape looming over him. *It won't end well.* For all the things that he struggled with, when it came to self-preservation, he was a natural. *I must see to the task that I'm charged with.*

The north lay ahead if he wished still to live.

1.5 / The Man's Quest

Leaving the presence of the Great Ape, the man made his way north as instructed, in search of the white rock that extends from the ground. As he traveled along in the country of Regulus, he noticed that the land was far more barren than other places he'd been to date. The forest was dominated by only a handful of members, mostly the hideous vines he knew so well, or the same type of tree repeating seamlessly along, side by side for as far as his eyesight could tell. Every which way, the view was equally bleak. There was little undergrowth other than the thorns, no berries to eat as before. There were no flowers growing anywhere to be seen.

Funny the ape should be so proud of a land so desolate. Perhaps the application of its rule is not as keen as its tongue.

Looking back on his earlier travels, he hadn't appreciated how opulent the forest really was; he was so focused on surviving, on reaching any form of safety in his stupor of fear. Now that he had seen this lackluster land, he realized how diverse it all had been, how full of different forms of life. While he hadn't seen many creatures the previous days, he'd heard them all around, calling out in a wide assortment of sounds. At the time, he tried to ignore them out of apprehension, but now he again longed for the company of life. For here the air was empty; there were no sounds to be heard but the crunching of a carpet of dead leaves as he stepped diligently along.

After a long time traveling through the mundane domain of Regulus the Great, he noticed here and there the hint of a burgeoning flower. Soon the small shoots could be seen all around him, and he picked up the pace in his excitement. There were no blossoms yet, but he could tell that new life was starting to spread into the tedious land through which he'd traveled.

As he made his way further, the green shoots slowly overcame the carpet of dead leaves, growing taller on average with every step he took. Eventually, when the height of the shoots had reached his knees, he stepped out into a lush field of fully bloomed flowers. All were slightly different, with their own unique designs; and each shone alone, with its own unique colors. But together, they radiated a comprehensive glow of pure white – a luminous beacon of hope. His body was once again overcome with total delight, as before when he first left the routine of his home. Every way that he turned was full of dazzling light and marvelous colors.

So this is the blight to the land, as perceived by the ape.

In a short while, the man could see a small glade up ahead where the canopy ended, and he raced forward at full speed. He would not have thought it possible, but the glow from the flowers grew even brighter in the unobstructed sunlight. Down in the center of the dell was a spring that nourished the land from its bounty. The spring fed into a large pool, and at the water's edge rose a single white rock, like a pyramid erected by ancient forces and unstable ground. The man could again hear the sounds of dozens of animals dispersed through the trees surrounding the glade.

He took a moment to cherish the beauty of the scenery, and only then did he notice it: down by the spring existed a magnificent creature. *How could I not have seen this at first?* It stood on four legs, and had long, flowing, silken hair of silver. Its long neck extended down to the grass at the edge of the pool where it grazed leisurely in peace.

He attempted to categorize it, to quantify its majesty in some way, but the effort was futile. In looking upon this unsuspecting animal, he was overcome by a suite of different thoughts. He vacillated between extremes, his conscience torn in two drastically different directions. Amazement was countered by an inexplicable fear; admiration was undercut by unbearable envy. *It's the most beautiful creature I've ever envisioned.* And shortly thereafter: *now is my chance to prove what I'm worth.*

Eventually, a third thought overtook both of the former, as he contemplated fight or flight. The sight of the huge pile of bones from the victims who'd presumably chosen to cross the Great Ape now appeared again in his mind, as did the ominous words it had spoken to the man as he left on his hunt. The warning resounded in his head in the deep voice of the brute: *by the beast's hand or mine.*

It was not fear alone, however, that drove him to settle on what he eventually decided. As beautiful as he acknowledged that the creature was, it stood on four legs and it fed in the grass. It couldn't possibly grasp the full weight of his mission, or appreciate the needs of a man such as himself. The man had no love for the ape; but whether he knew it or not, his instincts were guiding his choices now in full. *Is this what the Sage had in mind?*

The man stepped now from the shade of the trees into the grass of the clearing, the Blade of Entitlement strapped firmly to his waist. Approaching ever so slowly, he placed his feet softly at the start of each step. The beast appeared to take no notice of his advancement; its head stayed fixed in the grass where it grazed, its ears never turning to the sound of the man. Without warning he heard a voice, soothing and earnest, coming from no clear direction at all.

"It is difficult to know where we should turn, when the path of our life has encountered a split."

The man was stopped dead in his tracks. The beast had not turned even so much as its head. It kept grazing in the opposite direction, though the man somehow knew that it spoke to him.

"How did you know I was here?" he asked.

"Why, I could feel you walking on top of me."

The concept was laughable. Here, he'd encountered yet another incomprehensible lunatic.

"Don't be absurd," he retorted. "You've got excellent ears."

The beast didn't move; its ears still faced away. It answered thereafter with a puzzling song:

> *I have ears; I have eyes; I have more things besides*
> *I have deep roots, tall trunks, and a heart to forgive*
> *I have shade for the weary and food for the weak*
> *I have small shoots, and petals, and water within*
>
> *I have feet on the ground; I have wings in the sky*
> *I have leaves that indulge in the rays of the sun*
> *I have beauty in things you would never suspect*
> *I have fruits from the vine of more flavors than one*

The man stood motionless. Though he again did not understand the full mystery of these words, he was at least able to contrast them to the views of the ape. He was beginning to see why the Lord of the Land so hated the beast that stood before him.

"What is your name, my child?" asked the voice.

Without even a moment of hesitation, the man answered freely.

"It's Davis."

The words seemed to come from something other than himself.

"And how did you come to be here, Davis?"

"I ... don't know," he responded. "I can't say I know where here is."

"And yet, you have decided what it is that should happen here. You have chosen a path without seeing its end."

The words struck the man abruptly, resonating with the deep-seated discord in his subconscious mind about where he must go and what he must do. The voice of the beast continued in his head.

"But such is the plight of a man of your standing, though woeful it is you must flounder so far."

Again, the words weighed more than mere discourse. They implied a great impression of inferiority, and the man didn't take kindly to having the burden of judgement turned upon him. He was a man, sure enough, but this was a Beast here before him. What could it claim to know about the choices of Man? He was beginning to think the Great Ape might be right.

"The one who sent you here has polluted your thoughts," it continued, as if knowing the self-fulfilling trajectory the man's mind was following. "It claims to be the supreme ruler of all, though it has only just arrived here, and it knows not the Way. Its true name is Myops, though I doubt it would admit it. I gather it goes by a new name of late."

By now the creature had turned from its grazing and started approaching the man where he stood, lifeless and unsure of what would befall him. Only as he caught sight of its eyes was the man starting to understand that this beast may be more than he was suited to trifle with.

"Who are you?" he asked out loud, clearly nervous.

27

"I have several names, few of which would you understand. I am Custos, overseer of Amadea; I am Vilicus, Praestes, and Ostiarius; I am Coerator, Satelles, and Claustritumus."

It lifted its gentle eyes, wishing that the man would recognize even one of these names, but with little hope that he was in fact capable of doing so. After pausing to allow for a reply that never came, the beast started again.

"I see now that you must finish what you have come here to do. Before I will allow it, I would say but a few words to help prepare your troubled mind for the journey yet to come."

The man was curious what made it decide to cooperate with his quest so suddenly, but he was pleased nonetheless with his own apparent prowess. He reveled in his impending glory as the beast carried on.

"Though the allure of self-serving solutions may seem to benefit you at no cost, the poison you sow may be slow to be reaped. Real meaning comes from being a small, yet integral part of something bigger than You. What is good for the whole will aid all of its parts." *This, my poor man, is the Way.*

With that, the beast turned slowly away. Its words had fallen on deaf ears. It withdrew from the spring and lay down in a circle of small but vivid purple flowers. Their appearance sparked a dull reminiscence of his home by the sea where he grew one each day. At that moment in the glade, he realized that he hadn't bothered to question why the fish never moved, or ever put up a struggle. Seeing that the beast was not of the temperament to fight, the man approached it where it lay on the ground. It looked longingly at him one last time and silently shared its parting words.

You too know the meaning of sacrifice.
You have proven it once and shall prove it again.

It turned its head away and rested it upon the ground. The man grabbed by the hair, lifted it again to expose the beast's neck, and pulled the dagger from the sheath on his side. The Blade of Entitlement was as sharp as any razor, and it cut effortlessly through the thick hide of the throat. The man let go of the head and it fell to the earth with a thud. Viscous waves of blood were now spilling over the grass in the middle of the circle of flowers. The beast had been slain, and the Great Ape appeased.

The man rolled the corpse over to claim the trophy demanded of him. In the center of its chest was a small region of very short hair in the shape of an oval, in precisely the spot where he needed to make an incision. The blade dove deep into the torso, piercing through the bones with ease, and sliced along in the outline of the shape.

He pulled the heart from its chest and left an ill-fated hollow.

Looking up for the first time since focusing on his task, he discovered that all the beauty in the glade had disappeared. Spinning, he found that everything surrounding him had reverted to the same uniformity through which he had walked from the throne of the ape.

The flowers were now dead and wilted. There were no songs from any animals dispersed in the trees. The heavenly colors were replaced by only thin shades of gray. The spring was now dry, no more than a flat basin of dust. The rock by its side had turned the deepest shade of black.

It took but a single moment.

Only now did he begin to remotely understand the consequences of his actions. All the joy that the glade provided had withered away with the rest of its life. He wished that it needn't have ended this way, but even the beast evidently saw no choice in the matter. The man stared for a long while in disbelief, until finally consoling himself with what little solace he had.

"What's done is done," he said softly.

It was time to return and surrender his prize.

As he left the glade and entered the wood, he saw a small note pinned to the trunk of the very first tree. It was the same type of tree that filled all the ape's land, which stretched boundlessly now that the glade had been cleansed. The note was of a familiar make, though as he unfolded it, he witnessed an unfamiliar script.

Davis,

> *I see wisdom behind your eyes, though you know not it is sleeping. When it awakens fully within you, you may find me at Immolatio.*

Custos

On the outskirts of the glade, which at this point may as well have been a mirage, the man had great difficulty deciphering exactly for whom the note was intended. The name at the top sounded vaguely recognizable, but he wasn't quite sure if he knew who it was. He eventually settled on the idea that the note must be for him, though he was still uneasy being called by this name. He folded the note hurriedly and placed it in his pocket.

1.6 / The Heart of Custos

As dismal as the woods had appeared as he traveled north a short time prior, he found them to have deteriorated even further as he returned to the south with the Heart of Custos in his hand. His legs marched on, though sorely tired from all the walking he had done. At this point, the only reward he was truly hoping for was simply to rest and have nowhere else to travel. *What good would being placed on the trail I've lost even serve me?* After all, he had nowhere to go, nothing to do, and no one waiting for him anywhere in the world.

After walking on in this way for a time, the silence of the barren land was shattered by a tremendous shuddering of wings. The waves from their beating could be felt in the air around him. The man looked everywhere for the cause of the disturbance, and as he turned his back to his current direction, he spotted a large bird sitting high in a tree. He felt sure it had not been there just a moment before. As he stared at it, the bird flapped its huge wings a second time.

Astonishingly, instead of launching into flight as the man expected, the shape of the bird vanished completely in a quivering flash. His eyes scanned all directions again, searching for the place where the bird may have gone. Without a great deal of effort, he found it again, on a branch behind him this time, a good distance closer than it was only an instant before. The man stood perfectly still, unsure as to what this ominous meeting might bring him.

When hardly a few seconds had passed, it flapped its wings yet again and was gone. His head reeled around to each bearing but could find no trace of the bird this time. Just as he was about to give up in his searching, he turned back to his original direction, only to leap back in alarm with a loud and startled shout. The bird was sitting on a dead stump, just a few feet behind him as he turned around. It barely gave him a moment to catch his breath.

"I am here to ensure that you are worthy of the trust that my good Lord has bestowed upon you," said the creature. "I can see by your bounty that it was not misplaced."

Now that the bird was perched right before him, the man could definitively see that it was about his equal in height. Its wingspan, however, would have spread well over two of his lengths; its talons were sharp, and the size of the man's head. The bird could detect that he was shocked at its presence, and it backpedaled a bit to calm the man down.

"But forgive me in my haste. Often, I find I'm so focused on a task that I think not for courtesies. Allow me to introduce myself. I am Errol the Wary, Chief Vassal to Regulus, the Great Ape of Justice and Lord of the Land."

The bird paused to wait for his reply, but none came. His focus stayed fixed on each movement of the bird. Seeing that the man had no intention to respond, it continued.

"I followed your progress as you set out from the throne, though I doubt you have seen me until this very meeting." Of that, it was certainly correct. "You have done a great service to all of the Land. The beast has been slain, and its pestilence cleansed. Your heart should be proud, for you have conquered the unconquerable."

The man found this last use of words distasteful, as he held the heart of the beast in his hand. Still he spoke no word. As much as he feared the ape, he distrusted the eagle yet more.

"Well then," said the eagle skeptically, as if detecting this unspoken suspicion. "I will return to my Lord and tell him of your conquest. Regulus will be much pleased at the news of it. Good day."

At that, it flapped its huge wings and disappeared into nothing.

After a long and onerous walk to the south, the man was within a shout's distance to the throne. The time had now come for him to surrender the heart as a token of freedom, but the thought of it weighed heavily on his conscience. After everything he'd seen, he wasn't sure that he wanted the ape to have it.

Remorse had now joined the growing list of his emotions.

He combed his mind for all the possible options, though none seemed like they would play out to his favor. His feet had kept moving as he envisioned these various scenarios, and shortly he found that he'd run out of time. The ape could be seen by its throne up ahead, giddy with excitement as the man came to meet it.

"Welcome, welcome!" said the ape with glee. "Come, tell your tale!"

It could hardly contain itself. Without saying a word, the man approached the throne, fell to one knee, and held the heart out in front of him. It was not out of respect for the Great Ape, however, that the man had kneeled to the ground. The weight of his conscience had grown insufferable; it dragged him to the earth as he forfeited the Heart of Custos.

The ape reached out and seized the heart from his hand. It lifted it on high, spun around in an ecstatic daze, and began to dance wildly. When it was finally able to contain its excitement, it turned back to the man. He was still kneeling, his head bowed low.

"Rise, rise, proud Knight of Regulus," said the ape. Evidently it had knighted him in its head as it spun. "For your great service to my kingdom, I offer you the chance of a lifetime."

The man didn't know what to expect, though he suspected it was not an honor he wanted.

"You are to be my second in command, Chief Vassal to Regulus the Great Ape of Valor, Conqueror of Beasts, and Lord of the Land."

Apparently it had claimed more than a small part of the courage involved in fulfilling the deed.

"Our reign would be resplendent, our dominion unchallenged; we could own all the land for as far as we could walk in a lifetime. They will sing of our greatness for ages to come!"

The ape appeared to have entered a daydream full of its own glory. It would have continued, but for an interruption.

"Your eminence," replied the man, who had now risen from the ground. "You flatter me with your generosity."

On their last visit, the ape could not be fooled by fair words of this sort, but it was so enamored with joy and respect for its knight that it saw them instead as the words of a true servant. The man continued without pause.

"Even so, I cannot accept what you so graciously offer. My purpose lies farther ahead down the road." He did not know how truthfully he spoke.

The ape was offended by this, but its mood was too pleased to be insulted too greatly. Moreover, the visions of its daydream did not go away; they simply blurred out the part about needing a Vassal at all. Its supreme rule over all would be achieved with the aid of no one; there would be no others with whom it would have to share fame. As these delusions of grandeur continued to unfold in its mind, it fixed its attention on the heart in its hand. It was the doorway to everything splendid to come. Raising the Heart of Custos to its mouth, it took a large bite with its massive teeth.

As the Great Ape finished devouring the heart, it resumed its wild dancing while marching in circles, as if simultaneously creating and watching its very own parade. With each step it took, however, the ape shrank smaller, thinner, weaker. Every step became shorter as the length of its limbs decreased. It looked less and less human with each passing moment. *The ape is devolving right before my very eyes.*

As the man looked on, the words of the beast echoed again in his head. *The poison you sow may be slow to be reaped.* Their meaning, at first so misunderstood, was becoming clearer, though he was still far from knowing their deepest significance.

In seeing this, a confidence stirred within him that he'd not yet experienced. As the ape grew ever smaller, so too was the man emboldened to speak ever more truthfully. The remorse that he felt had bolstered his conviction. It still wasn't wise, but something was roused within him, and he felt a self-assurance come to his voice and his deeds. Regulus the Great was now a foot or so shorter than the man himself, and it continued to shrink at the same steady pace.

"You know," said the man, "before the beast died, it told me your name." The ape barely even heard him, continuing to march around in its self-satisfied way. "Tell me, Myops: why the need for the change?"

With that, the celebratory procession came to an abrupt end. The ape, now little more than a monkey, turned to the man in a furious rage. It shrieked a horrible shriek and beat the ground with all four limbs.

It never intended to hear its true name again.

The monkey charged at this intrusive man who dared challenge its authority, a man who by now had pulled the blade resting on his hip. He prepared himself to use the dagger for a second deadly deed, but he never got the chance.

The eagle had been sitting by, though not idle in thought. Its integrity had been sullied by the offer to the man, and the demotion did not sit well with its pride. It stewed in resentment from where it lurked in the branches but was quick to recognize a long-sought opportunity when it finally came.

As the monkey first started to rush at the man, the eagle swooped down from its perch, grasped it with its enormous talons, and slammed its body forcefully to the ground. One set of claws pierced the torso and held the squirming monkey in place; the other ripped off an arm of the prey as it wrestled in vain. The large powerful beak of the bird lashed downward like a bolt of lightning, delivering the final fatal strike to the monkey's neck. The lifeless body lay in the dirt, foiled by its own game of treachery, greed, and the lusting of power.

The eagle rose from its victim, with no intention to eat its prey. After all, it was no savage; in fact, it was the new, and self-proclaimed, Lord of the Land. It turned to the man, who was still very much braced for a fight.

"For your service, young Knight, you are to be my second in command: Chief Vassal of..." – the bird paused briefly – "...Nobilis the Righteous, Prodigious Bird of Prey and Lord of the Land."

The man bowed slowly, but returned the same reply he had for the bird's predecessor.

"You flatter me, highness, with your generous offer, but my purpose lies elsewhere, farther ahead down the road."

The eagle bowed in return. Its transition from terrifying predator to dignified nobility was unsettling to the man. He imagined that the line between the two was not thick.

"Then you may leave as you came," said the bird. "You will find the trail you seek farther still to the south. I bid you adieu and wish you good luck in your travels."

The man wasn't sure the bird meant it, or that he wanted its blessing, but to be rid of it for now was an ease to his nerves. He bowed one last time to ensure his safe passage, turned to the south, and started to walk.

1.7 / The Stranger

The man's feet carried him tirelessly on a course for the south. *If I could only find the trail, perhaps I could make my way back to the grove.* There were so many things he wanted to ask the Sentient Sage after so much had happened. At this early stage, he was still in the mindset to look backwards for answers to things yet to come.

The landscape at first was as bleak as before, coated in the curtain of gray that had first set in after the beast had been slaughtered. Eventually, however, the canopy overhead began to thicken, and the lush forest he'd remembered slowly started to make itself known once again. By now, the sun had long since gone down and the woods were so dark that it was again difficult to make progress. Even so, he suspected that the colors in this region would surely creep in come morning. *At last, I'm leaving the domain of Errol the Wary.* He had yet to adjust to the bird's newly christened name, and it would not have been happy to hear of this unintentional insolence.

Naively suspecting it to be a simple matter of ecology, the man rather preferred this section of woods. The thorns weren't as dense, and he no longer had to struggle with the start of each step. The berries were again present, though in the shadows he could only catch sight of them if they passed particularly close to his face. They tasted magnificent and satiated the pains that had grown in his stomach. They gave him new strength, which he would need at its fullest if he hoped to endure the perils of the following day.

After trudging along with no more guidance than a best guess at his original bearing, he finally came to what looked like the edge of a trail. The trees overhead had recently thinned, just enough that a small hint of starlight flitted down to the forest floor. In this dim light, much to his surprise, he found a man beside the trail with a very small fire. Upon first sight, he called out to the stranger, but they made no response. He went to greet the man and investigate the situation further.

"Hello, I'm Davis," he said naturally, unaware of his words.
The stranger again made no reply. *He must not have heard me.*
Davis moved even closer and examined what the man was doing. The thinning of the trees had evidently allowed enough light to reach the forest floor to afford a small bed of flowers at the side of the trail. The stranger was walking back and forth between the fire and the flowers. As he reached the flowers, he would bend down, pluck one from the soil, stand up, and turn around; he would then walk back to the fire, throw the flower in its center, and turn around to do it all again. The man repeated this cycle — over, and over again — every motion performed with robotic precision.

Davis could not help but focus on the fire. When a flower struck the flames, it burst out in a painful display. It curled and wilted, writhing in the heat of the blaze, hissing as the water left its crumbling body. It was equally distressing to him each time it occurred.

What's the point of this? He tried again to get the stranger's attention.

"Hello? Can you hear me?" he asked loudly, waving his hand in front of the stranger's eyes as they turned for another approach to the flowers. "Hello? Are you in there?" The stranger's silence only made him angrier. "Stop it," he shouted. "Stop! What are you doing this for?"

There was never an answer. *He's trapped in his own world.*

Ignoring Davis entirely, the stranger walked again to the flowers, bent to the ground, and plucked another from the soil. This time, Davis kept his eyes on the earth. Each time the stranger removed a flower, another shoot would take its place and quickly blossom. He had been so focused on the destructive force of the fire that he failed to notice: despite the insistent depletion at the hands of this human, the flowerbed never diminished.

Davis tried several more times to communicate with the stranger, but they could neither see nor hear him. Moving past anger, he grew increasingly saddened by the impassive routine of this stranger on the side of the trail. It was such a waste of time, flowers, and the heat of a fire.

Eventually, he gave up on his attempts to break through to the stranger. Turning away, he started down the trail and left them to their meaningless madness.

"The poor lost soul," said Davis. "He doesn't even know that he is."

He glanced over his shoulder one last time; the stranger slowly faded in the haze and passed out of sight. Davis looked back in pity, shrugged his shoulders, and continued down the path into the darkness ahead.

TWO

2.1 / Welcome to Inanimis

Davis awoke in a soft bed of moss by the side of the trail, unsure of how long he'd slept, or how long he'd walked after last night's encounter with the insensate stranger. He rose from the ground refreshed, brushed the dirt and remnants of plant matter from his clothing, and started again down the path to an uncertain destination. His mind was still focused on a single goal: *I must find the Sage.* He couldn't say where the thought had come from but was confident that it meant he was to find the grove once again.

Upon the long miles that he traveled that morning, he had plenty of time to deliberate over what he would ask the sagacious young boy. Countless questions plagued his mind, and he was sure the Sage would have an answer or two; that is, if he could comprehend them. He had no way of knowing, but his hopes were futile. He would never see the boy again.

He tried to recall the note he'd been left, for it might have held a hint about what he should do, now that he inhabited a different state of mind. *What did it say?* Most of the words were lost forever, but one sentence frequented his thoughts over the last few days: *I know where you've been and where our ending lies.* He chastised himself again for burning the note in his fit of frustration, yelling aloud as he traipsed along on his route.

"Two of the most pressing questions I have, and he outright told me that he knew the answers!" *How could I have been so foolish? Why do I always act before thinking?* He took a deep breath and exhaled a long sigh. *My only hope is to find the boy again and ask humbly for his help, now that I've got a better grip.* It wasn't a good one, but it was the only plan he had.

Many hours of trail passed by underfoot, and though his thoughts were running in circles, his feet led ever onward in a mostly straight line. His eyes were upon the ground as he marched, and eventually they noticed the dusty, irregular soil of the trail transition into the predictable uniformity of concrete. Lifting his view, he saw the path unravel into numerous parallel lanes only a few yards in front of him.

The sides were lined with shoulder-high barriers, to stop anyone from crossing over between rows. At the edges of the outermost lanes rose a high wall; its top towered above even the tallest trees, and its sides stretched in both directions for as far as he could see. In the center of the lanes, far in the distance, was a single opening in the wall. Aside from turning around, Davis would have no choice but to choose a line.

Ahead of him in the various rows were dozens of people, forming lines of different lengths in the separate divisions of the trail. Everyone was dressed in the same style and shade of clothing, and though he found this a bit odd, his spirits were lifted by the prospect of meeting new people.

Scanning to assess the least populated line, he finally chose one near the center. *I don't know what I'm waiting for, but the shorter the wait, the better.* As he reached the end of the line, he tried to engage the woman in front of him in conversation.

"Hello, I'm Davis," he said, sounding rather proud of himself to have discovered this much. "What's your name?"

The woman turned to him with a scowl and looked around suspiciously, as if she had something to hide. Davis checked to see if the people in the other lanes were equally reticent. They were. It seemed as though everyone but him knew better than to speak while in line. Having seen that the coast was clear, the woman glanced back at him a second time.

"I'm Tacey," she answered with a barely audible whisper. Taking the series of hints, Davis too began to whisper.

"Who are you?" he asked. "What are you doing here?"

"We're waiting our turn," she answered and promptly turned forward.

"Waiting for your turn to do what?" he asked again, a little louder.

There was no reply. Davis asked her again, followed by another question or two of a different sort, but all to no avail. The woman made it clear that she was done with the conversation. She would not risk being thrown out of line, having waited so long.

The line stepped forward a few paces, though he was still far from the front of it. He gave up on trying to pass his time pleasantly and hung his head. The concrete below was marked with yellow arrowheads aimed in the direction of travel. He wondered why they needed signs for such an obvious thing, obviously not considering the possibility of someone attempting to go the wrong direction in his lane. There could be no such discord in a place of this sort, a place so proud of its orderliness.

After a tiring and tedious wait, Davis finally made his way to the front of the line. Beyond each lane, in the side of the wall, was a window covered in a thick but translucent plastic. Above each window was a large black sign with plain white lettering that spelled a different word for each station. Davis turned to the window immediately in front of him.

"Registrar," the sign read.

By what seemed purely an accident, he'd managed to enter the line that was adjacent to the only entrance through the wall. The opening was guarded by an iron gate, itself guarded by a tall, fat man, in a too-small dark, blue suit. There was a long black baton hanging from his belt on one side; a strange, snake-like metallic device hung from the other. Davis squinted for a better view of the object, but his focus was shattered by an earsplitting scream from the window in front of him.

"NEXT!"

He jolted from the shock and stumbled awkwardly to the window.

"Welcome to the Registrar," said the man behind the plastic in an indolent monotone. "Identification please."

There was no emotion whatsoever in his voice, just an homage to the illusion of courtesy he was obliged to uphold.

Davis looked down at the base of the window to see a small gap through which items could be passed. He patted down the pockets on each of the articles of his clothing, in a feigned attempt at looking for whatever it was he was supposed to present through the slit. When his empty gesture failed to yield what it was that he needed, he shrugged to the Registrar and faked a timid smile.

"Oh boy," said the man in the booth. He turned his head over his shoulder and shouted back to the horde of important-looking people pacing behind the window clerks. "Got a Non-ID here!"

A large, intimidating woman in a darker uniform came over to his window. Leaning over the Registrar, she forcefully marked a small book to his right with a bright orange stamp. The Registrar looked back at Davis.

"Wait just a moment. I need a different set of forms."

Reaching under his desk, he lifted out an enormous stack of papers that were bound on the left-hand side. Davis cringed at the thought of wading through it all.

"Whoops," said the man in the booth, "wrong forms."

He placed the erroneous stack back under the desk and fished around for a while in search of the appropriate one. *At least it wasn't those forms,* thought Davis. At that very moment, the Registrar produced an even bigger stack of papers, twice the size of the original, and slammed it on the desk.

"There we are," he said in a satisfied manner. Though less adept with people, this man clearly loved his forms. He flipped open the first page and looked back at Davis. "Name?" asked the Registrar.

"It's Davis." A tingle of déjà vu overpowered his every sense.

"Date of birth?"

"Well..." said Davis, trying to buy time. "I don't exactly know."

"You don't know?" asked the Registrar, insulted by the possibility. His eyebrows angled down to a dubious point. "What's your number?"

"My number?" asked Davis, yet again in need of clarification.

"Your identification number..." said the Registrar, trying to jog his memory but seeming to know full well where this was headed.

"I'm sorry," said Davis. "I just don't know."

"Oh boy," whimpered the Registrar again. "Got a Non-Classified here!"

He shouted over his shoulder, the slightest hint of panic hiding ever so subtly beneath the calm, composed surface of the man in the booth. They were not supposed to feel emotion. An even bigger woman in an even darker suit came over once again and overlaid a large black "X" upon the initial stamp in the book.

"Wait just a moment. I need a different set of forms," repeated the Registrar with a sense of defeat. He rummaged about for a long time under the desk and eventually had to drop from his seat to take a much more thorough look. "Ah, here it is," he said from out of sight.

With great effort, he stood back up and heaved an enormous stack of papers onto the desk with his full strength. It was twice as large yet as the previous, and it proved a great burden for the scrawny pencil-pusher to lift. The Registrar turned the first page and looked back at his victim.

"No wonder the line moves so slow," muttered Davis under his breath.

"There is a registration fee of 1200 Units," said the Registrar.

I don't have any money if that's what he means. When he made his lack of funds clear, the Registrar slid the humongous stack of papers into a tray under the desk. Davis couldn't tell if he was frustrated because of the nuisance, or because he wouldn't get the chance to fill out the forms. As he pushed the tray shut, a door on the front of the wall beneath the window unfolded before Davis, presenting him with the huge stack of papers. He lifted them out from the tray; their weight was almost unmanageable. The Registrar informed him of his only two options.

"If you have anything of value to exchange, you may do so at the Broker, six lanes down to your left. If you cannot come up with the appropriate amount for the fee, you will be detained for Voluntary Service. Good day."

That doesn't sound very voluntary. The hand at his side rested on the hilt of his only possession while he considered his choices.

Davis made his way to the back of the lines, the very place where this whole process had started. Not knowing what else to do, he counted off six lanes to the left. The line was horribly long, but he rushed straight in to make the least of the wait. At the end of it was a young girl, dressed in the same garb as everyone else, though her demeanor appeared fairer and slightly less hesitant than the woman he'd met before.

"Hello, I'm Davis," he whispered coyly. "What's your name?"

"Mira," she responded with a gentle voice.

"It's nice to meet you, Mira. Might I ask what you're doing here?"

"I'm exchanging the gifts I was given for my birthday."

"When was your birthday?" asked Davis.

"It was today. It's a shame too. Some of them are starting to hold real sentimental value to me."

The poor girl. It was among the first of his encounters with empathy. To have to part with things for which she obviously felt an attachment seemed an unfair price for registration, or whatever it was the girl needed.

"Do you need the money that badly?" he asked.

"Of course not, I have plenty of Units," bragged Mira, appearing to have overcome her petty sentiments. "In fact, I have so many of them, I couldn't possibly spend them all if I tried."

"Well, why don't you keep the gifts for your birthday then?" he asked. "Or, at least keep the ones that you're saddened to part with."

She stared at him, unblinking, as if it were an absurd thing to even ask. "You can always use more," she said.

The sadness Davis felt now turned to pity. He wasn't even sure what sentimental value really meant, having little in the way of memories or sentiments. Still, he sensed on some level that it was an awful lot of something to give away for nothing.

The juncture at which they'd arrived left little in the way of a desire for further conversation on behalf of either party. After waiting for hours with the intolerable weight of his documentation burning away at the muscles of his arms, he finally arrived at the front of the line.

"Broker," the sign read, and he breathed a sigh of relief.

This was not an environment in which to slip up.

"NEXT!" the teller eventually shouted, and Davis approached the booth.

"Welcome to the Broker," said the woman behind the plastic. "What will it be: buy, sell, or trade?"

"Sell, I suppose," said Davis. He set the book down.

"And what do you have to offer?" asked the Broker.

He placed the Blade of Entitlement into the tray below the window and closed it shut.

The woman pulled it in, inspected it, then pressed one of the many small buttons on the side of her desk: "Tools, Utensils, Gadgets, and Devices." Each button had a different label for the myriad categories of things people could ever think to barter. Every item imaginable would have fallen into one of the categories, and in the remote possibility that it couldn't, there was always the failsafe: Miscellaneous.

In a short while, another woman in a darker suit came, leaned over the Broker, and placed some initials in a spreadsheet in the book by her side. Turning next to the item, the supervisor picked up the blade and put it through a series of tests. First, she took it out of the sheath and visually inspected it. It was flawless, beautiful in its way. She then placed it on a scale, wrote down its mass, and went to bend it with her hands to test its stability. She then left with the blade, returning several minutes later with a small slip of paper in her hand. She handed the paper to the teller and left.

"This will fetch you 1500 Units," said the Broker.

"I'll take it," said Davis, quite content that he would not have to either be detained or use that very blade in trying to avoid such a fate. Anyway, he was glad to see it go, for with it left at least a small part of the dreadful regret that had weighed on his conscience for the deed it had done.

The Broker slid Davis three small tokens through the gap in the plastic. *That's it? That's 1500 Units?* They were awfully small, and awfully few, for what sounded like such a big number. He followed the arrows to an exit and made his way back to the beginning, where he once again entered the line for the Registrar. There were people in front of him as before, but he was so exhausted from his ordeal, and so unimpressed by his previous conversations, that he didn't bother to harass any of them this time.

Now that he had enough for the registration fee, and with plenty of time to kill in line, he sat down on the ground and folded open the huge book of forms he'd been lugging around. The people nearby cast a whole host of disapproving expressions his way, but boredom and fatigue had gotten the better of him. He began flipping through the pages, pretending to pay careful attention.

The first part of the book was straightforward enough – demographics mostly: name, date of birth, number, height, weight, handedness, shoe size, etc. The list went on and on. He flipped through many more pages into the middle, the majority of which consisted of an exhaustive inventory of adjectives. As best as he could tell, each served as descriptions for the character of a person, and next to every line were blank boxes labeled one through ten, waiting to be checked.

...Doubtful, Dowdy, Down-Hearted, Down-Home...

He flipped through another inch of the book.

...Drunken, Dubious, Ducal, Dulcet, Dull...

Still in the D's. Grabbing a fistful of paper, he flung the weight of it over with a jerk.

...Insensible, Insensitive, Insidious, Insightful, Insignificant, Insincere...

The more he read, the more dumbstruck he became. He didn't know half the words, but of the half that he did know, he didn't have the faintest idea how he should score them. He didn't know who he was in the slightest.

He kept flipping pages, exasperated and angry. It would not be the last time he felt the lure of this oft-tempting impulse, and the crowd struggled to not let the turmoil upset their taciturnity. He caught sight of more descriptions as the pages raced by.

...Spiritual, Spiteful, Splendid...

He flipped yet further, growing ever more hysterical.

...True, Trusting, Trust-Worthy, Truthful...

The pages kept turning in a frenzy of despair.

...Wise, Wishful, Wistful...

And all at once, at this last word, he stopped.

Wistful, he read again.

Finally, here was a word he understood in its fullest, and knew without a doubt applied to his being. He closed the book shut and rose from the ground. There was nothing this huge stack of forms could do to fill in the pages of a life he didn't know.

2.2 / Panic at the Gate

The line advanced yet again, and the people behind him were further irritated by his delay; it was one of the only emotions they managed to muster in line. Slowly, he gathered his book of forms from the ground and moved on ahead with the rest of the herd. Hours passed, and finally he made his way up to the front once again.

"NEXT!" shouted the Registrar, and he shuffled on ahead.

"Name?" asked the Registrar.

Davis was insulted by the repeat question, though he'd been gone from this window for many hours now. After how hard it had been for him to finally remember his name, the least this man could do was the same.

"It's Davis."

A larger and even more unsettling sensation of déjà vu took root in the base of his brain stem.

"Ah yes," said the Registrar. "Davis with no date of birth."

Davis smiled, pleased to discover that the man in the booth did at least slightly remember him. He raised the huge stack of forms into view with the last waning remainder of his might, as a signal to the Registrar. The man took the clue, pushed opened the tray, and Davis set it inside with a loud crash. After pulling the book back in, the Registrar flipped open the pages, but not one of the forms was completed.

"That's right," he said, his memory spurred, "a Non-Classified in need of Registration. I see you haven't filled out any of the forms yet. It's no matter; we can take care of that together." Finally, the Registrar had his chance at the endeavor he so greatly coveted. "There is a fee of 1200 Units, as I'm sure you recall."

Davis handed over the tokens through the gap in the plastic. The Registrar looked them over.

"I'm sorry," he said. "This is only 900 Units."

"What? That's ridiculous!" Davis protested. "I was just given those by the Broker at the last window I was at. She told me they were worth 1500 Units. That's more than enough for the fee."

"Well, they were worth 1500 Units, but that was a few hours ago. Now they're only worth 900. It's a matter of Inflation."

"Inflation? It sounds more like deflation," Davis muttered disdainfully.

"Actually," perked up the Registrar, "Deflation is when–"

"Look, I don't care!" interrupted Davis, a bit louder even than he meant. "What am I supposed to do now? I don't have anything left to sell but the clothes on my back."

"Sir, I'm going to have to ask you to calm down," said the Registrar. The clerks at the desk were highly trained in the art of detecting the signs of a person about to become unhinged. It was a crucial skill in Inanimis. "Luckily for you, we'll be able to secure a loan for the remainder of the Registration fee, but you're going to need to fill out a few forms."

Of course I will.

The Registrar pulled out a stack of papers, though admittedly smaller than Davis had anticipated, and proceeded to ask him a series of inane questions. Davis was barely attentive, and he'd be lying to say that he didn't fudge an answer here or there. In any event, the Registrar finally submitted the loan to one of the large looming ladies behind him in the dark uniforms.

"Now then," said the Registrar, turning his attention back to the huge stack of forms, "let's start at the top." His excitement was palpable, and the mood was lightened now that he could finally carry on with the registration process. "A number," he continued. "Everyone needs a number!"

"Why can't I just be called Davis?" he asked, far less chipper.

It was a relatively new concept to him, surely, but he thought he'd at least gathered that a name was used for this very sort of purpose.

"Don't be ridiculous," laughed the Registrar. "Everyone here needs a number. How else are we supposed to know who you are?" One of them was missing the point entirely, but Davis wasn't sure which. "OK, a number," continued the man in the booth. "We'll have to assign a new one."

He looked down at the desk and flipped through a small box of cards. When he came to the front, his expression grew even more satisfied. Of all the many types of paperwork he enjoyed, this was one of the Registrar's favorite perks of the job.

"It looks like the next number to be used is: HSS-7-011-247-238" said the Registrar as he wrote it down on the form.

"Why can't you just call me Davis?" he asked again. He still wasn't sold on the idea of a number, having gone to such lengths to discover his name.

"Because it's simply less precise!" snapped the Registrar, quite firmly now. His system challenged, he began to shed some of the illusion of courtesy. "Even so," he said, regaining his composure, "a name can often say a lot about a person. What does it mean anyway: Davis?"

Names have meaning? Davis hadn't ever thought of that.

"I don't know what it means," he said.

He wasn't ready to admit that he'd only just learned he had one.

"Well let's see here," said the Registrar. "Let me consult our reference."

He glanced over his shoulder to check if any of the looming ladies were watching him, then he pulled out an encyclopedia of names. Even Registrars could sneak in a bit of fun now and then, so long as they didn't stray too far from protocol. He flipped through the pages and scrolled the length of them with his fingertips, all while keeping one eye on the workings of the supervisors behind him.

"Ah, here it is," said the Registrar, awfully pleased with his use of the alphabet. "It says here that Davis means: Beloved. Does that ring any bells?"

Davis didn't even hear the question. His world was swallowed by a tidal wave of emotions. The view of the small man with a huge book behind the thick plastic covering had vanished, and the scenery all around him echoed of familiar feelings as he'd had once before.

Like the first night in the wood, when he had first heard his name, his mind was again bombarded by the last words he heard. *Davis means: Beloved.* It grew louder with each passing repetition, spoken by a chorus of eerily reminiscent voices. *Davis means: Beloved.* Great searing pains of nostalgia and regret coursed through every vein in his body, flowing inward to the center of his being, overpowering all other thoughts. *Davis means: Beloved.* Then came the images again, like a swift blow to the head, but this time they possessed two outstretching hands as the visions unfolded.

First came the long face and deep eyes of a horse. It was black all around, except for the white of the feathers at the start of its hooves, and a single white stripe down the length of its snout. It was leaning over a wooden fence as the hands threw hay over top, into a trough on the other side. The horse came closer; the hands reached out and scratched behind its ears. Its eyes stared straight inward at him from the center of the vision. *Those eyes.* They looked right through him. The horse made little in the way of an expression that could be read by man, but an intense wave of something he couldn't describe flooded over him. It emanated out from the vision in a warm, comforting vibration.

He then saw a young boy standing beside him, his lips poised in a sarcastic smirk. A small set of hands reached out and gently struck the side of his shoulder. The boy fell away, grabbing the site in a fake demonstration of pain. Laughter could be heard over the rustle of grass as he fell to the earth and rolled on the ground. The viewer turned to leave but suddenly tumbled downward and again met the face of the boy; he had tripped up the spectator as they went to walk away.

Next, he beheld again two children: a small boy, and a girl, slightly his elder. The children sat on a pair of knees jutting out from his viewpoint. The hands — his hands? — reached out, poking and tickling the children's sides. They squirmed and wrestled away, immersed in the richest laughter. They fell off the knees and rolled on the ground in amusement. There were simply no words that could describe the joy he felt in that modest moment. He was complete — the polar opposite of how he'd felt of late. *I am home.*

Last came the face of a beautiful woman. He knew her somehow, though he couldn't say why. Her eyebrows were raised as if to say thanks. She leaned into the vision, her arms outstretched to both sides. His own hands rose and passed in to her through a blurry veil separating them. They gently stroked back the hair from in front of her majestic eyes and wrapped around her tightly in a deep and loving embrace.

The scene turned to gray, and while he felt the pressure from her body start to dissipate, the warmth of her presence did not leave him with the rest of the visions. It stayed with him, a part of him, as the rest of the cloudy daydreams blew away in a breeze that began from behind. Soon there was nothing left to see, only an inescapable sensation of longing, the name of which he did not know.

And though he could recall these few scenes among the visions, he got the sense that many more came with them that he couldn't remember. It was as if the extremes in a lifetime of emotion were distilled down to the size of an atom, condensed into an unspoken singularity in the center of his being. All the joy and elation, the sorrow and suffering, the totality of creation pierced into the soul of whatever he was in that moment. And yet, it was as large as the universe itself, unbound by any scale of space or time, all-encompassing in its scope.

Thus was he struck, overwhelmed by the profundity of what it really means to exist; for to exist is to depend upon others, including even those of which we have but the slightest conceptions. And so was he haunted again by these unknown apparitions. Despite the indescribable occurrences that accompanied them, they hinted only at the slightest suggestions of reminiscence.

The Registrar came back into sight.

"Sir?" he asked as he stared at Davis with a look of growing impatience. "Your height and weight, sir? If you don't know offhand, we'll need you to–"

His sentence was interrupted in a most unexpected way: Davis darted from the window in the direction of the gate, with no warning whatsoever. He knocked over the unsuspecting guard and pushed his way through the threshold. By that point, the Registrar had pressed a large red button on the underside of the desk and the call was out.

There was an emergency in the land of order.

Davis ran at full speed, barely aware of what had happened since the last of the visions faded away. The images had withered, but still he felt the heat in his chest from that last impassioned embrace, and it terrified him. He wasn't sure if his purpose lay on the other side of the gate, but he knew that it certainly wasn't to stand there and be turned into a number. As he slowly regained his senses, his mind focused in on the immediate issues at hand, as his feet sped along on the sturdy concrete. *Where do I run now?*

The guard he'd left behind was blowing a loud, shrill whistle from his back on the ground, his feet flailing in the air. The alarm rung by the Registrar churned piercingly in all directions. There was no hope of sneaking his way out of this one. The first question about the digits of his number and he would be done for. A few other men dressed in the same outfit rushed over to help the large guard off the ground, and he pointed in his direction as Davis looked back.

48

As he ran at top speed, he took a moment to scan his surroundings. He was in something looking very much like a city. There were buildings everywhere, though all were monotonous and appeared essentially the same, save the insignia on their black and white signs: "Labor Office, Expansion Division, Engineering, Waste Management, Special Operations, etc." The signs went on in a similar fashion at each one that he passed.

Ahead of him he spotted a central structure, the only one with any semblance of what passed for artistic flourish in the city. It was large, with a round dome on its top and pillars lining the front: "Council Chamber" the sign read. It was surrounded by guards and Davis changed directions again at the sight of them. The largest of all, however, was a massive building that dwarfed the rest of the city: "Corrections."

It all seemed very unnatural to him. *So, this is the place I was trying to get into? Is this the kind of place that people like me are supposed to live?*

He wasn't so sure.

Guards were rushing at him from all directions now, drawn by the sounds of alarm and the cries of their compatriots. Several lunged forward at Davis as he ran by them, but somehow he weaved in and out of their attempts to detain him. For a while he ran on in this manner, ducking and bobbing, darting and swaying, eventually even laughing madly at their efforts to ensnare him.

At last, the hilarity came to a close as several of the officers circled him from all sides. The circle got smaller, the hope of escape dimmer. One of the guards reached to his side and lifted the snake-like metallic device that hung from his belt. Aiming it at Davis, something shot out like a dart and struck him in the neck. There was a sharp shockwave of pain, as if every nerve in his body had suddenly short-circuited. He fell to the ground and was unable to move.

Now that their agile foe had been immobilized, the guards closed in further, and the one who'd made the shot stepped forward into the center of the circle. He turned a small dial on the side of the device to change its function, and it clicked as it arrived at its destination. The guard walked forward and lifted a small booklet from his back pocket.

"You are hereby cited as Under Detainment, by the power of the Department of Corrections. You have no right to resist, refute, or otherwise..."

The words droned on, but Davis didn't hear them. He would not intellectually comply with their game for even a moment longer. He could not have discerned if it was the strength or the meekness of his will that had caused him to give up; either way, he wasn't sure how this was all going to end. When the words of the guard were coming to a close, he tuned back in to see what he had missed.

"Thus, by the power of the Court of Inanimis..." *Evidently they went from detainment to sentencing in the short span of a minute.* "...your identity will now be Permanently Re-Assigned."

The guard stepped forward, reached out with the end of the device, and placed it upon the center of the criminal's forehead. The tip of this snake had several long protruding needles extending from the middle of a glossy chrome circle. He could feel the needles stinging as they perforated his skin and pressed against the front of his skull.

While he didn't know what it meant to have his identity Permanently Re-Assigned, he was fairly certain it wasn't a good thing. He'd only recently had the first inclinations that he might have one at all; it would be such a shame to lose it now. Just as the guard was about to flick the fateful switch, the fortunes of this traitor to Inanimis turned in his favor.

2.3 / Black Ashes

Davis lay on his back on the concrete, aching and unable to move, subject entirely to the whims of Inanimis. The weapon's prongs stabbed into his forehead, and his body was numb from a current coursing through him. But the pain was the least of his worries. The guard who had immobilized him lurked above, blocking out the sun, staring down at him with a sadistic smile, a little too enthused for the duty he was about to perform.

Davis closed his eyes and prepared for the end. He saw a glimpse of his home by the sea, by a vast field of purple flowers, and part of him longed for those simpler days. But not every part gave in so easily.

This cannot be the end, he protested.

Shrouded in darkness, for one brief moment, the world went entirely still. In the depths of that void, slowly he felt the warmth of the sun return to his face. The silence was shattered by a soft, sweeping implosion. When he lifted his eyelids again, a thick plume of black ash was raining down on him from above, and the guard was nowhere to be seen.

The feeling in his hands was slowly returning, and Davis propped himself up with his arms. He turned his head in all directions, attempting to discern what had happened, but what he saw next made little more sense. He lay in a pile of ashes, legs still useless, but the guards encircling him were cast into chaos.

Their circle was quickly broken as they panicked and fled for their lives. Others fought blindly with what little courage they possessed, trying in vain to ward off whatever it was that attacked them. One by one, the guards were struck by some formidable force; they burst outward in a black cloud of smoke and dust, and floated to their demise on the concrete below.

He caught sight of two bodies surrounding the commotion, dressed all in black, revealing nothing but their eyes. One figure was slightly taller than the other, but they were otherwise identical in appearance. The two shapes spun together in circles, back to back, side-stepping in a flurry, every motion harmonious and fluid. As the taller one was approached by a threat from the front, they would spin in unison; the shorter would reach out his hands, and the guard would be gone. *The tall one is sensing, while the smaller one strikes.*

This pattern went on for minutes: ducking, dodging, turning, sweeping, leaping, sliding, striking. They moved with an impressive grace that would be beautiful if it weren't so menacing. They evaded every attempt by the guards to hit them with their devices. Davis could see the darts flying past the figures, but each time, they contorted their bodies in avoidance, and another guard would be gone.

In the middle of the turmoil, Davis turned to find one of the tortuous devices laying at his side. It was the very weapon that had been an instant away from carrying out his punishment, and only at the sight of it did Davis realize that said punishment would not be fulfilled. He wasn't sure what would have happened, but for the first time, he found himself ecstatic to know that he had an identity. After all, this was proof that he must: *how could they reassign it if there's nothing to reassign?* To this end, he owed much to his unexpected visions, and to the grave effect they were starting to have on his outlook. As soon as he got out of this mess, he was going to find the meaning behind the mirage.

The last guard never even knew what hit him. Looking straight ahead at the taller of the strangers, he was just about to pull the trigger. In a rapid streaking motion that left only a blur, the shadows swung in another tight circle and snuck up from the rear. The shorter one reached out his hand and placed it upon the shoulder of the guard. Like so many before him, he crumbled away into a cloud of black ash. Without delay, the strangers turned their attention to Davis; he was still recumbent on the ground, though slowly regaining the feeling in his legs.

"Come," said the man who dealt the deadly blows. The taller of the two stood behind him, one hand on the shorter one's shoulder. "There's not much time."

"Who are you?" asked Davis. They may have helped him greatly, but he was not without fear of this rescue party.

"There will be time for that later," answered the taller. "For now, you must come with us if you hope to survive another day."

Davis tried to rise on his own but wasn't quite able. The two men helped him to his feet and propped him up until he regained his strength. As soon as he could stand on his own, they urged him onward. Davis followed as the men slid through dark alleys between the tightly packed buildings. Eventually they reached a wall where there hung a long black rope. Looking up from its base, the wall was enormous, much bigger than Davis had first appreciated from outside the gate. Then again, he hadn't been faced with the task of climbing it at the time. Without hesitation, the shorter one leapt in the air, grabbed hold of the rope, and began the ascent.

Not a chance. "I'm sorry," said Davis, "My arms are still weak from whatever they did to me. I won't be able to make it."

"We know," said the taller one. "That's why he went up first."

He's been in my position before, Davis realized.

When the climber reached the top, he sent a wave traveling down the rope with a flick of his wrist, and the man on the ground signaled Davis to grab hold of it. He secured the rope around his waist so that it took a minimal effort to hang on, and sent another wave back up the rope to the top of the wall. The man at the top immediately began to lift Davis off the ground, and with surprisingly little effort. *For being short, he sure is strong. Perhaps that's why he deals the blows.*

When Davis reached the top of the wall, the man helped him onto the ledge, untied the rope from his frame, and tossed it back down again. The top consisted of a platform wide enough to walk along, but narrow enough that Davis felt plenty uneasy with such a long fall so close on either side. The rope was anchored to a steel spike in the center of the platform, and so too was a second one; it ran across to the opposite side and plunged over the edge. And thus were his eyes led out over the landscape, out across the black forest far below.

From this high vantage point, Davis saw the forest stretch for countless miles, unbroken in all directions but one. From the sight of the sunset, now well underway after a day of mostly waiting, he deduced that the city's entrance must also be in the west. In that direction, a dark blanket of treetops rolled along until finally ending far away in the distance. There, almost as far as the horizon itself, was a large open region. It was darker yet than the forest, as if the trees fell over cliffs and into an enormous canyon, immersed in shadow.

To the east was also forest, but in it was a large gap in the trees, as wide as the diameter of the city, like the wake left by a stick that's been dragged through the sand − a vacuous cavity extending as far as the eastern horizon. The wall where he presently stood, however, faced north; only more forest lay that way, except for a darkness beyond it. To the south he could not see, for the city and its far southern wall blocked the view of any land beyond it.

As Davis took in his surroundings, the shorter man had been busy pulling up the outside rope as his companion climbed the inner wall. When he got the rope to the top, he again secured it around Davis and indicated that he should sit down on the edge. Davis carefully complied, wary of the long way down, and before he knew it, he was being lowered into the darkness below.

Davis fell quickly, so much so that he doubted whether his descent was still in full control. And yet, as the ground sped closer, his pace was slowed, and he was set down gently. He started uncoiling the rope, and by now the second man had reached the top of the wall. As soon as the rope was free of Davis, much to his surprise, both men grabbed hold of it with one hand; first one, then the other, they flung themselves carelessly over the side of the wall. They fell swiftly, slowing themselves only slightly by the grip of a single hand. The shorter came first, the taller no more than an instant behind. Their knees bent fully as they absorbed the impact from the ground. They rose, perfectly nonchalant, and walked over to where Davis was standing under the dark of the canopy.

Who have I gotten myself involved with? he wondered. But he would not find out until well past nightfall, for there were many miles to travel ere they were out of harm's way.

"We have a sanctuary not far from here," said the taller one, "but we must go around the city first."

"Go around it?" asked Davis, far ruder than he realized. "We ran this way from the city center, only to have to traverse the whole perimeter now? That will take all night! Why didn't we just climb the wall on that side?"

The men, though clearly not pleased with the skepticism of their passenger, humored him for the sake of moving on as quickly as they could.

"Keep your voice down!" answered the taller man in a stern whisper. "First of all, the north is where our ropes were." He layered on his own share of condescension. "You can't climb a wall with no ropes. That is, unless you are more skilled than either of us?"

Fair point, confessed Davis, albeit silently. He had no misconceptions about the level of his talent relative to these two.

"Secondly, we come this way on purpose. We enter from the north, precisely because it is the opposite of where we come from. The leaders of the city have spent a great deal of both time and resources trying to find us. They've scoured every inch of this northern hillside for miles, never finding even a hint of our presence. Still they press on, because the only signs we ever leave them are on this side of the wall. Resourceful as they may be, they're not creative enough to think we might be deceiving them."

The men looked around to ensure that no one had seen them make their escape. They signaled to follow as they ran through the woods to the north. *I thought we had to go south!* For once it wasn't worth the hassle of complaining, and he followed suit in silence.

There was very little light, the footing was difficult, and Davis struggled to keep up. A fair distance into the wood, the men finally stopped. They walked around the trunk of a particularly large tree and lifted two torches that had been wedged into the soil. The shorter man pulled out two small rocks and sparked them together to light the torches. Turning back to Davis, they began unraveling the black cloth wrappings that covered their heads. Even in the faint light of the torches, Davis could tell that there was a striking resemblance between the two men.

"Are you two brothers?" he asked them.

They looked at each other and the taller one replied.

"In a sense, yes."

What does that mean? At the moment, he was too tired to care.

"You don't say much, do you?" he said to the shorter one.

"Actions speak louder than words," he smirked.

"We need to keep moving," interjected the taller man again. "Now that we've made it out of sight from the wall, we can swing around to the west and eventually make our way back south."

All of that was acceptable to Davis except for the part about going west.

"The entrance to the city is to the west. Why don't we go east to avoid the chance of being spotted? Isn't that the better way?"

Though woefully uninformed, at least his knack for survival was starting to shine through, and that impressed the brothers well enough.

"Your thought is a good one, but the west is the only way," said the talkative of the two. "The east is occupied by a filthy, treacherous wasteland we cannot hope to cross. Even if we could, we would be completely out in the open, for no trees can grow there."

Davis had forgotten about the gap he'd seen from the top of the wall.

"Besides," he continued, "they don't send many citizens out very far from the wall, especially at night. When they do leave the city, they almost never leave the trail, except for the direst of circumstances."

I wonder if today's events might qualify.

"Most of their interaction with the west is through an army of Harvesters, typically sent out just beyond the wall, to the periphery of the forest to continue clearing trees."

"What do they need to do that for?" asked Davis.

"To make room for the next westward expansion, of course." He paused a moment, as if finishing a thought. "Once in a great while, they do send Prospectors to explore further out into the unknown, but I doubt very much that we'll encounter any."

The short one shot him a disapproving glance and his brother took note of its meaning. Davis pretended not to notice.

"Come, enough talk for a while," said the taller one to change his own subject. "We'll have plenty of time to catch up when we're in the safety of our sanctuary." He gestured west and led the way.

The traveling was easier now that the men in front had torches, but the forest was still thick, as it frequently is, and they moved at a very rapid pace. After a long journey in a westward direction, they came upon a small cairn of stones on an old fallen log. The shorter one led the way and signaled to the south with two fingers. Later they came to another small cairn, at which he looked back with a finger over his mouth as a sign for silence. He put out his torch and his brother did the same. For a few minutes, Davis could see nothing at all while his eyes adjusted, but eventually a dim image of the forest floor came to him.

They rested a while to allow their night-eyes to set in, and the short one passed him a small bar of grains to alleviate his hunger. In all the day's commotion, Davis hadn't realized how incredibly hungry he was. With this small bit to eat, however, it brought the pangs of hunger to his full attention, and he longed for more food to satiate them. When the men felt duly prepared to continue, they rose from their seats and signaled again to the south.

After a few minutes, they came to the edge of the path that Davis must have traveled earlier that day. It was dusty, as before, and unoccupied by anyone that the brothers could detect. *Now I understand the need to put out the torches.* Seeing that the coast was clear, they crossed the trail side by side, minimizing the time that their shapes could be seen from eyes on the path. After making their way well into the woods south of the trail, they again lit their torches and moved more quickly.

With most of the danger behind them, the brothers and their companion hastened far away and to the south. They must have ventured many miles according to Davis; but it was a crude estimation, for he carried on in a daze. Finally, just as his legs felt that they could very well give way for the second time that day, they spotted a large rock outcrop jutting up from flat ground.

The party swung around it to the west, then came back to the rocks from the south. *There's an awful lot of backtracking involved in whatever it is these men do.* The rocks rose in bursts, like staggered shelves, and as they climbed, they eventually came to the highest shelf of all. A long, flat stone projected upward in a point and hung out over a meager opening, facing south and away from the city far afield.

"We've made it," said the taller one. "You did well."

Davis managed half a smile. They climbed further up and went in through the darkened gap.

Entering the cave, they descended through a long tunnel that led deep into the heart of the craggy plateau. Davis could smell smoke, and as they made their way further, the orange glow of a fire lit the far wall of a curve up ahead. As they turned the corner, the narrow tunnel widened out into a large, round chamber, in which a third man, dressed the same as the others, sat by the side of a central fire.

"Come," said the taller one. "Meet our eldest brother."

Davis stood for a moment, taking in the scene, as his escorts walked over to the fire and sat down, one on each side of the man already there. Rather than enter, Davis stood still at the end of the tunnel, awestruck by the beauty of the refuge.

The cave appeared mostly natural, except for the occasional modification, to widen a turn or deepen a ceiling. The chamber, the innermost sanctum, was the most impressive of it all. It was roomy, yet warm and welcoming.

The low ceilings of the tunnels opened out into a tall and spacious dome, and in it were numerous holes, bored through the rock. They were small, not quite as big as a fist, but they reached up the long distance to the surface, so that the light of the stars just barely trickled through. As Davis was inspecting these puzzling alterations, a new voice broke the silence.

"They allow the smoke to escape, but in so many channels that it is not seen by any unsuspecting eyes."

It was the brother Davis had not yet met, although – oddly – he vaguely reminded him of someone.

He seems familiar, he thought; *but I must be mistaken.*

"Come, join us by the fire," he said. His voice was deep – gruff and determined, yet comforting and kind all the same. "I suspect we have much to discuss."

2.4 / Heroes and Heretics

Davis sat in a circle around the fire with three brothers.

"I see you have met my kin," said the man directly across from him, the tallest of the three yet. *Not quite,* thought Davis.

He gestured to the shorter one, seated to his right: "This is Manus."
He gestured next to the taller one, seated at left: "This is Cerebrus."
He folded his hands in his lap: "And I am Animulus."

He paused, assessing whether their guest had heard these names before. When it was clear that he hadn't, Animulus continued.

"We welcome you to our sanctuary, Davis."

Davis nodded his head in thanks. *How do they know who I am?* He waited for more to develop before speaking up. *Can I trust them?*

"My brothers tell me you have had a long and tiresome day," said Animulus, though no words had been spoken that Davis had heard.

Manus got up from his seat at once and walked to the side of the dome, where a small wooden table housed daily rations for their supper. *There are four bowls,* noticed Davis. Manus grabbed one and filled it with a thick steaming soup. He returned to the fire, handed it to Davis, and sat back down by his brother's side, all without saying a word.

"Eat this and recover your strength," said Animulus again. "I am sure you have many questions."

Of that, he was most certainly correct.

"Who are you?" asked Davis.

"You know our names, though our tale may be of more interest to you," said Animulus. "But first, you must come to know the city as we know it."

Davis said nothing, simply raised the soup to his lips. His hunger was too unbearable to distrust these men any further for now. Seeing this unspoken truce, Animulus began to explain things as best he could.

"Somehow, you had found your way to the city of Inanimis. But for the intervention of my brothers, I doubt you would ever have escaped it. Be glad that you have, for your spirit is still free.

"The occupants of the city care not for the world, nor strive for a better means of living. What they have, and what they have done to get it, are two very different issues to them. In fairness, they function with impressive efficiency within their walls, but it has come at the expense of all things outside them. They have shut themselves in from the world, and as such, they have lost touch with what it truly means to be alive.

"They harvest incessantly from the wild, without caution or care, and produce little sustenance of their own. They collect waves upon waves of the fruits of the forest, extract their essence, combine it with other corruptions of this sort, and add to it things that come not from Nature at all. They strive ever to be better than Nature, to improve upon it, in defiance of its rules. They focus solely on what they find valuable at present. They discard and discount all else whose purpose they don't understand, only to take more when they have need of it for differing purposes.

"The waste they produce through these dealings is foul and poisonous — toxic and unusable to any other living things. So too do they exhaust all the ample resources surrounding them. Once it has pillaged what it can from the adjoining frontier, the city moves forward a step in a constant expansion to the west.

"Both the western and eastern fronts consist of walls with two sections: an inner and outer. In the east, they place their filth between the walls. When the western forest is expired, or when waste fills the eastern space, the outer wall is demolished, leaving its contents for the forest to cope with. This is the Inviocassus — a futile, barren wasteland. The original inner wall becomes its replacement, and a new one is built further west of it.

"Much of the same happens on the western edge of the city: a new outer wall is built, and the innermost one is demolished. The earth is excavated deeply, and more footings are laid for the foundation. The city floor consists of a large slab, propped up by a series of underground beams. When all is set, great machines crank the slab forward and shift the city into its new position. In this way, Inanimis creeps ever onward in a single direction, leaving a trail of death and destruction in its wake."

Davis had already finished his soup and hoped for a second helping. He set down the empty bowl and looked over at the table, where the others were still neatly stacked. The irony of his ravenous hunger was lost on him.

"As I said, they function quite economically within the city, for they segment every aspect of society into countless factions and classes and divisions. In principle, this might have been wise; but in practice, each faction looks out only for its own interest and cares little for the good of any other citizens. The status quo rewards only ever-growing greed in the face of the constraints of reality.

"They live in a way that is linear and improvident, whereas the way of Nature is cyclic. They live as if they were separate from Nature, though nothing natural ever could be. They care not for the suffering of the world outside their walls, for they fail to think of it as a world equal their own."

Animulus breathed a sigh, battling despair, and placed a hand upon the shoulder of each of the brothers beside him.

"We three are outcasts — sworn enemies of Inanimis. They have branded us Heretics and know us by no other name. In truth, we are the Scrutatorus, for we search for a better way."

"How do you know so much about the city?" asked Davis, before pivoting to what he really wanted to know. "Who are you?" he asked again.

"We might ask the same of you," said Cerebrus.

Animulus silenced his brother with a single look.

"We were not always outlaws," said Animulus.

"Then how did you come to be outlaws – Heretics?"

Animulus looked again at Manus, who then rose, grabbed the bowl that Davis emptied, and returned to the table. He filled it, along with the other three bowls, then brought his brothers their dinner and their guest a much-hoped-for second helping.

"That's a long tale," said Cerebrus. "And one best heard over supper."

Soups in hand, the brothers bowed their heads in silence. Having already begun to slurp it down, Davis stopped, wiped his mouth, but didn't think to take after the others. When a minute or more had passed, they raised their heads again and took a sip from their bowls in unison.

"We know of the city because we awoke within its walls," started Animulus. "We were citizens there once, children really; and like all its children, we were donated by our parents to be housed with a cohort of others born the same year. After schooling, we entered standard rotations among the many professions, interning in a service division for a time before moving on to another. Apprenticeship, they call it. In this way, the youth of Inanimis are assessed for their optimal profession, one that suits their strengths while fulfilling the city's current needs.

"We did not know each other well in those days, though we each in our way showed the most promise as woodsmen. When the time came for our assignment, we were selected as Prospectors in the Expansion Division. We had good reason to be excited: though entailing much hard work, this is a prestigious assignment, awarded to only the most capable citizens.

"As you now know, as the city progresses along its inevitable trajectory, it emerges with each step into what was once the distant frontier. Thus, there is ever a need to scout further into the west. From that time onward, our task was to range far afield, uncovering more of the unknown wilderness. We spent long days on many essential tasks: marching, mapping the landscape, cataloging its flora and fauna, establishing an inventory of the many resources of interest, and otherwise gauging an area's worth and potential for expansion. Little did we know where this path would lead us.

"We labored on in this way for many years, becoming more familiar with the life of the forest, more at home in the wild. And then, one day, we discovered within it a secret that changed our lives forever."

Davis stirred, and at the sight of it Animulus paused, scrutinizing him, searching for subtle signs of understanding. For his part, Davis remained convincingly aloof given all he had experienced. Animulus shortly continued.

"The expedition began like so many others before it. Our team was assigned a grid far to the west of the city, and further north than we had ever ventured to date. Upon arrival, we began our routine chores: marking trees for harvest, surveying the landscape, digging soil samples, transcribing the species encountered, and so on.

"As the day advanced, however, the environment started to change, transitioning from a typical locale to one that was lush beyond anything we had ever encountered. Most of the team was ecstatic, realizing the rich potential this region offered for the city. As our work progressed, the forest grew more beauteous still, though such a thing seemed hard to imagine.

"Eventually there was an opening in the treetops; we arrived at a small glade, filled with wonder. A stream collected near a large rock and formed a deep, clear pool. The outlet continued to a gap in the far side of the glade, where it fell over a ledge into more forest below. The land beyond the cliff beckoned to us, somehow looking even more divine, but it was not clear if we could make it there from where we stood. Even if we could have found the way, our collective attention shifted to a singular focus. By the side of the pool stood a startling creature, the likes of which we had never beheld.

"We Prospectors could not believe our eyes, nor did our stories correspond. Some claimed seeing only a timid deer, others a towering horse. Others saw odd chimeras or half-beast hybrids. A few claimed seeing stranger things yet. Most simply had no words to describe it at all. All knew that our stories would never be believed. We waited, and when our surprise was finally exceeded by curiosity, we moved closer for a better view."

"Why did you think no one would believe you?" asked Davis, and Cerebrus answered for the brothers.

"Legends of this type of encounter had long been told in the city, passed down as folklore of the scandalous sort. The inquisitive among them call it the Guardian, while cynics discount it as the Farce of the Forest. The most scornful call it only the Scourge. To propose it as part of reality was to discard all hope of ever being taken seriously again.

"Some no doubt tried over the centuries, at which point their greatest outcome was to end up as a patronizing punchline, the moral of a story used to threaten children about the dangers of telling tall tales. Most had even less fortune. Those who would not recant their story were labeled as lunatics, the truly zealous as Heretics, should they rebel against the city. In either case, believers were reformed with cruel but effective methods."

He deferred again to Animulus, who continued their shared tale.

"In that inexplicable moment, there were as many reactions to the creature as there were perceptions. Many of the Prospectors were terrified by what they saw, while in others a great greed grew within them at the sight of it. Only we three looked on in awe, unsure of what we were witnessing, yet somehow oddly protective of it. The creature had spoken to us, barely audible; but on some level, somehow, we had each heard it. From that moment on, we were brothers.

"At last, the trance was broken. Our team leader shouted, commanding the crew to hunt the beast in the name of science. I suspect that sport was closer to his true motives. Our colleagues lurched forward in chorus, but we three raced ahead and stood in their path. The captain ordered us to stand down, and when we refused, flushed a deep shade of red. He threatened us with varied forms of discipline, but still we would not yield, for we knew what would happen if we did. Greatly outnumbered, our peers forced their way on at the orders of the captain, knocking us to the ground.

"With no words spoken, we rose as one and followed the others. Cerebrus tried to explain that we should proceed with patience, with respect, and I pleaded with them to listen. The captain confronted us directly as his men carried on, but Manus reached out and grabbed him with an irrepressible fury.

"Even anger was an extreme we seldom experienced in the mundane life of Inanimis, but this was something else entirely. This was a ferocious, unbridled rage that dwells only in the darkest parts of our humanity. How it erupted we could not say, but to our shock and dismay, we unleashed a power we had no idea we possessed, and it came at great cost. Before we had time to even process what had happened, our associates were annihilated, returned to the soil as ashes."

Davis had no reply; he simply stared at the brothers with wide eyes. He would not have believed it, had he not seen this terrible power in action earlier that very day.

"The sky was dark, the forest cheerless, and the creature we sought was nowhere to be seen," continued Animulus. "Our only memory of it came as a subtle voice, rendering blurry intuitions, faintly suggesting a different way of being, one for which we never knew we longed. We searched far and wide, but never again found a place of such beauty, or a creature so beguiling. Need and desperation eventually drove us home, to the only life we had ever known, and the vain hope that our kin would believe us, understand our inexplicable urges, and most importantly, forgive.

"Upon returning to the city, it was quickly apparent that none of this was bound to happen. We were immediately apprehended, and after a great many inquisitions and investigations we were reluctantly given a trial. That we were granted even that much still amazes me. When the time came, we told much the same story. 'The Guardian is real, for we saw it ourselves,' we said. The fact that three accounts corroborated one another gave an unprecedented credence to our tale, but even this could not overcome the engrained skepticism and stigma associated with so strange an experience.

"It became clear that no verdict would rise to our naive hopes, but still we would not back down, and we became only more emphatic in our assertions. We chastised the city for its unrelenting advancement, and fantasized aloud about a better way; but the Councilors overseeing the very public trial made sure to make a persuasive example out of those who would speak out against them in such a fashion.

"Our testimony was abruptly concluded, and the Councilors needed little time to confer. We were labeled as Heretics of the city and sentenced to Permanent Re-Assignment. Our memories, our personality – everything that made us who we are – would be lost forever. Our minds would be shocked, stunted into one that is barely competent, but entirely complacent.

We would be capable of only the most trivial jobs, of which the city had plenty. But never again would we slander Inanimis, or spout lies about what lies in the forest beyond the edge of the frontier.

"Our stupor slowly dissipated as we were dragged away for reformation, but when the shock finally fled, we were left with naught but contempt. We escaped captivity in much the same way as you witnessed today, driven by two of the deadliest emotions: self-preservation and vengeance. Few guards dared stand in our path after observing the fate of the first several who did. And so we came to leave Inanimis — by force, condemned to a life of exile.

"We were of course devastated by the ignorance of our own people, but sadly, it surprised us little. Who could ever believe such a thing without experiencing it for themselves? And of those few, who among them would side with our actions? Even of those who did see the creature, most reacted only with aggression toward it. Whatever made us any different, we do not claim to know, but we have sought for the Guardian ever since.

"We have come to learn that it is known by many names, though we know it best as Praestes. Since that day, we have neither seen it, nor heard more than rumors and whispers among our occasional acquaintances — that is, until yesterday, when all hope was finally lost."

For the first time, the otherwise stoic man stumbled, unable to muster the words. Animulus knew what they meant, but he had yet to utter them aloud. He finally managed it.

"The Guardian is dead."

"Dead?" said Davis, trying his best to act surprised.

"Slain by the hands of a man," quoted Cerebrus.

Davis was stunned. His spirits sank, dragged down by equal parts sorrow and terror. *They know.* A mass of dread sat in his throat, choking for now all hope of any other words. Frankly, it may have been for the best. He understood that he could not speak of what he knew to the brothers, for fear of what they would do if they found out.

Amazingly, Davis had not even remembered the note sitting in his pocket; his thoughts were too blinded by the scene of the bloody Heart of Custos in his hand. If he had, however, he might have been able to lift the spirits of the brothers, for the note had told Davis to come find the Guardian at Immolatio when his wisdom had awoken completely.

Then again, admission of it would probably have sparked a series of questions to which he didn't want to give the answers. What's more, even if he had remembered the note, he'd never heard of this place. He had no idea where to go. Nor was there any way of knowing whether Custos would even be there, for Davis had not yet met the only prerequisite. As it was, he sat idly by, as if having no knowledge of whom they spoke, his heart pounding nervously in his chest.

"What does this have to do with me?" he asked to change the subject.

The answer, of course, is that it had a great deal to do with him. He knew who was responsible for the slaying of the Guardian, for he could not escape the memory of wrenching the Heart from its lifeless body.

But now, what mattered to Davis was what his role in all of this could yet be. He had come to a crossroads, and as before, he wasn't sure where to turn next. His thoughts were again clouded with so many questions that they overwhelmed his ability to think clearly about any one in particular.

Was it the right or the wrong thing to do? What is even the difference, and who is it that decides? What had come over him at the sight of the beast? Why did he do it at all? More importantly: what was there to do about it now? Why was he drawn into that city today, and by what grace was he saved from its clutches? Surely the ways of Inanimis are extravagant and reckless; but isn't the murder of its citizens just as unforgivable? What were those images that overcame his senses, and why did they cause him such emotional distress? What was that overpowering feeling, the weight in his chest which had never left him since that last warm embrace?

This last question, above all others, dominated his thoughts.
And then, Davis remembered how this long day had begun.
The Sage might know the answers.

"We do not know," said Animulus, not entirely ignorant of his guest's internal strife. He detected the anxiety but could not discern its cause.

"But you two rescued me!" said Davis, turning to Cerebrus and Manus. "Now that I think of it, how did you both just happen to be there?"

"The tale is not fully told," is all Cerebrus would say. Animulus resumed.

"We heard news of the fate of Praestes through a note. The messenger evaded our detection, which was not the least of our surprises. We knew not the author."

"What does it have to do with me?" repeated Davis – louder, impatient.

The brothers looked at one another, hesitant. *They trust me as little as I do them,* he realized. In the silence, there somehow grew an understanding. Animulus pulled the note from his pocket and handed it to Davis.

Scrutatorus,

> *The creature you long sought is dead, slain by the hands of a man.*
> *An ally walks among Inanimis, but he does not belong there.*
> *Take heed, tomorrow afternoon, to the sounds of alarm.*
> *His fate is entwined with your own. Send him west.*

> *You will know him as Davis.*

> *The Gardener*

"What lies to the west?" asked Davis.

And as he asked the question, Animulus jerked, assailed by a shiver — struck either by odd recollection or unsettling premonition. He said nothing, but his disposition changed markedly, and instantly.

"We hoped you could tell us," said Cerebrus. He appeared not to notice, too focused on interrogation. "Come, we have told you our tale, along with much of what we know. It is time for you to explain yourself."

"Explain myself?" asked Davis, genuinely perplexed by the prospect. *I couldn't do that if I tried.* "What is there to explain?"

"Who are you?" asked Cerebrus, stern. "Where do you come from? And what were you doing in the city?"

"I lived by the sea," he said. Quickly he came to a dilemma, for so little had happened that he felt comfortable sharing. *How much should I say?*

"So you do know of the west?" prodded Cerebrus, in the nick of time.

"I suppose," he said. "I had never wandered inland before, but since then I've seen little more than trees, and I lost my bearings more than once. I'm afraid I won't be much help with geography."

"Geography is not our problem," said Cerebrus. "You say you had never wandered inland. What led you to Inanimis?"

"I was lost in the woods," answered Davis. It was a clever workaround: neither false nor fully honest. "I stumbled onto the city by accident. I talked to some people at the gate, and the next thing I knew, I was running from the guards. Then you showed up."

"So, you have no idea why someone would send us a note with your name on it? Do you know its author?"

"I have no idea," said Davis, and it was equally true for both items.

"He's lying to us," said Cerebrus, turning to Animulus. But the tallest man said nothing yet, for he was lost deep in his own deliberations.

The Heretic turned his ire back at Davis.

"You know more than you are telling us. Speak!"

The stare of Cerebrus was intense, and under its pressure, Davis was rattled. He was fairly sure he could not outsmart these men; and he was certain he could not outmatch them in arms.

He had little choice but to confess.
"I..." he started. The words did not come easy.
He had yet to fully confess it to himself.
"I don't know who I am."

"He's lying!" shouted Cerebrus to his eldest brother once again.

Davis would not be shaken now. He did not plead. He did not squabble. He simply looked Animulus square in the eye and told him the truth.

"I awoke by the sea, but I remember little else. I think there's someone who might be able to help me – a Sage – but I don't know where to go."

"Brother," began Cerebrus, even louder than before. "He is—"

"That's enough," said Animulus, rebuking his brother as kindly as he could. He hadn't spoken since he shuddered; and for a moment, all was still.

"You must go west," he said to Davis.

Cerebrus looked at his brother in disbelief, but he did not protest.

"You know the Sage?" asked Davis, optimistic for the first time all day.

"I have never heard of such a person," said Animulus. "But the note says you are to go west." He glanced at his brother. "It also calls you an ally."

"And you believe it?" asked Cerebrus. He was skeptical, but genuine, and he trusted his brother fully. If Animulus said so, his brothers would follow.

"Praestes is dead," he said. "I cannot explain it, but I believe it to be true. And the same note that delivered this ill news named Davis a friend. It then predicted when and where we should find him, predictions that proved true. It gives me no reason to doubt it, and the same goes for the man himself. Forget not the state in which you found him. Any enemy of Inanimis is a friend of the Scrutatorus."

He stared across the fire at Davis, weighing the make of him one last time before committing to bestow his full faith. His eyes were piercing; he too had seen more than he disclosed. His attention next alternated between brothers, to his left and then right, in the circle around the fire.

"Something tells me that fate did not send this man to us without cause. His is entwined with ours, the note told us also." Surprisingly, he smiled, and the mood was lightened. "If you distrust him so much, what harm is there in sending him away?"

The brothers nodded. The word of their elder was all that they needed.

"I know of no Sage," said Animulus, "but we are by no means the only ones living outside the walls of Inanimis. Free people, an ancient people, are to be found here and there – if you can find them. I have heard word of a wise woman, far away, in a canyon named Recordatio. I would start my search there."

"Will you join me?" asked Davis. He thought of black ashes blowing in the breeze inside the city. *They may prove useful allies, if allies we are.*

"We will help prepare you for this journey," said Animulus, "but it is one you must take alone. The note says only to send you west, not to lead you there. We have come this far on its word, and my intuition tells me that this too should be heeded. And with the events of the day as they are, we cannot leave the city unwatched. Our purpose lies here for now, to gather what news we can of the death of Praestes. Long have the elite of Inanimis spurned the Farce of the Forest; I suspect they had a hand in it."

Not Inanimis, but another. Of the Lord, however, Davis could not share, for there would be no way to absolve himself entirely.

"Then there is much to discuss," said Cerebrus. Manus rose from the fire, ready for action.

"Not now," said Animulus. "Our guest has had a difficult day, as have we. There will be time on the morrow for more answers, and the added questions they create. For now, we shall rest."

His brothers did not object, for they were more tired than they would have admitted. The men tidied the table and retired to their beds, which they rolled out on the floor of the chamber. They provided an extra mat for Davis, and at the end of this tumultuous day, he finally found the need to acknowledge their help.

"Brothers," said Davis, trying to find the right words.

He settled for the simple.

"Thank you."

They nodded in recognition and wished him goodnight. Manus threw some gravel over top of the fire, and they each fell away into slumber.

Davis awoke not long after dawn, well-rested for how late they had gone to bed. As early as he assumed he had risen, he sat up to find himself alone in the chamber. He walked out through the winding tunnel and emerged into the morning sun. There he found Animulus, sitting on the pinnacle of the large stone serving as the doorway, looking north. Without turning to face him, Animulus spoke to the newcomer.

"Good morning," he said. "I hope a deep sleep restored your strength. You will no doubt need it for a long walk and an arduous experience."

"Whatever may come, I see no choice but to carry on," replied Davis, trying to sound brave.

"Your words are wise, my friend. I only hope your heart is as steadfast."

Davis wasn't sure, and Animulus could tell.

"Come, join me on my perch," he said. "The view is quite remarkable."

Davis obliged and scrambled up the side of the rock. It was indeed pleasant upon its peak — more spacious than anticipated, with ample room for all three brothers to sit and survey the land around their sanctuary. In doing just that, Davis saw it for the first time: far in the distance, rising above the trees to the west was an immense, foreboding mountain. Its face glowed red in the rays of the ascending morning sun.

"Will I have to go over that?" asked Davis, realizing in the moment what stood in his way.

"By the power of Praestes — No," said Animulus, and nothing more.

"Then where am I going?"

"Cerebrus can no doubt tell you where things are in relation to each other, but in my experience, I see that you wish for more than directions."

Davis said nothing.

"What would you ask of me?" said Animulus.

"Directions are fine for now," replied Davis. *I have enough to worry about without troubling philosophical questions.* "Where are the others?" he asked at their mention.

"They have gone out to forage for breakfast," said Animulus. "They need not have gone far, and I expect them soon."

The two then sat in silence for a while, enjoying the fresh morning air, ignoring the chance for any further inquiries. In a few minutes the brothers returned, and the two men climbed down from the rock to greet them. Manus produced a gathering of berries and wild grains; he entered the caves to cook them, for no fires were to ever be lit outside the inner chamber. He boiled the grains, mashed the berries in a mortar, and combined the two together. He partitioned the meal into four even rations and returned outside. The men ate their breakfast atop the entrance stone, basking in the beauty of their surroundings.

I never knew how delicious such a simple meal could be. There was nothing fancy about it, just two of the most basic bounties of nature; but together they yielded something so divine that he could hardly contain his enjoyment.

"It's amazing how the meekest meal can satisfy the soul," said Animulus, in seeing his guest's delight. "The people of Inanimis break foods down into their ingredients, only to build it all back up again into something barely worth eating. It makes no sense. We prefer to eat the things Nature has given us in the way in which they were given."

"I can't imagine a means of making this meal any better," said Davis.

When all their appetites had been satisfied, Manus walked into the cave and returned momentarily with a deerskin bag.

"Here are the supplies we've prepared," he said, handing over the bag.

"As promised," said Davis. *These men have had a busy morning.*

"In it you will find rations of grains and berries for several days, two of the small rocks you've seen us use to start fires, a pot for cooking, a pouch for carrying water, and a dark green cloak to protect you – at least a little – from unwanted attention."

"There are things in these woods from which it is best to stay hidden," said Animulus.

With such a comprehensive set of supplies in hand, Davis couldn't believe he'd been wandering around in what was evidently a dangerous place without any form of provisions. The thought had never even crossed his mind to take such precautions when venturing out into the unknown world. Now that it had, he chastised himself for being so foolish.

It's lucky I've made it this far with the way I've been going. From now on, I must promise myself I'll be smarter.

"You should also have this," said Cerebrus. He handed Davis a folded piece of paper. "It might help you keep track of those bearings you keep losing." He mocked Davis, certainly, but in the way that a brother might do.

As he unfolded it, Davis viewed a crude map with odd labels. The coast was apparent, far away to the west, though nowhere was there a bay of the same shape as the one he vaguely remembered. He'd left the shore only a few days ago, but it may as well have been a lifetime.

Next to the coast was the outline of a canyon, twice in length what it was in width. A river flowed through its middle, twisting and branching, until eventually it met the sea. Southeast of the canyon was a sprawling set of hills, their images growing larger until culminating in a single massive mountain. To its west, below the canyon, was a glaring blank space in what was an otherwise detailed map. The lines in that direction faded, giving way to an enthralling opacity. *Terra Incognita,* the lone inscription read.

Cerebrus placed his finger in the middle of the canyon.

"This is your destination: Recordatio — the Canyon of Reminiscence, as some call it. The water flowing through it is the river Tenuis, which stems from a lake of the same name, not far to the west of our sanctuary." From the canyon, he slid his finger eastward across the whole width of the map, where it came to rest on a small triangular shape, looking very much like the angular rock at the entrance to the caves. "This is where we are, south and slightly east of the city of Inanimis."

Davis looked at the outline of the behemoth to the north, which he knew crawled ever steadily in a westward direction. To the right of it was marked the Inviocassus, stretching all the way to the eastern edge of the map, and beyond. His eyes traced back west and saw that the city was due east of the canyon, as he'd witnessed from high atop its walls. Should Inanimis continue in its course, it would be faced with a serious problem.

I suppose they'd simply change direction. He was probably right.

While not entirely sure of every direction he'd traveled the previous day, Davis estimated that he had walked mostly south from the throne for a long way before stumbling upon the city's western gate. Yet, the city was near the top of the map, and its far south was equally unknown. Thus, it seemed that this map would only aid him in the central region of the world.

From the sanctuary, Cerebrus dragged his finger back westward.

"Here is the lake Tenuis, only an hour from our doorstep."

To its southwest lay the eastern edge of the mountain's encircling hills.

"And those?" asked Davis. He glanced back over his shoulder at the mountain, glowing red in the distance.

"Those are the foothills of the Great Volcano — Talionis," said Cerebrus, but Animulus interjected at once.

"At no point should you ever travel that way, if you know still what is good for you."

"Why not?" asked Davis.

Animulus stared at the ominous peak above the trees to the west.

"The ash from the mountain is toxic," he said. "It can drive a mind mad. Some even claim Talionis is guarded by ghosts of the past. In either case, it is perilous. All those who wander that way are not long for this world."

"Another myth?" asked Davis with a smile.

"It is no myth," said Animulus, and he was not amused.

"Nevertheless," said Cerebrus again, "the hills leading up to Talionis serve as a useful landmark." He traced the route of the river until it met the Recordatio. "The river falls into the canyon here, northwest of where we are. You can descend to the bottom along a faint trail at the southern side of the river, though the way is unsafe. The spray from the waterfall renders the rocks untrustworthy, and the trail is incredibly steep. Together, it makes for a deadly combination."

"Footing is not the only difficulty of this endeavor," added Animulus. "You will need to keep grounded as you descend through the mist – both your feet and wits alike."

Davis would have wondered what he meant, but he didn't have time. Cerebrus immediately continued.

"When you reach the end and the ground becomes level, follow the river. Somewhere near the shore, you may find the wise woman, if indeed she is more than a rumor."

"It sounds like a fool's errand," said Davis.

"Then aptly named it is," said Cerebrus with a condescending smirk. "But yes, you will be on your own. We have never been to the bottom of the Recordatio, though we have surveyed it from above."

"The way is known to be treacherous," stressed Animulus again. "We find enough trouble without seeking it out."

Turning back to the map, Davis wondered again about its curious void.

"What's in this region here, where nothing is marked?" he asked.

"We do not know," said Cerebrus, "for neither have we ventured that way, nor heard of any who have."

"From where we have stood," said Animulus, "all there is to see is sand."

Ever a man of haste, Cerebrus drew them back to the practical. He pointed again to the lake.

"When you come to the Tenuis, you must make a crucial choice. As you see, the river meanders for many miles before finally flowing into the Recordatio. You could follow the river, but the way is long and laborious. Not only does it wander, the undergrowth is thick and makes for difficult terrain. As your way is long and difficult enough, I would recommend a different route."

Animulus looked on in disapproval, though he said nothing for now.

"Rather than follow the river, if you were to simply keep traveling west from the lake, you would meet the foothills of Talionis. If you skirted the edge of the foothills – without ever beginning to climb – you would be on a perfect northwest bearing, heading straight for the canyon.

"The way is far more direct, and the terrain less difficult. The hills are coated in ash from an ancient eruption, and neither tree nor weed will grow there. Even where the ash has ended, the vegetation is small and sparse. If I were you, I would travel alongside the Ashlands, as they are called."

Animulus could no longer bear his silence.

"If you choose to go this way, you must make sure not to climb the foothills, not even slightly, and do not disturb the ash. Steer clear of Talionis. Not only will it take you off your bearing, but you may lose a great deal more than your time."

With this stern word of warning, Davis looked as if he'd already seen a ghost. Animulus could tell that he'd been suitably cautioned, and he let the matter go. The look of gravity on his face quickly turned to a smile as it became time to wish his newfound companion goodbye.

"You had better begin if you wish to make your way down into the canyon by nightfall. You may have just enough time, should you keep a steady pace."

Davis refolded the map and placed it in the pack with the rest of his timely supplies.

"My friends," he said, "thank you again for all the aid and guidance you've provided. I am off to answer the most pressing of questions."

"May you find what you seek," said Animulus. His brothers nodded, and they too managed an unlikely smile as they bid the man farewell.

Davis looked one last time at the mountain in the distance. The sun had grown higher, but still Talionis radiated red. Without further ado, he made his way into the west.

2.6 / First Perceptions of Cohesion

Precisely as he'd been told, within little more than an hour Davis came over a small rise and looked out over the Tenuis. He sauntered down to the shore, where he envisioned drinking the remainder of the water in his pouch, to take advantage of the opportunity to fill it again.

Before he even reached the edge of the shore, however, a putrid odor knocked him backwards. Fighting through the discomfort, he made his way to the water to find that it was not clear as expected, but riddled with a filth that made him abandon all thoughts of filling his pouch. He turned and walked up the bank to escape the intolerable stench.

Finding a nice flat rock uphill from the lake, and out of the reek of the water, Davis sat down to rest before continuing. Having traveled only an hour, he paused more to delay his decision than recover his endurance; for he knew that he had come so soon to the point where he must decide which route he would take. As he sat in consideration of the two scenarios, he was pleased by the sight of an unexpected companion. A small newt was traveling ever so slowly down the length of a log beside him. The newt passed just to the left of Davis, but it appeared not to have noticed him.

"Hello there," said Davis.

At this unforeseen harassment, the newt leapt six inches in the air, rolled up into a ball, and plummeted down the rest of the log. It tumbled off the end and crashed into the grass below.

"I'm sorry," said Davis, rising from his seat to approach this visitor. "I didn't mean to startle you."

At the sight of the threatening giant, the newt curled back its spine, lifting its head and tail off the ground. All four limbs arched in the air as far as the newt could stretch, showing off its bright red underbelly in a rather humorous display of self-defense.

"Don't come near me!" it said in a panic. "Stay away!"

Davis found the scene amusing and bent down to get a closer look.

"I'm warning you, I'm toxic! Approach at your own peril!"

Now feeling sorry for the stress he was causing the creature, Davis stepped back and sat down once again on the rock.

"I'm sorry," he said in a soothing voice. "I meant no offense. My name is Davis. Who are you?"

The newt was not so sure it could trust this stranger. It waited a while but eventually, perhaps due more to fatigue than trust, it unfolded itself back to the ground and regained its normal gait. It stared blankly at the stranger in suspicion.

"Come here," waved Davis with a smile. "Rest with me a while. Tell me about yourself."

The newt, though still apprehensive, clambered back up the side of the log and turned to inspect the man that had surprised it so.

"How do I know if I can trust you?"

"Well," said Davis, "I suppose you could take my word that I've never harmed a newt before." This wasn't very convincing. "Nor do I intend to now," he added.

"You don't intend to," said the newt, "but that doesn't mean you won't."

"Why are you so certain I will?" asked Davis, a little insulted by the aloofness of the encounter so far.

"Just learning from the past," it said. "You can't blame a newt for that."

At the onset of these words, Davis was overcome again by an eerie sensation. *The past?* Something flashed in his mind, but he lost track of it as quickly as it came.

"What did you say?" asked Davis uneasily.

"I said you can't blame a newt for learning from the past," it repeated, slightly annoyed. It was beginning to think there might be something odd about this human – or at least more so than the others it had heard about.

"Right, sorry," said Davis. "I've been having trouble with my ears." *Among other things.* "Well..." he said with a moment's pause, thinking of a way to refute the newt's fairly good point, "...you've never met me before. What's your name, and what brings you here on this fine day?"

By now the newt had calmed down, convinced that, at least for the moment, the stranger meant no harm.

"My name is Nemus," it said. "I lived here in this lake – until recently that is. My kindred are all leaving, though we have nowhere to go."

"Leaving?" asked Davis. "But, leaving why? Isn't a lake the perfect kind of place for someone like you?"

Apparently he'd forgotten his own reaction to the status of the water.

"We don't want to leave, but our home is no longer fit for our presence. We're a very sensitive lot, you know. As soon as we heard from some of our furrier friends about the presence of the Tall Ones, we knew it was only a matter of time."

"The Tall Ones?" asked Davis.

"That's right. The ones who walk on two feet. The ones who look like you. I've never actually seen one of you before. I'd like to say I'm pleased to make your acquaintance, but I'm not in the brightest mood of late."

"You mean people are the reason you're leaving your home?"

"We're told that the Tall Ones live a great distance in that direction," said the newt, nodding his head to the northeast. Of course, what was a great distance to a newt, Davis knew as a few hours' walk. "What happens upstream, happens downstream."

The words again struck a painful, powerful chord, somewhere deep inside of Davis. The dreadful sensation was back all too soon.

"I'm sorry, what did you say?" he asked the newt for a second time.

"I said: what happens upstream, happens downstream."

And so it was that Davis had his very first glimpse of how everything he witnessed was connected. He'd previously seen the world as only a collection of separate entities, but now had the faintest glimmer of insight into the way things actually are.

He thought of Animulus, denouncing the exorbitance of Inanimis. He thought of the wastes of Inviocassus, and the stench of the tainted Tenuis. He thought of Regulus the Great, dancing around in its very own parade. He thought of Errol the Wary, who now sat on the throne, all too eager to have slain its former master.

But most of all, Davis thought of the bloody Heart of Custos resting in the palm of his hand. He was beginning to understand in earnest that there might be dire consequences to the actions he had taken, as well as those that were to come. The newt continued, not appearing to notice the effect it had on its companion.

"And what happens downstream often comes back to affect what happens upstream again, now that I think of it," said Nemus. "The Tall Ones have never seemed to be bothered by that notion, but it's something we've come to know well. They may not care, or even be aware of it, but their presence has poisoned our waters. We're left with no choice but to leave our home or die in its grime."

"I'm sorry," said Davis. "I would never have wished this upon you."

"You might not have ever wished it," said Nemus, "but it happened nonetheless."

Davis was not without empathy, but neither was he willing to take the blame for the actions of others.

"You don't understand," he said. "I may look like the ones who are responsible for this, but I am not one of them."

The newt stared at him skeptically, not entirely convinced. Davis couldn't really blame him, for he wasn't entirely convinced of it himself.

"In any event, I'm sorry," he said, and he left it at that.

The two took an impromptu moment of silence, both contemplating in their way the severity of these events. Davis eventually spoke first, for he wondered what was to come for Nemus.

"Where are the rest of your kind?" he asked. "What will you do now?"

"Most of my kin have already left. We divided our numbers into small groups, each heading out in different directions away from the lake. The hope is that at least some of us may one day find a suitable new home, even if the rest of us cannot be there to join them. That way, hopefully, a small remnant of our kind can live on – to die another day, as it were."

"Well, I don't think you'll have much luck to the northeast," said Davis, knowing what dwelt in that direction. "If it's not too late to tell those who left, they may have better luck on one of the other bearings."

"Thank you for your concern," said Nemus, "but I'm afraid it's too late for me to get word to them. Most of my kin would be well on their way. I should already be far from here myself, but I couldn't bear to part with my home so easily. I hesitated, stayed back while the rest of my group pressed on. I've always been more on the sentimental side, I guess. I just found it so hard to convince my legs to move. I have so many memories from my life here, and memories are such a heavy burden to bear."

As Nemus spoke, Davis was overwhelmed by a torrent of grief. All the inexplicable images he had seen earlier unexpectedly washed over him in a single wave of recognition, as if they were something he might have once known. *Memories? Is that what those were?*

This time around, he didn't see any of the scenes that had tortured him twice before; but he most certainly felt them. Their enormity pressed down on him, practically crushing him under their burden. Somehow Davis knew exactly what the newt meant. He understood what a crippling sadness these types of thoughts can cause, though he barely knew what they were. He appreciated how hard it must be for Nemus to leave everything that he knew and loved behind. It was as though, for the briefest moment, he was dimly aware of what it meant to love something at all.

Then he had another thought, posed to himself in the form of a question. *What would the man who stood over the slain body of the beast have thought of himself now?* Here he was – a man – crushed in his sorrow over the woes of a newt! *To hell with that man,* he decided. Unfortunately for him, however, this was also the part of him that had acted last.

"I wish there was something, anything I could do," said Davis, but he knew that there wasn't. *I can't even change the choices I've made, let alone the choices of others.* He felt powerless – the victim of having to observe the true victims.

"Thank you for your kindness," said Nemus. "But you and I both know that all either of us can do is move forward." The newt looked back at the festering lake. "In fact," it said with spirits lifting, "I don't think I need to dwell here in my own misery any longer. I think it's about time I take up my journey to the southwest."

"The southwest?" asked Davis with alarm. The warnings of Animulus reverberated in his head. "I don't think you should head that way."

"Why not?" asked Nemus.

"The mountain Talionis lies in that direction. I've been told it's not safe. 'All those who wander that way are not long for this world,' I was told."

Nemus just laughed at the concerns of the man.

"I may have never been there, but I know of Talionis. It might prove perilous for people like you, but I have nothing to fear. The only dangers that lurk there are those which you already carry." It grew as much of a grin as a newt could ever muster. "Besides, there might just be a mountain spring up there somewhere waiting for me."

Davis could tell that he wasn't going to convince the newt not to head that way, but thinking about it made him realize that his own path was still undecided. The choice was not an easy one: take the long but safer route, or a shortcut that flirts with the edge of disaster. The one thing he did decide was that sitting around wasn't going to help him figure anything out either way. The only thing to do was to consider the choices and make the best of the possibilities provided.

Following the river to the northwest was strenuous and overly-long, while the way to the west through the foothills was easier and more direct. Animulus did not approve of the latter route, but Cerebrus didn't seem to think that it was altogether hazardous. *Anyway, if a newt can face the terror of Talionis, what could I possibly have to fear?*

Thus was his internal strife settled. So long as he didn't begin to climb the mountain, as Animulus warned, the path to the west was the best way to go. Just as he had resolved this dilemma, he noticed that Nemus seemed equally ready to depart.

"Thank you for helping me finally come to terms with the fact that I have nothing left in this place," said Nemus.

"It was my pleasure," said Davis. He didn't know what he had done, but he was glad the newt had begun the process of looking forward. "I don't know what you will find to the southwest, but I hope it's the mountainous spring your heart desires. Farewell."

So did the two creatures part ways: Nemus setting out on a more southerly bearing, while Davis headed west to the Ashlands, his back to the morning sun.

The morning was well underway, and a short shadow stretched before Davis to the west. He moved steadily in that direction, enjoying the easier passage foretold by Cerebrus. He remembered well enough the inaccessible understory he'd so often encountered, and it wasn't difficult to imagine the tedious terrain should he have chosen the path of the river. From his limited interactions with the brothers, he knew at least that none were of a delicate constitution, or of the mind to overstate the difficulty of a passage. He recalled as well how easily they had moved through the dark woods after their escape from the city, and how hard he had struggled to keep up. *If even they find the river tough to navigate, I wouldn't stand a chance.*

Before long, the trees were almost completely absent, and little else stood in his way. As he moved along swiftly, any lingering uncertainties about his route were left behind him. *What took me so long to decide such an obvious thing?* His thoughts drifted lightly about from one reassurance to the next until finally wandering off into altogether irrelevant places, which aided in the passage of time. His shadow grew yet shorter as he strode confidently along, entirely unaware that the ground beneath him had started ever so slightly to rise.

Davis stopped to catch his breath. To his left were the vast rising foothills, so close that they blocked any view of Talionis. The hills were adorned with no vegetation, but they were littered with boulders of various sizes. A thick gray dust coated everything in sight, the ash of a long-forgotten eruption. It choked out any hope for the rejuvenation of new life.

The sun burned directly overhead, and as he rested, he shielded his eyes and looked down to the ground. Only then did he learn that his feet stood in the very same substrate. *The ash...* The sun continued to rise. His shadow was now but a small circle beneath him, growing shorter with every passing second. And then, at the stroke of noon, it vanished.

The sun straight above made it impossible to discern his orientation, though he certainly knew which direction not to travel. He spun, trying his best to calculate a northwest bearing as instructed. There were trees behind him, but far in the distance, and far lower than anticipated. *Did I wander too far?* Before he had the chance for these ill omens to sink in, there came a rustling in the dust of the hillside. It sounded like footsteps.

He turned around quickly and shouted: "Who's there?!"

There was no answer. A dark cloud made its way between him and the sun, concealing all the land in a thick shroud of gray. Not a moment before, there hadn't been a single blemish in the blue of the noontide sky.

"Show yourself!" he said in a timid voice intended as strong. "I know you're out there!" Once more, there was no response.

He spun again, but this time there were no trees to be seen. The same dreary landscape continued ceaselessly in all directions. There was nothing to be seen but boulders scattered in the ashes. The dust swirled in the distance; a circle of haze surrounded him which could not be penetrated.

He tried not to think of the warning he'd been given, but it was not a thought he could repress. *You may lose a great deal more than your time.* At that very notion, the rustling was back. The footsteps echoed, shattering on the boulders, dispersing in a way that made it impossible to tell from which angle they came. They sounded closer, however; of that he was sure.

From over his shoulder he started to hear faint cries in the distance — sounds of intense pain, longing, and distress. They haunted his thoughts, like the shrieks of a banshee outside your window, whom you know is not long from coming in through the door. With each passing breath, the voices grew more numerous, diverse, and distraught.

Most screamed in dire agony; but some, he suspected, were whispering his name. He circled in terror, trying to defend all directions at once, sweat dripping from the sides of his face. The footsteps grew louder, though he knew not to whom they belonged, or from where their maker would appear.

Davis finally ceased his spinning and stopped to listen more closely, determined to make sense of this madness. Just as he did, the footsteps grew even louder yet and quickened in their pace. But at last, he could sense their direction: they were coming from directly behind him.

He turned to face his adversary. The commanding figure of a man emerged from the whirling wall of dust. He was cloaked in darkness and rapidly approaching. Davis hardly had time to assess his foe, for he was only a few yards from him now, rushing forward at full speed, a knife held in his left hand.

Davis tried to brace himself for any sort of defense, but he was taken utterly unaware by the sudden assault. The man reached out to stab him, but at the last possible chance, Davis was able to grab the leading hand, and he wrestled with his assailant. The men grappled back and forth, each vying for control of the motions of the other. *He is too strong*, Davis feared. *I can't stop him.* Without a warning, Davis lost his grip on the man's wrist; and within an instant, he felt a piercing chill in his ribs.

His senses decelerated, the sight of his surroundings passing in snapshots as he fell to the ground in slow motion. He felt everything and yet was equally numb to it all. He felt his right lung collapse like the bursting of a balloon, his last remaining breath leaving his chest in a single great wave. He felt the warm stream of blood running down the front of his abdomen. It meandered from side to side, like the waters of a flood when they first breach the levee, unsure of where they should turn now that they finally taste their freedom. Last of all, he felt his head crash into the earth, lifting an enormous storm of dust as he fell into the ash.

The gray sky grew dimmer, and his sight was no more.

How long it was that he drifted about untethered in the darkness of his nightmares, Davis could not say upon waking. Nightmares they were, however, for his torment did not cease when he blacked out from pain. Images of war, death, depression, heartbreak, jealousy, and hatred plagued his thoughts, overpowering the existence of any other emotions. In that moment, negativity was all he had ever known. Every terrible thing a person could ever have done to them, or that they could ever do to another, was condensed into a ruthless deluge of suffering – and he was drowning in it.

What troubled him most, however, was the unrelenting implication that he himself had a hand in bringing it all about. Such an unfair suggestion he could not abide. Near the end of his delirium, the sight of his assailant came back into his mind. His first thought upon opening his eyes was how badly he hated this man, and how desperately he needed vengeance.

As he came to his senses, the terrible aching in his ribs was still present, though by now it had spread through his whole body. He reached down to inspect the severity of the wound, but to his surprise he felt nothing at the site of the puncture. There was no cavity in the place where he'd felt the knife enter, no river of blood streaming out from the wound. He shot to his feet in alarm and lifted his shirt over his head. There was nothing there – not so much as a single scratch.

He scanned everywhere for signs of his attacker but found only a single set of tracks in the ash which led to where he currently stood. The trees below him had returned to his view; a cloudless sky above shone bright blue. The sun had moved on, and a small shadow stood behind him to the east. He grabbed his pack from the dust and rushed down the slope as quickly as he could.

As he reached the start of the trees, he took a long drink from his pouch. This helped cool the ache of his injury, but it would not fully go away until he slowly began to accept that it must not have happened. *The dust is toxic*, he reminded himself. That must have been it. *Or maybe I'm just exhausted, dehydrated. Whatever the case*, he admitted, *that's one hell of a brave newt.*

After resting for a few minutes on grass well beyond the foothills, Davis slowly started to recover his strength. The most important matter now was to keep moving, not out of a desire to arrive at his destination – he'd almost forgotten why he was going this way in the first place – but out of a need to get as far away from here as quickly as he could.

Now that he was paying more careful attention, from this lower position he could clearly see that the ground did slowly start to rise. *This must be the place Cerebrus described.* Truly, he needed to turn northwest, and avoid continuing onward into higher ground. Carefully checking the placement of every step, he made his way slowly along on the proper course until the threatening hills of Talionis gave way to a wide, level plain.

The grasslands continued across the vast plain before him; and in the distance, Davis could see where the steppe fell away into the Recordatio. To the north, the forest carried on unbroken, until it came to the cliffs of the canyon. He could not yet see water, but he heard it roaring, and Davis knew this to be the place where the Tenuis rushed over the precipice.

As he walked towards the sound of the waterfall, he looked west and wondered again what lay in that direction, in the uncharted regions of his map. The sun was now well into that part of the sky, and Davis knew he needed to pick up the pace if he was to get to the bottom of the canyon by nightfall. Still, he hoped that soon enough his adventures would die down, and that he could find peace in exploring the great unknown that lay out there beyond his sight.

2.8 / The Path to Recordatio

The sun had begun to set by the time Davis stood at the edge of the canyon and looked out over its expanses. There was little room for delay if he intended to make it down the allegedly treacherous trail, but he took a moment anyway to savor the sight of the sea. It was the first time he'd seen it since embarking on his adventure. For some reason, it comforted him to know that it was still out there. The canyon was equally stunning, filled with lush fields and clusters of trees. The river wandered through them wildly, branching and reconvening often as it fed down to the shore.

Turning north, he walked along the boundary on his way to find the Tenuis. The forest to the east slowly dwindled as it approached the cliffs, the river emerging from its cover and rushing over the falls. The spray from the falling water filled the whole sky about it with a dense mantle of mist, concealing any actual sight of the river, and making it darker than the dusk alone. As Davis approached the southern bank, he scoured everywhere for the entrance but had little luck in the heavy fog so close to the falls.

Long did he struggle, but at last he stumbled upon a spot where the sharp edge of the cliff crumbled away into what looked like the start of the trail. By its side was a large post, a piece of paper pinned at its top. He plucked off the note and found an old familiar script.

Davis,

> *If ignorance offers one bliss, as they say*
> *Then why are you troubled so much every day?*
> *You came to this canyon for things you know not*
> *But herein you will find only what you forgot*
>
> *The greatest of riddles is hardest to solve*
> *To strengthen your chance, you must build your resolve*
> *Fear for your safety and sanity too*
> *Fear you will lose more than hope from this view*
>
> *Promise yourself you'll endure the dark night*
> *For the past will come haunting your soul into fright*
> *The greatest of puzzles is worth all attempts*
> *Come to terms with the Self and admit the past tense*

> *The Self-Aware Sage*

Davis crumpled the paper in his hand and closed his eyes in a rage. The pressure had been welling up beneath the surface ever since his journey began, but it mounted now to its highest level yet. He could feel it swelling, like a flood on the verge of breaking a dam incapable of containing it. It wouldn't take much more, he suspected; soon it might burst. Instead, he let this wrath flow from his body, to the taunting note clenched in his fist. When he opened his hand again, there was nothing left but ashes.

The cinders drifted off with the breeze, and Davis was taken aback by how effortlessly this ability had come to him. *So that's how the brothers do it.* Though now only ashes in the mist, the note was still a challenge, and it was a challenge he was ready to accept.

The path down the cliff was even steeper than he envisioned, and the rocks were indeed unworthy of trust. More than once he felt the grip of his footing start to loosen, forcing him to cling to the side and regain his composure. Despite the danger of doing so, Davis moved quickly, flirting closely several times with being entirely out of control. He had fallen subject to a headstrong intention to face whatever it was that awaited him at the bottom of the Recordatio.

The visibility only got worse as he descended, and the canyon floor could not be seen through the fog. Below him was nothing but swirling mist and a dense darkness beyond it. Soon he could no longer see the trail to place his steps. He would have likely continued in his obstinacy, groping blindly with his feet for their next stable placement, but for the sudden bombardment of unsettling stimuli.

A large rock slipped out from underfoot, bounced off the trail, and plunged into the abyss below. Davis waited, expecting to hear it hit the canyon floor, but it didn't make another sound. Instead of a crash, there came the sound of childish laughter from the fog – a laughter he'd heard more than once before. *I know those voices.* Davis reached out and waved his hands through the mist, trying to clear a path to view them, but in shifting his weight, he again almost fell. He lunged back, gripping the cliff barely in time to save himself. But still he would not give up.

"I'm over here!" he shouted in desperation. He now knew without a doubt that they would recognize him too. "I'm this way – come to the sound of my voice!" *The sound of who's voice?* "Come to your father!"

His shouts echoed off the walls of the canyon, but they led to no joyful reunions. Instead, the sound of laughter melted away into terrified screams, the likes of which a parent hopes to never have to hear. Both children were wailing at the tops of their lungs, horrified by some new turn of events.

"Joni! Evan! – It's OK," he cried. "Daddy's here. Everything is OK..."

Davis tried to comfort them, though he knew deep inside there was a cause for their sorrow that he could not rescind. The tips of his fingers barely grasped a rock on the side of the cliff as he leaned, his other arm stretching as far as it could through the mist in pursuit of their pleas.

As he continued calling out to them, they were joined by a third set of woeful screams. It should have been the sweet and soothing voice of a beautiful woman, but it was full of fear and despondency. She cried wearily, repeating his name as if trying to wake him. He knew he'd heard it not long before. Rolling ceiling tiles flashed again in his mind, the light fixtures racing by, pulsing like a strobe light. Her weeping whimpers never left his side as he sped down the length of that long and unknown corridor.

Though shattered and sobbing hysterically, her voice was still somehow full of unyielding resolution. It was as if, in spite of all the pain the world would inevitability engender, she would not ultimately be defeated by it. And yet, in this moment, she had never been so terrified. The joining of this last voice pushed his distress to the point of insufferable. He shouted out to her, but her cries never abated. He reached his arm further yet — stretching desperately — until his fingers slipped from their feeble grip, and he fell.

Davis plummeted through the haze, and the little light that existed was entirely extinguished. He sensed people around him in all directions, but none could be seen. There was only a thin circle of fog in front of an infinite blackness. He spun uncontrollably in its center, falling at terminal velocity. Every person he had ever known was shouting out to him from behind this thin veil, and they were inconsolable.

He couldn't discern a single voice, but he knew not one was missing. They pined for him — needed him. Their pain and despair were palpable. No words could describe the intensity of their mourning. In the center, he suffered the sum of all their grief, and it was excruciating. It weighed him down, a lead stone tied to his very essence, and he fell ever the faster for it.

At first, he tried to hide, but they were drawn to him too strongly, and him to them. Spinning rapidly, tumbling through the nothingness, he tried to reach out to the calls of these phantoms. They asked him where he'd gone, but he was right here in front of them. They begged him not to go, but he was waiting right here and always had been. He shouted answers to each of their questions, but he was never perceived, and it was never enough. The ring of voices in the fog constricted steadily inward as he fell, until the spell was finally broken by the dull thud of the ground.

Davis opened his eyes into the light of the setting sun, recovering slowly from the blackness that had consumed him only a moment before. His bones ached, and his head was ringing from the impact. He felt that he'd fallen forever through the fog, but when he looked up from his stance, he could see the spot on the cliff where the voices had started.

His mind raced. *How did I fall for so long? Where's all the fog? How is the light so different? Who were those voices? Where did they come from? Add those to the list of odd things that have happened today.*

He rose and brushed the dirt from his clothes. The journey so far had been difficult on his nerves, though the real work hard hardly begun. And yet here he was, in the Canyon of Reminiscence, in search of the Sage. He clenched his teeth; his face was grave. *It's time for answers.*

2.9 / The Self-Aware Sage

The glow of the sunset filled the canyon, illuminating the spray from the waterfall. Davis stood, gazing up at the top, still baffled by his odd descent. The mist was present, but it was far less thick than only moments ago. He couldn't see the canyon floor on his way down, for it was hidden in fog and darkness; but from here he could see the whole cliff face, burning orange in the last rays of the day. *It's in the past*, he decided. *It's time to move on.* It was a novel sort of thought for the man.

He was not far from where the waterfall crashed into a pool at the base of the cliff, and he rambled over to the river to clean himself up from his trials. The pool was large, and the water at its edge was calm and cool. This far downstream, it showed no obvious signs of contamination, unlike the lake at its headwaters. He kneeled on an overhanging bank and leaned out over the pool to splash his face. The chill was refreshing and helped rejuvenate his failing senses. Drops from his body fell back into the pond, and he watched as the ripples disturbed the surface and radiated outward.

The calm returned and Davis paused, peering into the water. There was no one looking back at him – only the deep, dark blue of the pool – but this didn't strike him as odd. In fact, he thought nothing of it at all.

"The water reveals what you most want to see," said a strange new voice from behind him. "It seems as though you wish to see nothing."

He rose, turning quickly to find that an elegant woman had approached undetected. She seemed familiar somehow, and he eventually placed it as a familial resemblance to the young boy that he met first on his journey.

"Are you the wise woman I was told I could find here?" asked Davis.

"That depends on what you consider wise," she said. It was no jest.

"Are you ... the Sage?" he asked more plainly.

"I am," she said.

"So you're the one who wrote the note at the top of the cliff?"

"Also true," answered the Sage. "I hope you have had a meaningful trip. I tried my best to warn you, but it is not an easy thing to describe."

"What's not easy?" He tried to be coy, but it wasn't convincing.

"You mean to say you do not know? I find that hard to believe."

"And why do you find that so hard to believe?" he asked.

"Because you are standing here at the base of the canyon, and there is but one way down."

Davis looked again toward the top of the cliff. The orange on its side was growing dimmer by the minute as the sun continued sinking. He remembered the journey well enough. There was no choice but to deflect.

"And that makes you think you know something about me?"

"One of us must," she retorted. "You made it clear that you do not."

So soon upon meeting Davis, the candid nature of this woman was playing into his preconceived aversion to her. He was in no mood to be patronized after the sort of day he'd had.

"How do you think you know anything about me, when even I don't?"

"We are not so different, you and me — except for one key point."

"And what's that?" asked Davis.

"My name."

"And what is that?" he asked again.

"I thought you said you read my note."

How was it signed? It could only come from memory, for the note was now but a scattered mess of ashes at the top of the mesa.

"The Self-Aware Sage?" said Davis reluctantly. "Is that supposed to mean something to me?"

The woman looked at him with the first expression since their meeting that could have been considered welcoming.

"In time," she replied, "I certainly hope that it will."

"And you don't have a real name, other than that?" asked Davis.

"My name is Ævitas," she said.

"It's nice to meet you then. Mind telling me what I'm doing here now?"

"You do not already know?" she said.

What little patience Davis had left was cast aside by the dodging of so simple a question. He tightened his fists, unsure how else to cope.

"This isn't a game anymore," he snapped. "I'm tired of being treated like a child. I'm sick of all the symbols and metaphors and ambiguous advice. I want answers! Who are you, and what do you want with me?"

She took a moment, looking long and hard at the presumptuous man standing before her. This angry and arrogant nature did not truly suit him, and she knew that fact; she had to remind herself, however, that he simply didn't. She justly perceived that he was fishing for any sort of personality he could muster. She said nothing, but she walked slowly past him and sat on a rock near the side of the pool. This caught him off guard and diffused his frustration; he followed and sat beside her. The Sage tried a different tactic.

"You are finally beginning to understand the gravity of your situation, and for that I commend you. You have started, however, by asking the right questions in the wrong direction. Unfortunately for you, I have no answers." She gestured to the water. "For I am like a mirror; I can only reflect your questions back to you. It is you who must answer them." He followed her attention to the pool, confused by the notion. "And so, Davis, I will ask you: who are you, and what do you want from yourself?"

"I don't know who I am!" he said defensively. *I'm sick of having to admit that.* "Right now, I just want to find out what I'm doing here."

"You are here for the very reason you just conceded," said the Sage. "You do not know who you are, and that makes it very hard to undertake what you are here to accomplish."

Davis was too intent on the first part to take much notice of the latter.

"You know that You Are, and that is something – but it is not enough. You have proven on more than one occasion that you can survive on instinct. You are only starting to understand, however, that there is a lot more to living than simply responding to stimuli."

"I seem to be doing just fine," he said; and as soon as he did, he knew it wasn't true. The Sage paused and waited patiently for him to come around. He quickly hung his head, conceding defeat, but slowly raised it again, determined. "So, what do I do now?"

"You must face the most difficult of challenges," said Ævitas. "You must confront the Self and learn from its lessons." Her lips turned from flat to frowning. "I have to admit, I am not confident you will succeed."

"You know, the last Sage was a lot friendlier," said Davis. He was only half-joking. Her disposition reverted in an instant, from having begun to show the first shred of patience, to suddenly having none left for him at all.

"It was you who said that the time for games is over," she said sternly. "The light-heartedness that comes from waking at the start of a leisurely day has long since passed. You have glimpsed into the heart of your most profound inner mysteries, yet you hide from them in denial, like a coward, wrapped in the self-pitying illusion of confusion. If you cannot rise to this challenge, then go back to the place from whence you came. Perhaps there is a chance you can shrink back into the pitiful complacency of insentience."

Davis was shocked by her bluntness, but not by the truth she spoke, for he knew it as such. *She's right,* he admitted silently. *I am hiding. This is the whole reason I came here. What am I waiting for?* he asked, and he already had an answer. *I'm afraid of what I might find,* said something else inside.

The Sage took a deep breath, and she spoke softer and more sweetly.

"Should you choose instead to go forward, though the way is turbulent, the rewards will be greater than you could ever imagine."

The man's eyes widened.

"Where do I start?" said Davis.

The Sage could not help but produce the faintest beginnings of a smile.

"You have already started but at first could not see."

I have already started? he wondered. *Where did I start?*

"The water?" asked Davis.

The Sage nodded her head.

"Beside you is a hallowed place – the Lacuna Speculis," she said. "You must confront your reflections. Though not all will be easy to endure."

Davis was visibly mystified as he looked out over the pool. *Confront my reflections?* The mirror was an inconceivable concept for him.

"What do you mean?" he asked, turning back to the Sage. "I'll see visions in the water of the things that I'm thinking?"

The Sage laughed at his naivety, jovial for the first time since they met. Davis might have been pleased by it, but he was lost too deep in thought.

"You will see," said Ævitas, and she nodded her head.

Intrigued now, Davis rose and walked closer to the pool. He glanced behind him one last time, as if looking for encouragement from the Sage, but he found to his dismay that there was no one there. *I am on my own.* Davis had little love for this Sage, but now that she was gone, he almost missed her company. He turned back to the water and kneeled on the bank for the second time today.

The water was so blue that it almost looked black, and he couldn't tell how far down its depths extended, for he could not see beyond the glare of the surface. Upon it, there was no one below him where his own image should have been, only the subtle twinkling of the evening's first stars.

What am I supposed to find? At first, there was nothing but silence and stillness. Then, to his great fortune, his thoughts echoed the first thing the Sage had said. He could still hear it spoken in her voice.

The water reveals what you most want to see.

Perhaps that was the key to it all. Perhaps all he had to do was decide what it was that he actually wanted from all this. He stared into the pool, straining his eyes in the last fading dusk light, wondering what secrets were hidden on the bottom beyond his view.

Well – he reflected – *what do I really want?*

Without any conscious effort, something came to him. He heard the laughter of children, then the sweet soothing voice of a beautiful woman. They were all he needed now. His awareness turned again to the feeling in his chest that hadn't left him since it arrived at the gates of Inanimis.

"I want to know who they are," he said aloud into the water. "I want to know how I know them. I want to find them again and fill this great void."

At once, an outline slowly faded into view in the deep blue of the water. Having summoned them, Davis expected he might again see the images accompanying those old conversant voices that pursued him. But to his surprise, it was only a single person that began to appear directly below him. The features of the figure grew sharper the longer he gazed into the waters. Soon he saw the face of the most unfamiliar person of all.

It's ... Me.

A tear ran from his eyes and splashed upon the face in the water. The ripples refracted and distorted his image, and he was overwhelmed again by a set of unexpected recollections. At the sight of his reflection, a lifetime of memories filled every crevice of his consciousness. They contained love and joy, happiness and prosperity; but these emotions were intrinsically coupled with fear and misery, misfortune and regret. Every component of his ego was thrust back upon him after a long age of slumber. Every positive and negative aspect of his life existed concurrently, like two halves of a whole.

As these remembrances flooded back in a single momentous wave of recognition, he found it odd that anyone could ever forget such a profound thing as the Self. But that didn't really matter now. He was whole again.

Davis had found himself at long last, at the bottom of the Recordatio.

He turned around, overjoyed, wanting desperately to have anyone with whom to converse. He'd been lost for so long in some amnesiac reverie; it was only natural that he needed to share his elation with someone. For he was complete again; he was himself. He had stories – a lifetime's worth of stories – memories that brought him so much happiness that he felt it a shame that they should dwindle away in his brain all alone. Memories were meant to be remembered; and how better to remember them than by sharing them with a friend by the fire?

"Ævitas!" he cried loudly. "Ævitas it worked. You can come back now."

There was no reply but the chirping of insects in the last lingering rays of the sunset.

"Ævitas, please," he shouted, louder this time for the lack of replies. "Where am I? I need your help – I remember! I remember it all. Please..."

His shouts broke down into little more than a hesitating murmur. He fell to his knees at the edge of the pool and began to weep softly. A tear for the people he'd known in those stories; a tear for the places he'd been; a tear for the fact that he'd truly been with them all once, yet now they were mere shadows of their former selves, rattling dimly around in the waning mind of a lonely man on his own in the wilderness. *How quickly we lose them*, he lamented. The bittersweet veracity of nostalgia had already caught up with him, only moments after his very first recollections.

Even the happy memories only bring me pain in the end, for they have all passed away. His whimpers had now subsided into a slow series of long and steady breaths as he tried to regain his composure. *If this is what it brings me, I don't see the point in remembering.* He wiped his cheeks with his sleeves and rose from the ground.

"I want to give them all back," he said. He barely knew what he was forfeiting. "If I can't be in them anymore, then I don't want them at all."

The water in the pool began to ripple on its own. The ground began to rumble, and the cliffs began to shake. Boulders toppled down from all sides of the Recordatio. The last sliver of the sun sank beyond the horizon, and the sky went dark. Davis closed his eyes and hoped for the end.

He saw a flash of purple flowers by the shore so far away.

But then, in his utmost despair, the most important memories of all called out to him from the darkness. He remembered his wife and children, his three best friends, his purpose on earth. There was nothing in the world he would trade for those memories, save only the chance to relive them all over and stay in them forever. *I would do anything just to be with them.*

Whether or not he would ever find them again in this vast maze, he didn't know. Deep down in the furthest recesses of his latent wisdom, a part of him knew that what they shared could never truly go away. If only that part could speak to him now. Of all the questions he had – the innumerable uncertainties existing at each step – the one thing he knew without a single doubt was that he loved them with every ounce of his soul.

Now that he remembered who he was, he finally had a name for the unshakeable feeling that sat like a weight in his chest. It was Love. For to be a person is to know it by name, and a person he was after all.

The melancholy of nostalgia did not go away, nor did he suppose that it ever would. For a moment, it had threatened to thwart his great progress, but he was learning by necessity how to cope with this heavy burden, one tedious step at a time. For now, he tried to steer his thoughts in a more optimistic direction, as to do anything otherwise would lead only to peril.

After all, he had gained more than he bargained for over the course of this disconcerting day. He had found the exact sense of purpose he was aiming to discover, and much more. Davis needed to find his family again, to do whatever he could to provide for them — to protect them from harm.

The sun may have set, but the waxing halfmoon had begun to rise. Much of it was cast into darkness, but the other part of it was shining with a bright, white light.

2.10 / The Stranger

Davis had stumbled unwarily upon a newfound devotion to an ambitious endeavor. Yet, as was often the case, his principle problem was that he hadn't the slightest idea of where to begin.

He stood at the edge of the Lacuna, entirely alone, cold from the damp and the darkness. He lifted his head to view the pathway out of the canyon, but he couldn't see much through the mist from the falls, let alone the blackness beyond it. Even should he have found it, he doubted he could muster the strength for such a climb.

For now, the best course is to wait out the night.

Knowing little of the canyon's layout, and seeing nowhere that suited his wishes, the only immediate comfort he could conjure was the sight of the sea. *The first steps of this journey started there,* he justified. *Perhaps that's where I'll find the next ones.* He had traveled a long, winding, wearying road since he first left his home by the shore. *Having come so close to it now, at the end of this troubling day, it would be such a shame not to see it again.*

The sunlight was now entirely absent, but this caused him for the first time to really consider the night sky without it. *The stars are so bright – so beautiful.* Once upon a time, he would admire them often; but of late, he hardly thought to appreciate them. The longer he waited, the more attuned his eyes became to the nighttime, and so did he embark on the last remaining leagues of the day's western march.

From his earlier vantage at the top of the mesa, it was not difficult to underestimate the length of the canyon, for everything looked so small and accessible. From its floor, however, this did not appear to be the case. Luckily, the trees were scattered, and the ground was sandy enough that little grew between them other than the irregular bunches of grass. Thus, by following the river and moving rather slowly, he could make his way well enough toward the sound of rolling waves.

Davis traveled for what seemed like several hours in this manner, climbing slowly up and down the rippling hills, accumulated over ages under a constant barrage of ocean winds. Finally, he climbed one last mound to find the sands of the shore. The beach stretched far and wide, splaying out from the delta of the Tenuis, and it disappeared into the night in both directions. His legs ached from the day's long miles, and he limped in pain down the dune to place his feet into the cold water.

Standing in the sea, Davis stared into the distance. There was nothing but stars, shining from the sky and reflecting off the surface. He stood at the edge of the world, staring into what lay beyond it, but he could travel no further – only look. The game quickly grew tiring, and he turned back to take his seat upon the shore. Only then did he notice that he wasn't alone.

Not far down the beach was a person, sitting up on the bank with their arms around their knees, sheltering themself from some unspoken ailments. *How did I not notice them?* Whatever the answer, Davis was glad for the company, still keen as he was for the chance to share a conversation.

"It's a beautiful night," said Davis. "Can I join you?"

The stranger turned quickly in alarm, not having noticed him approach until then. They were either not used to the company of others or not expecting any on a sudden.

"I – uh..." said the stranger, taken aback. "...of course. Please, sit down."

Unsure at first, they couldn't help but revert to their manners when entertaining guests, unexpected though they may be. As the stranger turned to greet him, Davis was faced with a man no more or less his very own age. He sat down a few yards away and buried his feet in the sand.

"My name's Davis," he said to the man. "What's yours?"

The stranger stared back awkwardly, unprepared for the inquiry.

"I – well..." he hesitated, but he couldn't continue.

What's wrong with him? All I asked was his name.

"I don't know," he said finally. Utterly dejected by the prospect, he turned back to the sea and hung his head in shame. The man hadn't been able to fully confess it until now, let alone accept it. "I suppose I just have to face the fact that I don't know who I am."

"I see." *I wish I had something I could tell him.* "It's one of the hardest things to know," managed Davis in a consolatory tone. He spoke from experience. "I'm sure you'll remember eventually. Just give it some time."

"What if I don't?" asked the man, nervous of the implications.

Davis hadn't thought of that.

"Well..." he said, buying time to think, "I suppose you can always decide on a new name for yourself. Who's to say we're bound by what we were? The way I see it, all that we'll be is what we do."

The man just stared, comforted little by the idea. These were not the answers for which he had hoped. Davis turned back to the water and the shape of the moon shining brightly upon it. The moon, itself a reflection, seemed to shed a little more light.

"You know," said Davis, "in all my travels lately, I haven't seen very much of the moon." The stranger lifted his eyes to the sky. "It's a shame too. I've always felt this great sense of wonder when I look at it."

Thus was a memory sparked, fundamental and familiar, but deeply buried. His past had surged back to him in the depths of Recordatio; but once the initial ecstasy passed, it settled into a fog that made it difficult to access. He could sense that his memories were with him somehow – that they would never truly leave – and yet he couldn't be confident he would find them when he wanted. Some were too trivial, others too routine; some were far too sacred, experiences too profound to explain in mere words; others still, too sorrowful to dare bring to the surface. But here was one that was just right, unwittingly uncovered, and free for the sharing.

"A long—" started Davis, but he froze. Only now did he truly come to terms with just how far away these memories were, and how disconnected from the present. *I need to get back to them,* he vowed. *I need to get back.*

"I'm sorry, what?" asked the stranger.

"Sorry," mirrored Davis, snapping out of it. "What seems like a very long time ago, my wife and I used to lie out on a blanket sometimes, in the big meadow down the road from our home, when the moon was bright and full. We would stay there for hours, sometimes talking, sometimes just lying there together, looking up at the stars.

"I remember one night in particular; it's clearer in my mind than yesterday. The moon was as full as it gets — low in the sky too — the kind of moon that gets that deep, orange glow. It was so big, we said we felt like we could reach right out and touch it. We laid there, drank a box of cheap wine, and wasted away the night just being with each other."

"It sounds like a beautiful memory," said the stranger. "It must have been an incredible night."

"It really was. It was one of those nights that just seemed to happen to you. And it was over before you ever thought to stop and appreciate it."

"At least you can think back and appreciate it now though," lamented the stranger. His envy was hard to miss. *He's right about that, I suppose.*

At this, the conversation died down, for the stranger had little to contribute in the way of fond reminiscence, and Davis was suddenly sensitive about pointing that out. When enough silence had passed for it to no longer be awkward, Davis fell back in the sand and stared up at the rich night sky.

As he lay looking up at the stars, his eyes squinted so that their lights reached out or retracted at the slightest of his movements. He entertained himself for a time with this panoply of wavering starlight — moonbeams dancing back and forth among the constellations. It was a game he had played as a child, he remembered, protesting the need for sleep until he could no longer resist it.

All the while, his mind had not strayed far from the beautiful memory. As he looked at the sky, he could almost feel his wife's presence right there by his side; but when he felt the urge to turn and speak to her, he knew she was no longer there. Her body was gone, but the weight in his chest had never expired. Of the children, he couldn't bring himself to purposefully think, for to be apart was far too painful.

I miss them all so much, he confided in silence. The water welled in his eyes, and the starlight danced all the grander. *I need to be with them again, whatever the cost.* He wondered for whom the companion beside him would long, if he could only recall that he loved someone at all.

He wondered this, and many more things, until the weight of the day finally caught up with him, and he drifted someplace else. The stars stopped their dancing as his eyelids shut one last time for the night.

THREE

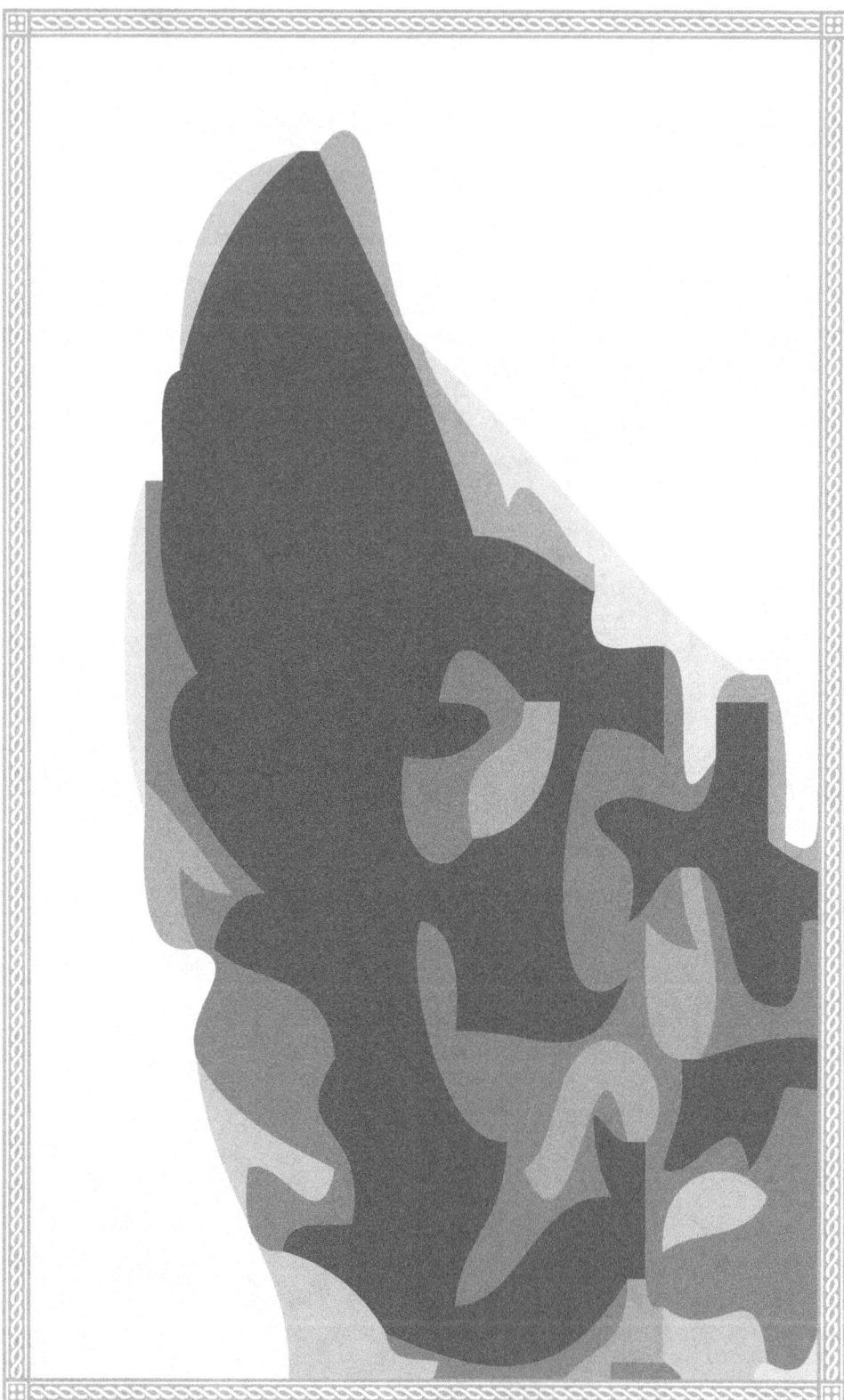

3.1 / A Dream of Something

The first rays of sunshine peeked over the edge of the canyon far to the east, basking the beach and the ocean beyond it in the warm glow of morning. Davis awoke with a start as the light touched his face. He hadn't realized he had drifted off. He woke late, as the sun took longer to clear the height of the canyon wall to the east and the tall trees atop it. The extra time without daylight afforded him a much-needed period of convalescence. Many of the aches and pains from his long travels had passed, and he felt surprisingly good after all he'd been through. It was a new day.

He sat up, expecting to greet his newfound companion, but there were no signs of one ever having existed. There was no indentation in the sand where the stranger had sat, no footprints leading away where he must have once walked. As much as it puzzled him, it was arguably more disappointing that he couldn't share what he wanted to share. Normally the first thing he recalled in the morning was the last thing he'd thought on the previous night, but this morning was different. He had dreamed.

I was lying on the sand, looking up at the stars. But then, slowly, everything changed. I had this overwhelming sensation that my body was only an illusion – not that it wasn't real, but that it wasn't all. My surroundings faded away entirely, and I rose like mist, burning off the ground in the heat of the bright morning sun. My body wasn't whole anymore, yet I was more complete than I've ever been. I wasn't contained within just one place; I was diffused throughout the atmosphere, spread over an infinite distance, but never once was I stretched too thin. I was everything, everywhere, all at once. The walls that divided me fell away. Nothing was separate anymore. I felt no emotions – no petty thoughts, needs, motives, desires – but it wasn't unsettling. No: it was a comforting reminder, but of something I can hardly remember...

But that was then, and this was now; and here he was, awake, sitting on the very beach he departed in his slumber. In recalling it, he realized how ridiculous it would have sounded to another person, had anyone been there to have heard it. *Oh well,* he thought. *It's just a dream.* And like dreams do, its memory and meaning faded more quickly the harder he tried to recall it.

Davis rose, brushed the sand from his body, and stared out at the ocean. The sight of it cast his thoughts back to his previous life by the bay in the north. This time, there were no footprints before him on his course through the sand; he could turn any which way he pleased.

Basking in a fresh sense of confidence, this fact was no longer disturbing, as it once was. Rather, Davis was excited by the prospect of the endless possibilities. At long last, he put his lingering unease about the various turns of the road to rest. He could no longer be bothered by which may be the best objective path to follow, for there was no way of knowing ahead of time anyway. It was such a pointless waste of energy and a needless cause of worry.

All I can do is pick one and make the most of the path I have chosen. After all, one can take the right road from the start and still stumble before the end, just as one can always make the most of a difficult road. He turned his attention back to the landscape and scanned it in all directions. *So which way will it be?*

He had not forgotten his mission, but neither could he make much sense of it. He had to find his family, but he didn't know how or where that could happen. He'd gathered that most people lived in the city; if his family were here, they would likely be there. Then again, the thought of returning to Inanimis was about the least appealing option he could imagine. Quite frankly, it didn't seem like much of an option at all, thanks to the way he had left it. Alternatively, he could return to the brothers and bring tidings of what he had found in the Recordatio, but it didn't seem as if anything that occurred would be of much interest to them. He had as few answers for them now as the first time they met.

Of all the options he considered, the one that appealed to him most was that which made the least empirical sense. He thought often about the large void in the map to the south. There was something alluring about it, something intriguing that he couldn't explain. He felt a dim hope that what he sought lay onward in that direction. In a sense, it did, though not in the form he expected, nor was he ready to reach it of yet.

Davis moved quickly along the beach to the south. The soft sand took more effort per step than seemed fair, but the going was open and flat, and thus easy compared to most of his previous travels. His mood was upbeat overall, bolstered by the recent sense of direction, but his thoughts turned repeatedly to the visitor from the night before.

I wonder who he is, and why he couldn't tell me. That the man could not be accounted for on the following morning was a fact he largely chose to ignore. And so it was that when a silhouette emerged far down the beach, Davis assumed he had caught up with the stranger at last. He quickened his pace and called out as he came closer.

"Good morning!" he shouted.

The figure turned, tilted its head, but soon twisted back to face the ocean. Before long, they bent down, grabbed a rope from the beach, and began to reel it in hand over hand. With a smooth and leisurely effort, a small net was dragged up onto the beach, its contents flopping and flipping from within. Having finally arrived at the scene, Davis came to a stop and tried his hand a second time at a greeting.

"Good morning," he repeated, but he had no better luck.

96

Before him was a man well into his years, wearing only a rough-cut cloth covering on his waist. His limbs were long and gaunt, his muscles well defined. His skin was darkly tanned and deeply wrinkled, weathered by what must have been many years under the sun. The man reached down to the net and loosened the cinch to reveal a day's haul of three large fish.

The man turned, looking right past Davis, and gave a sharp whistle to the east. Lit by the sunrise behind, the silhouette of a woman appeared over the edge of the bluff, and without delay she came down to meet her partner. Her appearance was much the same as his, and she was no less hardened by the passing of the seasons.

"Hello," said Davis, somewhat surprised.

She walked right past him, without so much as making eye contact, and approached the net. By now the man had grabbed the two largest fish, one in each hand by the gills. Davis admired their size and imagined them searing over a fire.

"Those two should cook up nicely," he said, trying whatever he could to strike up a conversation.

Instead – much to the surprise and disappointment of Davis – the man turned to the water, bent down to place the fish in gently, and swirled them around for a moment as they caught their breath. He watched in evident satisfaction as they swam into the distance and disappeared into the deep.

"What did you do that for?" asked Davis, but again there was no reply.

The woman stooped to free the smallest fish from the net. She turned, closed her eyes, and lifted the fish with both hands over her head and into the sunrise. The two figures stood with bowed heads, their lips moving in unison, uttering an inaudible invocation. When it was done, they nodded and walked back up the bluff. Upon reaching the top, the man paused and turned around.

"You come?" he asked Davis in a slow, deep voice. Davis nodded, thankful for his inclusion at last, and followed them away from the shore.

Not far away was a small encampment fit for two. A simple wooden frame leaned against a tree, covered in fronds woven together to form a crude roof. Beside it was a small fire pit dug down into the sandy bottom of the canyon floor. There were no structures other than a stone by the fire, and it was on this stone that the woman slaughtered the fish with a single, precise strike with a wooden club. The sharpened edge of a clam's shell was used to strip the muscle from the carcass, resulting in two beautiful slabs of meat. Having done the butchering, the woman handed one filet to her partner. Without a word, both cut a third from their half and handed it to Davis, and thus were all three afforded an equal share of the bounty. Flattered, Davis nodded again with a smile.

"Thank you very much," he said. "I'm Davis, by the way."

The two looked at each other, confused, but said nothing. Davis glanced at the empty fire pit and wondered how to best go about cooking his meal. *I guess I could start a fire with the rocks from my* – but then he realized it

— *the pack!* It was nowhere to be found, nor could he recall where he'd lost it. After all, there had been plenty of commotions yesterday that could have accounted for the mishap. *All that thought the brothers put into it, and I couldn't keep track of it for a single day.* Such was the result of his plans for greater caution upon receiving the set of supplies. The irony didn't escape him, and he derided himself silently for his foolishness.

Whichever way it happened, for now he was still left with cold fish and no fire. He didn't have to wonder long as to how he would solve this dilemma, however, for his companions did not hesitate; they bit into the raw flesh and peeled it away from the skin with their teeth. Noticing their guest's reluctance, the man brought his fingers together in a point and gestured to his mouth.

"Eat. Eat," he said.

"You don't cook it?" asked Davis.

"Cook? No," said the man. "Fresh. Fresh."

"Fresh," confirmed the woman matter-of-factly.

Davis stared at the fish, shrugged, and bit into it decisively. He was no stranger to eating fish, but never like this. Having tried it, he had to admit how amazing it tasted. It was salty, yet sweet, and had far more flavor than any fish cooked over a fire. *Fresh, indeed.* For some reason, he hadn't been hungry upon waking, but now that he was eating, it certainly felt good.

"Thank you again," said Davis. "I have to ask, though: why did you let the two largest fish go?"

"Big fish, more babies," said the man.

"One fish enough," said the woman. "Half for me, and half for me." She pointed first to herself and then to her partner.

"Half for you and half for him?" asked Davis, but the woman just furrowed her brow at her partner.

"No. No," said the man slowly. "Half for me" — he put his hand on his chest — "and half for me" — he pointed to the woman. There simply was no distinction.

"I don't understand," said Davis, but the two just stared, alternating between odd looks at him and each other. He returned to his fish and let the matter go. "Are you two alone?" he asked between bites.

"Alone?" said the man. "No. No. Never. Never."

"So, there are more of you? Where are the others?"

"Others?" said the woman. "What is others?"

"The rest of you."

"We understand," she said. "We are elsewhere."

"And who are you?" said Davis.

"Who are we?" she said. "We are people."

"Yes, but what kind?"

"What kind?" she grimaced. "What kind of question?"

"I'm sorry," said Davis. "I meant no offense. I mean: you aren't from the city, I take it?"

"City?" said the man. "No. No. We live free. Free like fish." He rolled his hand toward the sea in a series of waving motions. "Long time we live free. Forever. Forever."

"And you've always lived here?" said Davis, looking around at the meager campsite. Other than the fire pit and makeshift roof, there were hardly any signs of habitation.

"We live here. We live there. We live elsewhere."

Though appearing largely uninterested until now, the woman was first to ask a question of Davis.

"Where are you?" she asked.

"Where am I? I don't understand. I'm right here."

"No," she said, shaking her head. "Where are you?" she said again, as she gestured to her partner.

"Oh," said Davis. "I'm alone."

"No. No," said the man. "No alone. Never. Never."

"I wish you were right," said Davis, though he didn't understand the man's intention.

"No. No," he insisted. "You find you."

"I'll do my best," joked Davis, trying to change a sore subject.

"No. No," said the man, having noticed the levity of the response. "You find you. You must."

Clearly uncomfortable with how swiftly and astutely they had narrowed in on his problem, he resolved to at least make the most of it.

"How do you suggest I do that?" he asked earnestly. "I don't know where they are."

"They?" asked the woman. "What is they?"

What is so hard to understand about this? He considered a translation.

"I am here" – he pointed to himself – "but I don't know where I am" – he pointed to the man, then waved his hands outward at the landscape. "Can you help me find them?" – he quickly corrected himself – "can you help me find me?"

"No. No," said the man. "You find you. You must."

Davis had a thousand other questions, but little confidence at this point that they would bring him any further clarity. He soon finished his fish and took after his hosts in returning to the beach and tossing the skin back into the surf for the scavengers to scavenge. Standing at the water's edge, the man and woman again turned to the east, spit into their right palms, and raised them on high for the sun to behold.

"We thank," said the woman.

"Thank. Thank," said the man.

Taking their meaning, Davis too turned and raised his hand to the sun. The others made it clear that this would not suffice and feigned spitting into their hands again. Davis relented. He spit into his palm, raised it to the sun, and at last they were contented. Having partaken of their meal, the least he could do was partake of their grace.

"You go," said the man, evidently as eager to get back to their own life as Davis was to get back to his. He spoke bluntly, as was their custom, but there was no ill will in his words. Rather, the man and woman both smiled at the parting, wishing their odd companion well, wherever he was headed. "Be free. Be free."

"Thank you," said Davis, though he wished in that moment for a better way to express his gratitude for the meal. He spit a second time in his palm and held it out to face them. The two shook their heads, smirked to each other, and wandered back up the bluff. At the top of the bank, the man turned and pointed to the sun. He waited, as if ensuring that Davis understood – he didn't – before turning again and descending out of view.

3.2 / A Tale of Two Fishers

A short walk down the beach, a long pier came into view, extending out over the water. On opposite sides were tied two boats, one of which was enormous when compared to the other. Still a great distance away, Davis could barely make out two people upon the dock. As he neared, he discovered two men in a heated debate. One man was much larger than the other, yet the presence of the smaller one seemed to loom over him in an imposing manner. As Davis reached the end of the dock, the men hardly took notice, so engrossed were they in their own affairs.

"I'm here 'til I'm done and there's nothing you can do about it," said the smaller one. He spoke in an aggressive and unintelligent accent, or so it seemed to Davis. He was a wiry, bent, and crooked little man, hunched and bowlegged from long years at sea.

"I've been fishing this shoal for years!" said the bigger one, sounding gentler but equally daft. "There's no way I'll surrender it just because you make some outrageous claims about new permits and rights."

He was tall and fit, quite muscular even. At first glance it was unthinkable that he could ever be pushed around by so scrawny a foe; but even when speaking in defiance, his voice was timid and deferential.

"It's not my problem," said the crooked one in a mischievous jeer. "I've got the permits right here." He was quite pleased with his stance as entitled by law. "If you have an issue with it, take it up with the bureaucrats."

It seems everyone's aware of them, whether they want to be or not.

And while the bureaucrats appeared to be on the wiry one's side for now, anyone who's dealt with them knows how fickle an ally they can be. The two would have no doubt carried on with their argument, as they had been doing for a while now, had Davis not intervened.

"Excuse me," he called out. "Hello. Can I ask what the problem is?"

The fishermen turned simultaneously, both surprised and unsure as to whether they wanted to bring anyone else into the matter.

"Who are you?" asked the short one.

"My name's Davis."

"Well, Davis," he retorted, "it's no business of yours."

"Look..." he continued in an apologetic manner, "all I meant was that I might be able to help if you tell me what's going on."

"I'm sure you can," said the short one again. "Now scram."

The bigger one, however, had far more to lose. Having had a chance to process, he didn't hesitate in making his plea to a third party.

"I've been fishing this shoal for years," he said. "Avidus here" – he referenced the wiry one – "shows up today and starts telling me I can't fish it anymore because he's obtained rights to the whole zone."

"Rights from where?" asked Davis, though he suspected what the answer might be.

"From the Court of Inanimis and the Department of Resources," said the wiry one. He held up the piece of paper with scorn. "Providus here" – he swung a snooty arm toward the bigger one – "is in Contempt of the Court for refusing to comply."

The choice of words amused Davis. *I have a fair bit of contempt for the court myself.* He tried his best to be objective, but one can only do so much.

"If he continues to stand in my way," said Avidus, "I'll have no choice but to send for the Court – to have him forcibly removed!" He stood on his toes, barking the last line as close to his rival's face as he could reach.

Wanting as little attention from Inanimis on the western front as possible, Davis had to think quickly on his feet. *It can't hurt to stretch the truth a little, as long as I remain fair and balanced.* He did have one idea, but it would take an audacious performance. *How would they act?*

"My friend, there's no need for that now," he said. I myself come from Inanimis. I'm an appointed representative for the Court..." – he paused briefly: *it would have a fancy title* – "...an Arbiter. We've heard news of quarrels of these sorts all along the coast." *How?* "Ever since the redistricting, there has been some understandable confusion." *Good save.* "I've been sent to resolve these disputes appropriately. You're lucky I found you." *Not half bad.*

Having experienced it firsthand, he found the aristocratic language came rather naturally. Unfortunately, the men were not as convinced by the character he'd created and so readily embraced. Davis could tell they hadn't quite bought it; he had to act fast to resolve the lingering inconsistencies.

"You see," said Davis, "when I first met you, I wasn't aware that this was a business affair. Now that I know, however, I have no choice but to get involved." He didn't give them a chance to contemplate their doubt. *Be the lie.* "Please, Providus: continue. Avidus: you will have the chance to rebut when Providus has spoken his piece."

"I don't–" started Avidus, but the Arbiter was too good a moderator.

"Please," he interrupted sternly, "Providus has the floor."

Providus, still eager to be heard, didn't delay, and the game was set. Davis did feel a little guilty for the hoax, but if it kept the gaze of Inanimis from spreading, he felt that the lesser of two evils had been committed. Plus, in a way, he found the gamble a little bit fun.

"Oh – well..." said Providus, still a bit stunned, "...thank you, Arbiter." He leapt at the chance but was unsure where to begin now that he had the undivided attention of the Court. "I – well, as I said, my family has fished this shoal for generations. For years we've maintained a healthy population of fish. It's the whole basis of our subsistence, and we take good care of it. We take only what we need to get by. We don't ask for much, just enough to endure. I have but one small fishing boat."

He pointed over to the humble vessel, afloat under the shadow of the monstrosity on the other side of the dock.

"I pull all my catch by hand, while Avidus uses great trawling nets that decimate the ocean floor. They scrape along the bottom, gathering everything in their path, destroying the habitat with a single trawl. They pull in any species in the way, harvesting more in bycatch than the fish he actually wants. He destroys the whole seafloor for miles on end. The populations take decades to recover, if they recover at all. His whole system is rigged with winches and pulleys; he hardly has to lift a finger! With so little effort, he's devastated the ocean everywhere his fleet travels.

"And that's not even considering the number of fish he takes. With his system, he catches more fish in a day than I do in a whole year. He drives the local populations to extinction, but it doesn't matter to him, for he just marches into new regions he has yet to deplete. He doesn't care for the people who live nearby, and who depend on those fish – people that manage not to cripple the seas that provide for their supper.

"On top of all that, he outcompetes me in the marketplace, for he has greater quantities to sell and can do so for lower rates by the pound. He takes more than his fair share, defiles places that aren't his – that belong to us all – and drives those of us with a sliver of ethics out of business for practicing what we believe to be right."

Davis was surprised by the impassioned and articulate argument Providus could make in a pinch, once he got going that is. He turned to Avidus and allowed for a reply, but at first the man just held out his permit.

"Think whatever you want about the way I do business," said Avidus. "All I have to say is business is business, and may the better man win!"

Apparently, it wasn't literally all he had to say, for he carried on in defense of his practice. *He's one of those people who uses expressions without realizing the words have a literal meaning.*

"I've got mouths to feed, the same as anyone else," he continued. "Sure, I pull in bigger profits, but I've also got more expenses. It takes a lot to run this operation. You're just a single man on a single ship; you don't need to catch as many fish to make ends meet. What's more, you act as if people don't have the need for a huge number of fish. Forgive me for being the one to supply them."

He shook the outstretched permit, lifting it up high for Providus to see.

"At the end of the day, the only thing that matters is that I've got a permit and you don't. You're obligated by law to forgo fishing this bank. What do you have to say to that, Arbiter?" His voice was thick with derision as he emphasized the title. "Kindly tell this man to cease and desist."

Davis deliberated for a moment, struggling with how he was going to provide a resolution for these two drastically different opinions. There were good arguments on both sides, he had to admit.

The wiry one has a point. There were certainly a lot of hungry mouths to feed, and someone had to do so. A bigger operation would also come with bigger costs, so that much made sense to Davis. *And yet, Providus has a point as well.* The harvesting method was destructive, disturbing, and otherwise disgraceful. It's also true that the land belongs as much to one as it does to the other.

Why should one have the right to take more at the expense of all others? Is this how we should manage a shared resource? May the first one to take as much as they can before it's all gone win?

Davis could see exactly why Inanimis would have written such a permit. This time, however, he was in a position where he just might be able to make a difference.

3.3 / The Arbiter's Judgement

The silence was awkward. Davis stood motionless, hand on his chin, staring down at the dock, lost in thought. The fishermen both glared at him, awaiting his judgement. To their great confusion, the Arbiter made no immediate verdict, but began instead with something entirely off topic.

"My wife and I had a house once, with a beautiful yard. It was lined with fruit trees, and when we first found the place, we couldn't get enough of it. We were enamored with the prospect that, in our very own yard, we could grow something of use, right out of the thin air.

"The first season in the house went very well. We ate fruit fresh from the tree every day, and we made plenty of preserves for the future. We even brewed a large batch of delicious homemade cider. We had more than we could use, and as hard as we tried to keep up with it all, much of the bounty went to spoil on the ground.

"That winter, the trees continued to grow. I imagined a huge harvest in the coming fall, and I was convinced to take full advantage of it. I had plans for mountains of jars, whole closets full of bottles. The next year, the limbs hung low to the ground, each tree absolutely teeming with fruit. At first, I was ecstatic, envisioning my glorious plans coming to fruition."

Davis couldn't physically hold back a chuckle at the play on words.

"No pun intended," he smirked. He always loved a good accidental pun. Little did he appreciate that the deadpan performance of his character was slowly starting to crack, for the representatives of Inanimis knew nothing of humor. The crooked one looked on in suspicion but said nothing for now.

"As the summer progressed, however, and the fruit continued to grow, the branches started breaking – just a few here and there at first, but before long it was an all-out epidemic. Not knowing what else to do, I cleaned up the fallen limbs and hoped for the best. By the time the fall came along, we had hardly any fruit left on the trees, and a few of them died altogether.

"Instead of pruning the trees as I should have, I let them grow too large, in hopes of an exorbitant harvest. Little did I know that my greed had ruined our chances for even a meager harvest that year. I never forgave myself fully for that, and by the last time I saw them–"

His voice broke and he coughed. An eerie paranoia crept over him. *I can't remember when that was.* Neither could he recall what turn of events led him to move away from the house with the beautiful yard, the house he loved so much. He faltered in his story, losing track of what he was saying, his mind wrestling with this most disquieting question. *How could I have a gap in my memory where such an important event should reside?*

He realized, for the very first time, that he couldn't reconcile the past — a past he'd only recently remembered — with wherever it was that he found himself now. He picked back up, trying to conceal the great deal of worry that this sudden realization raised.

"—by the last time I saw them, they still hadn't fully recovered from the loss," he said shakily. He'd almost managed to salvage his composure. "None of the trees ever had quite as much fruit as they had that first summer."

The crooked fisherman just stared at him with a cross look. *He must have missed the point.* In truth, the wiry one was on to his ruse. *I should clarify the moral of the story.*

"You see," he said slowly, "by being too greedy, I had even less in the end than if I had only been modest."

It almost pained him to reiterate it so bluntly. *It just isn't poetic.* Only yesterday he would have condemned such an impulse as the evasive and obscure tendencies of the self-proclaimed Sages. Regardless of the point's brevity, it didn't appear that his message was going to get through.

"That's ridiculous," said the crooked fisherman. "If you were smart, you would have rigged up a large series of structural supports for the branches." His pace quickened; his voice was almost cheery. "You could have built a framework of metal scaffolding around each of the trees, or ... put up a series of tall poles with—"

About to be carried away by his own fantasies to bleed every last fruit from the soil, Avidus was harshly cut off in a most unexpected fashion.

"You're missing the point!" shouted Providus, his timid nature temporarily overtaken by a dire need to fight for what is right. "At some point, the well must run dry! Can't you see that you cannot simply take and take forever, and never run into any of the consequences?"

"You two are absurd," scoffed Avidus. "You're just being paranoid. We're not talking about overharvesting, just maximal harvesting." His lips curled into a crooked smile at the notion. "And," he confessed, "if it does happen at some point down the line, it's going to be long after we're dead and gone. Let someone else worry about it. They can surely plant new trees."

This was quite a predicament for Davis. *I can either do what's right or do nothing at all.* Seeing no other option, he pushed his luck to the brink.

"I have no choice, Avidus, but to revoke your permit for the rights to this zone." *It should at least sound official.* "Under clause 47-C-115, the permit should never have been issued outright, due to a conflicting claim to the rights of the area. Furthermore, your failure to disclose the conflicting claim is in violation of clause 66-D-119. I may, however, be willing to overlook the offense, if you comply fully with the original zoning."

In all fairness, he did a pretty good job mimicking the rhetoric of Inanimis. *The beauty of bylaws: nobody actually knows when you just make them up.* He might have even gotten away with it, but for the dead giveaway that was the moral of his speech. The meaning had not been lost on Avidus; he simply saw through the disguise. No representative of Inanimis would have ever sided this way.

"Keep quiet, so-called Arbiter!" said Avidus. He was through being told what he couldn't do when he knew full well that the city would back him. "You may have this fool duped, but I know you're nothing more than an imposter. Now leave me, both of you, or I'll be forced to call on a real representative of the Court."

Whether due to fear of retribution for his duplicity, or anger at the man who so clearly deserved to pay for his crimes against the sea, Davis wasn't sure. Either way, the words of the fisherman stirred a tremendous amassing of wrath, buried carelessly, somewhere deep down inside. What once had been patience, perhaps even understanding, was overwhelmed by a sense of sheer hatred for those who live in this way – voraciously taking, with no regard for the earth or the others who depend upon it.

Overtaken and out of control, Davis lunged forward at Avidus. The man's boastful demeanor from a moment ago was now scared and pathetic – a helpless old victim in the arms of a vigilante madman. Davis clenched the fisherman's upper arms, shaking him, and the assemblage of anger made its way to the surface. The flesh of the little man singed and smoldered; a black cloud of smoke fumed out from the edges of the deathly grip.

Davis had a flashing thought of Manus eliminating the city guards he so vehemently despised. He thought also of his own reaction to such hatred. *I don't want to become that. I cannot become that.* He loosened his grip on the crooked old fisherman, who fell to the ground in searing pain.

The sleeves of the man's shirt had been burnt away entirely. A large piece was missing from both arms near the shoulders, the edges blackened as if scorched by a fire. The flesh underneath was bright red and covered with blisters, the site of a terrible burn. Aghast, Avidus recoiled on the dock and fell backwards. Looking down on him, Davis couldn't believe the deed that he'd come so terribly close to completing.

He thought of apologizing but didn't see the point. *What good could that possibly do now?* There were differences here that could not be reconciled, especially after he had been first to choose violence. Aside from finishing what he had started – a terrifying prospect to his conscience – the only option he saw was to drive the man forth from the land. In his heart, however, Davis wasn't sure which of them – vigilante or victim – deserved his abhorrence the most.

"Leave this shoal," said Davis. "Don't come back. You are not to fish here. Bring your death and destruction to the other parts of the sea. I doubt it will be long before your ventures wreak havoc here anyway."

The man had been cowering in terror of the expectation that Davis would escalate still further. In hearing this pardon, this liberation from the fiery hands of the Arbiter, he scrambled backwards down the length of the dock. When he deemed himself far enough that it was safe to turn his back on his assailant, he rose to his feet and ran to his boat in trepidation. The boat cast off from the dock faster than it had ever done before. Avidus was free to live another day, at great cost to the sea.

Davis turned back to the second fisherman. In the heat of the moment, Providus had steadily recoiled in fright at the sight of the violence.

"I don't know what to say," said Providus. "Thank you, I suppose, though I worry that this will not bode well for me in the end. I know your heart was in the right place, but I have a terrible feeling that I may yet be held accountable for this."

"When they get word of this, as I'm sure they will, you must tell them it was me. They should know the name Davis if they have any sense. I'll leave you at once." He frowned. "I'm sorry things ended this way."

Davis began to walk down the pier, but he looked back over his shoulder with one last question before the men parted ways.

"Do you imagine he'll ever change?" he asked Providus sadly.

He already knew the answer.

"No," said Providus. "No, I don't imagine he ever will. Then again, that doesn't mean it can go on like this forever. There are only so many fish in the sea."

As Davis reached the end of the dock, he looked back one last time at the scene of the crime. By now, Providus had made it to his boat, and the sight of it sparked an awareness of something that should have been obvious. *If he travels the sea for a living, he must know the lay of the land.* Davis needed as much information about the local geography as possible. The irksome void in the map had yet to be filled.

"Providus," he shouted as he trotted back out onto the pier. "Providus, one last thing."

The fisherman turned his attention again to the man whom he wished was well on his way.

"What is it, Arbiter?" he said. *He still calls me by my title,* noticed Davis.

"Before I go – and I promise I'll be going – I was hoping you could tell me a little about where I am."

The fisherman nodded.

"I came from far away, from the east – most recently anyway. I had a map, but I lost it. And even if I hadn't, it didn't account for everywhere I've traveled, or where I might want to go. I once lived near a bay in the north, but the map didn't show much above the northern limits of the canyon. It also had a vast blank space to the south." He pointed over his shoulder in the direction he'd been heading. "What do you know of the shore on either side of us?"

"I have to confess, I don't travel very far from this area," said Providus. "From what little I've explored, the shore on either side of the canyon is made up of tall, steep cliffs that fall down from the highlands. If you're thinking of heading north or south, you'd best find a better plan. The shore isn't passable in either direction without climbing back out of the canyon."

Davis scratched his head and strained his eyes to the south.

"As far as I know," continued Providus, "there's only one way in and out of the canyon by land. I'm guessing it's the way you came, since you came from the east. To the south, I can't speak; as far as I can tell, those cliffs go on for miles on end. But as for the north, I have heard rumor of a bay on the coast, after the highlands work their way down to sea level over many long miles. I've never been there though."

"That makes sense," said Davis. "From the bay, I climbed up a great distance before entering the forest to the east. It seems that I've been wandering around the highlands until yesterday, when I descended into the canyon." He paused, stumped by the situation, before steering back to his most pressing question. "So, you know nothing of the south?"

"I'm afraid I don't," said Providus. "It sounds to me like you need to find yourself a better map."

Even the map that I had would be nice.

"Indeed, I do," said Davis with a smile. "Thank you. I'll leave you in peace." *Poor choice of words, Davis.* He extended his hand, but the fisherman leaned back instinctively. *He still doesn't trust me.* Davis pulled it back quickly before things had a chance to become too uncomfortable. "I'm sorry again for the trouble I caused you. As I said, if the time to answer for these deeds should come, don't hesitate to turn the hounds of Inanimis towards my trail." There was a brief ensuing silence as the severity of his actions continued to sink in. *It's no less than I deserve.*

With that, Davis left the fisherman for good, to return to his duties and some semblance of normality. Davis tried in his way to do likewise, carrying on with his amateur orienteering. The thought of ascending the trail in the east was no less unnerving in the daytime than it had been in the dark. For some reason, his heart urged him onward to the south. *At the very least, I can get a closer look before turning back – if I must.*

He marched on as before down the length of the shore. By now, the sun had climbed to the middle of the sky; its glaring heat was only made tolerable by the cool westerly breeze blowing in from the sea. The events of the morning kept replaying in his head, and it made for a difficult walk. As disturbed as Davis was by how he handled the wretched little fisherman, he was perhaps even more tormented by the unwelcome epiphany he had during the telling of his story.

Why wasn't he able to reconcile the past with the present? How had he gotten here from there? Where was Here in the first place? Somehow, he had oddly omitted that question with each of the wisest people he'd met. How did he come to leave his family? Why couldn't he remember such an important turn of events? How could it be that here – in the very Canyon of Reminiscence – he was unable to connect the pieces of his past? The fact that he couldn't answer this basic set of questions was beyond disturbing to the man who'd awoken in a state of such tranquility.

Davis carried on in his travels, afflicted by thoughts of this sort all the while, until eventually he arrived near the base of the cliffs at the southern edge of the Recordatio. The cliffs jutted out well into the sea, and the waves crashed violently against them. Even if he could survive the dangerous swim around the head, he'd have nowhere to go, for according to the fisherman they carried on for many miles.

He inspected the rock face for any form of a safe passage up it, but he knew it wasn't climbable. Both the Self-Aware Sage and the trustworthy of the two fishermen had said as much. His own observations only confirmed this, despite a stubborn wish to the contrary. Ultimately, he came to terms with the fact that he was going to have to turn east and exit the canyon the same way he'd come in.

I only hope the passage this time is easier than the last.

3.4 / Mole Problems

Heading eastward along the bottom of the ravine, Davis came across a series of strange sights. Large mounds of dirt began to populate his surroundings, appearing slowly at first but soon littering the canyon floor in every direction as he carried on. Most were taller than the man himself, leaving him perplexed as to what force could have possibly made them. As they grew in frequency, so too did his curiosity, until eventually he was driven to inspect one more closely.

Davis crawled to the top of the great mound and poked his head over the pinnacle. To his surprise, he found its center hollow, opening into a large tunnel that led down into the impenetrable darkness of the earth.

"Hello!" he shouted.

Rather than bounce back at him, the echoes of his voice shot out from the top of the hills all around, like steam erupting from a network of geysers. *They're all connected*, he realized. *Interesting.* He scrambled back down the mound and, upon arriving at the bottom, was greeted by an unexpected sound that was much too late for an echo.

"Hello," said the strange reply from behind him.

Although the voice surprised Davis, it had no hint of aggression, annoyance, or any other such emotions as he was prone to inspire. He turned around to find an enormous mole staring down at him, its front half flopped out of the top of the hill. Flailing its huge claws, the creature crawled fully out of the tunnel and slid down the dirt to greet him. The mole was even longer than Davis was tall, and much greater in volume due to its rather stocky build. The man didn't know how else to respond, other than to repeat a hesitant "Hello."

"But you're the one who said 'hello' in the first place," said the mole. "I was responding to you, so you needn't say it again." Davis just continued to stare in disbelief. "That's why you said it in the first place, wasn't it?"

"Oh—" he started awkwardly. "Thank you — yes, I'm sorry. I was just rather ... surprised to see you."

"Well, what did you expect when you wished me good-day?" it asked.

"I — well, in fairness — I didn't know you were down there."

"Then who did you mean to wish a good-day?" The mole was clearly a little hurt that its new friend hadn't intended to greet it.

"I didn't know there was anyone down there," answered Davis. "I was just testing the echo."

"I see," it said, dismal. "It does have a lovely reverberation, doesn't it?"

"Quite nice, you're right."

And with that, Davis looked for his chance to escape from the company of the strange creature. Something about it seemed lonely and sad. Davis was troubled enough as it was without the sorrows of a mole being piled upon him. Moles were awfully good at piling, after all.

"OK, well, I guess I should be going then," he said. "Sorry to bother you, though it was nice to meet you. Good-day."

"Is that a 'good-day' as in 'I must be leaving'? Or is that 'good-day' as in you felt sorry that you hadn't meant to wish me 'good-day' and thought that now was as good a chance as any?"

"Good-day, as in I'd better be going," said Davis.

"But we've only just gotten over the hassle of greetings!" said the mole. "It's not polite to leave now, nor is it particularly efficient."

"I mean no offense," he said as an attempt at consolation. It was clear from the start that it wouldn't be working. "But I really must be going," he pressed on. "I have a long way to walk."

"Why walk when you can dig?" asked the mole.

"I'm really not much of a digger. We humans are better at just walking."

"Well I, for one, am an excellent digger," it said, quite proud of the fact. "Why, here are whole scores of molehills that would gladly attest to that, I should say."

"Yes, it does seem that you're an excellent digger," humored Davis. "Anyway, I really should be off. Nice to meet you again."

At the persistence of this new friend in trying to avoid its good company, the mole grew even more visibly saddened. It may have been a bit slow, but it could tell well enough when its presence wasn't wanted. Its whiskers sank down to a dejected frown; its head sagged lower to the ground than it already hung. It tried its best to fight them off at first, but eventually it couldn't stop itself from letting out the saddest series of whimpers you could ever imagine a mole whimpering.

How do I get out of this?

Davis truly wasn't trying to be rude; it's just that the idea of having a conversation with a gigantic mole seemed incredibly bizarre at the moment. Prior to coming to this place – whenever and however that may have happened – he had never experienced anything of the sort. For the time being, however, he was trying his hardest to ignore the uncomfortable discordance between the types of realities he had known. In the meantime, in this one, the mole continued whimpering on in its pitiful display.

"I'm sorry," said Davis reassuringly. "I don't mean to offend you."

"You said that already," said the mole through its whimpers. "And just because you don't mean to, it doesn't mean that you won't."

The words sounded awfully familiar. Davis was pretty sure he'd been patronized by another lesser vertebrate in a similar fashion.

"Look, I don't know what else to say," snapped Davis, frustrated at this point. "I said I was sorry, but I really do need to get going."

"You could say that you'd stay for a while," said the mole. "Give me a chance! I think we have a lot more in common than you realize."

I don't see what I could possibly have in common with a fidgety, flea-ridden, fossorial fit-thrower. His growing sympathies for the beauty of Nature's creations were now stretching terribly thin.

"Don't take this the wrong way..." started Davis. *What are the odds of that happening?* "...but I don't see how we have that much in common."

"Well, for one, I'm a mammal," said the mole. We've got lots in common there. For instance, I've got fur on my skin just like you."

A technicality, thought the man. He said nothing for the moment.

"And we moles give birth to live young to be nursed by our mothers. That's true for humans too; or at least, I think. Let's see..."

It squinted its eyes even further than normal, contorted its face, and racked its brain, but found little else to support its claims of commonality.

"I guess I don't know much about people after all." The mole whimpered a single whimper, slowly spiraling into another bout of self-pity. "I mostly spend my time rummaging around blindly in the dark, destined to find only whatever I might run into. I can't see much more than what's in front of me, and even that's a blurry mess of perception. I never know what I might find; I don't even know what it is I'm looking for. All I know is that I've got drives that are driving me on, even though I can't begin to understand what they are. I might delve a while in the darkness here, dig a tunnel through the darkness there – no real pattern other than wherever my fancies might lead me."

The mole hiccupped as its sniffles settled down. It widened its eyes again, straining to see the person in front of them. The mole could barely focus on him, but it made out the faintest glimmer in the side of the man's eye, and it could tell that his disposition had softened.

"But every once in a while," it said with a hint of optimism, "I run into someone like you – someone that I can try my best to make sense of, but might not ever really understand." It seemed to quickly forget that it was trying to look on the brighter side. "You see, we can never really understand another creature in the way that we understand ourselves. Heck – we can barely do that in the first place!"

Davis wasn't sure what the digressive insectivore was rambling on about, but he was certain it was rambling. Nevertheless, more than a few of the words struck Davis as unfortunately apropos.

"The way I see it, you've got it all wrong," said Davis. "Here we are, in the bright sun on a beautiful afternoon. Don't be bothered by the fact that you don't know where you're headed. Just be grateful for the places you end up that you're happy with."

"And what about the other ones?" asked the mole.

Davis shrugged, painfully unaware of his lack of self-awareness.

"I've been trying my best not to worry about those."

He couldn't help but look east toward the edge of the canyon.

"And how's that working out for you?"

"Tough to say," smirked Davis. "I have mole problems than I used to."

Davis couldn't resist the wisecrack, trying to lighten the conversation and bring it closer to any sort of conclusion. And anyway, the mole couldn't possibly have seen that it was the brunt of this bad play on words, especially considering all it had said about its vision.

"Well, it must make you wonder why you even try any mole," it retorted with a surprising sarcasm.

"Very good," laughed Davis genuinely. *Perhaps there's more to this mole than meets the weakly-seeing eye.* He thought they might have even made a breakthrough in their so-quickly-uncomfortable relationship, had he not been able to tell that the mole's feelings were again a little worse for wear.

"Come on," he said. "I was only making a joke. Don't take it so hard." He practically pleaded with the mole to not start whimpering again. After numerous overly apologetic assurances of this sort, the mole finally relented.

"Alright," it said, "just so long as you promise not to tease me any mole." Its frown slowly turned into a wry smile.

"You have a deal, my friend. I won't make even one mole joke of the sort." Davis wondered how much longer the terrible quip would continue, but he dared not question the only thing in their entire interaction that had caused the mole to smile. The conversation lulled, but the thought of the east still weighed on Davis.

"You know," he said, "maybe it was more than blind luck that led us together." He immediately regretted his choice of words, but the mole seemed, surprisingly, not to be bothered by it. "After all, I need to get to the top of the canyon, and as you pointed out, you're an excellent digger."

"And you pointed out how good humans were at walking," said the mole shortly. It rightly inferred that this friend might be using the animal for his own devices.

"I just mean—" *How am I going to get out of it this time?* "You seem to be looking for some company, and I need to get out of this canyon." He gestured up the side of the cliff not far to the south. "What do you say? Care for an expedition?"

The mole watched the man wave vaguely into a very fuzzy distance, slightly intrigued at the prospect, but more than a little hurt that its new friend only seemed to bribe it for the use of its talents. Even so, the mole had little to do and even less when it came to people to converse with. At the end of the day, that's all it really wanted.

"I may be shortsighted, but I'm not stupid," said the mole. "If you need a favor, just say so already."

The poor thing is right, confessed the man. He glanced far away into the east again, desperate to get out of this canyon as quickly as he could.

"You're right," said Davis. "I'm sorry. I could use your help, if you would be kind enough to lend it to me."

For its part, the mole dragged out the suspense for as long as it could. It didn't get to feel useful very often. The creature feigned reluctance in a most transparent manner.

"I suppose I could do that," said the mole at last. "It would be good to have some company for a little while longer. Besides, I do like a good dig."

Farewell, fair Recordatio, sighed Davis. *Good riddance, more like it.*

And so, the two journeyed to the edge of the cliff, where the mole began the significant endeavor of digging a tunnel up through it. Now that they stood at the base, it seemed like an impossible undertaking to Davis. But the creature was large and strong, and its shovel-like forearms were formidable; they made short work of the task. It started the process with a wide entrance. That way, there would be plenty of room for Davis to keep the mole company while it shuffled dirt past him and out the opening.

Along the way, the mole told Davis of one adventure after another, though each sounded similar to the others and all were equally mundane: dug a tunnel this way, connected with another tunnel that way, ate a delicious grub over there, and so on it would go. It seemed a monotonous life, but it was all the mole had ever known. When the stories had become so redundant that even the mole started to notice, it finally turned its attention to Davis.

"So, what about you? What's your story? How'd you wind up here?"

In its very first inquiry into the man's life, the mole had already hit upon a very sore subject. Davis didn't answer at first. He didn't know how.

"I wish I knew," he confessed. "I guess I just found myself here one day."

"Ah yes," said the mole. "I have that problem every once in a while. Sometimes you find that you've been tunneling along in the darkness for so long, that when you finally poke your head out through the surface, you have no idea where you are anymore."

"Pretty much sums it up," said Davis. "What do you do then?" *I can't believe I'm genuinely asking for the advice of a mole right now.* Still, the creature did appear to have been in this plight once or twice before.

"My solution? Pull my head back underground and keep burrowing!"

"That doesn't sound like it really helps solve the problem," said Davis.

"No," chuckled the mole, "but it helps me keep my mind off it!"

"So you don't have a solution then; is that what you're telling me?"

"It doesn't sound like you have one either," it said. "I guess that's one more thing we have in common." Of every similarity the mole could have pointed out, this one was perhaps the most unappealing to Davis. The mole continued thinking as it scooped another load of dirt behind them. "Well, what do you remember from the last place you poked your head out?"

Davis was stopped dead in his tracks. This had yet to occur to him.

"Everything," he said, and then waited for that to make sense. It never did. "Every single thing," he said again slowly. *That's what I find so unsettling about it,* he almost admitted in this moment.

"Then where was the last tunnel you entered?" said the mole. Davis briefly wondered if it meant to speak in metaphor, or if it was genuinely incapable of understanding the world in terms other than those for its own mode of living. Ironically, it clarified: "What's the last thing you remember?"

Davis tried as hard as he could to reach into his memories, and in them find the answer to this inexplicable riddle. *Where was I?* He stood there in the darkened, sloping tunnel, stewing in silence, wrestling with hazy images and shadows of the past. Ahead of him, the mole dug steadily upward, toward a long-awaited surface, clear blue skies, and the light of the sun. Davis grappled with this turbulent internal struggle, finally answering with what he felt must be the most recent of his former memories.

"I said goodnight to my wife and kissed her on the forehead. I told her I loved her, rolled onto my side, closed my eyes – and then nothing." He took another moment, searching in vain for certainty. *Is there really nothing else?* "It's tough to put all the pieces in order, but I'm pretty sure that's it."

By now, the mole had stopped tunneling, entirely ensnared in the curious melodrama of this sad and wandering primate.

"You must have spent a long time underground," it said. "That must have been one very long, very dark tunnel."

"I guess I must have," said Davis, conceding for the time being the perpetual metaphor of the mole. "I guess it probably was."

After this impasse, the conversation lulled, and eventually the mole reverted to discussing the tedious events of its subterranean existence. Apparently even a short reprise was enough to forget that it had already covered every aspect of its life at least once. After a long and excruciating set of stories of such similar nature, climbing ever upward at a steep angle through the cliff, the mole took a final scrape with its claw, and a blinding beam of sunlight shot into the tunnel. Both animals squinted as if they had never basked in its likeness before. With a few more swipes, the two were able to scramble out of the tunnel and stand again on level ground. Finally, they had broken through to the surface at the top of the Recordatio.

"I can't thank you enough," said Davis, overjoyed to see the sunshine once his eyes adjusted. "You've saved me a great deal of time and trouble."

"It was my pleasure," said the mole. "For the time that was spent was spent well, as I see it."

Having achieved his goal, Davis didn't know how to break the inevitable news. *Best to just put it bluntly.* The mole did seem to appreciate sincerity.

"I hate to take my leave of you so quickly, especially after you've done me such a great service, but I really do need to press onward in my quest."

"And what's that?" asked the mole, sad but unsurprised.

"I have to find my family," said Davis. He choked at the thought and the words didn't escape unscathed. "I hope you can at least understand that."

The mole again hung its head but nodded it slowly. It was clear that the man meant this more than anything before it. Still, it couldn't help but feel a little bit used. And yet, it had managed to have quite a good visit with this human by the end, and ultimately let him go with only a moderate measure of guilt. The two said their goodbyes, and it was a sadder parting for Davis than he expected by far. With no further fanfare, the mole climbed into its tunnel and was gone – descended again into the depths of Recordatio.

∞∞∞∞∞ ∞∞∞∞

3.5 / The Gardener

∞∞∞∞ ∞∞∞∞∞

With his most recent companion finally allowing him to take his leave, Davis could at last turn to see what lay in the southerly direction. To the southeast were the rising foothills he had walked past, and from this vantage point he saw the monstrous volcano at their pinnacle.

Upon initially approaching from the east, his view of the mountain had been blocked by the trees, or else by his proximity to the foothills as he made his way around their perimeter. From his current perspective, however, there was nothing to block his view of the ominous mountain, and the sight of it shook him to his core.

Talionis must have been a massive undertaking for even the powerful forces that had crafted it. It rose further into the air than any mountain Davis had ever beheld; but it was also wide, and seemed in that moment to be more a series of mountains than a single volcano, each peak daunting in its own right. His heart shuddered at the thought of what had occurred on even the mere foothills of the mountain, and he thought briefly – as this was as long as he allowed himself to dwell on Talionis – that he never again wanted to wander that way.

For the time being, Davis was able to ignore the Great Mountain, for his true interests lay to the south. Before him in this direction sloped an arid grassland that ran far away into the distance and cut off any further sight. He was beginning to understand why no one had ever traveled this way, for it was a lonely and desolate landscape.

Quite sure that nothing behind him held any better answers than those already provided, Davis felt little choice but to investigate the mysterious void in the map. It wasn't a rational compulsion, but whatever drove him onward proved stronger than reason. And so it was that his feet carried him over the sandy grassland to the faraway hill in the distance, to see what he could see.

When Davis finally reached the top of that distant overlook, he found a land beyond it that transitioned completely into desert. Any last remnants of parched grasses dissipated on the far side of the hill, its scenery occupied by nothing but rolling dunes of sand. Davis sat on the brink, both saddened and bored by the answer to the great mystery of what lay in this region. Just as he was about to rise and commence the odious task of deciding where he should return, Davis discovered that he was not as alone as he initially thought.

There in the desert at the base of the hillside stood a figure, a watering can clutched in its hand. On noticing this stranger, Davis was puzzled by how he could have missed them during his initial reconnaissance. The figure was hardly inconspicuous: it walked slowly, leaning every couple of paces and tipping the can ever so slightly. The idea of watering the sands of the desert was laughable, and Davis couldn't resist the urge to see what sort of creature would practice such a futile gesture in this infertile land.

"Hello," called out Davis. "Do you mind if I ask what you're doing?"

The figure looked over its shoulder at the sound of this intrusive guest. It made a dismissive wave, indicating an awareness of the question, but turned back to its task in an effort to finish the last bit of what it had started. Davis carried on down the hill, and upon closer inspection this stranger struck him as impossible to place — an amalgamation of countless different creatures.

It stood upright on two nimble feet attached to large, strong legs, themselves adorned with a flickering tail. Its trunk was broad and housed long arms with lanky fingers. Its face, however, appeared strangely human. The fur on its head was mostly short, but longer on its chin as though it wore a beard. Likewise, a curly moustache rested upon its upper lip, stretching out like a vine in both directions in search of the light, with only the tips reaching up to the sky. Its eyes were large and bright, and they would ensnare you in amazement if you took the time to study them.

Despite these disparate pieces, the creature blended together into a whole that was surprisingly coherent. It could no doubt be broken into its various components when scrutinized; but when taken together, the creature had a certain cohesiveness about it. It was as if, after one had looked at it for long enough, they would no longer view it in this piecemeal manner, but simply see it for the inimitable and exceptional entity it was.

The sight of the creature shocked Davis as he first drew near to it, and he thought more than once about taking to his heels and heading quickly back north. Still, there was something earnest about this creature before him — something pure. Something beckoned him to stay and ask it all the questions that had entered his head at first sight of the stranger, and the futility of its task. When it had watered the last section of sand in the row it was tending, the creature looked back again at Davis and responded in turn.

"Hello Davis," it said. "It's good to finally meet you."

"It's good to finally meet me?" repeated Davis in surprise. *How could it possibly know who I am?* It wasn't the most articulate response, but the creature knew perfectly well what he meant.

"I've heard a lot about you," said the stranger, doing no better job at creating any clarity.

"You've heard a lot about me? Well, I don't know anything about you."

He paused, allowing time for the logical response. None ever came.

"So ... who are you?"

"My name is Hortulanus," said the creature as it took a slight bow. "I tend the gardens of Amadea, though sadly they have grown barren of late."

"Amadea..." muttered Davis. *Have I heard that name before?*

He might have, although he knew not when, where, or why. He thought it best to ignore it for now, for the name touched on a discomfort so profound that he didn't dare awaken it.

"You tend the gardens?" asked Davis, even more oblivious to the name on the note which had driven him west in the first place. That frantic day may as well have been a lifetime ago. "This doesn't look like much of a garden to me. It looks more like a desert."

He also didn't seem to realize that Hortulanus had just said as much, stricken as he was by curiosity and apprehension at the mention of Amadea.

"You couldn't be more correct," said Hortulanus. "Once upon a time, however, all you see before you was the lush and fruitful Garden of Elisium. You'd be hard-pressed to find a more beautiful place on Earth."

"How could such a thing have happened? It doesn't look like anything could have ever lived here."

"You couldn't be more wrong," said Hortulanus. "Everything-that-ever-was once lived here. And to answer your question, such a thing could have happened by the workings of your very own hands.

"For in the not-so-distant-past was the dreadful Day of Darkening, and on this day occurred the Death of the Guardian. It had long been foretold, though all those who walk in the Way hoped above all else that it would never truly come to pass."

At the mention of the death of Custos, exactly as before, the man's heart sank within him. Overwhelming feelings of fear, distress, guilt, and remorse flooded into the forefront of his mind, liberated in an instant from their hiding places deep within his psyche.

This time, however, he couldn't hide behind a wall of ignorance. This time, his deeds were somehow already known. Davis had nothing to say in response, and the Gardener continued without pause.

"While we mourn in our way for the Death of the Guardian, we dare not despair; for it was also foretold that Praestes would rise once again, on account of the deeds of the very person who brought about its demise."

The eyes of Hortulanus peered directly into the thoughts of its visitor.

"I know you feel a great sense of regret, but contrition can only be true when it leads one to acts of atonement."

Davis no longer dedicated any effort to the guise of innocence. He knew how greatly he had wronged the Guardian — the very symbol of righteousness in a world so eager to stray to iniquity.

"I'm sorry," he said, tears welling at the verge of his eyelids. "I'm sorry. I really am. I can't say it enough." His words poured out quickly, desperately, pleading for forgiveness but without ever plainly saying so. "I have prayed with the passing of every single day that I could take back my actions. I don't know what came over me. It's like I didn't even have a choice."

"There is always a choice," said Hortulanus. "There is always a choice; but you are not exactly in control of what your own mind will choose. It is one of the Great Paradoxes: The Curse of the Sentient Being."

The Curse of the Sentient Being? He had worked so hard to break out of the daze of unconsciousness; how could it possibly have been for nothing? Again knowing the man's intent without the need for a clearer question, Hortulanus continued.

"The waking mind is at the center of this paradox, for it is precisely what creates the illusion of conflict between the Fates and the Will. Free Will does exist, but you are not the one in charge of employing it. The workings of the mind that decides are complex; and despite all your pride, you are but an observer of its outcomes. And as for Fate, it is little more than the eventual actuality, borne from a set of potentialities among which the waking mind decides.

"This is not to say that you are helpless, but rather that You are not quite what you think."

The Gardener stopped abruptly, as if having spoken out of turn, and tried to backtrack to the best of its ability.

"But alas, we are getting ahead of ourselves," it said. "For now, it can suffice to say that you are what you are; you will choose what you will, and it leads you to the fate that you are fated to discover. With a powerful enough resolve, you can steer yourself out from even strong currents, as you drift toward the many channels branching before you; but you can never expect to arrive anywhere other than downstream."

"And what makes any of this a curse?" asked Davis.

"The other creatures of Nature simply <u>are</u> – and that is enough. Very few of them feel the need to wonder why they exist, or to what end it all will lead. Those who try to take control are the most likely to stray from their purpose. With wonder comes doubt, with doubt comes despair, and with despair comes the falling of angels."

Hortulanus aimed its attention to the ground it had recently tended.

"Take this plant, for example."

The man hadn't yet noticed, but dozens of tiny shoots had emerged from the sand in the places where the Gardener had been watering. Davis had found himself on the edge of the very same despair that Hortulanus described; but at the sight of these small plants, there bloomed along within him a faint glimmer of hope.

"When the time is right, a seed will germinate, though it knows not why, for it knows nothing at all. It will reach up through the soil, towards the rays of the sun, growing ever upward to bask in its warmth. It will take what it needs from ground and air alike, and convert this great potential into something of worth.

"When at last you have fulfilled your task, and this garden is once again a place of abundance, an animal may very well come and eat of the fruit or the flesh of this very plant. It will eventually die, either in service of another connection in the food web, or having provided in some other way for the creatures of Nature; but it will wonder not why it existed at all. It simply was. It lived, and died, and fulfilled its purpose to the utmost perfection.

"Should the plant have wondered what the world above may have had in store for it, or should it ever have realized that one day it inevitably must die, it may have never desired to emerge from the ground at all. It may have despaired, and strayed from the reason it lives in the first place."

"But to wonder is a wonderful thing!" replied Davis, desperate to not accept that all the effort he had exerted was only going to waste. "There has to be some greater good that outweighs any drawbacks of the conscious mind. Surely there is good to come from being sentient."

Davis searched in all directions for a situation in which it would not have been better to have never been conscious at all. He mostly failed, but settled for the best he could do.

"If I'd never been conscious, I would never have known that I am, and I think that's a blessing in its own right."

"You are quite correct," said Hortulanus. "And we arrive therefore again at the paradox. I did not say wonder leads only to doubt; for it leads also to illumination."

"So, to be conscious is both a blessing and a curse?" *Now that I can believe.* "But to what end?" he wondered aloud. "What's the point of it all?"

"To your place in the ground — to give back what you've been given. A new shoot will emerge from the bounty you've buried, and the cycle continues on ever anew."

Davis pursed his lips and shook his head.

"No," he protested quietly. "There must be something more."

He couldn't accept this as the most satisfying reason for his existence, but neither did he possess the means to refute it. *It seems so nihilistic.* Was he really only here so that he could live briefly and then die? Did he live only to consume things, so that he too could become fuel for those who will feast on his flesh? Surely these things were inevitable, but was this the sole reason he existed? *No.*

"I know it in my heart," he said. "There must be something more."

"Perhaps," said Hortulanus. "After all, I'm just a Gardener. I look for what's best for the growth of my garden; and a garden is always in need of good soil."

After what felt like a long journey down an existential tangent, the man's thoughts naturally made their way back to the immediate concerns weighing on his mind as he struggled to make sense of his journey. Though he longed for more profound answers than Hortulanus had provided, Davis nevertheless sensed an aura of wisdom around the strange creature — a creature who evidently knew at least part of the mind of the Guardian.

"I wonder..." said Davis upon breaking the silence, "...things aren't adding up as they should." He searched for the right words. "I was hoping you could, maybe, share some insight on something." He rubbed his neck awkwardly. *How do I even say it?* He weighed all sorts of options, but none felt any less clumsy. *Just come out with it already,* he rebutted. "I was hoping you could help me figure out how I got here."

"Go on, my friend," said Hortulanus.

The Gardener knew precisely from whence this unrest stemmed, but thought it best to let Davis explain it himself. Davis, on the other hand, was hoping for exactly the opposite. Yet all it took was this gentle nudge and the words came pouring out, along with a drop of water from his eyes.

"Well, that's just it: I don't know," he said. "I don't know how to go on, where to go on, what to go on to. Nothing is making sense. I've never been this lost in all my life. And when I think back to all those times, most of them I can see as clear as day; but there's this huge vacuum in the middle, between then and now. It's been eating away at me ever since I first tried to connect the pieces. All I want is to get back to where I came from – back to the people I love."

"You could try," said Hortulanus softly, "but it isn't going to work." The poor man's lips started to quiver as the words of the Gardener slowly sunk in. "That doesn't mean that you can't be with them though."

"What do you mean?" asked Davis.

"Instead of looking back, you need to look forward. Instead of asking how you got here, you should be asking where to go next."

"But how am I supposed to have a clue where to go next when I don't even know where I am?"

This was a good point, from the perspective of a mortal anyway. The Gardener tried to find a better way of explaining it, without saying something Davis wasn't prepared to hear.

"You're in the very place that you need to be," said Hortulanus, "though you still have much to discover. I can't be the one to teach you, however. You have to learn these things for yourself, through the medium in which you have chosen to teach yourself."

"What is that even supposed to mean?" asked Davis, half offended.

"It means that you must continue to visit the Sages, for they can help lead you along on the path of discovery."

"Then where do I go?" asked Davis bluntly.

At least he had asked the right question.

"Far to the North there is a great tower that looks out over the whole of this land," said Hortulanus. "It sees all, though I doubt you have seen it from your place on the ground. The Tower of Transpectus, it is called. There you will find a wise old man who will have many more answers than you currently know."

"In fact..." said the Gardener, "...he left this for you."

Hortulanus extended a note in its outstretched hand.

"Wait a minute," said the man.

He stepped back and raised both palms in a mix of disbelief and self-defense. His demeanor towards the Gardener had only moments before grown to that of a trusting confidant, but it now deteriorated to that of an all-out skeptic.

"I'm supposed to believe that I just happened to find you here, and that you just happened to have met with this Sage in some faraway tower, who just so happened to leave you a note in the off chance that you should run into me? You then expect me to march on blindly to the north for miles on end, in the vague hope that I should find someone there to help me? Don't take this personally, but this is all starting to sound a little ridiculous."

He squinted his eyes, as if trying to read through some clever bluff.

"You really don't understand, do you?" said Hortulanus sadly. The Gardener had secretly been hoping its visitor had a keener sense of insight into his current surroundings. "I don't expect you to walk anywhere."

With this last peculiar comment, Hortulanus waved its right hand in an arching motion over the eyes of the unsuspecting traveler, and a powerful spell overcame Davis at the execution of the gesture.

The world around him grew blurry and dim. He staggered and felt seasick, as if the ground on which he stood was no longer solid. He fell into a ravenous blackness, and his senses were laid for the moment to rest.

As Davis opened his eyes, he looked up to see faint stars nested deeply in a dark blue dusk. He rose from the ground and tried his best to make sense of what had happened. *That wretched trickster of a gardener!* he cursed. *He must have drugged me somehow and dragged me to this place.*

When he was through objecting to the means of his arrival, he finally thought to look around and figure out where it was that he'd arrived. Around him in a circle was an open ring of trees, for he had again come to a large grove in the middle of a dense forest. In the center was a fire pit with two large stones beside it, which could be used as makeshift seats.

"Wait a minute," he said aloud. "Is this...?"

Sure enough, Davis quickly discerned that he was again in the Grove of the Sentient Sage – the place he'd arrived on the first day of his journey; the place that had sent him so decisively down the path he was now on.

He scanned around for a view of the Tower of Transpectus. *If it has a view of everything in the land, why haven't I seen it from wherever I am?*

In gathering his composure, he rubbed his aching head and massaged his sore chest. It was then that he felt the unwelcome volume of something in the pocket of his shirt. He reached his hand inside and grasped a folded piece of paper, on which he imagined was written a familiar script.

To Davis (for now):

> *Your mind is on fire for things that are gone*
> *The freest of spirits shan't linger so long*
> *Let go of your yearning for things that evade*
> *It's time now to shatter the mighty charade*
>
> *The motives that drive you are on the right track*
> *But the place that it leads you will never lead back*
> *While it's hard all at once to confront a clean slate*
> *It's time now to face the harsh truth of your state*
>
> *The place that you long for is not to be found*
> *The time that you pine for is nowhere around*
> *The love you encountered in life comes along*
> *Whilst worldly you were, somewhere else you belong*

Forever in search of clear sight,

The Surmounting Sage

Great, thought Davis. *Here we go again.*

He turned around, deciding which direction he should head in search of this elusive tower. Sure enough, just as he spun – there it was. The Tower of Transpectus could be seen over the trees at the south edge of the grove, in the very same place where only moments before there was nothing to see. It reached an immense distance into the waxing moon's sky, and for once Davis was certain about something: it had not been there.

Davis headed into the trees, and before long he came to the ancient stone base of the tower. In the center facing him was a large and dark wooden door with a heavy metal circle resting on it. Davis reached his hand out to lift the ring and knock upon the door, but before he could even make contact, it lurched and swung open slowly with a croak.

I guess someone's expecting me.

The fading light of dusk was quite faint under the trees from which the tower emerged, but it was dark inside the tower – very dark. Davis hesitated one last time, but he ultimately took a step inside. A wide staircase could barely be seen lining the perimeter, and as he peered upward, the stairs dissolved entirely into blackness.

The climb was long and arduous, spiraling ever upward. The stairs circled the inner wall of the tower, an otherwise hollow chamber with no ending ever within sight. While the surroundings never grew brighter, the blackness somehow receded as he rose, just enough to see what lay before him in the same faint glow. Every several hundred feet was a landing upon which he could take a much-needed rest to regain his endurance. Under the tremendous strain of hours of climbing in this fashion, Davis collapsed at the most recent of them, perched by now thousands of feet in the air.

As he lay looking up at the never-ending spiral, a small piece of paper flitted slowly down from the darkness above and landed lightly on the platform. He picked up the paper, albeit reluctantly, and read.

You know, you really don't have to walk.

Feeling again as if he were the brunt of some cruel cosmic joke, a genuine anger – no mere annoyance – was roused from within. He shouted as loudly as he could into the blackness of the ascending tunnel.

"What is this, some kind of game for you people?!"

He closed his eyes and exhaled sharply.

I wish I was just at the top of this godforsaken stairwell already.

Davis opened his eyes again, expecting to resume the long ascent, or else give up entirely and make his way back downward. Instead, he found himself in the middle of a large, round room. Windows lined all edges, and the sunset far away basked the whole space in a deep and gorgeous orange hue. The only embellishments were a modest wooden table, a tall hourglass in its center, and an old man in dark, flowing robes, sitting at its far edge.

"Who are you?" asked Davis. He was in a demanding mood again, annoyed as usual by this Sage's trials, even so early in their acquaintance.

"Do not ask who I am," said the old man evasively. "Who are you that comes knocking on my tower door?"

"You don't know who I am?" asked Davis, genuinely surprised. "You wrote a note addressed specifically to me."

"I know who you are," said the Sage. "Don't be ridiculous." He was as curt as his guest. "But it is not me that matters when it comes to knowing you. I wanted to know if you knew who you were."

"I responded to the note, did I not?" replied Davis. "I think it's safe to assume that I do."

"Excuse me," said the old man. "Please allow me to rephrase that: I wanted to know if you knew who you <u>were</u>."

A sharp pain rocketed through Davis, starting in his center and quickly radiating outward. With it came an entire lifetime's worth of memories, flashing in front of his eyes in bursts of vivid reminiscence. *Not again – not like this.* Countless perceptions of people and places swirled around him in a cyclone of excruciating emotion.

They shouted to him, but despite many desperate attempts, he could not bring himself to form any words. They longed for him, but he could not console them. He longed for them as well, but they had no way of knowing it, and neither could they comfort him.

This had happened to Davis before, but with each new experience it became far more unbearable than any of the former. And this time, the storm would not subside, nor succumb to taking pity on the man. It only swelled in intensity, picking up speed between passing flashes.

Davis was soon knocked to the ground by the mounting force of the tempest. He writhed in pain and closed his eyes in fear, but every sight could still be seen. The winds raged, the sound swelled, and he felt the pressure of an entire ocean bearing down on him.

He thought it couldn't possibly grow worse, and yet it did so in a great crescendo. The wind howled, faster and faster, the noise growing louder and louder; the ground rattled, stronger and stronger, tossing him violently. He feared that the very tower beneath him might collapse at any moment.

It was only when Davis was about to lose consciousness that the storm finally gave way, culminating in an epic climax in which the many sights and sounds were extinguished in an instant – like a candle at the onset of a windstorm. The images faded, and all grew dark. Slowly, the orange glow of sunset began to filter in, and the room at last became still.

"Who I was," barked Davis, hardly missing a beat as he pulled himself up from the floor. His head still throbbed. "What do you mean who I <u>was</u>?"

"You know exactly what it means," said the Sage. "But just as before, you are afraid to admit it."

The old man had the same sense of brevity as Ævitas before him; but as was also her way, there was a subtext of deep-seated affection hiding beneath the surface of his words. But Davis was not ready to follow him down this path, and both men knew it. Trying to restore any order he could, Davis changed the subject to aim for a more proper introduction.

"What's your name?" he asked, taking care to establish a calmer tone. "I can tell you're known as the Surmounting Sage, but it seems fair to know more about you than some foolish old nickname."

"My name is Vincentus," answered the old man. His voice now had the warm tenor of a loving grandfather: quick to scold, but as quick to forgive. "Welcome to the Tower of Transpectus, Davis. I hope that you are truly here for the reason it exists."

The Sage had still not risen from his seat, and he did not do so now. Instead, he reached out to the elegant hourglass sitting on the table and gently turned it upside down. The grains of sand pooled in the funnel, and slowly, one by one, they began to trickle through to the lower chamber.

"As far as my name is concerned," he continued, "to surmount is precisely the challenge you're currently facing. And I, on the other hand, have already achieved it. For all the differences among the Sages who have come before me, we have all accomplished, at the very least, the thing you are seeking at the moment. One would think you might come with a slightly more accepting mindset."

The last statement was delivered with a smile, but Davis could still tell that he was being subtly rebuked.

"What do you mean?" he asked, ignoring the slight. "What exactly do I have to surmount?"

"You know what it means," said the Sage again. "And you would do well to start answering as many of your own questions as you can." His eyes shifted briefly to the hourglass, and then back to Davis. "You must confront the cause of your distress – and you must overcome it, if you can."

"And what's the cause of my distress, exactly?" said Davis.

The Sage lifted his bushy eyebrows high in an even more subtle rebuke; but being not without pity, he played along for now.

"You once had a life that you'd almost forgotten," said the Sage. "But now that you haven't forgotten it, you can't seem to connect the pieces of yesterday with those of today. Does this not sound familiar?"

Davis simply turned his head, and his lack of protest made it known that the Sage was perfectly on point.

"You will have well-earned my title when our work is complete," said the Sage, "for it is by far one of the most difficult things to overcome."

Davis again did not answer, but instead walked slowly to the window and looked out upon the landscape in a second attempt to ignore the imposing words of the Sage. The view was remarkable, and only now did he realize exactly how remarkable it was. He turned as he scanned, walking the edge of the room in a clockwise motion, taking in the land on all sides.

In all directions, he saw many of the landmarks he'd already discovered, but he viewed their relationships even more clearly from this vantage. The city was not all that far east of where he was now, or at least it seemed close from as high up as he was. To the south, Talionis towered over the rest of the land, including the Recordatio to its west. And to the north of that canyon rose a large plateau, which eventually made its way down to the bay he once called home, before he was even capable of questioning where his true home lay. But in the north and far east, the forest stretched on without end, as did the desert in the south, and the ocean to the west.

Perhaps this tower can't quite see everything after all, he thought.

Davis eventually came to a stop at the window in the west. He gazed out upon the land silently, though his mind was not idle. As he stared at the stunning scene of the sun setting across the ocean, he couldn't help but think about the darkness that would soon follow, and the storm that had most recently overtaken him. The pieces that weren't adding up were now unfortunately beginning to make sense from the far-reaching view at the Tower of Transpectus. In the meantime, however, his denial fought as hard as it could to persist. Taking his cue, the Sage pressed at his cause.

"Tell me, Davis: how did you come to be in this place?"

Davis had no reply. He couldn't even concoct a believable story. He simply had no idea.

"I don't know," he said.

"And where do you think you are then?" asked the Sage.

"I don't know," he said again, slowly losing grasp of the calm tone he had worked to establish. He caught the mounting anger and tried to collect himself, but it was never far away. "After I remembered who I was – who I am, I mean..."

Davis faltered, grappling for the moment with which of these two tenses was correct after all. He never came to a consensus.

"Now that I remember," he continued, "this place just seems so..."

"So what?" asked Vincentus.

"Supernatural."

The Sage let out a hearty laugh, and for a moment it broke the tension.

"There is no such thing as the supernatural," said the Sage. "There is only the natural which we do not understand."

The Sage pressed on, for there was little time for philosophical tangents.

"Think back," he said in encouragement, "far back to the edges of the oblivion that has filled such a large part of your mind."

Davis tried as before to recall, but he once again had to fight his way through the dark, dense cloud of amnesia. With great effort, he made his way back to the last place he left off.

I said goodnight to my wife and kissed her on the forehead.
I told her I loved her, rolled onto my side, and closed my eyes.

128

And only in revisiting these thoughts again did Davis realize that these weren't the most recent memories he possessed after all.

He'd forgotten about the horrifying screams of his children. He'd forgotten about the rolling ceiling tiles as he passed down the length of the hospital corridor. He'd forgotten about the wound that had pierced through the depths of his chest. He'd forgotten about the face of the beautiful woman – his wife Constance – the face upon which he would look as the last breath of his body slowly expired. The most painful epiphany he would ever endure took hold of his thoughts at long last.

"No..." he started. "It isn't true. None of this is true!"

He started pacing nervously, waving his arms like a madman, raising them to his head, throwing them down again, and waving them some more with every new raving.

No, no, no.

"You're all in on some sick scheme to... – to make me doubt my sanity!"

This is all a joke. This is all just a joke.

He closed his eyes to hide from the pain, but it didn't go away.

"None of this is happening," he mumbled. "None of this is here!"

And when he opened his eyes again, he was sitting calmly on the beach, in the bay to the north. The sight of the tower had vanished completely, like the changing of a channel in the frequencies that comprise the waves of his consciousness. He fell back to the sand and closed his eyes again in defiance.

"This is all a hallucination," he muttered to himself in consolation. "I must be sick, or – or, I must have hit my head." *This isn't happening.* "This isn't happening," he said firmly as he slowed his frantic pacing. "It's going to be fine," he repeated softly. "It's going to be fine – I'm probably at home right now." *I just want to go home,* he thought as he started to sob.

And when he opened his eyes, he found himself lying in his own bed, in the home with the beautiful family and beautiful yard full of fruit trees. The ceiling fan he once installed was turning overhead, and he knew the feel of home immediately. Overjoyed, he shot out of bed and rushed out of his room to find the others.

"I'm home!" he shouted madly, as if that were a normal thing for his family to expect upon him waking from his slumber. "I'm home! Where is everyone?"

He raced from room to room, searching every nook in the house for any sign of his loved ones. He shouted for them by name, but no one ever answered, and he could never find them.

He ran back into the bedroom, where everything was otherwise exactly as it should be. On the dresser was his wife's wedding ring. *She takes it off at home*, he thought. *She has to be here.* He clutched the ring tightly and wouldn't let go.

"Constance!" he shouted as loud as he could. "Constance!"

129

Again, she never answered.

He ran a second time to Evan's room, the next one down the hall, and yet again to Joni's. Everything was exactly as it should be, but as with his wife, neither of his children were present. He fell on the ground, his chest pounding, throbbing in the physical agony that is a broken heart.

They're gone, he thought. *No, they're not* – He sobbed. – *don't say that!* *They're gone,* he thought again. *No, they're not,* he realized slowly; *I am.*

He rolled over on the carpet to the view of a plush green frog, nose to nose with him, staring him straight in the face. He fought back the tears and rose to his senses, picking the frog up as tenderly as he could.

"I gave this to her when she was born," he whimpered through the tears. "It was one of the single happiest days of my life." *And there were so many happy days,* he admitted. He looked over at the chest of her toys but couldn't bear to put the frog back. He dragged himself pathetically across the floor toward the chest of toys and went to open up the lid. Each item, a sign of someone's affection for her; each item, a memory, or more. He put his hand on the lid, but the voice of the Sage shot loudly through the house.

"Don't open it!" he said. "You won't be able to bear it."

The Sage was deadly serious – anxious; scared even. It was not like him, even given how little Davis knew of him. Davis would have no doubt defied the Sage as a matter of principle, but the command startled him so much that he let go of the lid and recoiled backwards into the center of the room, dropping the frog and leaving it behind with the rest of her belongings.

But his hand was still clutching something, and in his manic state, he could not remember what it was. He opened his fist to find the wedding ring, and the world began steadily collapsing.

The walls began to shake. The wind again began to howl. The pressure mounted and his ears began to pop.

"Let it go!" echoed the voice of the Sage, desperate. "Let. It. Go!"

Davis couldn't bring himself to do it. He rose to his feet, clutched his fists ever the tighter, and defied the storm to come. He would remain here. He would die here, if die he must.

The shaking grew more severe. The roaring wind grew louder. It stabbed at the shutters, ripping one from its hinges and flinging it away. The fruit trees outside could no longer tolerate it, uprooting and pitching over under the strain.

Davis was stunned, exhausted, and filled with longing for all that was, and all that could have been. But most of all, he was filled with fear – the fear of what might now come.

The whole house trembled more viciously. Just then, a large oak from the yard creaked and crashed, ripping through the ceiling, tearing a gaping hole in the side of the house. The wind reached in and tried to drag his very body away. And as it pulled at him, he could no longer hold on.

His hand let go, and the ring fell to the floor.

Davis ran from the room to escape from the terror, but the storm, for its part, had started to lull. It was deathly cold, and it had grown dark with the onset of the clouds that accompanied the inclement weather. And worst of all: he was all alone.

When it was clear that his search had failed to yield what he wanted most of all, he collapsed on the floor of the hallway in agony, sobbing for those he had somehow lost. He curled into a ball and closed his eyes as hard as he could.

"No, it can't be," he cried. "Something is terribly, terribly wrong. I never got the chance to – I never even – I didn't get to..."

All the unfinished business he had yet to fulfill in the earthly realm – the love, the laughter; the plans, the dreams, the wishes; even the heartbreak and sorrow he had yet to attain – all of it was weighing down on him, and he doubted now that he could ever find closure.

He closed his eyes again in the hope that one of these times he would wake up somewhere that he actually was.

He opened them again to a view from his crib – a view he had seen long ago when his memories first started. It was such a long, long time ago. Yet now, in this moment, he knew that what he'd perceived as so long a time was in reality but a momentary sliver – the tiniest slice of time in an endless universe that was far, far bigger than he could ever be.

To him, it was so painfully long ago; but here he was right now, a child, on the verge of exploring a brand-new world into which he was born, and all the potential that it offered. He thought next of his family: his loving parents that had fed him, sheltered him, loved him, given him everything he ever needed – nay, wanted. He thought of his brother, tripping him up and wrestling with him in the grass in that bright sun, out in the fields.

He could hear them all, calling out to him, as if once again a child. But here too, despite wanting nothing more than to be with them all again, he had no choice but to ignore them. He knew this time, without so much as a dire shout from the Surmounting Sage, that if he entertained those memories – if he entertained that sorrow – he would never overcome it, for the love he bore for all of them was far too great to witness in earnest.

And yet there he was again, standing up, reaching out over the side of his childhood crib, trying to conquer the world as only a toddler could do.

How could it have passed by so quickly? In his occasional musings on Death during life, he had hoped that when the time finally came, it would feel like it had lasted for ages on end – that it was finally his time to make his way into that greatest unknown. He hoped that it would seem as if life had persisted for a just and satisfactory duration, and that he would march on in dignity through that fateful transition. He now found that it was nowhere near long enough, nor was he anywhere near dignified.

He aimed all of his thoughts at the blanket in the meadow, when and where he might look up at the full moon. He wanted more than anything to wake up with his wife and a box of cheap wine by his side. As he opened his eyes, he indeed saw the stars, the meadow, and the blanket where he lay; his wife, however, was nowhere to be found.

He closed his eyes one last time, though he had run out of memories he was willing to denigrate. None of the scenes from the movie of his life were occupied any longer by the actors whom he longed the most to embrace. There was nothing left but old sets, slowly falling into disarray from disuse, for the filming had long since concluded.

He opened his eyes once again; he was standing in the western window at the top of the Tower of Transpectus, staring out over the Endless Ocean. He had indeed confronted Death, but by no means did he feel that he'd surmounted it.

3.7 / Living on as Light

"As I said," spoke the Sage, "it is one of the hardest things to confront. I am proud that you allowed yourself to do so at last."

"What do you want from me?" shouted Davis.

Tears still streamed down the side of his face, for they had never yet stopped since they had begun, as he ran through the wraith of his house in search of his family – the things in the world that he loved most of all.

"What do you want?!" he repeated, shouting angrily this time at the unassuming approach of the Sage. "Why can't you just leave me alone? Do you get that much joy at the sight of my suffering?"

Davis couldn't have misunderstood the role of the Sage more. The old man simply continued to walk over to him, and gently placed his hand upon his weeping guest's shoulder.

"I know how you suffer, and it brings me no joy," said the Sage. "In fact, it brings me back to the sorrow I felt when I was in your very position. For I too have been through this ordeal. It was the most desperate sorrow I have ever endured. But when I arrived at the end of what I thought I could bear, I survived. I overcame. And you will do so as well – if you let yourself."

In a sudden, unpredictable burst, Davis lunged at the Sage, his own sorrow turned to madness. He grabbed the old man by the front of his robes and flung him hard against the window.

"Stay calm, child!" said the Sage, but Davis was done heeding his warnings. Davis slammed him against the window a second time and pressed against him with all his weight.

"Or what?" shouted Davis, blind with rage. "What's the point?"

Yet again, he was not abiding reason, but this time the stakes were far higher than most. This time, Davis had pure wrath in his eye – a wrath the likes of which the Sage could not hope to control. Davis slammed him again.

"Calm down," the Sage said sternly. "Calm down!"

Davis lifted him up and heaved the old man into the window for a fourth and final time; for this time, the window gave out.

Glass shattered every which way as the old man crashed through it. The Sage was bent backward over the stone that formed the base of the window, his upper half dangling out into the cold night air, for by now the light of sunset was nowhere to be found.

The Sage moaned in pain and pleaded with his assailant. Still, Davis would not relent. He pressed harder, bending the Sage's back yet further over the edge. The Sage's eyes were wide open, his pupils fully dilated, and he turned his head quickly, back and forth between Davis and the ground so far below. *He's afraid*, the man noticed.

"Why?" shouted Davis. "Why are you afraid?!"

He was right. The Sage tried to hide it, but terror had seized him.

"You expect me to just let go of everything I love, just like that?" shouted Davis. He shoved the Sage again with another wave of force. "You think I should just let it all go?" He would not relent. "You think it's easy?"

"Please," groaned Vincentus, but it was to no avail.

"Easy for an old man, maybe!" he chided. "I had a wife, children, a family. I had my whole life before me!" His voice broke. "What about you?"

"Please," the Sage pleaded again. "There's no time."

"You say you've surmounted Death?" Davis shoved him again. "So why shouldn't I just throw you from this window?" By now the Sage had regained his composure, and his expression had shifted to one solely of pity. "Answer me!" shouted Davis, irate and losing touch with any humanity he had left. "Answer me!" he shouted again. "What do you have to live for?!"

And with these final words, the undeniable irony took hold of Davis and mustered a different part of his madness. He smirked, began to slowly chuckle, and then began to laugh in full — a deep, cruel laugh that would have been unrecognizable to any of the loved ones he seemed to think he was avenging.

Before long, he was in hysterics. Rather than pushing, this time Davis pulled; he wheeled the Sage around and flung him into the center of the room. The old man stumbled and crashed onto the table, which slid forward under the weight being heaved upon it. A trail of blood lined the floor behind him and stained the whole back of his robes, drawn out by the shard of glass that had pierced deep into his body from behind.

The table came to a stop, but the hourglass did not. The last meager grains in the top circled around the funnel as it toppled; it careened in chaotic spirals until it found the edge of the table, tumbled slowly over the brink, and shattered into pieces upon the floor.

The room went black, but Davis had a flash of an inexplicable image. He was by a fire on a cliff, perched between the sea and a rolling field of purple flowers. He knew nothing. He wanted nothing. He had nobody. The vicious storm again raged, only now he barely noticed. The sky over the ocean churned in an ominous shade of red, and the world began slowly to fade.

But before the blackened sun could fully set, Davis snapped out of his stupor, as if it were but a momentary vision, and stood once again at the window in the Tower of Transpectus, side by side with the Surmounting Sage. Davis could still feel the trace of the tears that ran down his face as he searched his house in vain. The Sage gently put a hand on his shoulder.

"I know how you suffer, and it brings me no joy," said the Sage. "In fact, it brings me back to the sorrow I felt when I was in your very position. For I too have been through this ordeal. It was the most desperate sorrow I have ever endured. But when I arrived at the end of what I thought I could bear, I survived. I overcame. And you will do so as well — if you let yourself."

"So, what now?" asked Davis, somewhat scornful but mostly sarcastic. "I suppose you're here to tell me that I'm just supposed to move on – that it was all just a façade, and that this is some truer reality?"

Actually, telling him to begin the process of moving on was precisely what the Sage was there to do, though he had more tact than to try it so soon. The old man simply let this anger run its full course. Like the denial before it, eventually it too would wane. After a time, the bulk of it had slowly receded; or at least, it was no longer aimed outward.

"Not a façade – no," said the Sage. "The life you knew was real in every sense of the word. But so is this place."

He pointed out the window to the wide lands far below.

"Every place that you go, every creature you see, every person you talk to – each of them is appearing to you for a reason. You must remember that fact as you maneuver this realm. There is no such thing as coincidence in your world anymore, for the world in which you live is exclusively Mind."

"This place; this land," repeated Davis. "You say that as if this is a place at all – as if there is any land to stand upon."

"Everyone needs a stage on which to carry out their saga," replied the Sage. "You have crafted this realm for that very purpose."

"I have 'crafted' this realm," mocked Davis. "I haven't done anything! I find myself the pawn in a game that is far beyond my control. The only thing I want now is to be alone." *I just want to be alone.*

He didn't even mean the words, not really; but the very instant he uttered them, the world all around him faded away, and he was left with exactly what he asked for. There was no one to be found, for there was nothing at all. There was nothing left but himself, all alone, on the most basic of planes in an unfounded dimension.

His sight scanned aimlessly in the void, and he came to grips rather quickly with the fact that this was no sort of existence to covet. Then and there, in the absolute absence of anything, Davis changed his mind. In a surprising display of his very own sagacity, he decided to begin the process of putting the past to rest. Though he was far from finished with this onerous enterprise, the first step was to accept that it had to occur.

He wasn't ready to let go of the past – not by far. But he at least reasoned that there was no sense in wallowing in the filth of self-pity. There was simply no good that could come of that. After all, he was still here, wherever Here was. Thus, Davis chose to instead focus on the only remaining thing he could: the journey that still evidently lay before him.

The interior at the top of the tower faded back into view; the Sage was again sitting by the table at the far end, as the sand trickled slowly through the hourglass. Davis faced the window, staring out across the sea, but he said nothing for now. Upon the return of his apprentice to his presence, Vincentus broke the silence.

"I don't expect you to forget, you know. I could never do that myself."

Davis did not turn, but he nodded slowly. He couldn't manage to contain the one last tear that made its way down his cheek.

"I know," confessed Davis. "It's alright. I hope I never will."

The Sage smiled and afforded him as much time as he needed. Never turning from the window, Davis was stuck – lost in his countless conflicting thoughts about all he had discovered.

By now the sun had long finished setting, and all that remained was the glow of the stars and the moon. The moon was still waxing, but it was almost full, and it hung high in the sky. The soft white light blanketed the trees and the ocean beyond them, and Davis looked up at the familiar celestial body reflecting it from the sun and back down to the land, kindly taking pity on those who would otherwise walk only in darkness.

Finally, he broke the long silence.

"Sometimes, when the moon was big and bright, like tonight, my wife and I would lay out on a blanket in a field down the road from our house. It's where I asked her to marry me, one night when the moon looked very much like this one." *Another one of the best days of my life,* he realized.

"It sounds like a beautiful memory," said the Sage. "Memories are fragile things," he warned. "Cherish them or else they die."

Surprisingly, lost in his own deliberations and with little explanation, Davis laughed aloud. It was the sincere kind of laugh that comes with fond recollection – the kind that all his many loved ones would recognize and recall fondly long after he was gone.

"What's so funny?" asked the Sage.

"We had a friend," answered Davis, appearing to change the subject. "She was a real physics buff. She used to talk about how, if you were looking from far enough away – and I mean really far – with a powerful enough telescope, you could still see dinosaurs roaming Earth."

Davis couldn't help but laugh again in thinking about it after so long.

"The first time she brought it up, I thought she was joking. But she was serious; she really meant it. It's like how, when you look at the sun, you're actually looking at the sun from eight minutes in the past, because that's how long it takes the light to arrive.

"She explained that light from the earth was forever beaming out across space, into the faraway reaches of the universe; and while it travels very fast, it still takes millions of years to get somewhere. If you were far enough away, she said, and if you had the means to see far enough through space, you could literally look backwards in time.

"My wife would joke sometimes, as we would lie on that blanket under the moon, that if we ever had to die, at least our likeness would live forever among the stars. Living on as light, she would say."

The smile slowly faded from his face. *Living on as light.*

"I guess that's all I've got now."

"We're certainly a long way from Earth," said the Sage as he joined Davis by the window. "And while I may not have a telescope, you stand now atop the Tower of Transpectus. The view from up here is quite astute."

Davis said nothing, just continued to stare out across the sea at the reflections of the moonlight shimmering on its surface. The Sage hesitated, torn between giving him the space he needed, and not letting him fumble backward into despair.

"Take your time," decided the Sage.

Davis appreciated the thought, but he needed no more time — at least not to be ready to depart.

"The view from up here is quite astute indeed," he said. He turned to face the Sage again for the first time since arriving back in the tower after confronting his vacant memories. "Thank you, Vincentus."

The Sage smiled and nodded approvingly, proud that he had somehow succeeded at last. He could tell that his apprentice was prepared to take his leave, and so he attempted to pass on any parting wisdom he could, to ensure his success in the trials that were to follow.

"Do not treat this revelation as a curse, my friend. You have seen through the most powerful guise of all, one that your own mind had crafted to deceive you — to detain your progress in a state of static inertia. You must never give in to such treachery. You must turn the tides, Davis. You must garner a momentum so powerful that inertia works instead in your favor, to hinder the chances of ever coming to such a stagnant demise."

Davis didn't understand their full context, but his emotions faithfully tracked the impassioned words of the Sage.

"I know that it's hard," continued Vincentus, "but you will find a way to move on. I am sure of it."

I'm not so sure, thought Davis. As of this moment, the person he is — no: the person he <u>was</u> — it was all he would ever be in his mind. It was all he remembered; it was all that he could know. To claim that letting go of it would be little more than an inconvenience was an egregious insult to the value of his life and the love he had known. He humored the Sage for now.

The Sage, not entirely unaware of this hesitation, had nevertheless achieved all he needed, and more. All that he ultimately needed was for Davis to ask the very next question that followed — a question he had asked many times before.

"Where do I go now?" said Davis.

The old man smiled — in part at his accomplishment, and in part at the humorous fact that this was a question for which he didn't have an answer.

"I can't say," he said. "Wherever it is, it seems you're ready to find out."

Davis waited quietly for a moment before again letting out an unexpected laugh of his own, for he reflected on just how appropriate the metaphor of the mole truly was, now that it came back into his mind.

"I guess I will just carry on then," he said, "and keep tunneling ahead on my way through the dark."

3.8 / The Stranger

Having come to terms, in a way, with the nature of his situation, Davis was now mostly focused on the meaning behind it all. *If I'm really gone, then why am I here?* For as much as the old man had done for him, Davis had correctly sensed that there was little more in this regard with which the Surmounting Sage could help him.

For now, there was nothing else to do but head off in some other direction, and let the passing of time wash away the woefulness that comes with realizing you're no longer living. He walked to the stairs at the corner of the room, and upon reaching them, waved an appreciative wave to the Sage in parting.

As he began descending the stairs, the thought of the long journey down was far from appealing, and it was then that Davis had the mischievous thought that he should put his current understanding of his surroundings to the ultimate test. *What could I possibly have to lose?*

He approached the edge of the stairs near the tower's central chamber, and with no visible hesitation whatsoever, he leapt from the edge and plunged down through the chamber to the ground far below.

As he fell hundreds of feet at freefall speed, Davis quickly began to question whether he had just made a horrible and irreversible choice. The confidence in the feet that had flung him from the edge was evidently no longer shared by his brain. The staircase circled him like a tornado as he fell; its spiraling shape created a dazzling illusion as it whirled around him, while he, on the other hand, seemed perfectly motionless.

It was certainly unsettling, but if this test had any hope of succeeding, he had to believe in it without question. *Even if I'm wrong,* he reasoned, *and my body should break under the fall, what's the worst that could happen? I'll finally leave this place, or else wake up somewhere equally frustrating.*

The time for the final test had come, and Davis tried diligently to quell any remaining doubts about whether it would work. He closed his eyes as he plummeted and envisioned the first place that came to mind: The Grove of the Sentient Sage. The sound of the staircase continued to whirr, and the ample doubt remaining screamed at the prospect of imminent extinction.

Soon, the sounds of the stairs swirling all about him blended with those of a crackling fire; the two fused until any distinction between them was irresolvable, and Davis could no longer tell which was which, nor what to expect when he opened his eyes.

Just as the ground was about to surprise him in the worst possible way, he opened his eyes to see firelight. Davis sat on a rock by the side of the pit, and he looked to his left to see a handsome but troubled young man.

"Are you the one who wrote the note?" the stranger asked nervously.

"Not – no, not that I know of," said Davis.

Davis had only just arrived here, but this man did not look well.

"Are you alright?" he asked.

"Not really, no," he replied. "I'm desperately seeking for answers in this place. I can't seem to make sense of it all. I need to get home, but I don't know where I am."

The words of the stranger struck him as dreadfully sad, for Davis understood all too well what this poor lad was grappling with.

"Calm down, my friend," said Davis. And without even knowing what came over him, he found himself speaking in a pleasant, rhythmic meter. The words had come all at once like a vision.

What you face now is one of the hardest endeavors
You'll need all your wits to confront your own ghost
Be prepared for the onslaught of turbulent weather
Be prepared to let go of the things you love most

"So it was you!" said the stranger, obviously annoyed by the elusiveness of Davis – a man who, from his perspective, had unexpectedly appeared in the grove from the edge of the trees. "That was the last verse of the note I was left," he protested. "You obviously wrote it. What kind of cruel trick are you trying to play?"

Davis certainly didn't remember writing any note, but he supposed that didn't really matter now. What mattered most now was pointing this lost and lonely soul in the direction he needed to travel.

"Not far to the south is the Tower of Transpectus," said Davis, gesturing over his shoulder to the spire extending now out of the trees.

The man looked up to find the tower looming over the grove, visibly alarmed that he somehow hadn't observed the enormous monument earlier.

"The answers you seek are at the top of the stairs," said Davis. "It's a long walk up, so I don't recommend it."

"If the answers I seek are at the top of that tower," said the man, "then there is nothing stopping me from climbing those stairs. I don't care if it takes me a decade."

At least his resolve is commendable.

"I think you misunderstood me," said Davis. "What I meant was that there's no need to walk."

As he spoke, Davis waved his hand in an arching motion in front of the eyes of the unsuspecting man.

The stranger was overwhelmed. He staggered and felt seasick, as if the ground on which he stood was no longer solid. He fell into a ravenous blackness, and his senses were laid for the moment to rest.

From where Davis sat, the stranger vanished from sight, dissolving slowly into a faint outline of smoke, which mingled with that of the fire. The plume rose into the cool night air, to dwell forever among the stars.

As he sat alone by the fire in the grove, Davis closed his eyes to wait out the rest of the night. He opened them again immediately – it took no longer than a momentary blink – and the dark evening sky had converted to bright morning sun. A new day had begun, and he felt as refreshed as if he'd slept through an unbroken night's rest.

I think I'm starting to get the hang of this.

While there was a great deal left for Davis to learn, somehow, in this very moment, he had finally discovered without question what his next move should be. He wasn't sure from whence the inspiration had come, but he didn't need to question it.

The words of Hortulanus resounded in his head: *contrition can only be true when it leads one to acts of atonement.* It was time for him, at last, to find the way to Immolatio.

FOUR

There was only one major problem with the confidence Davis felt at the conception of his plan: he didn't know where Immolatio was. He didn't even really know what it was; how could he hope to find it? As quickly as he asked the question, the answer appeared in his thoughts. He reached into his pocket and found exactly what he expected. He pulled out the note and unraveled it to find an old familiar script.

To the fledgling at rest on the edge of a ledge,

> *To take now to flight you must first make the leap*
> *You cannot return and the edge is too steep*
> *While your fears have been urging your feet to remain*
> *Your heart is in need of releasing the pain*
>
> *The walls in your mind are quite like a cocoon*
> *The truth you won't find lest the edges are hewn*
> *When your eyes start to focus on what penance brings*
> *The soul is set free with a set of new wings*
>
> *When questions have answers you cannot expose*
> *Quite often they're found with a moment's repose*
> *When you pass through the verge of this interim door*
> *At last will you know what your trials were for*

The fully transformed,

Transcendent Sage

"Does that sound reasonable, Davis?" spoke a gentle voice from behind.

Davis turned to behold the shape of a tall and slender woman. There was a magnificent radiance about her. A very soft light glowed about the edges of her skin and a warm smile of compassion rested upon her face. Her presence alone was a comfort to Davis. She was clearly corporeal, but there was something otherworldly about this Sage as well. The aura around her made it look as though she were residing in two places at once.

As he attempted to take in the scenery, Davis learned that there wasn't any. He stood on a lone patch of grass in the midst of an encircling fog, beyond which he could not see. It was only he and the Sage, who had answered his call without even the need to have placed it.

"The Transcendent Sage," he said. "Do you have a real name?"

"I am Janua," she answered, "though I am also Aditus." She began to walk slowly around Davis in a circle as she spoke. "My title, however, is perfectly fitting, for Transcendence is precisely the reason I am."

"And what, might I ask, have you recently transcended?"

"Why, the illusion which you presently personify," said the Sage. "I represent the transition between Lesser and Greater. This is the very transition that you must also make — to emerge from the cocoon, as it were, after a complete metamorphosis."

The Sage of course meant no offense, for in this form she had no way of realizing just how much she was asking of him. Nevertheless, Davis was again insulted by the insinuation that his whole life was only a nuisance to be shed before he could truly be free.

It wasn't an illusion — not in the least.

He could still feel the air in his lungs, the touch of his body; he could experience the pangs of hunger, the delight of satiation. The blood that flowed in him was more real than the grass growing under his feet, as far as he was concerned. He bore sorrow and joy, anger and empathy. And there could be nothing more real than the bond he still felt for his family. He had no plans to go about shedding any of it.

"You said I'd understand these trials," he reminded her.

"I did," she asked, still circling.

"What's it all for then?" he asked clearly. "Why am I here?" Without even offering a chance to reply, his frustration had grown. His voice steadily rose, and his true feelings made their way out. "And why should I have to endure having my whole life belittled? What's the point of making me relive these painful experiences? Why can't I just go peacefully to rest, with my bones in the ground?"

"You want to know why you're here?" she asked peacefully.

"Yes," he said after a sigh.

"Not long ago, you called yourself the Arbiter. I could not possibly have come up with a better term for it. You are here to make peace between the parties you find here. There's a great deal of unrest in this realm, as you have no doubt discovered."

"What does any of it have to do with me?" he asked, frustrated again.

This was a rather patient Sage in comparison to some of the others he had encountered. Not minding that he had recently been given this answer, Janua stayed entirely calm and composed. She was almost detached from the waves of emotion which Davis was experiencing, as if she were only partly capable of even perceiving them at all.

There was no scorn in her voice — just a simple explanation.

"The individuals you find here have everything to do with you," she said. "It was you who awoke their troubles; it is therefore upon you — and only you — to resolve them."

How did I awaken their troubles? He was open by now to at least a degree of self-reflection; but even so, that didn't seem entirely fair. *They all had plenty of troubles before I showed up.* He was struck by a brief flash of the corpse of Custos on the ground below him. *At least, some of them did,* he corrected.

Thus did Davis begin to reflect back upon the various individuals he had met during the course of his travels. As he left them behind, he was under the foolish impression that he'd hardly ever have to think of them again. Here he was now, however, placed in the undesirable position of having to reconsider them — to try to understand them in a way he hadn't previously attempted.

Many were in conflict, with themselves or with each other, even if not overtly. He remembered the Heretics and the guards of Inanimis. He thought about the fishermen, two kinsmen at odds. He thought of the beast in the north that he'd been sent to slaughter by another more fitting of that title. He thought also of that creature's own demise, and the vassal who had so swiftly seized on its weakness.

"There are forces out there in extreme opposition," he reasoned. "It reaches down to the very core of who they are and what they stand for. How can I possibly make peace between such bitter nemeses?"

Many needed something he could not provide, or had issues he could never dream of resolving. He thought of the newt in its undeserved exile; he thought of the mole longing only for companionship. He thought of the people in the city, some of whom had surely suffered at his hands, for doing only what they knew. He thought also of the suffering they inflicted on the world outside their high walls.

"How can I possibly be expected to mend the misfortunes of others? How do I decide who to help? And how am I supposed to go about helping them? It's hard enough to carry out my own actions without causing a greater commotion. How do I ensure that I don't only make things worse?"

Lastly, he thought again of the Guardian and the words of the Gardener.

"How am I to reconcile conflict when even I am so subject to falter? How am I supposed to decide what is truly right and wrong, or know which decision is best? How do I bring to justice those who have committed misdeeds, and how do I make amends for the misdeeds that I myself have committed?"

Davis stopped to catch the breath eluding him. It was a lot to worry about, for certain, and the Sage was not able to provide answers directly. She was not privy to the means of forging peace between parties at war, resolving the hardships of strangers, or atoning for a lifetime of sin. No, those were the realms of other Sages. She was here for the sole purpose of aiding Davis on the path of ascension; and at present, that lay in the form of a simple set of directions.

"I am sorry," she admitted. "But I truly can't say." She tried to comfort him, as was her nature. "Something tells me it is your destiny to find out."

Her answer was hardly a comfort to Davis, for it was hardly an answer at all. He tried again, focusing on some of his most practical concerns.

"What am I to do when confronted with people whose philosophies I genuinely abhor? I try as much as I can to relate to them — to try to understand things from their perspective. I can concede an issue here or there, but eventually I find myself torn between compassion and contempt."

Conflicting notions she knew well, and his pleas had moved her to help however she may. She would try to channel all the insight she could muster.

"To begin, you must learn that all things in Nature depend upon the balance of opposites. As such, we must try to approach things in as holistic a light as we may. For where these entities of which you speak are in opposition to each other, so are you forever at war within yourself."

And as the Sage circled, her own holistic light began to slowly fracture and frizzle. The light at first grew brighter, with sparks flickering around the edges of her aura, and Davis had to look away. He closed his eyes. The Sage continued to circle.

She walked gracefully around Davis, almost as if dancing; and as she did, her body slowly sundered into two. A second copy of herself pulled gently away and lagged behind the first, mimicking the same fluid dance. Soon, the two women were on opposite sides, with Davis between them.

When Davis deemed it safe to try opening his eyes again, Janua stood before him, though her light seemed lessened somehow. And although the Sage continued, her lips did not move, for there was not one voice, but two.

"It is in our very nature," said the second voice.

Davis spun to find a second Sage standing behind him, identical to the first in almost every way, and yet different somehow.

"Aditus?" guessed Davis.

She nodded, then carried on as if there was nothing odd about the arrangement.

"The only requirement for perpetual progress," added Janua, "is to acknowledge the truth of our polarities, and to have the patience to endure the slow ascent."

The Sages resumed their circling, always on opposite sides from each other, with Davis in the center, spinning occasionally to keep track of them. They spoke as they walked, and although it was always Aditus who began, it was Janua who would finish the thought.

"For where I have wealth..."

"...where am I poor?"

"For where I have freedom..."

"...where am I shackled?"

"For where I have peace..."

"...where am I of chaos?"

"For where I have faith..."

"...where am I in doubt?"

"Nothing in Nature ever exists entirely alone," said the Sages in unison.

Davis wasn't sure how any of this was relevant to his question, but he was enthralled all the same. The calming presence of the Sage was finally having an effect; he listened patiently, despite his tendency to the contrary.

"Often what one thinks of as opposites..." said Janua, "...are in reality just the presence or absence of a certain phenomenon," continued Aditus.

"To light..."

"...there is darkness."

"To heat..."

"...there is cold."

"In other cases, there is a true duality," said Aditus. "Two forces of opposite, but complementary natures," continued Janua, "entwined in an endless struggle for equilibrium."

"To positive charges..."

"...there are negative."

"To entropy..."

"...there is order."

"Only through acknowledging its many dualities can one ever hope to truly understand reality," said Janua.

"I take your point," said Davis, his patience beginning to slip a little, "but I'm not here to discover the intricate secrets of the universe."

"Not yet," replied Aditus. "Since you are so eager to get to the point, let me state it quite clearly." Janua continued: "The same truth can be seen in the forces at work in your actions every day."

Again, the Sages circled Davis, each responding to the other in turn.

"Only through attention to the fact that I am selfish..."
said Aditus from his left.

"...can I ever discover the obligation to give,"
continued Janua from his right.

"Only through acknowledging my envy..."
said Aditus from behind him.

"...can I ever discover all the many things
for which I have to be grateful,"
said Janua from his front.

"Only through admission of my hatred..."
said Aditus from his right.

"...can I ever discover compassion for all those
whom I am initially inclined to hate,"
ended Janua from his left.

"Normally, things in Nature are drawn into an irresistible attraction between opposites," said Janua. "Witness, for example, the force of two magnetic poles as they collide. Together, they yield an equalized whole; whereas alone, they would forever be seeking a stability which only the other provides them."

"In humans," said Aditus, "an awareness of differences unfortunately tends to lead us only to fear – a fear that can lead to such terrible conflict."

"You must learn to let go of this fear," said Janua. "And you must start by first being aware of its presence," ended Aditus.

I don't understand, thought Davis.

"So, only by admitting that I feel contempt for others can I discover..."

He assumed that perhaps an attempt at sounding wise would somehow reveal an insight of genuine value, but his thoughts of this sort were quite clearly misguided.

"I don't get it," he admitted. "What exactly are you trying to say?"

Before daring to continue any further, however, the Sage was compelled to offer a disclaimer. The two entities were now once again united, her aura fully restored in an instant; she spoke as one, and more firmly than normal.

"You must understand, Davis: you are confronted with a tremendous dilemma that cannot easily be solved. Do not mistake me to mean that there are simple answers to complex riddles.

"The answers you seek are paramount, integral to the very meaning you barely realize you are seeking. This way will be perilous to your progress, and you should tread carefully upon the path laid ahead of you.

"I must also admit that I myself am only barely capable of understanding the things of which I am about to speak; and you are likewise not yet ready to comprehend. Quite frankly, it is ill-advised for a Sage to engage in such affairs."

In her unique position, the Transcendent Sage tapped into all that she knew from the other side to guide her.

"And yet, I sense that it might do you well to be exposed to these things sooner, rather than later. I hope this decision does not prove to be unwise."

She looked deeply into the man's face, studying him carefully; she hesitated once more but eventually nodded, and the gamble was settled.

"I will do my best to pass on the teachings of Sophias, who was the Master of my Master. I regret, however, that I will inevitably be an insufficient conduit."

Davis perked up, intrigued by the Sage's willingness to indulge his haste.

"I will need all my power if we are to succeed, and this fruitless void will not suffice. We need hallowed ground, not hollowed."

She took him by the hand.

"Follow me."

4.2 | Imprecise Insights

When Davis awoke, they were sitting by the water's edge of the Lacuna Speculis. Each half of the Sage peered back at the other from opposite sides of the reflection – two halves of one Sage, speaking with one voice. The light she possessed now was far greater; it encompassed Davis, and indeed the entire pool, shining like a spherical halo of golden white mist.

The pond rippled gently, at the same frequency as the shimmering dome that was her aura, and it became increasingly difficult to tell where water ended and sky began, or which way was up and which down.

The Sage then commenced with her best attempt at a comprehensive treatise on the nature of good and evil, both within and without.

"Like you, Davis, I too am torn between an infinite, boundless love for all people, and a disdain for those in opposition to my own way of being. Part of me transcends this vice, but another part still shelters it."

"Aditus?" asked Davis, himself now a part of this treatise.

"She is but my Lesser Self," confirmed the Sage.

"And Janua, the Greater," reasoned Davis.

"There are so many triggers that manifest this tension in us," she continued. "The way others act; the way others speak; the way others think. Their differences are often taken as an affront; we might even be inclined to think them intentional – as if they were devised in order to divide.

"Our Lesser Self is eager to facilitate this schism; it sends us messages of discrimination, to perpetuate and justify its own individuation. It infers an inherent inferiority of others, to build itself up in return.

"It is in our very nature to compete for dominion over the world, and these glimpses of rejection that we catch ourselves sensing are the means by which the lower part of us strives to conquer. It is this very hubris that we must work to defy. Even so, the kingdom of matter must have its due, and ever too often we are tempted to stray."

Davis had already missed much of the insight she provided, but he nevertheless felt a deep bond forming. He was beginning to think that she may truly be the bridge between his own mindset and something a great deal wiser than it. She was torn in two by the gravity on both sides of this problem, and that was a feeling Davis could certainly understand.

The Sage continued.

"Part of the reason we judge the actions or values of others is that they are in opposition to our own moral or spiritual path. If we even bother to question our own actions and values in the first place, and if we then still feel justified, it is hard not to succumb to contempt.

"If we are to continue along our own spiritual path, however, we must refrain from these lesser instincts. We must exercise acceptance and forgiveness. Still, it is hard for the moral person to observe those in the world who actively choose to rob, rape, and murder their kin.

"Do not doubt that there are truly those in existence who embody the deepest meanings of the word Evil – those on the path of greed and envy, hatred and aggression, or domination over the powerless. How could the moral person not feel contempt for those who walk down this path willfully, at the expense of the others around them?"

The Sage, true to her nature, also saw the other side.

"And yet, are these not traits we all possess? In truth, the contrast between Good and Evil are not differences in kind, but differences in degree. That is, the vices of humanity are shared by all, only differing from person to person in their degree in the continuum.

"When we observe these vices externally, is our contempt entirely for others? Or, is it enhanced because we see these traits as a reflection of ourselves? If we are afforded the luxury of forgiving ourselves, so too must we learn to forgive those that we see as our reflections.

"Furthermore, being ourselves but human, and possessing these same traits, who are we to judge the behavior of others? We are not responsible for Creation; we are merely a small component of all the Created. How then can we bear the weight of the stones raised for casting?

"At the same time, we are capable of self-reflection; we can compare the actions of others to the relics of our own history. We too may be imperfect, but that does not mean we cannot oppose those who do more harm. We may be flawed, but perhaps less so than some.

"Take yourself, Davis."

"What?" At the mention of his name, the man practically jumped. "Me?"

"You are by no means the pinnacle of all that is good."

Why, thanks for the compliment.

The Sage knew his mind. *None of us are,* she consoled him.

"And yet," she continued aloud, "would it not be fair to say that you would stand in defiance of Evil if you were ever confronted with it?"

"I'd like to think so," he replied, sounding both vulnerable and unsure.

The Sage paused in what was an otherwise speedy diatribe, and she smiled at him. Given her perspective, she had forgotten just how sad and scared this man still was.

"Time may yet tell," said the Sage as she smiled. "And I hope, if that time should ever come, that you are able to triumph, in whatever way one might triumph over evil."

"What way is that?" asked Davis.

"I suspect that is for you to learn elsewhere," she admitted. "As we have already discussed, this is no simple question. But if people do not dare to stand for righteousness, then who will? Yet, how might Good triumph over Evil without falling victim to its very ways?

"The solutions to these dilemmas are not quite clear," mused the Sage. "Should good people simply do nothing, for fear of being sanctimonious, or judgmental of things that are not theirs to judge? Should good people do nothing in the vain hope that the universe will eventually settle the score? Is the only remaining choice to lie down in the path of destruction, in an act of self-sacrifice? Can non-violence ever triumph over violence when it has no means with which to combat it?"

Davis was utterly overwhelmed. These problems worried him already, but the more he considered them, the less clear the answers became.

"I don't understand," said Davis. "And I'm not sure this is helping."

The Sage at least appreciated his honesty, and it was clear she was losing her audience. What's more, she had gained about as much insight as she was able to discern through the shroud separating wherever they were and whatever lay beyond.

The large dome of light surrounding them shrank back down, merging with her body and restoring her to her original, much more humble form.

"I told you at the outset," said the Sage. "I do not have all the answers."

"But what exactly am I supposed to take away from this?"

The Sage thought for a moment, struggling almost as much as Davis to process the many facets of this puzzle. After a moment, she spoke.

"It seems that the answer must inevitably involve compassion and understanding. Empathy is essential, for to forgo the foundation of a moral code in defense of that very code is to unfold a hypocritical paradox."

She thought again while Davis tried to translate that.

The Sage had already moved on, speaking mostly for herself.

"The answer must also somehow involve raising awareness through an open and honest system of communication. And that takes time, and trust."

"Slow down," he said, but she was swept away in her own deliberations.

"Only through reflection, implementation, and iteration at the individual level can one hope to truly embody these values, and nourish the growth of virtue; and only through the gradual transmission of consciousness among individuals can such a transformation ever hope to reach the scale of the entire collective."

"Stop!" he said bluntly this time. "You're not making any sense."

The Sage complied, having worked out at least the piece of the puzzle she was attempting at the moment. She backed up a bit for Davis.

"We must hold ourselves accountable as individuals, and work to attain our values in practice," she said. "But we also need a mechanism to agree upon those values, spread them broadly, and hold each other accountable."

"So, what do we actually do?" asked Davis, stressing the final word.

"For now, your path must spiral upward, as must all our paths. Your focus must be on truthful self-reflection, and exemplifying the virtues you hold in high esteem; and then, by the grace of the Great Soul, may it grow."

"So..." hesitated Davis, unsure if the Sage had provided him an actionable answer as requested. "So, you're telling me that I should just act as I wish the world at large would do, and hope that over time all the rest will follow suit?"

Technically, he was asking for clarification, but his tone implied that he didn't quite buy it. *There has to be more to it than that.*

In seeing that this was still entirely unsatisfactory to him, the Sage soon realized that she had little choice left but to send the man on his way, to do as he can to find these answers himself. She was confident enough that she had given him what he needed, or else that he possessed it himself.

Her demeanor changed, as did her tone; and while she was not exactly cold, she was certainly direct. The man wanted clear direction, after all.

"Davis, the only practical advice I can provide you is this: you must try, in whatever way you can, to peacefully reconcile the dissenting forces you encounter here. Only in the salvation of others will you ever find salvation for yourself."

While Davis didn't know it, salvation was the very reason he was here.

"Thank you," said Davis sincerely, followed by a smirk. "I'm not sure I'm any better off than I was when I arrived; but then again, I seldom feel that way after an encounter with a Sage."

Davis laughed, testing this Sage's capacity for humor for the first time. She smiled politely, but that was about it.

"Still," he realized, "I think I could use your advice one more time."

"Go on," said the Sage.

"For once, I think I know where I need to go, but I'm not sure how to get there."

"You have already been upon its doorstep," she said. "This time, however, you must step through the door."

Davis racked his mind regarding all the possible places to which the Sage could have been referring. Everywhere he had traveled already seemed so well established; it didn't make sense that any of them could have been the so-called doorstep of Immolatio.

That is, all of them but one.

"The desert?" asked Davis.

"Precisely," said the Sage.

4.3 | The Way to Immolatio

Davis opened his eyes to view rolling dunes of far-reaching sands.

"It's good to see you back so shortly," said Hortulanus.

The Gardener had been busy at work in tending the grounds. The greeting sounded sincere; and in a way, Davis was glad to see Hortulanus again as well.

"You know," said Davis, "you really could have told me."

"But what fun would that have been?" grinned the Gardener.

"I'm glad you had fun, but it would have saved me a lot of distress."

"Would it have?" asked the Gardener. "I think it would have been quite a shock, should you have believed me at all. The wiser part of me tends to think that the latter was hardly possible. Some things are learned best when discovered by the self, and not taught by another."

The Gardener leaned to spare some water from its can.

"In any event, you're here now; and now is all that we have."

At the notion of time, Davis suddenly laughed.

"Now," he said in sardonic fashion. "Something tells me that Now doesn't exist any more than Here does."

"It seems that your insight has grown, even should your foresight be lacking. Time indeed means something different here, but that does not mean you can dawdle about. The realm is in urgent need of attention. Should you fail to attend to it, there will be calamitous consequences." Davis swiftly began to take the situation seriously at the mention of this dreaded last word. "Like a garden, it needs tending, or it will become overrun."

"What do you mean?" asked Davis.

Hortulanus looked grave for the first time in the current visit with this naïve young soul.

"Do you not see the desert that stretches before you?" asked the Gardener. "You should know it well, for it was built by your own exploits. The majestic Garden of Elisium once stood where you currently stand, but it is withered now into naught but a desiccated domain of despondence.

"Should you fail to right the wrongs you have committed, it will never again flourish, despite all my best efforts to irrigate it with affection. Should it never again flourish, you will never find your way to Amadea, and the cycle cannot complete, to all of our detriment."

The name of Amadea was still an unsettling occurrence for Davis to endure, yet he was focused enough on his task that he finally mounted the courage to inquire.

"What cycle?" he asked. "What is Amadea? And why is it so crucial that I should make my way there?"

"These questions aren't my place to answer," replied Hortulanus.

At the insistence of Davis, it responded with only repetitious remarks.

"Some things are learned best when discovered by the self, and not taught by another," said the Gardener.

An impish simper on the creature's expression implied that it got a moderate delight from its more edified position.

At even further insistence from Davis, it provided only a warning.

"Suffice it to say that, if you don't make it there, there wasn't much point in existing at all." The Gardener hopped lightly along as it went back to its watering. "And that would be a dreadful and dreary doom to discover," it said.

Davis agreed. The whole practice of living practically begged for something worthwhile to eventuate somewhere down the line. It would be such a shame to come so far and still leave so much undetermined.

"Well," said Davis, "I'm here now, and now is all that we have." *Two can play this game,* he grinned. "If you would kindly stand aside, fair Gardener, I have somewhere to be."

Despite both parties having good reasons to the contrary, their encounters had somehow managed to forge the beginnings of an unlikely friendship between the Gardener and the man who depleted its garden. Hortulanus simply took a single sidestep, bowed its head low, and waved its arm sideways, as if leading the way in the direction of the horizon.

"As a matter of fact," said Hortulanus after Davis had walked past, "I have some business in Immolatio myself."

The Gardener put down its watering can.

"I think I'll join you," it said. "That is, if you don't mind the company."

"By all means," smiled Davis. "The more, the merrier, as they say. And now that I think of it," he laughed, "I don't exactly know the way."

As the sun burned down upon Davis on his way through the desert, the jovial disposition from his reunion with the Gardener had taken a turn toward the serious. The severity of the situation began to sink in with the remembrance of why he needed to undertake this voyage in the first place.

Nor was Davis sure what he expected to find there, for he was quite certain he had slain the Guardian once and for all. Yet somehow the creature had managed to leave one last note, imploring him to seek it in the place he was currently seeking. With each step further into the desert, the guilt of the slaying of Custos redoubled. He knew that the time when he would be judged for his deeds was nigh.

"Have you met the Guardian?" he asked his companion as they made their long way over the sand.

"In a manner of speaking," replied Hortulanus.

"How about in the manner in which I'm speaking?" asked Davis.

"Then no, I don't believe I have."

"You don't believe you have?" asked Davis.

"I don't believe so — yes."

"That doesn't sound very convincing," said Davis.

"Well," said the Gardener, "I'm not entirely convinced. You see, the Guardian you know takes on many forms. It is Custos, overseer of Amadea; it is Vilicus, Praestes, and Ostiarius; it is Coerator, Satelles, and Claustritumus."

"So I've heard," said Davis. "What's the difference?"

"There isn't a difference, though none are quite the same. You saw it somehow, as have I; but I doubt that I've seen it in the same way as you."

"What other way would you have seen it?" asked Davis.

The Gardener stopped, as if to think about how to put this tactfully.

"In a way that's a little closer to the truth."

"Whatever the case, I'm not really sure what to expect," said Davis.

"Well, what are you expecting?" asked Hortulanus.

"Custos told me to come to Immolatio when my wisdom had awoken completely, but there was little left in terms of an explanation. I'm not sure that my wisdom even has awoken completely; still, I feel something urging me on – somehow, I just know the time is right."

"I do take pity on someone with so little an idea of what to anticipate," said Hortulanus. "Let me try to extrapolate."

As they spoke, the travelers arrived at the top of the most recent dune, and it was higher than any they had traversed so far; but even from here, the sand stretched on as far as they could see in every direction.

"As I've said," continued the Gardener, "rather than desert, these dunes were once the rolling hills of the Garden of Elisium. You'd be hard-pressed to find a more beautiful place on Earth."

The full meaning of this redundant remark chimed through clearly now to Davis, upon the chance of a second listen from a fuller perspective. The Gardener continued without pause.

"Eventually, as the hills rise, they give way to a bluff at the edge of the sea, due west of where we currently stand. Immolatio is this bluff, and from its high seat in the clouds, it looks out far across the unending waves of the Infinite Sea. Upon the edge of this cliff is the altar of Expiatio. It is said that whatever is placed upon the altar shall be cleansed and born anew."

"The Heart!" shouted Davis. He could barely contain his excitement at the onset of this potent epiphany.

"I'm sorry my friend, but I have to go. I'm not quite ready to make it there after all. I have an errand to run first. I'll meet you there when my detour is complete."

Davis didn't even allow for a reply. He closed his eyes and envisioned the place where the Great Ape had fallen. The Gardener watched as the man vanished at once from his place beneath the bright desert sun.

4.4 | Return to the Throne

Upon arriving at the throne in the north, Davis realized that this unfortunately meant he was once again in the domain of Errol the Wary.

Or was it Nobilis the Righteous, Prodigious Bird of Prey?

He didn't think it would have been possible for this land to have become any more desolate, but somehow it had managed. Almost everything had fallen into complete disarray. The thorns that had brought him here on his very first visit were practically the only living things left. They encroached inward toward the throne, as if even the wicked plants themselves were considering a mutiny.

The seat of the throne, however, was currently empty. Davis ran over to the spot where the Great Ape had fallen. There was nothing left but the skeleton of a small and pitiful primate.

Poor Myops, he thought, in an unexpected bout of empathy. *In life it was selfish and arrogant, but in death it simply seems sad and alone.*

In looking down upon the rotting remains of the ape, some of the wise words of the Transcendent Sage were finally starting to make sense. There was so much about this ape that was like himself; so many of its fatal flaws were shared by Davis and all his kind. Though he was hardly conscious of it at the time – for he was only barely conscious at all – it was precisely for this reason that the Guardian was dead.

Perhaps there was a way to right both of their wrongs.

Now that he was here, however, Davis wasn't sure what he thought he might be able to accomplish. Myops had eaten the heart, after all; how was he going to obtain it, so as to make his amends? He hadn't quite gotten that far. It was almost as though the mere thought of this scene had caused the landscape to change, without any intentional input necessary. But he was here now, and he desperately wanted to find some kind of solution.

His desires were answered by the deafening shudder of wings.

"What business brings you here, yet again, to my kingdom?" hissed an ominous voice from behind.

Davis rotated in an instant and beheld the Great Bird of Prey, perched on a branch in one of the many dead trees nearby. The shreds of civility that had existed at their last parting were all but a memory. The eagle seemed desperate and paranoid, mad and maniacal.

Things were obviously not going well for the Lord of the Land.

"My liege," spoke Davis humbly, as he bowed his head low. "I have come for something I lost. I was hoping your great wisdom could help me."

The bird could no longer be flattered by soothing words of this sort. It bowed as a requisite gesture of courtesy, but its eyes were menacing, and they hid a great suspicion.

"Go on. What is it you seek?"

"All the realm is aware of your generosity, my Lord." *This is not going to go over well*, he predicted; but he had no better ideas. "I was hoping that I could, perhaps, recover a souvenir I once possessed – but a small token for the great service I have done for the land."

"How did you know about that?!" shrieked Errol. Its eyes opened widely in a frenzy of panic. "That cursed weasel!" shouted the bird to itself. "It has betrayed me – I knew it! That pathetic varmint told this stranger of my most prized possession. I knew it was only a matter of time!"

The eagle was lost in its own furious deliberations, but its attention soon turned back to Davis. It flapped its wings, and with a second deafening shudder, the bird had vanished from its place in the tree.

Davis turned around, remembering the propensity of the bird to appear from behind. Sure enough, there it was, down on the ground and walking rapidly towards him in a very awkward fashion. It didn't resort to walking very often.

"You have betrayed your Master," hissed the bird. "Your only hope for a pardon is to confess your crimes and reveal the plot of this traitor."

By now it was only a few feet away, and there was no sign of it slowing its enraged approach. Without having a moment to think of some courteous remark which would still get his point across, Davis reached forth his hand and shouted forcefully at the bird out of fright.

"Stop!"

Amazingly, the eagle was immediately frozen in place, only inches from ensnaring Davis with one of its monstrous talons. Davis stepped back several paces from the bird, almost as shocked as it was by his stunning display of power.

Errol slowly retracted its talon and placed it again firmly on the ground. It tried to regain its civility, and pretended that it was for this reason, and not some other, that it had been stopped dead in its tracks. It lifted its wings, ruffled its feathers with a shake, and nervously preened the worst of them as briefly as it could.

"Excuse me," said the bird. "I seem to have momentarily lost my manners. As I was saying, your only hope for a pardon is to reveal to me, in full, this treacherous plot of betrayal. Speak."

"My liege," said Davis, doing just as good a job at regaining the civil pretense with which they had operated, "I'm afraid that I truly don't know what you mean. I've never met a weasel, nor spoken with one. Who is it?"

It ignored the question, for the bird's thoughts were too focused on how this stranger could have known about its most valued treasure.

"How did you know about the stone then?" said the bird suspiciously.

"My liege," said Davis, "I didn't know there was such a thing. I have heard of no stone until you yourself just spoke of it."

The bird glared at him, squinting its powerful eyes.

"Then what did you mean when you spoke of a token for the service you have done for the Land?"

Here goes nothing.

"I seek news of the Heart of Custos," he admitted.

"So you do know about it!" shrieked the bird. Great desperation still lingered on its face; but as it spoke, it sounded at least a little bit satisfied that its previous paranoia was justified.

"The last I knew, it was eaten by Regulus, who lies now in the dirt."

"I will never surrender it, for it is a symbol of the death of the treacherous beast – a memento of my noble rise to power. It represents everything that is just in the world."

Davis knew the bird meant something entirely different by these words; but from a more enlightened perspective, it was true.

Again, he had no good strategy; he tried to say it as politely as he could.

"My Lord," said Davis, "I think it only fair that I should be rewarded with this prize. For it was I who slew the beast; and it was I who led to the downfall of your master."

At this grave offense, the bird broke out into an inexorable rage. Here was an explicit admission that its guest had come for its most valued treasure. Here was another claiming the honor for its own glorious deeds. Here was someone with the presumptuous notion that they had been responsible for the spoils of war which the bird now enjoyed.

"How dare you challenge my authority?!" it squawked. "How dare you challenge my power?! It was I who claimed the throne triumphantly. It was I who cleansed the Land of its filth. It is I who rules as Lord of the Land!"

Reeling from the unforgivable insult to its honor, the eagle launched into flight, swooping down upon Davis, its deadly talons outstretched.

There simply wasn't time to think of a peaceful solution, nor did Davis believe one could have existed. As the bird came within reach of its prey, Davis stretched out his hand in a powerful motion driven by instinct alone.

The bird ignited in midair and fell to the ground, engulfed in flame.

The squeals and shrieks and screeches of the bird were unbearable, and the stench was just as bad. It writhed in agony, back and forth on the ground. At the sight of it, Davis again felt pity sink in. With it came an enormous wave of regret, for he had failed so readily at his charge.

The bird screamed in desperation and distress, pleading with the world to end its intolerable suffering. Davis waved his hand over the sight of the bird; it turned to black ashes which fell to the earth.

At the end of the horrendous scene, another creature poked its head cautiously out from behind the large throne. Davis didn't notice it at first, still reeling in his shock and remorse. It slinked around the side of the throne cautiously, staying as low to the ground as it could.

Eventually, Davis did see it, for the creature came near to the site of the slaughter, once it finally deemed the scene safe. It was a guileful and devious weasel, though larger than any Davis had ever seen, reaching over half his own height. It stretched itself up on two feet to full stature; standing by the large mound of ashes, it cleared its throat and began to speak.

"Why—"

Its voice cracked immediately, and it cleared its throat again, for the weasel was trying its best to sound kingly. It had mostly only sounded deceitful and dubious before this moment, and it wanted it to be special.

"Why, thank you, my good sir!" said the weasel awkwardly. "You have done a great service to this land."

"And who are you?" asked Davis.

"I was Ancipitis the Astute, Chief Vassal to Nobilis," said the weasel, slipping unintentionally back into the sound of a wily underling. It cleared its throat a third time in an effort to regain its authority.

"But now — now, I shall be known as..."

It hesitated, searching for the most glorious name it could concoct.

"I shall be known as ... Callidus the Cunning, Lord of the Land."

"Good to meet you, my liege," bowed Davis.

"For your service, I would reward you with the treasure you seek, for I want it not. Its very presence is unnerving to me, for some reason which I cannot explain."

The weasel bent back to all four feet and slunk its way over to the side of the throne. It opened the very same chest from which the Great Ape had produced the Blade of Entitlement. It pulled out a small black bag made of felt, holding it only by the string which cinched the bag shut, as if the weasel dared not even touch it.

"Here you are," said Callidus, and it hastily handed Davis the bag. "Good riddance, I say. Furthermore, for your great service to your Lord, I would award you with the title of Chief Vassal. What do you say?"

"You flatter me, your eminence, with your generous offer. Still, I cannot accept it, for my purpose lies farther ahead down the road."

"Very well," said the weasel.

Davis bowed one last time, closed his eyes, and envisioned the desert.

Lifting his head from the depths of the curtsy, he opened his eyes to see the sun setting far away in the west, over long leagues of sand. He raised the bag in his hand and turned it upside down. A resplendent gemstone fell into the palm of the opposite hand.

The stone was circular in shape and heavy in weight, yet it didn't even fill the width of the hand that grasped it. Davis could tell why one such as Errol would covet such a treasure, for it shimmered with a wondrous shade of red. It drew Davis in with its beauty, practically lulling him into a trance as he took in its glow.

As Davis continued to stare into the stone, however, the red began changing into a deep shade of black, as if old and overly oxidized blood were trickling down the edges on the inside of it. Soon, the whole stone shone no more – covered from within by a dark, opaque black. He placed the stone into the bag almost as hurriedly as the weasel had handed it to him, and slid the bag into his pocket.

Looking again over the sand, he realized that he didn't fully know the location of Immolatio: there could be no shortcut this time. The long miles before him, and the weight of the Heart, would make for a tedious walk.

4.5 | Terra Incognita

The trek across the desert proved to be the first instance in all his travels to date in which Davis genuinely thought that he might not make it. He'd encountered despair before; that aspect was nothing new. At times, it felt like his whole journey was little more than one long, drawn-out, melancholic wallow in it. This time, however, he was under the impression that he might drown in it completely.

The environment itself was unwelcoming and hostile, to the point where he couldn't have imagined a garden of paradise ever residing in the place. Even in the last remaining hours of sunlight, the heat of the arid air seared his skin with every movement. The only moisture he encountered was his own precious fluids escaping out into the desiccated atmosphere. He longed more than ever for the cool, quenching relief of water. Despite his discarnate status, he still felt the need to appease his worldly requirements.

He had yet to fully shred his way through the silk of the cocoon.

In addition to the unpleasant sensations he wasn't yet able to disregard, Davis was also troubled by the fact that his only directions consisted of a straight line through the sand, towards the setting sun. The most distressing part of all, however, was the great burden in his pocket – the fateful reminder of his purpose far away to the west.

Though he didn't have any way of guessing exactly what awaited him, he was aware on some level that he had come all this way to pay for the crimes he had committed. The blackening of the Heart of Custos weighed heavily on him, and it was this very omen which ultimately caused the pessimistic turn his outlook had taken.

In spite of a sincere belief that he might be undone in the unending desert, its end did finally come. As Davis came over the penultimate dune, he beheld the bluff of Immolatio in the distance, looming over the sea. He gathered the last of his strength, ignored any remaining discomforts, and raced into the valley between it and his present position. When he eventually crested the final hill, he stood upon the entrance to Immolatio at last. The cliff shot straight down into the sea; but upon its top, only a short distance from the edge, dwelt the altar of Expiatio.

The altar was pure and simple, yet divinely elegant in its austerity. It was composed of a solid piece of rock. Whomsoever had carved it had taken great care that all its edges were exactly even; it was level and symmetrical – a truly perfect shape.

The only embellishment whatsoever was the presence of two interweaving lines encircling the outer edge, carved directly into the stone in an intricate manner. They complemented each other completely, so that as one was at its maximum, the other was at its minimum. The lower would then rise by the same degree in which the upper would fall, until they had crossed over one another, and their roles became reversed. This same process repeated along the perimeter of the altar until each line eventually connected back with itself – two infinite sine waves, dancing ever around each other in a flawless harmonious display.

The hour was late, and the sun was now touching the western horizon. It formed a perfect half-circle over the top of the altar, and in its center was the shape of a familiar figure. On the far side of Expiatio was the silhouette of the Gardener, the creature's edges glowing from the sunset behind it. Davis couldn't make out any details, but had he been able to, he would have seen an expression that was grave and dejected.

Hortulanus was not alone either, for on both sides of the altar stood three dark figures, shrouded by their shadows from the sun far away. Davis could not determine who they were, but he could hear them shouting at one another, and see them gesturing aggressively in the fury of debate. Having taken in the scene, he stepped forward to engage with it directly.

"Who is it that stands here shouting, arguing in anger before the very altar of atonement?" He didn't know the inspiration for his words; they came effortlessly. "Have you no decency? Have you no respect for even sanctified places?"

Davis looked back and forth at the shadows, but their shock from the entrance of this visitor didn't allow them to answer of yet. He looked instead at the Gardener; its head was simply bowed low in sadness.

"Hortulanus, who are these people? And what are they arguing about?"

"I have summoned them here, on behalf of all your interests; and it is good that I have, for try as they may, they would have never found their way here on their own.

"Some are people whom you have met before; some are people who have sought to meet you. All are people who cannot agree. Even in Immolatio, they argue about the things which they would argue about elsewhere. Even here, in the most sacred of places, they have come seeking both blood and vengeance."

The Gardener looked first at one group, and then the other.

"They have come in search of someone other than themselves to blame."

Davis stepped forward even further to identify them if he could. To his left were the Scrutatorus – Animulus in the center, Manus and Cerebrus on either side. To his right were three individuals he had never met before.

"Who are you?" he asked the strangers, ignoring for now any salutations to the brothers, even after all their time apart. "Why have you come here?"

The figures looked male and all were equally tall, though the two on each side gave way to the one in the center, as he stepped forward to speak.

"You may not know of us, Davis; but we know of you. So should you also be familiar with our authority: we are the High Council of Inanimis, and we have come to demand that your associates are put to death for their crimes against our rule."

"What crimes?" asked Davis with his best attempt at sounding ignorant.

Before the Councilor could reply, Cerebrus shouted back in revulsion.

"You dare accuse us of transgressions?! What about the crimes of Inanimis? What about the countless victims of its selfish and reckless ways?"

The hands of Manus were shaking with anticipation as he heard his brother speak; they were burning for the chance to incinerate their foes. His brother was not done; not by far.

"We are simply doing what must be done to protect the world that we love from the vile petulance into which your kind would turn it. We shall not stand idly by to be accused of treason by the greatest traitors to Nature the world has ever seen! Nor will we rest until the walls of your city are laid completely to waste, its people are free from the shackles of enslavement, and the Inviocassus is once again replete with green trees touching the sky."

The Councilor started to defend himself, but he was again interrupted, this time by the interjection of Davis.

"Cerebrus, please! Let me try my best to get to the bottom of this. From what I've gathered so far, it doesn't appear as if you've made any headway with talk of that sort."

He turned calmly to the men from the city.

"Councilor: do be so kind as to introduce yourself and your compatriots. I'm sure that we can find a reasonable solution to your quarrels, if we would commit ourselves to the respect that each in their own is due."

The Councilor had obviously not encountered a proposition of this sort from the brothers, and for the time being, he reverted back to the air of decency and dispassion with which the people of Inanimis perform all of their duties.

"My name is Legatus; I am the Chief Councilor of Inanimis. At my left and right hands are Politicus and Exercitus respectively. Together, we are the principal ruling body of the city. As I said, we have come to demand the surrender of the Heretics, for their copious crimes against humanity."

"What crimes?" repeated Davis.

He shot a glance at Cerebrus to imply that he was not to interrupt.

At the request for a full account of their wrongdoings, the Councilor was visibly excited for the chance to consult his official documentation on the matter. He produced a rolled scroll from his large robes and slid off the ribbon that was binding it. It sprung open with a jolt and uncurled all the way to the ground. Evidently, there was a long list of official grievances.

"I, Legatus, Chief Councilor of Inanimis, on behalf of the High Council and the Court of Inanimis, hereby present Article 1348-C, which documents the known instances of infractions, as committed by the defendants."

Davis had already practically stopped listening. It was hard not to, for it felt as though the Councilor had been talking for ages, yet he had not yet begun to begin. The man licked his fingers, flickered them in anticipation, and slowly began unfurling the scroll.

Get on with it already!

"Infraction One: violation of Code 19-48-J, subsection 56.1 — Desertion and Defamation. Infraction Two: violation of Code 92-21-F, subsection 6.2.5 — Hindrance of Progress. Infraction Three: violation of Code 36-15-D — Assault on an Officer; six-hundred and thirty-eight counts. Infraction Four: violation of Code..."

Having seen the far end of the scroll make its way to the feet of the Councilor, Davis was not of the mind to withstand the recitation of every last bit of administrative jargon at this pace. He cut off the Councilor before the man was able to fully enjoy the duration of his own official narrative.

"Councilor, while I don't doubt that your parliamentary designations are important to you and your associates, for the sake of time I must implore you to make a more succinct summary of your grievances with these men."

The Councilor came to a staggering halt as he was disrupted in this fashion, and he was not pleased with the interruption of his official business, especially by someone not officially appointed by the Court. Nevertheless, he was indeed taken in by the patrician language of the man who had somehow taken on the role of adjudicator.

"I'm sorry," he said awkwardly, still a little unsure whether he should be succumbing to demands of these sorts from someone like Davis.

Regardless of his hesitation, he yielded for the moment; the scroll fell from its raised position as his arms gave way to disuse.

"In short, the defendants are charged with Desertion, Interference of Official Business, and numerous accounts of Assault."

This was as much as Davis had gathered from only the first three in a very long list of infractions; he now began to wonder what composed the remaining great length of the scroll, though he did not have long to wonder.

"Most recently, they are accused of Assault on a Merchant of Inanimis, one Avidus the fisherman. He appeared to the Court with burns on both arms and described how he had been harassed, threatened, and assaulted, and how his business had been hindered by the wrongful expulsion from his permitted fishing grounds."

Davis would have clarified the issue of this last transgression, but his tongue sunk, like a rock lodged in his throat. He tried to get any words out on the matter, but the Councilor continued without a moment's delay.

"Perhaps most importantly, they are in violation of Code 11-16-77: Veneration of a False God."

Apparently he couldn't resist the official designation for this, the most heinous of crimes in all of Inanimis.

"They freely follow the ways of a deity they call Praestes," he continued. "We know this beast only as the Scourge of Progress, and all those citizens who follow in its teachings are to be apprehended immediately."

The Councilor began rolling up the scroll most carefully.

"Thus, in light of these copious insults to our Official Code of Conduct, the Heretics are to be brought back to Inanimis for Incineration."

The change of subject freed his tongue from its paralysis, and steered his thoughts to this much more pressing matter. In the commotion to which he'd arrived, Davis had almost forgotten about the Guardian. Now at its mention, however, he felt the purpose for his presence there nag at the back of his mind.

"I'm sorry, I must have misheard you," said Davis. "Do you mean they are to be brought back for incarceration?"

"A Councilor of Inanimis never misspeaks," said the man. "They are to be brought back for Incineration. Permanent Re-Assignment is far too lenient a punishment for unspeakable crimes of this magnitude."

At these accusations, the wrath of the Scrutatorus could no longer be contained, regardless of any intervention by Davis. Their entire system of values had been disregarded at best, and desecrated at worst. To hear the Guardian spoken of in this way unleashed an explosion of anger in the brothers that would not be easy to subdue. Even Animulus, the most composed of the three, wore an expression of sheer detestation.

The brothers stepped forward rapidly in unison, each of their hands aflame with a deadly lust for revenge. Davis recognized the mounting tension immediately, and had he not physically inserted himself between the two sides of this debate, there would almost certainly have been ashes afloat on the breeze from the sea.

All three Councilors wore the snake-like metallic devices on their sides, the same as those worn by the officers in the city. At the advancement of the Heretics, each of the men reached their hands to their weapons, though none of them drew as of yet.

At the blockade made by their ally, the brothers did not advance any further. Instead, they resorted once again to shouting and threatening the High Council, who just as quickly cast aside all remaining delusions of decency and shouted in turn at their enemies.

Sounds of hatred and wrath swirled around Davis from all sides; it made it impossible to think. It felt like he was drowning in a sea of spiteful malevolence, with no hope of ever breaching the surface.

The brothers demanded the death of the Councilors, for they were convinced that the city was responsible for the death of the Guardian. The Council, of course, demanded the death of the brothers, for following the ways of the Guardian, and attempting in any way they could to hinder the progress of the city.

In the midst of this mire of malice, Davis looked up to see the Gardener on the opposite side of the Expiatio. In the chaos surrounding him, Davis had quite forgotten that Hortulanus was there. Ever since Davis had arrived at Immolatio, however, its eyes had never once broken their focus on him. While its heart was obviously heavy with sorrow, it said nothing; it simply looked on patiently to see how Davis would respond.

4.6 | Immolatio

The shouts coming from either side of Davis grew louder with each passing sentence, and it would not be long before words would no longer suffice. He feared they may give way to action.

His ears were bombarded by hatred from both sides, but his eyes remained locked with those of Hortulanus. They looked deep down into the very depths of his being, in a way that he had only experienced with one other creature to date. While Davis had certainly inferred the allegiance of the Gardener, it was not until now that he truly observed any meaningful similarity between it and its Master.

In the same way as he had heard the Guardian on that fateful Day of Darkening, he heard the voice of Hortulanus now, though no words were spoken aloud. It dimmed the clamor of the adversaries all around him, replacing the multitudes of madness with a singular sentiment.

Contrition can only be true when it leads one to acts of atonement.

The meaning of the words no longer needed any clarification for Davis; it was the will to act on them at last that he needed to muster.

Both sides inched their way closer, their threatening motions literally reaching over Davis. In a sudden culmination of their loathing, all words had finally lost their purpose.

Almost as if working in unison, each group thrust Davis aside viciously and reached out to strike at the other. The two forces clashed with a violent collision, all members on either side grappling with one from the other: Animulus to Legatus, Cerebrus to Politicus, and Manus to Exercitus.

Each Councilor held their weapon at the head of the brother opposite them, while each of the Scrutatorus grasped the neck of their counterpart Councilor. Just as all parties were in danger of total, simultaneous annihilation, Davis rose from the ground where he'd been thrown, reached out his hands, and shouted a spell of stillness and silence.

"Stop!"

Exactly as before, when faced with the onslaught of Errol the Wary, every action of the assailants was completely arrested. Each stood frozen, immobilized in time — the needle-like prongs of the High Council's weapons digging into the foreheads of the Scrutatorus; the glowing red hands of the Heretics searing the necks of the Councilors.

For now, however, there was nothing but peace.

Davis moved his outstretched hands in a parting motion, and in perfect accordance, the bodies of the combatants were dragged away from one another, back to their original positions from before the escalation. Davis let his hands fall to his sides, and all at once, the combatants were freed from the spell.

Free to speak or act as they pleased, for now all six of them simply looked around at each other, then back to Davis, in complete disbelief over what had just happened. The display of his power had shocked each of them enough that they yielded to him the right to speak first.

Having been given the floor — or having demanded it — Davis turned his attention first to the Councilors.

"Legatus, Politicus, Exercitus: the acts of Inanimis are imprudent and imposing. Your city lives like a parasite on the host that provides for you, for you take and you take, but you never give back. You care nothing for things outside of your walls, for you refuse to see how they affect the workings within them. You have strayed from your purpose, and it will come at great cost."

He then turned his attention to the Scrutatorus.

"Animulus, Cerebrus, Manus: you claim to honor the ways of the Guardian, but you do not exemplify the principles for which it stands. You seek peace, yet you so readily give in to your hatred; you use death and destruction as a force for revenge and requital. You seek to rid the world of the evils of Inanimis, but in doing so, you have employed the means of a different evil entirely. You have strayed from your purpose, and it will come at great cost."

Davis paused.

He knew what must be done, but not how to bring it about.

"It's quite clear that your differences are not going to be easily reconciled. Indeed, something must change; but I will not let change come from a battle of force. While each of you has so obviously erred, it is I who has sinned most greatly — I see that now."

Again, he spoke first to the High Council.

"To you, Councilors: I offer myself as ransom, in exchange for the misdeeds of my brothers. For it was in defense of myself that they attacked your guards, at least during the most recent confrontation. And it was I, not my brothers, who assaulted the fisherman Avidus. I take responsibility for all of their deeds, and I implore you to absolve their crimes, on the condition that I surrender myself to the fullest extent of your punishment."

As before, he spoke next to the Scrutatorus.

"To you, my brothers: I admit myself as the greatest wrongdoer of all. It was I who slew the Guardian, not the dwellers of Inanimis. They are guilty of much, but they are innocent of this. I do not fully understand the motivations that led me to commit such a treacherous act, but a stroke of the blade can never be undone. I take responsibility for all my deeds, and I submit myself to your judgement for this wicked offense."

What before had seemed like the most extreme form of rage in the eyes of the brothers, in comparison now only seemed like annoyance. To learn of this dreadful news after all this time, and when already in a state of such vexation – it tipped all three over the brink into lunacy. The wound was made all the more grievous by the fact that it came from someone they had considered an ally.

To hate an enemy was tolerable, but the news of this betrayal unleashed within them a true maleficence that they dared not think they possessed. They had wanted blood before, but from those whom they wanted to bleed. It was too late, however; there was no choice in the matter. The brothers still needed vengeance. But despite their bloodlust, they made no sudden movements. Animulus gathered his composure to the best of his ability and spoke only a single sentence.

"He who has slain the Guardian must in turn be slain for his sins."

Davis had no intention of escaping his unfortunate fate. Instead, he simply glanced toward the High Council for a nod of approval that his surrender would afford a complete resolution of all pending issues at hand. Without a word being spoken, Legatus made it clear that his offer had been accepted. His death would serve as a suitable replacement, in retribution for the crimes of the brothers, and the crimes of his own.

Seeing that his sacrifice would appease both disputing parties, Davis walked slowly to the altar, his head hanging down to his chest. Before he turned around to face his sentence, he looked up to find the face of Hortulanus. The Gardener's expression had changed from sorrow to solace; the creature found an elegiac comfort in the path Davis had chosen.

Meanwhile, the executioners had been arguing over who would be the one to carry out the execution. Each party vied for the chance to bring their transgressor to justice, and no agreement could be made as to which of them was more deserving of the task.

In hearing the conversation turning again to a quarrel, Davis turned back to the men and made their decision for them.

"Not one of you will carry out this deed, for I will not allow you to claim blood in the name of spilled blood."

Davis turned back to the Gardener.

"Hortulanus will do it."

He stared silently, again seeking approval for the decision he had made. Hortulanus simply bowed its head to Davis, and turned its back to look upon the sun setting far away across the sea.

Davis spoke to the crowd as he prepared for whatever was to come.

"Gentlemen," he said softly, "at least do me the decency of allowing me a moment to compose myself."

The men consented, and all six walked a short distance down the bluff, where they waited eagerly for the time of their bloodthirsty redress.

As they did so, Davis walked around the Expiatio and joined Hortulanus on the far side. The two stood only a short distance from the edge of the cliff and stared out at the beautiful scene.

"You must know that I do not cherish this burden you have placed upon me," said Hortulanus. The Gardener leaned its head around Davis and peered down the hill. "And yet," it smirked, "it does give me great satisfaction to know that at least none of them will get to enjoy it."

"What's going to happen to me?" asked Davis tentatively.

"Soon you are doomed to die the Second Death, and no one can say for sure what lies on the other side of so great an unknown. Perhaps there is nothing at all; perhaps there is naught but blackness, rolling on forever like the very sea here before us." The Gardener smiled again at Davis. "Then you could finally get the peace and rest you so desperately desire."

"After all that I've gone through," said Davis, "I'm not so sure that infinite blackness is all that I want." He remembered how he felt when he was afforded that very request, not long ago in the Tower of Transpectus. "I miss things. I miss feeling like I was a part of something. In life, I felt connected; with my family, I felt home. Here, I feel only alone and adrift. Whatever it is that awaits me, I hope it brings me back there."

I want to go home.

The Gardener reached down and plucked a small flower that had grown near the altar in Immolatio. Somehow, even high in the air on this desolate and arid plateau, it had found what it needed to grow.

"You might find that it indeed leads you there, though you may not necessarily recognize it," said Hortulanus. "You might find that you have been there all along. Never forget your place in the cycle, Davis, for it is this very place that you belong."

A familiar voice spoke softly in his mind, and it put him entirely at ease.

> *The suns rise and set, while the moons wax and wane*
> *Things will keep changing, but still stay just the same*
> *From the dust of the atmosphere, you have appeared*
> *Fear not this kind fact, which your kind tends to fear*

"Sometimes," the Gardener continued, "like this very flower, life can be plucked prematurely from its place. The tragic reality is that, at any place, and at any time, something may come along and uproot you in life. It isn't fair, and I won't patronize you by saying that it's for some greater good.

"The truth of the matter is that Life is stochastic, and navigating it all is a matter of statistics. Some people get more than their share of good fortune, while others may hardly get any at all. Unfortunately, we don't always have as much control over these fortunes as we would like. Our only control is in making the most of the choices before us; and today, you have chosen the road of peace.

"Who's to say if you will ever benefit from it directly? I can't promise you a land where the streets are paved with gold, or grant you rewards in the next life for having done what's right in this one. The truth is that you may simply die now and never know any differently one way or another.

"The good that can be done in the world, however, is far greater than all that. It is our duty to leave things better than we found them. Sometimes, this means fighting our hardest to get them back to how they were before we messed them all up. I can't say where you are going, but I can tell you to go there in peace, for you have managed to do exactly that. Good luck my friend."

With these words did Hortulanus leave Davis alone on the far side of the Expiatio. The Gardener walked around the altar, and the men far away took notice of the sign indicating the beginning of the highly anticipated event. All six men made their way back up to the altar, though Davis was still staring out at the sea. The sunset was now almost expired.

"I may not be able to perform the act myself," spoke Legatus, "but I think it only fair that the deed be done with this."

The Councilor produced from within his robes a long and glistening dagger, which he presented to Hortulanus.

"At one point it belonged to the defendant, though he traded it for currency when he arrived for the first time in Inanimis. The Court obtained it as evidence after he departed. As I see no other means by which you could perform this execution, I suggest it as the logical option."

The Scrutatorus looked on in awe at the Blade of Entitlement.

"This must have been the very blade he used to slay Praestes," said Cerebrus. "We eventually heard news that its heart was cut from its chest, though we knew not who wielded it. We concur; the knife should be used. It will be a fitting end to die by the same blade that caused us so much harm."

The Gardener took the blade from the Councilor and walked up to the front of the Expiatio. Davis turned from the sea and faced east once again. He stepped forward to the altar, climbed on top of its smooth upper surface, and stretched out upon it to pay for his sins.

In his hands, he clasped the Heart of Custos. The Blade of Entitlement fell swiftly through the air and pierced the one still in his chest.

The jolt from the puncture shook his body, and his arms flailed out to the side. The Heart of Custos was flung from his grasp and it smote the ground on the far side of the altar. The force of the fall sent it tumbling to the cliff, where it took one last bound – and leapt over the edge.

After a long descent from the heights of Immolatio, the stone splashed into the waves crashing fiercely against the cliff face. It sank down steadily through the water into the utter black of its great abyss. When the stone finally came to rest in the sand at the bottom of the sea – though no light was cast upon it, nor were there any eyes to see – the black slowly began to give way once again to a magnificent shade of radiant red.

The next thing Davis knew, he had opened his eyes and was looking up at the stars. There was no pain to be found anywhere in his body, if he could even be considered to have one at all. He sat up to scan his surroundings, unaware of when or where he was. All he knew was that it felt not like the hard, cold stone of Expiatio, but rather like the soft and forgiving feel of grass.

He recognized the place immediately, though indeed it was not Immolatio. To his right was the Lacuna Speculis; by its edge was a creature, the likeness of which he'd never before seen, though he knew in an instant what it was.

"I've traveled a long road to find you again," said Davis. "I'm glad that I have and that the journey is over."

The voice of the Guardian responded in his head.

Your wisdom has grown greatly since the dreaded Day of Darkening.

The creature did not turn to face him; it stood once again on four legs, but the form it took was difficult to pin down. Each time Davis looked, its appearance seemed to change slightly, while always remaining precisely what it was – what it had always been. Its head was bowed low to the water, but it was not drinking from the fountain.

"You see clearer now than before," said the Guardian, "though you still have much to learn."

"Why wasn't I able to recognize you in all that time?" asked Davis.

"We can only see that of the world which our senses provide us; and we can only know of the world what it is that we see. Through clouded eyes, you looked upon me and saw only a Gardener; for you believed me to be dead, and thus invented other forms in which to seek guidance."

"But you were dead," said Davis. "I saw it with my own eyes."

"I can never be slain," clarified Custos.

"I thought all things must pass," said Davis; it was solemn, not sarcastic.

"In one sense," said the creature. "And yet will they simply change their fleeting, mortal form. Unlike your earthly body, I am not mortal."

"What are you then?" asked the man.

I am many things, sensed Davis, before the creature spoke aloud.

"You may think of me as the liaison for that which has no form in which to walk amongst you; for I stand before you as a mere personification of what it is that I actually am."

Davis didn't understand – not yet; or perhaps, not anymore – but that didn't really matter to him at the moment. For now, he was glad to learn that the creature he'd belatedly grown to consider a friend had been with him all along, in the form of a friend.

He smiled, recalling in a new light all that Hortulanus had told him.

"I suppose if there's anything a Gardener does, it's to act as the Guardian of the Garden it loves."

Davis looked for even a faint hint of amusement on the expression of his companion, though no such sign came.

"This is indeed true," commented Coerator, "and Elisium is the most beloved Garden of all. From its bounty does all other life flourish. That it withered and vanished is surely a great sadness; but, as difficult as it may be at any time, we must never forget that life is cyclic.

"All too often, it is easy for things to fall from the graces of equilibrium – when not enough has been given, or too much has been taken. Sooner or later, however, things come back into balance; and thus is Elisium replenished, owing thanks to your own deeds of recompense."

"But I never placed the Heart upon the altar," said Davis. "I don't understand how it worked."

"It was told unto you that whatever was laid upon Expiatio would be cleansed and born anew," continued Claustritumus. "In your innocent ignorance, you presumed that meant the stone; in truth, it was you who needed rebirth. You could not see the Garden for the very same reason you could not recognize me as its Gardener. Neither one of us had been lost; you simply had to learn for yourself what it was that we meant."

Davis certainly felt different – 'freer' being perhaps the only word he could have used to describe it. Nevertheless, he was surprised to still find himself in the place where he was, and in the form that he was.

"I find it an interesting choice of words," said Davis, looking around. "It doesn't seem like I found any rebirth at all. I'm sitting here with you, at the edge of the very same pool I visited only a short while ago."

"You take me to mean that you would be clad with new forms," vied Vilicus. "I am referring to something much more important. The atoms you hoarded have long been recycled, and they have given the chance for many other things to exist. What matters now is that you have let go of the part of you with which you arrived here – the part you acquired on Earth; the part which so readily tried to stray from its purpose."

Davis lifted his hands and pondered them. They felt lighter somehow, and yet more whole than ever. They were still there, as was the rest of him.

"You said I still have much to learn," he said. "What else must I know?"

"For one," proposed Praestes, "despite all you have accomplished, your journey is far from over, as you mistakenly stated. In a sense, it has only barely just begun."

"How can that be?" asked Davis in dismay. "I know who I am; I know where I am; I have died the Second Death. I'm ready to be done with it."

"You have indeed discovered who and where you are," stated Satelles. "And yet, you still do not understand why you are here; and Why is the most important question of all."

Davis knew the truth of these words from their very inception, for this was precisely the last lingering question that troubled him. The answers he had received from the Sage along these lines were far from satisfying. Reconciliation of the disparate forces at work in this place was the last thing he was invested in, or thought to be possible.

"Why am I here then?" asked Davis. "What am I to do?"

He pleaded for clarity, though he would receive no direct reply.

Come and join me by the mirror; there is something you should see.

Davis did as he was asked: he walked over and sat down next to the Guardian by the edge of the pool.

"Look," offered Ostiarius. "Look deeply into your reflection, and tell me what you see." Davis glanced down at the pool but saw nothing out of the ordinary. "You have been here before, as you pointed out; and though you stared at the surface of the water, you did not delve into its depths."

Davis had no means by which to refute this analysis. On his first visit, he took as little time to truly reflect upon his reflection as he could manage in the moment. It was too unsettling at the time, the discovery of a life that had long been forgotten. Simply discerning that he had a reflection at all had been a monumental triumph back then. Now that it would no longer suffice, he stared into his own eyes and searched for an answer within.

What do you see? asked the Guardian silently.

"I see—" he began slowly, "I see my face; or rather, the face of a lifetime I've left far behind." He breathed deeply — partly in unrest, and partly in relief. "As much as it pains me to say so, I have to wish it goodbye. It was a life of joy and grief — a life of great fortune and terrible loss. I see its triumphs and failures carved into the face of its foolhardy protagonist. I see a deep sense of regret for the dreams he was never able to manifest. I see remorse for the fact that he died with little warning or closure, and that he never managed to discover the meaning of Life before he reached its end."

The Guardian finally made the joyful expression Davis had looked for — the only one he had ever seen it produce. Until now, its presence had solely embodied composure and serenity; but at this very moment, its eyes looked proud, its countenance gratified.

"And thus have you arrived at the answer to the question, for this is precisely the reason you are here."

"Oh, well at least it's a reasonable undertaking," mocked Davis. "I only spent my whole life trying!"

"Did you?" asked the Guardian. It was once again somber and skeptical. "It seems to me that you spent most of it keeping busy with one triviality after another, in denial of questions that run too deep. You spent it in search of only worldly experiences, with no appreciation of a grander purpose or reality; yet it is only out of a connection to that grander reality that any meaning will emerge."

"What now then?" asked Davis. He conceded the point without protest, for he had no defense.

"The answers you seek are still before you on your path; but in order to reach them, you must look for them where they lay."

The Guardian turned its head back down to the water and stared deeply into the pool, just as it had been doing when the man first arrived. Davis understood, and he needed no further direction. He did the same.

No more words were either spoken or sensed; and before long, Davis found himself alone with his reflection. The trees in the distance; the earth under his feet; the full moon; the stars; the entire sky above – all else faded without Davis even noticing. Soon, there was nothing surrounding him but the surface of the water, stretching out forever in every direction.

So too did his viewpoint shift, again without effort, and without him recognizing it. No longer did he stare down at the pool; his view shifted in orientation, so that he was facing the surface of the water in a perfectly upright position. Or so he might have thought, for as before, it was impossible to tell which way was down, and which way was up.

The water before him trickled over the front of some invisible doorway, as if the pool were a portal through which he could walk, should he so desire, and should he so dare. His reflection wavered ever so slightly, rippling not on the surface, but rather somewhere just behind it. He reached his hand out to test the illusion, and so too did his reflection. When his hand made contact, it broke through the plane; water spilled around it to either side, and the two images merged into one.

Soon, his whole arm had passed through the barrier, disappearing into the midst of his own reflection. Next in went his elbow, and then his shoulder; but having come to the core of his body, Davis hesitated. He may have reached beyond the surface, but he couldn't see what awaited him there. All he observed was his reflection, staring back at him, its body merging with his own with every inch that he pressed on.

The time had come to decide once and for all. Davis would have no choice but to reel his arm backward and turn away from the passage, or take one confident step and pass fully through the portal.

He lifted his foot, placed it before him, and stepped through the mirror to find what lay on the opposite side.

FIVE

5.1 \ Retributio

His feet touched down on cold ground; little but darkness lay ahead. Davis turned to see the portal through which he had stepped. His reflection once again glared back at him from beyond its surface, but from this side of the doorway, it looked different somehow − a bit less like what he truly thought he was.

Only but a moment ago, this figure and face before him looked like everything he had ever known to represent himself. It had been the perfect image of what he was. Back then, the other side of the mirror was no more than a playful thought experiment, wherein dwelt only a philosophical possibility, one which could be no more than a shade of his true essence. Now that he found himself on that imaginary other side, however, it was the person staring back at him who appeared as such − the shadow cast on a wall from where he undoubtedly stood at the moment.

Davis pondered his reflection deeply, but for no more than an instant before the smooth forgiveness of the rippling water through which he'd stepped began to change. The water grew viscous and the rippling slowed, then ceased, as if freezing into a rigid plane of glass.

He reached out to touch it, secretly reluctant − unsure whether or not he wanted to stay where he was and leave his likeness behind. His fingers pressed down with only the slightest force, but the instant they did so, the glass shattered violently into millions of tiny pieces. His reflection vanished, for the broken pane left nothing behind it but a wall of bare rock. Wherever he was, he certainly wasn't going to get back the same way that he came.

The shock of what happened quickly transitioned into practicality, and he turned to examine the rest of his surroundings. Davis was in a long tunnel, its walls made of the same rock as exposed by the shattered mirror. There was little light by which he could navigate − not even enough to cast a shadow, should there have been any possibility of one forming at all.

After a short while stumbling along by the feel of the walls, Davis saw in the distance a faint light coming in from the end of the tunnel. Racing ahead more quickly with the luxury of even this slight degree of vision, he quickly emerged from the initial chamber into a perpendicular pathway. As he stepped out into these new surroundings, the air became unbearable; it was a sweltering, muggy heat, which formed a stark contrast to the cold, clammy feel of the walls. To his dismay, he found nothing more than a long hallway, stretching on endlessly in either direction.

These hallways, however, were not quite so dark as the former, for they were lined with torches, mounted on the walls with ancient iron brackets. Pairs of large doors were spaced evenly between them, punctuating the length of the corridor. Every ten feet or so was another pair, staring across from each other, both perfectly identical in that they had little in the way of any detail at all. The doors were made of the same dark metal that matched the torch mounts, but they were smooth, had no openings, and bore no clues as to what lay behind them.

Quite the welcome, thought Davis. *This place is like a dungeon.*

As he dithered back and forth over which of the identical ways to start walking, Davis turned to discover that the dark tunnel from which he'd emerged had vanished entirely, covered over without a sound by the same monotonous rock that coated the linings of this comfortless maze. Neither direction looked particularly appealing, but he was urged on by the troubling inclination that if he stayed in one place too long, he might himself become devoured by the very walls around him.

Davis started walking. *The direction doesn't matter,* he decided, as there were no clear indications to suggest one over the other. He passed by the pairings of doorways on either side of him as he made his way down the length of the tunnel; but each time he did, he had the strangest sensation. He had never once opened any of the doors, as far as memory could tell, yet he continued to have the peculiar impression that they were closing behind him as he went.

I need to get out of here, no matter how long it takes.

As he made his way tediously through these unnavigable halls, he began to notice a pattern emerging. After every eleven sets of doors, he would come to a four-way corner with identical hallways extending in every direction. After passing several intersections of this sort, he began turning, either out of curiosity or perhaps in the vain hope that he might blindly make his way to some kind of meaningful destination. Regardless of which direction he turned, the hallways carried onward, and seemingly forever – an infinite matrix of halls filled with doors filled with heaven-knows-what, for he never recalled having opened any.

How long he had wandered through this maze he did not know; it seemed to be almost eternity. Perhaps out of sheer luck, or perhaps out of pity on behalf of the Universe for playing such a cruel trick for so long, Davis did eventually arrive at something worth finding.

After progressing through untold hallways in this mind-numbing manner, finally he came to a welcome anomaly in that laborious labyrinth. This particular hallway extended far beyond where an intersection would have normally occurred, and there were no longer any doors taunting him from either side of it. Instead, at the end of this tunnel rested a single door of a different kind altogether.

Davis rushed ahead and began to examine the intricate inscriptions that covered its face. Unlike any before it, this door was made of wood; into it were carved beautiful patterns that escape any attempt at description. The previous doors were cold, dark, and monotonous; they were reminiscent of Death, whereas this door was inspired, to the contrary, by Life.

The carvings were elegant and elaborate; they were chaotic, yet cohesive, suggesting some sense of order that was not perceptible when standing so close, nor could it be scrutinized closely enough to discern it from afar. Davis spent so much of his attention admiring the many engravings that he almost entirely failed to notice the small piece of paper pinned to its center.

"The Sage," said Davis enthusiastically, as if only just now remembering what he should have been looking for all along. He pulled the paper from the door and unfolded it to reveal its recognizable penmanship.

To Our Lesser Self,

At last, your long slumber has finished my friend
At last, you have found who you were in the end
At last, you've surmounted your sad earthly bonds
At last, the great mirror you have stepped beyond

Lost deep in the maze, you closed every last door
Yet now you have found there is still so much more
The Lesser is shed, so the Greater can gain
Yet another ascent towards the end of the game

Gather to you every ounce of your Will
For the contest before you may conquer you still
The Great Soul will welcome you, should you succeed
And with all of its grace, may you do this great deed

Ever anon and then gone,

The Steadfast Sage

"Well, there's no need for name-calling," said Davis.

In any event, he was glad to have some direction after his long and lonesome purgatory. There was no handle anywhere on the surface of the door, so he reached out and pushed firmly upon it. As the door swung open, Davis could see the flickering colors of a fire dancing about on the walls of a different sort of tunnel altogether.

This one was just as deep, or even deeper, in the midst of wherever he was, but it was brighter and warmer — more natural. In a short distance, there was a bend in the passage, and as he made his way around it, he came upon a collection of people in a circle around a large fire pit, embroiled in a fierce debate.

Davis had entered ignorantly, if not innocently, into a room with a great deal of commotion, and he wondered as to what was the cause of it all.

The conversation around the fire was raucous, as if an enormous dilemma had arisen and each had their own ideas of how to go about solving it. Chairs lined the vaulted room and encircled the whole fire, but not one of them was used, for their occupants were too busy standing, shouting, and pointing angrily at one another.

At the opposite side of the circle from Davis stood a ragged old man in a ragged old cloak, with a large pointed hat on his head. At first, Davis was content with only observing this ordeal as it unfolded, but the gaze of the old man was intent upon him. He felt he had no choice but to come closer.

As he walked toward the fire, the people around it didn't even seem to notice him; they were too caught up in their own wild and cogent deliberations, which became ever more turbulent the longer Davis watched. The intolerable cacophony swelled, approaching a tumultuous climax just as he reached the outer edge of the ring. Right before it could do so, however, the uproar was halted by the swift action of the only member of the circle who had noticed his presence.

"All of you, silent!" shouted the old man with a voice that could shake the foundations of mountains.

The words echoed just as loudly as they began, booming and bellowing through the chamber. And as he spoke them, the old man reached his hand out in a wide, sweeping motion in the direction of each entity at the edge of the circle. Each of its members was frozen in place, in the exact pose they'd been posed in when this wizard spoke his words.

Silence filled the room. The old man spoke again, but softly now.

"The savior has come."

The words were not expectant, nor were they awe-struck; they were spoken simply as a matter of narrative fact to the beings that did not seem to notice the newcomer's arrival.

Neither had Davis seemed to notice their meaning, for he was too impressed by the display of such great power over such an unruly assortment of entities, even while not entirely forgetting his own aptitude in feats of this fashion. He had been able to exert his will over some of the others he met in his travels, but never had he done so over so large a crowd, and especially not one comprised of individuals who all struck him as so powerful in their own right.

"How were you able to make the others stop?" he asked the old man.

"You are ignoring the most pertinent question," he replied, "and indeed the most obvious."

"The most pertinent question?" repeated Davis. "What's the most pertinent question?"

The old man stared at Davis with an odd grin, suggesting a preemptive satisfaction in the response he hadn't yet given.

"You should clearly have asked why the spell didn't work upon you."

Davis hadn't thought of it that way; but now that he had, he did find it a bit odd.

"Why didn't the spell work on me then?"

The old man scoffed at so foolish a question, and replied with an air of confusion as to why he would even need to ask it.

"Such a spell could never work on one so powerful as you."

"Someone as powerful as me?" asked Davis, genuinely confused by the notion. "I don't understand. I'm just a man."

"You are far more than that. You are many things."

"Then what am I right now?" asked Davis, not fully understanding the meaning the old man intended. Still, the wizard had an answer for him.

"You are the High King of the Archetypes."

At the outset of these words, a commanding surge of empowerment overcame Davis. He stood up to his full stature; and simultaneously, he felt exactly what he had always been, and yet entirely different. *There is something at my side,* he noticed; and when he looked down to see what it was, he beheld a long and magnificent sword, housed in an ornate sheath. In a way, he was shocked by its presence; but in another way, it felt comfortable where it rested – familiar even – as if it had been needed there all along, and the man somehow hadn't noticed it was missing.

Tentative, Davis reached down, pulled the blade slowly from its sheath, and stared at it, shimmering radiantly in the light of the fire. As he gazed into its gleam, however, another sensation overcame him. He fell into an unsettling trance, worsening the longer he stared at it; for deep in its reflection, Davis saw something troubling which he could not explain.

He jumped backward once the trepidation turned to terror, and the blade plummeted to the ground with a loud metallic clang.

"I don't understand," said Davis, shaken by the sudden premonition and unsure what to ask first. "What is this? Where am I? Who are you, anyway?"

"Calm down, young one," advised the old man. "Relax, and let the fire soothe your spirit."

Davis turned closer to the blaze and breathed deeply; the flames began to breathe with him, fluttering in sync with every in and out. Before long, the panic had mostly passed, and he inspected his surroundings more carefully now that the preceding commotion had calmed.

The chamber was almost perfectly circular, but for the opening of the entry tunnel and a second, shallow indentation on the opposite side. It was rounded at the top like a doorway, and about the size of one, although it was filled with only bare rock, the same as the walls on all sides of it. The room was not particularly wide, and while the ceiling was low, it rose in the center to form a large dome, which gave the impression of being more spacious than it really was.

Deep shades of crimson and orange danced about the sides of the roof and bounced around its ring, reflecting and amplifying the light of the fire so that the chamber was as bright as it was warm. Davis might have almost considered it homely, were it not for the tone of the gathering upon his entry into it.

And although that gathering had happened only a short time prior, in all his careful contemplation of the scenery, Davis somehow failed to register that the two men were now entirely alone by the fire, so focused was he on the countless questions competing for his attention. The old man could tell that his guest had regained his composure as much as he may, and he set out to answer each of his questions to the best of his ability.

"As for where you are, I would remind you that only a short while ago, you had become quite content with knowing that there simply was no answer to such an uninformed question. But this is not to suggest that you should fall back into nostalgia; no, far from it. Rather, you should enjoy the view from outside Space-Time, for you will find it to be far wider, and full of fascinating scenery you'd have seldom been able to imagine."

The old man paused for an almost undetectable moment, sensing the degree to which he held his companion's interest captive. It was of the greatest importance that he didn't lose Davis now. He showed not a sign, but he feared ever so slightly that a seed of indifference had begun to set in with the weight of his guest's fatigue.

"As to the question of what you held in your hand: that is your sword — Validus the Mighty, the legends call it. With it may you fulfill your Quest."

"What quest?" asked Davis nervously. *And legends?*

"All in good time," said the old man, "for I have yet to answer the last of your previous questions."

"Go on then," said Davis, pleasantly surprised that for once someone was interested in answering his questions as thoroughly as he was.

"Concerning the matter of my identity: Firmus is my name. I am the Steadfast Sage."

"In that case, it is nice to meet you. My name is Davis."

At this, the Sage stopped, either surprised, confused, or both; he replied with a slow, deliberate, yet consolatory tone.

"That's not your name," said the Sage.

"What do you mean it's not my name?" *I remember.*

"It is a name – one that you bore for a while. But it is not Your Name."

"Then what is it?" asked Davis frantically. "Who am I, if not who I was?"

"You are much more than any one name," said the Sage. "You are much more than a name in general."

At this prospect, the framework for understanding his existence – a framework which Davis had only recently constructed – began to crumble into pieces around him. It took a monumental effort to recall and cope with as much of his life as he had; and that is not to mention the difficulty of navigating its tribulations in the first place. To think that everything he was, was not all that he was – it was a horrendous possibility in this moment.

"Well ... I've grown pretty used to it," said Davis sadly. "I think I'll go by it for just a little while longer."

"How old are you?" asked Firmus, ignoring the self-pitying of this still-homesick young soul.

"Let's see..." started Davis. He actually had to think about this for a minute. "I'm 38," he determined.

"Wrong!" said the Sage abruptly. "Try again."

"Wrong?" asked Davis defiantly. "So how old am I then?"

"You were 38 – when you died, that is. But you are as old as the Universe itself, for you are made of the very same pieces. And yet, you are as young as the air you inhaled, the water you drank, and the food you ate on that last fateful evening; for the pieces of you are forever shedding and replenishing. The pieces of you are not static, for Life knows no such state. Some of those pieces could you see, for they would look back at you as you stared into the mirror. Others, however, you could only barely sense, if you could even have sensed them at all. It is within those parts that you now exist, and shall continue to exist, as you always have."

"Then why do I still feel like myself if I'm not really me?" asked Davis optimistically. He thought, momentarily, that he had found the single flaw in the old man's hypothesis.

"Excellent question, old young one!" answered the Sage. "Now you're starting to think, and therein lies the truth. But first, your question: if you are in fact no longer bound by the laws of the physical realm in which you dwelled, for a time, why then do you still feel like yourself?"

"Typical," said Davis. He hated it when they turned his questions back around on him. "I'm going to guess it has something to do with the process of death."

"Indeed, you are correct," said the Sage, "albeit only because you provided such a political answer; for it is obvious that everything you're experiencing is a part of the process of Death. To find the more precise answer, you must consider the place from which you are dying. Surely you would not be so bold as to say that only humans die."

"No, I suppose not," conceded Davis. "Though, to be fair, I've never really wondered about it from any other perspective."

"Precisely," smiled the Sage. "A great part of the reason you're here is to discover what other perspectives there are. But to answer your question more accurately, your spirit is undergoing its detachment from the human form of consciousness. All other beings die, as we've already established, and they would experience things in a manner that most suits their own means of existence. You are not charged with undertaking each and all of their journeys; not yet anyway. For now, you must find your way out of the halls of your ancestors, and back to the place where you belong most of all."

Davis said nothing; he simply stared at the Sage, and the silence spoke volumes of his skepticism.

"I take it that you think this all a bit outlandish," preempted the Sage. "I don't blame you; I felt the very same way when I once stood in your stead. Perhaps I am leading you too far afield. In due course, Sophias will guide you from the ghastly grasp of the perceptions and preconceptions of your forebearers. For now, it will suffice for you to understand a few simple things about the nature of your being. Let us begin with where you are — though you and I both know that such an explanation is insufficient."

"So you can answer where I am!" mocked Davis. "Not such a foolish question now, is it?"

The old man let Davis have his due, and he carried on instead with another question of his own.

"Where did you find yourself, once you made your passage through the mirror?" asked Firmus.

"I entered an enormous maze, each tunnel a part of a seemingly infinite series of halls full of doors full of heaven-knows-what."

"Its name is Retributio — the Maze of Recompense — and it dwells deep within the bowels of the Great Volcano, Talionis."

Davis shuddered instantly at its mention, a coincident blend of dread and disbelief. *How could I have made my way back to Talionis without even knowing it?* This was the one place in wherever he was that he had no intention of ever visiting again; and yet somehow, he had managed to unwittingly find his way into the very depths of its dungeons. *It certainly explains the repressive atmosphere.*

The Sage continued without affording Davis the chance for despair, for that was a chance neither of them could afford.

"You probably have no recollection of it at all; but nevertheless, you have come to the far side of a tortuous and perilous maze. Its chambers are filled with each and every one of the events of your life, whether you wanted to see them again or not."

"The doors?" asked Davis sheepishly.

"That's correct," said Firmus.

Once again, the seasoned Sage waited, attempting to assess how the implications of this revelation would register.

"You don't remember, do you?" said the Sage.

"I think you must be mistaken," said Davis. "I saw the doors, of course, but I never actually opened any."

"Don't be absurd!" scoffed Firmus. "If that were true, you would have never stood where you currently stand. No one reaches the Final Door without opening all the prior. Know it or not, it matters not now; but you were faced with a lifetime of lessons, learned from each of your days clad in physical form. It should not surprise you, for so was this true for every day you walked the Earth. The only difference is that you rarely stopped then to listen to the lessons your actions provided.

"So many of us fail to ever learn; we fail to ever admit the many errors of our ways, let alone repent them. And if we do not repent, we cannot grow. Give yourself some credit lad, for to have come through Retributio is a noble and notable accomplishment! Something tells me that you've graced its long hallways before – more than once, perhaps – yet this is the first I have seen of you. That you have come out on the other side of it speaks highly of your promise for the tasks that still await you."

Again, Davis said nothing; and again, Firmus detected the disbelief on behalf of his young apprentice. The Sage spoke harshly now, in a rapid change of tone.

"Do not take my word for it then, if you have even the slightest shred of doubt." He waved his hand angrily toward the tunnel from which Davis had entered the chamber. "By all means, turn around and revisit the long and lonely halls if you have not faith in the veracity of your own triumphs."

"No, no," insisted Davis. "I think just the once is fine." He still wasn't quite sure that he believed it, but it was far safer to entertain the fable than to risk even one more minute in the halls of Retributio.

"Just the once," muttered the Sage to himself, as if reciting a jest that only he would understand. This was not a battle he needed to wage, and he regained his focus as quickly as he lost it.

"I have faith in your potential," he continued, "but if you are to succeed, it is essential that you remember, and remember swiftly: you are in control of your own Mind! Do not let the others whom you meet take hold of your destiny, for they will ever attempt to steer it to their own devices."

Davis cast his thoughts back to his conversation with the previous Sage.

"The others whom I meet..." he said. "I've come to think that they are not necessarily so different from myself."

"Well done again, old young one!" smiled the Sage. "They are not so different from you indeed, for they are not at all distinct from you."

"What do you mean?" asked Davis.

"Each entity you've encountered is the embodiment of an autonomous part of your own psyche — a set of ways in which you think, feel, or interact with the world. Some of them know of the Way, while others represent the lesser parts of your mind — those that must change for the better, ere any ending can come.

"The latter are the ones of whom you must be the wariest, for they will fight tirelessly to become the Master of your Will. They fear growth in any fashion, for they know that with it comes only their surrender to a greater authority. It is up to you to maintain balance among the components of your Mind. You must take guidance from the wiser parts of you, and teach the lesser parts to grow, despite all their fervent resistance."

The fire roared; chunks of red-hot embers exploded outward from the center with a loud crack. Davis hopped back, dodging the cinders assailing his legs.

"And how exactly do I go about doing that?" he asked.

"The same way in which you have dealt with them all along," said Firmus. "Yet now, you have the greatest power of all on your side."

"And what power is that?"

"The power of Knowledge."

"But the knowledge of what?" asked Davis.

The Sage straightened his spine and his stature seemed to grow, from a meek and modest old man, to one with a great deal more vitality than he initially let on.

"Knowledge of the fact that each one of Them is only a part of You; knowledge of the fact that you are in control of your destiny here, if you are only strong enough to accept that simple fact. You can summon them or vanquish them, through exertion of your Will. You can invoke them for your guidance or evoke in them the Truth."

The Sage rose up yet higher still; it both unsettled and inspired Davis.

"I told you once already, though you did not heed me," he said firmly. "You are the Master of your Mind: The High King of the Archetypes!"

186

5.3 \ Archetypes

The Archetypes, mused Davis.

"You keep using that word, but I don't know what you mean by it."

"Quite clearly!" said the Sage, practically offended.

"Well what are they?" insisted Davis.

Firmus balked, and he walked around the fire. The flames followed him, spiraling upward in the same direction as the wake of his air. His face was strained, and Davis didn't understand the need for such evasiveness when asked only to explain a word the Sage himself had used.

Finally, the old man spoke with a melodramatic wave of his hand, and again the flames danced in his breeze.

"Would you ask the stones of a foundation to describe the sight of the tower where they dwell? I could not describe what you ask any better than they, for I am merely one brace in the scaffold upon which your Ego rests."

"My Ego?" asked Davis.

"That's right: you. We are all You, but who does that make <u>you</u> then?

"Me who?" *What?* "Which me?"

"The part of You right here, talking to me – another part altogether."

"How am I to know?" asked Davis. "I would have thought I was Me, but now I'm beginning to wonder."

"We are all You, but <u>you</u> are the peak of the pyramid. You stand upon our shoulders, and help not to hold the weight. Yet, for all your flaws, you unite all the constituents together as one. You rest upon our foundations, standing therefore at the greatest height, and look out furthest of all towards the unknown horizon."

This didn't appeal to Davis as a satisfactory explanation. He was used to ambiguous answers from Sages of this sort, but at this point in the game, he was in need of some candor.

"We speak not of towers or pyramids," said Davis. "We speak of the Mind. What part of Me does that make <u>me</u>?"

The Sage resumed his stroll around the fire, his hand on his chin as he searched for any way to make this make sense. He found a circuitous route; but it just might work, he reasoned.

"Let us think for a moment on Instinct," said Firmus, appearing to ignore the direct question for now. "What is Instinct if not an innate and autonomous capacity of a brain to act in a certain way in a given situation, refined over the millennia to yield mostly reliable results?"

"I guess that–" started Davis.

"It was a rhetorical question," interrupted the Sage with another wave of his hand. "There is not really any ultimate difference in the way the process works at the higher levels of consciousness. We couldn't be so naïve as to think that only reflexes are a product of Evolution. For even the higher forms of consciousness are products of the same fundamental processes.

"Networks of neurons are what dictated your actions in Life, though you mustn't let this dishearten your view of what it means to be alive. There are many forms of things that had not a brain of your sort at all, yet you would do them great insult to imply that they were any less alive than yourself. To think is not to Be; but rather, it is a bonus."

He paused awkwardly. He seemed lost — because he was.

"Alas, I digress..." The Sage resumed his pacing, circling back toward Davis on his side of the fire. "Where was I?"

In all fairness, Davis didn't really know.

"Networks?" he asked with uncertainty.

"Ah yes, networks. It is the very way in which the brain works: higher networks made of lower networks, with the former created by integration of the latter — by synthesis. The parts of the whole function somewhat independently; but somewhere at the top, something is needed to put their narrower existence into a broader perspective. That is where you come in. Yet, the whole would not exist but for the contribution of its parts."

"What exactly are we talking about here?" asked Davis in frustration. "What are the parts?"

"Well, most immediately, the parts of what you think of as You — at least some of them — are the Archetypes of human consciousness. And thus, we arrive at the heart of your question."

"Finally! And I'm still no closer to understanding what they may be."

"Well, old young one," said the Sage, "it simply is not simple; for You is made of a great many parts, across a great many levels of scale. If you seek to understand what dictates the way you navigate the world, then you must first seek to understand the components of your own personality. There can be no doubt that there are things that make you truly unique; yet, there are also aspects of your personality that are not quite so personal as you may have supposed."

"How so?" asked Davis.

Precisely as the Sage had hoped, under the guise of indifference, a spark of intellectual intrigue had indeed begun to spread. Thankfully, somewhere among those many components of his personality, there was a small minority that was just barely patient enough to endure things that were just barely pertinent enough. Davis was still reserving judgement in that regard, but for now the Sage took advantage of the opportunity.

"You were a person, and people are people. You're really quite a predictable lot actually. If you want to know what makes You, you must consider not only the components of your own personality, as we've mentioned, but also the components of human consciousness in general. Your consciousness is the type of rock found on a beach, while your personality is the shape into which the ocean has carved it.

"We could talk all day long about why you took on the particular shape you had taken; but what matters more to us now is what type of rock you were in the first place, and what makes it different from the others on the beach. If we were to zoom in far enough, we would find that the answer is very little at all; but from a more distant view, there seem to be a great many differences. And despite this, all of the many disparate shapes of the same type of rock share the most in common with each other, for they share the same origin, from the even greater forces that created their type of rock in the first place."

Davis didn't say much, nor did he reject the premise entirely. He simply bent his knees and squatted, to peer intently into the fire. He was contemplating, but at least he was doing so earnestly. Firmus wasn't sure if his analogy had worked.

Perhaps something closer to home, someone thought.

"Let us think on the concept of culture for a moment" suggested the Sage, again appearing to enter down an unexpected and unrelated tangent. "One need not look far in life to notice the differences between cultures. At first glance, they can seem unquestionably unalike. Yet, if we look closely, we find that they share a great many commonalities.

"Various peoples across vast stretches of time and space contain startling similarities in their customs and habits, symbols and myths. While there are idiosyncrasies which no doubt differ, it is fair to say that cultures largely engage in the same basic types of activities. The reason is that these behaviors are descended from the same core set of pathways in the brain that are common to the very nature of human existence, and which predate the subsequent divergence of the different groups."

Davis couldn't resist the temptation of his own attempt at philosophical discourse, in an effort to synthesize the maddening metaphors of the Sage. He was anxious to get on with things, in spite of any enduring reservations regarding all that awaited him ahead on his journey.

"I essentially take you to mean that the Archetypes are the foundations of human consciousness – the tendencies to think or behave in a given way which are common to all humans, even though they may be expressed in different ways in different people."

"And so has the stone described the shape of the tower," laughed Firmus. "At the heart of it, they are the underlying structures of consciousness. We cannot see these structures, and we therefore create symbols that allude to their nature. Their existence is universal, but their particular form is determined by the learning experiences of an individual burgeoning mind – the cultural and environmental context in which said mind develops."

Davis kept staring into the fire and thought for what seemed like a long time on the implications of this concept to his current pursuits. He never found any obvious connections. He rose from his pose, as there was little more he could decipher on his own.

"I have to admit, it makes for an interesting topic," said Davis, "but I still don't understand what it has to do with me."

He smiled, as if knowing that he might disappoint the expectations of so insightful a Sage. The old man did not give up on him.

"The archetypes have everything to do with you," said Firmus. "Ever since the dawn on which you first awoke from your insentience, you have been faced with the challenge of confronting them, in order to grow from their wisdom, or to grow beyond their limitations. Some have you learned from; some others have you conquered. In both cases, you have indeed become stronger and wiser for it."

The old man gestured around the room at the circle of chairs where the raucous crowd once stood.

"Some others," he continued, "you have yet to address."

Davis followed the gaze of the Sage, and only in this moment did he realize that the others had mysteriously gone missing. How he could have possibly overlooked this can only be explained by some degree of willful denial, whatever depth it came from within him.

"Where did they all go?" asked Davis. It was an ominous omen, for he feared whether he could contend with so large and ferocious a crowd.

"You have yet to confront them, and they bend not to your Will."

Davis scanned the room nervously, as if expecting the others at any moment to jump out and wrest from him the Mastery of his Mind.

"Who are they exactly?" he asked. "And what were they arguing about?"

"It matters not," said Firmus, "and yet it matters most."

"Enough with the riddles," said Davis. He rose to his own full stature and approached the Sage head-on, for the old man was not the only one who could speak firmly when no other options would suffice. "Enough with philosophy for the sake of itself. Speak plainly."

The Sage did not respond, only turned toward the fire, and approached it much more closely than either of them had yet. He raised both palms toward the flames, which bent backward at his command. And as the flames receded, no mere coals lay at the heart of this fire, but the very magma that flowed through the veins of the mountain. Davis was drawn to the sight of it; he followed the Sage, stood at his side, and stared into the fiery abyss.

"Who they are, exactly," said the Sage — and a vision was revealed, deep within the molten rock. "The plot of their squabbles is arbitrary, or at least much of it is; for if it were not about This, it would be about That. But the cause of their squabbles, and the means of its resolution — now those are questions that matter most of all."

And in the depths of the fires that burn in the depths of Talionis itself, Davis saw them; and he knew them all for what they were.

That is, all but one.

5.4 \ The Final Door

The Sage lowered his hands and stepped away from the fire. The flames launched back angrily to regain their lost ground, clearly unhappy with having been made to bend to the wizard's will. A dull silence grew between the two as the fire settled back down and resumed its steady flickering.

Davis didn't know how every subject they discussed was relevant to his endeavors, though this was mainly because he knew so little in the way of what his endeavors would entail. This is not to say that he did not reflect upon that which he and the Sage had deliberated. In contrast, his mind was filled with these issues; they circled his thoughts tirelessly, but their most important insights were those which Davis could not yet fully grasp.

The Sage sat idly by, watching and waiting, hoping beyond all else that his efforts would not be in vain, and that his acolyte would rise to the unseen challenges before him. When at last Firmus could see that their debate had lodged its way furtively, yet fervently, into his inner state, he awakened Davis from his daze and showed him the way that he must walk.

"For all of your travails over the long paths you have traveled, I commend you," said the Sage. "Yet, in spite of the countless recollections you've collected in the depths of this dark maze, there is one more door which you must open."

Davis was engaged in an uncharacteristically focused contemplation; he was slightly startled by his arousal, and he was greatly put off by the prospect of exploring the Great Volcano any further.

"Recollections I've collected?" he asked cynically. He had yet to overcome his incredible propensity for incredulity. "I don't remember opening a single door; why should I bother with any others? I haven't collected anything down here but a healthy dose of confusion."

The truth is that he was scared, and no excuse was too peripheral.

"Just because we don't remember every event of our lives doesn't mean that they haven't affected us," said Firmus. "Quite the contrary, in fact: sometimes those that lie beneath the surface of our awareness affect us most greatly of all."

The allusion to the surface cast his thoughts to the Lacuna Speculis, as it was the fateful plunge into its depths that had led him into this very dungeon. Davis let down his guard and spoke his feelings honestly.

He was still not ready to let it all go.

"What good has this maze done me? If anything, it was on the other side of the mirror that I finally remembered the events of my life. Back then, I was blinded by complete denial of who and where I was; but the memories returned despite all of it. Now, I just find myself without any of them, all alone in this dark and dreadful place."

He looked up at his only companion.

"No offense," he said. "It's just that, you're claiming I've gathered all these memories. It seems to me like all this place has done is rob them from me once more."

The Sage nodded; he knew quite well what this ordeal entailed.

"Again, your thoughts lead you in the appropriate direction; but again, it is your outlook upon them that is lacking. That you stand here before me is a testament to your conviction. You have indeed gathered your memories here; rather than run from them, or succumb to them, you have faced them head-on – in a manner in which you would never have been able upon conscious reflection. You have confronted them here so that you could progress beyond your regressions, and having done so, so that you might fully let them go. Take solace in this truth, old young one."

"The Lesser is shed, so the Greater can gain."

"Thus spoke the verse on the door; and while it was written in my script, it is not of my conception. It is a fate that is woven into the very fabric of living; and while you have stopped living in one sense, you have begun living in countless others. The cycle never truly ceases."

"Well I for one am tired of it," said Davis. "Ever since I arrived, I've been faced with one tedious trial after another, endlessly climbing an ever-receding ladder. And when I finally came to a place where I expected to find peace, I'm told that my journey has only barely just begun. I'm just about through with it. I can't take any more taunting by the weavers of this fate."

For one so Steadfast, the Sage grew nervous, and it showed on his face. Even he, in his eternal sagacity, feared losing Davis in this moment.

"You have said thoughts of this sort before," said Firmus sternly. "I assure you: they lead nowhere that will aid you anymore, for you have dwelled in that destination before, and the days are as long and insentient as the nights."

Davis turned to the fire in procrastination, his spirits sinking. Here and now, of all places and times, his fear was masquerading as exhaustion – and it was winning. Firmus knew the signs. He lifted his hands slowly as Davis stared into the fire, and the flames followed his command. Rising up and spreading outward, they soon reached into much of the dome overhead.

Davis stumbled back at the shock and the heat. He mistook the meaning of this show of power, but it was not without effect. Firmus mustered every ounce of his energy, for he feared it would be the only way to encourage his acolyte to do the same.

"Hear me now, Davis. You must rally your resolve! You must fortify your fortitude! For I am the Steadfast Sage, and that is what you must become. Rise now to the challenge, and drown not in your fear; for with you, we too shall all drown." *Or perhaps we shall burn.*

192

Firmus raised his hands yet higher; the flames rushed against the roof like a geyser, filling the dome and flooding out along the ceiling towards the edges of the chamber. Davis stumbled back, tripping over a chair at the edge of the ring; he scrambled on his hands and knees, shielding his eyes as much as he could, but too amazed to look away entirely. The Sage continued, and for a second time his voice thundered through the chamber.

"Rise, Davis! Exert your own Will." He had warned Davis of this very thing. "You must create the peace within yourself that you so desperately desire. It is only your hesitation that affords its long delay."

Davis inched back with another shuffle, and the Sage lifted the flames higher. They poured outward yet more, and the heat was almost intolerable. The Sage, for his part, seemed entirely unaffected by it. The flames streamed over the roof above him like lava and lashed out in all directions.

"Rise!" shouted the Sage. The echoes boomed; the mountain vibrated. Davis was pinned against the edge of the chamber now, and the flames showed no sign of relenting. "Rise now," shouted Firmus. "Rise, or perish!"

"Enough!" shouted Davis. He lunged up from his cowering and waved both hands towards the flames assailing him; the fire receded immediately, recoiling back into the pit in a flash and returning to its equilibrium.

The Sage breathed deeply; the flames only flickered lightly, and a wave of cooling and calmness washed over the chamber. Davis said nothing. He merely brushed off his clothes, leaned down to pick up the fallen chair ever so gently, and calmly placed it back in its rightful place in the circle. He walked back toward the center of the room, where the Sage had been standing when he awoke the beastly blaze. Davis cast a sideways glare at Firmus to let the Sage know he had made his point. Firmus resumed without delay, speaking softly, as if hardly anything had happened.

"And yet, you are right: the road ahead is lengthy. But that is no cause for you not to walk along its course. Before you may once again begin, however, you must remember why you are here, in the depths of Retributio. You have closed every last door behind you in its maze; that is, every last door but one. It stands now before you, and I beg of you: Enter."

True to his name, the Sage's conviction was unwavering; and somehow, against the odds, he had managed to transfer at least part of it to Davis and rouse him from his despair. Firmus simply pointed over the man's shoulder and stared ahead at whatever lay in his line of vision.

In all the fanfare, Davis had gotten turned around. He spun to see what the Sage was suggesting, and sure enough, there it was. Through the fire, in the strange archway across from the entry tunnel – where there once had been only bare rock – there was now, indeed, a Final Door.

This was odd, but very little surprised Davis anymore. And in any event, there it stood before him now. He said farewell to the Steadfast Sage with only a passing glance as he walked around the fire and headed for the door.

5.5 \ Lives Collide

Davis opened his eyes slowly, as one has the tendency to do at the start of the day. He tried with the usual defiance to linger even a moment longer in that senseless, soothing state of slumber, but his eyelids eventually gave way to the inevitable need to awaken.

The sheets were exquisitely comfortable, and he reveled in their security for a few more precious minutes. He stared up at the circling motion of the ceiling fan in procrastination – in denial of the breaking day. Rolling over to his left, he found no one there, and the blankets on that half of the bed had been cast aside. He rubbed his hand over the bedsheet, but there was only the slightest residual warmth in the place where his wife had slept.

He walked down the stairs to the stirrings of excited voices from the kitchen, but it was the smell of simmering coffee that held the majority of his attention. Emerging last of all into the room, he was greeted by the emphatic salutations of his children.

"Daddy," they shouted in almost perfect unison.

It escaped his amazement at the moment, but his children never failed to greet him, each and every day, as if they hadn't seen him in a lifetime. It isn't until we're older that we come to view the gift that is the presence of our loved ones with mere complacency.

"Good morning, little monsters," said Davis in response. He was happy to see them too, but for now his thoughts were limited. Despite a full night's sleep, he was simply exhausted.

"It's pancake day!" said the youngest in excitement. "On a school day!"

"I believe you, Evan." Davis lumbered over to the coffee pot. "Coffee..." he said slowly, with a long, drawn-out ending.

The steam rose from his mug as he filled it, rejuvenating his senses and providing the much-needed motivation to start yet another trying day. In the pursuit of the morning's first ambition, he almost failed to notice the third voice he'd heard from the hall.

"Aren't we forgetting someone?" asked Constance. She'd been busy flipping pancakes as Davis entered the kitchen with his own set of priorities.

"Good morning, my love," he said. He walked over, leaned in, and planted a sincere but mechanical kiss on her cheek.

"These are for you," she said, turning around with a plate of pancakes.

Davis sat down at the table and flipped open the paper. The kids went back to their own entertainment: Evan was building a castle out of plastic blocks, while Joni pretended to eat as she pushed pieces of pancake around her plate. They were conditioned by years of experience to know better than to attempt engaging too seriously with their father as he first cracked open the news.

Having selflessly served everyone else, Constance remained by the stove and poured the last bit of batter into the pan for her own breakfast. The news consisted of the typical tragedies. One story in particular took the headlines on this day.

SHOOTER DEAD AT THE SCENE AFTER KILLING TWENTY-TWO

"Can you believe this?" asked Davis, partly to his wife, but partly just for the sake of saying it aloud. "At least they got the guy, and we don't have to watch him plead to the jury with fake remorse. It's a pity someone didn't kill him before he had the chance to do it."

"Davis!" scolded Constance. "Nice way to talk around the kids. Thanks."

"What?" he asked defensively. "All I'm saying is I'm sick of people being able to do this kind of thing. The guy walks into a mosque and starts firing off rounds? It's a pity no one returned the favor any faster is all."

"Dozens of people lose their lives, and the first thing you can say is that you're sorry someone didn't kill him faster? If we're throwing around wishes, what about wishing it never happened in the first place?"

"I'm obviously sorry it happened," defended Davis. "You know that's not what I mean."

"Either way, it doesn't make for nice breakfast conversation," said Constance as she turned over the last pancake. "Besides, any loss of life is a tragedy as I see it — victim and criminal alike."

"You can't be serious," said Davis. "You're not actually going to tell me you're sad this guy is dead, are you?"

The kids pretended not to listen, but the pace of pancake-pushing and castle-construction had slowed somewhat in the meantime.

"I'm absolutely sad — just as sad as I am for the rest of them. That man had a mother too, and now she has to live with not only the loss of her own child, but the added grief of every soul he took from this earth."

"The man's a killer, Constance. Leave it to a woman to take his side!"

Davis was joking, but he was always much less funny than he thought he was. He could tell instantly that his joke didn't have the desired effect.

"Very funny," she said flatly. "The world isn't so black and white as good and bad. People aren't born killers; they're made that way. Yesterday, he might have been a murderer, but a long time ago, he was a child — a child that, with a little help, or a better lot in life, could have probably been steered from the path he eventually took."

Davis turned back to the paper and flipped the page.

"It's a horrible thing that he did," she continued. "No one's arguing that. But every time something like this happens, society is too eager to place the blame on the sick person who did it, so that we never look ourselves in the mirror and question our own role in fostering the illness. Instead, we're content with the easy solution, and we never confront the truly difficult issues. Then we have the nerve to wonder why it keeps happening."

Davis was not unaccustomed to rebuttals of this sort, but he was always quick to brush them off with a joke, in the place of having to actually reply.

"I should never have married a psychiatrist," smirked Davis to Evan.

"I should never have married a businessman," she smiled towards Joni.

"I'm sorry, my love," said Davis. "You're right, as always."

"Thank you," she said with a gratified smile.

"Or at least, that's what you've trained me to say," he muttered.

She shook her head as he teased her.

"Just eat your pancakes," she said. "You're welcome, by the way."

The monotony of the workday felt like a blurry haze as he drove home. It seemed to pass by in a flash, now that it was over; and this was especially paradoxical, considering how painfully protracted it felt while it was reluctantly unfolding. In reality, it was a long and tiresome day of checking in on clients, updating progress reports, and cold-calling businesses which their research group had indicated as prime candidates for their new product, plan, policy — whatever they were selling at the moment. All these chores were interspersed with meetings with various bosses, to discuss the company's plans for total global domination. If they weren't getting bigger, they were failing, they would say.

Davis scrolled through the radio as he sat in idle anxiety, a slave to the traffic light. The numbers reeled around on the console like a slot machine until they finally landed on an occupied frequency.

There's nothing you can know that isn't known
Nothing you can see that isn't shown
There's nowhere you can be that isn't where you're meant to be
It's easy...

"Easy my ass," jeered Davis.

He hit the scan button with a stab before the chorus came around.

The next time the dial landed, it fell upon the relentless predictability of talk radio. From what he could discern in the short time it was on, the show involved a panel of experts discussing the same vile mix of news he'd read about that morning. He rolled the volume knob all the way down until it clicked, resigned to listening only to the drone of cars rolling slowly down the freeway, stopping-and-going ad nauseum.

His car door slammed shut behind him where he stood in the driveway, pausing momentarily to reflect upon the status of his lawn. A series of dirt mounds were scattered throughout the otherwise pristine uniformity. Despite his most ardent efforts to combat the indomitable insectivorous invader — traps, poisons, even a series of sonic nuisances that appeared to annoy only the neighbors — the beast had bested him at every turn.

"I have got to find a way to kill that mole," he said in desperation.

He stumbled wearily into the house, tossed his coat on the rack, and fought the urge to slump into the first chair in his path. At the sound of their father, his children ran into the room. They greeted him again with an excitement he could hardly fathom, let alone muster in return after a long and grueling day of fulfilling the American Dream.

"You'll never believe what we did today for science activity," started Evan. His voice was young and naïve, blind to the worries of his father and the woes of adult life. He spoke in an innocent tenor that perfectly personified the innocence inherent in his story.

"Oh yeah?" said Davis impassively. He parted the incoming embraces of his children and made his way toward the living room. He could at least try to hold out until the second seat available. The apparent indifference hardly fazed his son, who was so excited for the chance to finally tell his story that he could barely space his sentences.

"We walked down to the pond down back behind the fields and had to count how many different species we could find and..."

Davis clambered over to the couch and fell into it backwards, a lifeless feather on the wind.

"...it was this thing that looked like a lizard and I shouted to the teacher and she told me it was a newt which I guess is like a salamander or amphibian or something and..."

The moment Davis hit the cushions, his thoughts were flooded with the long list of things he should really be accomplishing, but hadn't the strength to even start.

"...and Matthew said I shouldn't but I did and I got it and it barely even squirmed and I was so..."

The bills to pay; the taxes to file
The things to clean; to fix; to find for a while
The errands to run; the appointments to keep
The people to call; the people to meet
The clients to please; the boss to appease
There were places to go and things he should see...

There was hardly an anxiety in his life that wasn't drowning his senses, as he tried halfheartedly to fulfill even his most basic fatherly obligations.

"...but it really didn't matter because we found a bunch anyway..."

"That's great, Evan," said Davis, with no interest evident anywhere in his voice. He wasn't entirely sure what he was encouraging, but from the small amount he gathered, it sounded like a feat he should probably congratulate.

Meanwhile, Joni had not been idle throughout her brother's long and breathless story. Rather, she had been biding her time, like an anxious racehorse waiting for the gate to lift. Finally, her brother couldn't help but catch his breath, and she was off.

"My day was interesting too," she started. She had the voice of a young child, but as always, maintained a deliberate effort to sound as elegant and noble as a queen of old.

"Is that right, Joni?" he responded in the same trite and tired tone. "And what did you do today?"

"Well first, on the bus, my friend Rebecca..."

The problems at work; the projects at home
Finding time for his wife; finding time of his own
The big plans coming up for which he needs to prepare
The feud with the neighbors since they'd stolen his pears
He had questions, concerns, careful contemplations
He had fears, doubts, and frantic anticipations
He had thoughts to think and things to do
But no time left for any at all...

"...and I told her what Mom always says — that everyone is special in their own way — but she was upset because..."

His thoughts ricocheted inside his skull like a manic pinball, and there was little he could do to control it. To say that he intentionally tried not to listen would be entirely unfair; then again, to say that he tried as hard as he could to heed the concerns of his daughter would be giving the man a tad bit too much credit.

"...and I said I'd tell the teacher about the way they treated Rebecca, but they said no one likes a tattletale..."

Davis emerged momentarily from his stress-induced delirium as he realized that, on this particular day, his daughter's story might have been more important than experience had led him to predict.

"Did you tell your teacher?" he asked with his best attempt at the parental concern of someone who'd been providing their undivided attention. *Miss ... what's-her-name?*

"Well," she said methodically, "they told me they'd stop teasing her if I didn't, so I didn't tell on them."

"And did they stop?" asked Davis.

"For a while. But then, after recess, when we went back into class, they were throwing erasers at her from behind. I finally picked one up and threw it back at them, but it hit one of the boys — right in the face!"

She sounded almost as startled by the retelling of this part of her day as when it had happened in the first place.

"The teacher saw me do it, and she yelled at me. I tried to tell her that they started it, and they were picking on Rebecca, but she said that it didn't matter, because all she saw was me throw it at them. I had to sit in the corner, and every time she turned her back to the class, the boys were laughing, and making faces at me."

"Well," said a now thoroughly concerned Davis, "it sounds like we should have a talk with this teacher."

By now, Constance had finished her obligations in another room, and she came in to greet him as well.

"She told you her story?" she asked.

"She just did," replied Davis. "That's ridiculous!"

"Yes, it is," said Constance, before turning to her daughter. "But haven't I always told you that it's not OK to retaliate, Joni?"

"I know," said Joni. She gazed at her feet, ashamed and dejected.

"I think it's great she stood up to them," interjected Davis. "She can't let them bully her and her friends like that!"

Constance glared at him with an eye that said more than any words would have accomplished.

"But," yielded Davis, "your mother's right. You should have raised your hand and told the teacher what they were doing."

It was obvious that the young girl was still saddened by her reproach.

"It's OK honey," said Constance. "It's not nice what those boys were doing to you and Rebecca. You just have to remember not to sink to their level. Just because they act inappropriately doesn't mean you should too."

"Well, if I see them picking on my big sister, they'll never know what hit them!" said Evan, jumping up and flexing his arms above his head – the superhero the world has always needed.

"Oh, I bet they'd be sorry then," said Davis. He jumped up from the couch with his only remaining energy, grabbed his son, and threw him over his shoulder. He paraded around, the young one laughing and squirming, trying to escape the clutches of this friendly giant.

When Evan's flailing reached the point of risking being dropped, Davis spun him downward along his side and set him lightly on the ground. Evan sped off like a top and disappeared into the hallway. Davis turned to his wife, who'd been watching the commotion with a warm smile that masked a faint fear for her child's safety.

"What's for dinner?" he asked, as if he couldn't have arranged it himself.

The reassuring sheets surrounded Davis once again after a fleeting evening of banality – a small slice of the time we too often take for granted.

During dinner, he and his wife played the usual couples match of catch-up around the contributions of their children. Afterward, the kids occupied themselves with various invented games in the twilight of the yard, while Davis labored over taxes and Constance cleaned up in the kitchen.

As the last waning rays of the sun threatened to expire in their entirety, she went outside to begin the long process of convincing the children it was time for bed. Once they had gone through all of the appropriate stages – denial, anger, bargaining, etc. – she got them both inside and mostly settled for the night.

As the toil associated with so troublesome a task ensued, Davis was roused from his study and gave up on the form-filling for now. He caught up with the children after they had finished washing up. He gave each of them the usual goodnight farewell before they crawled into their beds.

"Goodnight, little man," said Davis to Evan. "I love you."

He made his way to the room next door. Several stuffed animals were scattered across the floor, while the rest slept peacefully in their chest. He picked up a plush green frog and handed it to Joni where she lay.

"Goodnight, my darling daughter," he said to her. "I love you."

The latent lovers passed the last brief hours of their night together in a state of mutual fatigue. Davis helped with the few remaining things to be done in the kitchen, as Constance had finished almost all of the cleaning, from breakfast that morning and the dinner she had also made. He kissed her on the temple as she rinsed the washcloth in the sink. Her wedding ring was safe and sound on the dresser upstairs.

"Thank you, love," he said gently. "You never cease to amaze me."

In no manner was this sentiment untrue, for he knew his own level of exhaustion could in no way outdo hers after an equally long day. Yet, somehow, she managed to carry on indefinitely, and without complaint – with an unwavering fortitude that continually impressed and inspired him, whether he said as much or not. They curled up on the couch to read their respective books, and before long, the evening had come to pass.

But now that it had come and gone so quickly, Davis slept peacefully in the stillness of night; that is, until this night – unlike any other before it – was no longer still and peaceful.

Davis jolted awake to a crash that was far too loud for his slumbering mind to justify within the context of his dreams. He turned to his left to find Constance confirming his suspicions. They stared at each other in confusion for a moment, unsure what could have made such a noise. She slid the covers to the middle of the bed and started for the door to investigate. Davis fell back into his pillow, ever quick to assume there would be an easy explanation.

Only moments after he did so, there came a second noise from far beyond the hallway, and it didn't sit well with his spine. Constance hadn't yet made it out of the room and Davis shot up in a flash.

"Get back," he whispered nervously.

He squeezed past her through the doorway and motioned for her to stay put. His heart was pounding at a pace he scarcely experienced these days, for there could be no mistaking it: there was definitely something stirring on the ground floor below.

It's a raccoon, he thought. *No: a bird. It's most definitely a bird.* He was rationalizing it now in whatever way he could. As he slowly approached them and the noises continued, however, none of his rationales were quite able to allay the growing realization that all was not well.

When he reached the bottom of the stairs, he peered once around the corner for a view of the living room. Just as he did so, a series of shuffling sounds shot out from the kitchen. By now, his adrenaline was fully at the helm, and he turned the corner to confront the source of the disturbance.

Davis scanned the room for whatever he could use to defend himself, but there wasn't much that would make do. He plucked an unsuspecting vase from its tranquil resting place, leaned around the doorframe, and beheld the shadowed figure. His worst fear had been confirmed: facing away from him, in the center of the kitchen, was an intruder.

He had no chance to think twice; or if he did, he certainly didn't take it. All in one fell, irrevocable swoop, Davis ran into the room, lifted the vase high into the air, and brought it crashing down upon the head of the stranger in a forceful, vase-shattering blow.

Dazed, the man stumbled forward, and Davis immediately began to grapple with him from behind. The men tumbled into the countertop, and the unsuspecting victim of this ferocious floral assault was sent into a state of panic. Unaware, and under attack, he scanned the counter for whatever he could use to defend himself, but there wasn't much that would make do.

He pulled a knife from the storage block and spun around to confront his assailant – but fate would intervene in other ways. The moment he turned, the knife drove effortlessly into Davis, piercing the side of his chest with the full length of the long blade.

The whole scene was over in a few seconds, from the conception of his impulsive plan to the perception of his repulsive wound. Davis looked down, already in shock from the situation and hardly able to process what had happened. Only a few short minutes prior, he was sound asleep in an ignorant bliss; in the greatest possible contrast, he was now awake, downstairs, in the kitchen, with the carving knife that his wife had dried and put away earlier that evening sticking out of his side.

If there was even a sliver of time in which to think, he would have noticed the cold, searing pain, pulsating throughout his entire being. Davis might have also noticed that the stranger was equally horrified – perhaps even more so – by the tragic turn of events taken in those brief moments. The man staggered away, literally bracing himself on the table, in shock and disgust at the events he had both witnessed and abetted.

Davis took no such time to contemplate his condition, nor would he have taken any chances. He didn't know this man, a stranger who had broken into their home – who must have surely come to harm them. His entire family was upstairs. Without the slightest hesitation, Davis extracted the knife from his ribs, turned it on the man, and plunged it into him repeatedly.

Over and over, he sent the blade into the stranger. The man gasped, but had no strength to fight back. Blood poured out of him and gurgled from his mouth. He slid sideways off the table and came crashing to the floor.

Davis likewise stumbled backward. He lowered his hand and dropped the knife as he came to the slow and painful realization of what had transpired. The blade hit the linoleum floor at an angle, teetering back and forth before coming to a cold and bloody rest amid black and white checkers. Davis promptly followed, toppling lifelessly to the ground. He was bleeding – a lot, and quickly. He could hardly breathe, owing to the abrupt collapse of his lung. The sudden calm in the kitchen lasted only an instant.

For the short time in which Davis had been investigating downstairs, Constance was content to remain in the relative safety of the bedroom. But at the ensuing sound of the scuffle, against her fear and better judgement, she ran downstairs to discover its cause – and, unfortunately, its outcome.

At the sight of the scene, she shrieked in terror. It was the sound of a person broken – shattered by complete and unexpected horror – a sound which Davis had never heard before, nor would have ever wished she would make in all her life. By now, the children had also been awoken, and both had groggily made their way downstairs to ask their parents what was wrong. They arrived to see their mother sobbing, consoling her husband, and wailing in a panic on the phone with emergency services.

Davis had little time left in the realm of consciousness, but he lingered there just long enough to see his children look down at him, lying wounded on the floor, with a stranger dying at the far side of the room – and to hear them scream. It was an even more painful scream, scarier than any of the most terrifying scenes from even his most vivid and powerful nightmares.

The next thing Davis knew, he was lying on a hospital cart, racing down the length of a long corridor. He stared at the ceiling tiles, rolling past him overhead, woozy and mesmerized by the sight of the lights, as they flickered by in rapid succession. He could hear his wife sobbing intensely from somewhere behind him, trying her best to keep up with the frantic pace and stay by his side no matter what.

The only intelligible words he could decipher were those of the paramedics, informing the nurses that a second patient had died in the ambulance. Davis had no recollection of it, but the two men had ridden to the hospital together, side by side – both in the flesh, and at the brink of death – their fates forever intertwined.

The gurney slammed into the double doors at the end of the hallway. As soon as it passed, an attendant stepped in the way of the entrance and instructed Constance to wait there. She strained from afar, through the small windows in the doors, leaning left and right to see past the surgical team. She couldn't stand to watch, but she would never give up hope.

Davis stared deep into the bright light above with only the slightest shred of cognition, and he thought his last remaining thoughts: *I hate that man so much,* he vowed. Over and over again, it echoed in his mind. It was all that there was anymore. *I hate that man so much.*

The world went fully black, and there was nothing left to think.

5.6 \ In Search of a Shadow

Davis staggered forward and fell to his knees on the dirt floor of the cave. The heavy door behind him slammed shut with a menacing thud. A bright light radiated through the cracks around its edges, and as the light flickered and faded, the outline of the door did the same. The metal melded seamlessly back into the original stone which had occupied the archway.

He rose to his feet as quickly as he could, reeling in circles as he tried to get his bearings. Before long, he began to realize where he was, but it took some time for his vital signs to stabilize after all that he had seen. Davis turned one more time to face the center of the room, and it was then that he noticed the old man, sitting calmly by the fire. He inhaled deeply, brushed the dirt from his pants, and spoke once again to the Sage.

"I think I ... understand," he said slowly, as if coming to grips with something as he formed these very words.

"Then your progress has not been in vain," said the Sage.

"Tell me, though, Firmus: what do I do next?"

The Sage revealed a wide and satisfied grin.

"You have walked through the long, and oft inimical, halls of Retributio, in the depths of Talionis. But there is work yet to be done upon its surface."

"Then how do I get there," asked Davis. *All in due time.*

The Sage stared up at the ceiling, though he was looking far beyond it.

"There is one who dwells there in the shadows, though no trees there grow to cast any shade. His name is Indignus. You have met him before."

A sharp, excruciating pain exploded again in his side; it spread through his body like a lightning strike. He reached his hand down to quell the pulsing agony, but it was not of the sort that could be easily stifled.

"How do I get there?" asked Davis again, in gasps through the pain.

"Not so quickly," said Firmus. "You have forgotten one important thing."

The Sage walked over to where Davis once stood. He bent slowly to the ground and lifted the sword from the dirt where it lay.

"You may need this," said Firmus — and there was something odd about the way that he did so. It struck Davis as deliberate, but he couldn't tell if it was meant as eerie or ironic.

The old man turned the blade straight into the air, and it glistened once again in the glow of the fire. With a flick of his grip, the blade pivoted; it spun downward and came to a rest with its point aiming at the ground. The Sage reached out his hand to offer the man his sword.

Davis hobbled over and reluctantly took hold of the hilt.

"And now, I will bid you farewell," said the Sage. "Although, it is clear that my spirit will be with you."

The Sage smiled. *Ever anon,* it seemed to say.

The old man walked to the side of the fire once again, and he bowed his head low for a moment's meditation. When he lifted his gaze, his hands followed in unison; and with them, a great plume of smoke and ash rose from the center of the fire, as a pillar of flames had done not long ago.

The column whirled in cyclonic fashion, like a mighty tornado rising from the fire; but as before, its great power was controlled – contained for now to the area above the pit, at the center of the room. When the plume hit the ceiling, however, it quickly filled the dome and spilled out equally in all directions. Like the flames before it, the cloud crawled along the ceiling, but when it reached the outer rim, it began to settle downward. Ash fell like snow throughout the room, obscuring much of his sight, while the funnel in the center continued rising steadily.

Despite this grand display, Davis fixed his eyes on those of the Sage. When at last, the ash had grown so dense that it filled the entire chamber, only the stare of the Sage remained, piercing through the haze. The ash continued falling. Soon, even the eyes of Firmus eventually faded, and Davis could see nothing but a deep, dark gray.

That impenetrable smoke lingered for quite some time, but eventually a cold wind began to stir in the stagnant air of the cave. The dark cloud reluctantly started to clear, and when it had fully settled to the earth, it transformed into the thick coat of ash on the surface of the mountain.

As the final particles set down amongst the rest of their kindred on the barren slopes of that forsaken mountain, Davis needed no clarification as to where he stood at present. For better, or for worse, he had found his way there once before, and the memory undercut his nerve at the sight of these desolate reaches once again.

High on the mountainside, the only sensations he perceived were the chilling oppression of a vicious wind, an irritation in his lungs from the treacherous dust, and the barely tolerable pain still pulsing in his side. *You must create the peace within,* he reminded himself, and it seemed to work – at least a little. The pain persisted, but it was slightly duller than before.

There was no life anywhere of which to speak, but something didn't feel right to Davis. No one else was near him, but he was not alone. An ominous awareness of another presence was omnipresent.

"Indignus!" he called out in defiance.

There was no reply.

"Indignus! Show yourself!" Nothing. "I know you're here." He let out a primal roar, as one mad with power, or else wracked with fear. "I've come to cleanse the haunting of these hills!"

Again, there was no reply.

Nothing stirred in the parched, ashen air, except the echoes of his own affronts. He had issued a clear challenge, but the lack of its acceptance did not dismay his resolution. Long did he walk the surface of Talionis, carrying on in this manner: daring, goading, insulting, demanding – even pleading with Indignus to show. But alas, the prolonged provocation was to no avail.

After countless long hours of his search had proven fruitless, his shouts gradually grew less frequent, until finally they came to a reluctant expiration altogether. It was then, in the silent onset of the sunset, that he first heard a voice in the distance.

While infertile in every fashion, the surface of Talionis was not entirely without feature. Great boulders were strewn about the ground, and canyons were carved like wounds into the mountainside. Both structures made navigating the meandering paths unsafe and unpredictable. It was in this complex habitat that Davis searched frantically for the source of the unfamiliar voice out on the breeze.

The airwaves resonated off the rocks, but would be silenced by the dust; they rebounded off the cliffs, only to be lost in the open air once they shot out from the mountain. In the fleeting bits he could capture in its passing flight, the voice wasn't at all as he expected, for there was nothing menacing about it. The voice was deep, yet lighthearted; it was loud, but it was warm – jovial even. It was the last disposition he was anticipating from the foe for which he was certain he was searching.

He heard the sound often, emanating each time from different, unknown, and unreliable locations; but never once could Davis comprehend any meaning. At this point, he wasn't even sure the sounds were intended as words. The only thing Davis could ascertain for certain was that, as it became loud enough for him to suspect he might soon find the source, the voice would swiftly stop completely.

In the midst of this futile searching, Davis walked across a ledge overlooking a wide ravine. The large, flat rock spanning its upper edge was all that remained standing when some unknown force carved it into the landscape; this, the most recent of the many erratic chasms he traversed. There seemed to be a way down, and perhaps through, so he turned the corner and descended the path into the gully below. Silence overtook the dismal landscape once again, and Davis was lost in confusion as to what it was that he was doing.

And then someone spoke perfectly clearly.

"We see that we are not the only one searching for something that we cannot quite explain," said the voice from the air.

5.7 \ The Bush Doctor

For once, Davis was certain that the voice was coming from a single direction. He turned to face it — and sure enough, there stood a strange-looking, but straight-speaking figure on the ledge above him. He had an affable appearance: tall and slender, dressed in robes of red and yellow — a welcome discrepancy in the bleak uniformity all around them.

"Who are you?" he asked.

"We are the Bush Doctor," said the man. "We have come to the mountain on a journey for our people."

"And what is your name?" asked Davis.

The man twisted his neck and raised a prominent eyebrow.

"We just told you," he said. "We are the Bush Doctor."

"I understand," said Davis, "but don't you have a proper name?"

"Ours is the most proper name," said the man. "We have no other. It is exactly who we are. Why should we be called anything different?"

"Where I come from, each person has a name that is unique to them."

The Bush Doctor let out a hearty laugh.

"And why would we do something so foolish?" he asked.

"Well..." started Davis, unsure how and if he should justify the concept. "That way, everyone is recognized as a separate person — as a separate individual."

"A separate individual," said the man. "We know no such thing."

"I see. Anyway, my name was Davis. You can call me that if you wish."

"Where you come from," repeated the man. "And where is that? We have never heard of such silliness."

"It's a long story," said Davis. "I've been on quite a journey of my own."

"Well — Davis," said the Bush Doctor, making a deliberate attempt at his name. The concept clearly did not come easily. "Then, that is two things we have in common; though we suspect there are a great many more."

Davis began ascending back out of the ravine he'd only recently descended, approaching the man calmly and signaling only friendly curiosity.

"And how do you know what I'm doing?" asked Davis.

"There are only two reasons why someone would come to this mountain," said the Bush Doctor. "Either we are looking for it or it is looking for us."

"I'm not exactly looking for the mountain," said Davis. He meant of course that he was looking for someone on the mountain, though this detail might have been lost in translation.

"Then evidently it has been looking for you!" said the Bush Doctor. He again erupted into laughter as he spoke the only logical deduction, amused by one with so little comprehension of the workings of Talionis.

In a few short moments, Davis reached the top of the ledge where the shaman stood. Upon his arrival, they exchanged a series of motions indicating an agreement to take a seat on the overhang above the path. The two men sat with their legs dangling over the edge, to take in the view of the ravine, and so they might carry on with their conversation in earnest.

"Which is it for you then?" asked Davis.

Again, the man contorted his face at the obtuse nature of his visitor.

"We have come on a journey for our people," he repeated. "We are their Shaman, and we are the one whom we entrust with our collective spiritual responsibilities."

"What responsibilities?"

The shaman gestured in both directions with his head, gazing around into the rapidly diminishing daylight of the atmosphere.

"We have come to thank the Sun for having blessed us on this day, and to ask, in our humility, for it to come again tomorrow."

Davis laughed at the notion that the man could affect such an astronomical process. He tried his best to contain his condescension, but the effort wasn't enough. The shaman gave him a look which suggested he was entirely serious. The last few rays of the sunset were already almost gone, and they would soon be leaving the men in total darkness. A cold wind whipped past them and raced down into the ravine below.

"And what do you think of the night?" asked Davis, his tone now blatantly anxious. Only then and there did he become abruptly aware of what the setting of the sun might forebode for his travels upon Talionis.

"When the darkness comes, we mourn the absence of the Sun; but we give thanks to the Moon for its reflections, which shrewdly guide us through the shadow. At times, her light is bright, for she is far out of the shadow. In those times, she looks down on us in sympathy, and empowers us to have no fear. But at other times, she is with us in the shadow, and has not the strength to shed much light. And in those times, she looks down on us in empathy, for she knows then of our plight."

Davis looked out into the dim sky in search of the state of the moon. It had shone full and bright when he had lain down upon the cold stone of Expiatio; but as of now, he didn't know what to expect. As if understanding his very thoughts, the shaman continued.

"Tonight, the moon is dark, for it is far within the shadow. She sheds no light to guide us on, but we thank her nonetheless — for the promise that she bears, to lead us into it again."

"Let's hope she keeps her promise," smirked Davis.

"Hope?" he said, solemn and unsmiling. For someone so good-humored, he was surprisingly unmoved by the effort to make light of the situation. "Hope is but a fool's game," he continued. "Hope leads only to disappointment, should we be failed by our desires. We choose instead to be thankful for the Fates, wherever they may lead us.

"Should we hope above all else to have a long and happy life for those we love, what are we to do when they are taken from us prematurely? Should our beloved be taken in the night by some predator, we would feel cheated by the Fates that made this happen, and turn quickly to anger and frustration toward them.

"Yet, if we had no hope of the sort, we would feel no such betrayal at the turn of these events. Instead, we would be able to see that our beloved has contributed something of great importance to the world. It was not a self-serving desire; it was even more important.

"The predator is to live another day, and may yet breed more of its kind, to play their own role in the world. Our beloved has then provided for us from above the soil. The remains of our beloved will also go to rest in that very soil, and out from the ground will grow the fruits of the earth. Our beloved has therefore provided for us from below. They may have left us prematurely, but they have attained the greatest honor that any of our tribe may attain: the state of Dationis. There is little else in the world that we can do that is as great a service to our Giver."

"Who is your tribe?" asked Davis upon realizing how little he knew of this shaman – or rather, how little he had thought to ask him.

"We are the Gratius," said the shaman. "The Children of Limbus."

"Limbus?" said Davis. "What is Limbus?"

"Limbus is where we are," said the shaman. "It is all we sense around us, though it is far from all there is."

"What else is there?"

"Why, there is all that came before, and there is all that comes after!" The shaman let out another whole-hearted laugh. "Then of course, there is all that is here now, but which falls outside our understanding."

A momentary silence set in, but Davis did not so much ponder these peculiar words as he pondered their peculiar source. In regretting how little he had asked of the shaman at their meeting, Davis was reminded of the odd manner in which they met. The words of the shaman, at first so readily overlooked, now struck him as suspicious.

"When you first called out to me, you said you were searching for something you couldn't explain. Yet, it seems as though you know exactly what you're doing, and why you're here on Talionis."

"We said that we could not explain it; we did not say that we knew not what it was. You may find the same is true for you; or perhaps not."

That aptly led Davis to the even more pressing aspect of his question.

"Your words also implied that you know what I'm searching for."

"You may find the same is true for you," repeated the shaman.

"Then you do know what I'm seeking?"

"We do."

"How?" asked a suddenly circumspect Davis.

The Bush Doctor only gave him yet another puzzled look.

"We heard you shouting about it," said the shaman.

"I see," said Davis, feeling foolish. "Do you know how I might find him?"

Validus the Mighty remained yet in its sheath; but while Davis didn't realize it, his hand rested upon the handle. Hidden in the darkness, under the cover of leather, the blade flickered once in anticipation.

"Certainly not by wandering aimlessly about the mountainside," said the shaman. "You will not find what you seek on the surface."

"I don't understand," said Davis. "I was told by one I trust that this is exactly where I would find him."

I've also met him here before, he did not confess out loud.

"You will not find it here because you do not truly know what it is."

"And how do you know then?"

"We told you," said the shaman. "We are entrusted with the spiritual responsibilities of our people."

"And what does Indignus have to do with the spiritual responsibilities of your people?" asked Davis. He wasn't so sure they were talking about the same thing after all.

"Which of them doesn't it have to do with?" asked the shaman.

Davis waited for more to follow, but the Bush Doctor simply stared back at him, apparently likewise awaiting a reply; and it was the shaman whose patience won the day.

"I wouldn't imagine Indignus had much to do with you," said Davis. "Not based on what I know of him anyway."

"You obviously know very little about it," said the Bush Doctor.

Davis shot back: "And what do you know of it?"

"Indignus is the fire that burns our crops, when we have watered them too sparsely. Indignus is the flood that drowns our fields, when we have watered them too deeply. Indignus is the Taker of the gifts of our Giver, but it knows not of Dationis."

"Your Giver?" asked Davis, recalling another of his many questions.

"Known by many names of course, all of which are still unfit. We use no names for it at all, for it is not of the sort for which names will do justice."

"And Indignus?" asked Davis, veering back closer to the issue that worried him most at the moment. "What does he want with me?"

"He?" asked the shaman.

The Bush Doctor raised a hand to his squinted brow to form a grave and disconcerted look. *This Davis does not yet understand.* The shaman closed his eyes, and as he did so, the light on the mountainside dimmed yet further – like candlelight in a wind just bold enough to threaten to exterminate it, but not proving strong enough to do so. The fading remnant of daylight, which even before was far too faint for the likes of Davis, was restored to its previous level as the shaman opened his eyes.

"We see," said the shaman at last.

"What does he want from me?" asked Davis again, quick as always to return to practical matters over the spiritual insights of Sages or Shamans.

"The last we knew, it was you who were searching for him. We think the better question is: what do you want from Indignus?"

Davis sighed, conceding a fair point, and asked himself the same question in earnest. Despite his contemplations, he gave no reply. He either didn't entirely know the answer, or he was too reluctant to share that which he found. He scanned the ever-darkening atmosphere, which was slowly settling into a diffuse red glow with the disappearance of the sun.

"The last time I saw him, it was in bright midday – not at all like now."

"And what was the nature of your interaction?" asked the shaman.

The pain from the wound in his side lashed out at him again. It had never departed, despite his ability to ignore it improving over time. He had no choice now but to think of it again; and in doing so, Davis was overwhelmed by a sudden surge of aching and anguish.

"He attacked me," he said reluctantly, grabbing at his side to stifle the sting. "He wounded me; I grew dizzy, and then fell. I was certain in the moment that I would die, though I now know such a fear to be needless. When I finally rose from the ground, there was neither injury nor adversary to be found. I didn't know his name then, but I've since learned who he is."

Davis clenched his teeth, biting down on his pain and anger alike.

"I have come to end his reign," he said with dark determination.

"Have you?" asked the Bush Doctor. He stared at Davis, as a father would a wayward child, saddened by their ignorance but sympathetic all the same. "Tell us: what do you think Indignus is?"

Davis knew whom he sought: his assailant – the man whom he blamed for his unfortunate fate; the man who had taken his life; the man who had taken him from his family; the man who had taken his family from him. And yet, this stranger had become so much more than that. He had come to symbolize everything Davis feared and despised; he had come to encompass all that was wrong with the world.

"He is the fire and the flood," echoed Davis. "The devil in the darkness."

"And yet, you were attacked in broad daylight," said the shaman softly.

Davis still grasped the hilt of his sword, but by now his grip was twisting, tightening down viciously on the handle in his slowly swelling rage.

"The ghosts of Talionis," argued Davis. "A hallucination ... brought on by the toxic dusts of the Ashlands. It is exactly as the people of the world say."

"And what exactly is the world of which you speak?" asked the shaman. "We have told you its name; have you so quickly forgotten what it means? You have only arrived at the surface of the mountain; have you so quickly forgotten what you learned deep in its foundations?"

In his unspoken yearning to search for the simpler solution, his pride ignored the broader context for which he fought so hard. The instincts he so long ago first trusted – and only recently outgrew – were fighting with all their might to pull him back into the land of the living. Torn as always in two directions, Davis didn't know which emotion to follow, should emotion be followed at all.

Do not forget all you have learned, old young one, he heard the voice of Firmus say. At the shaman's allusion to the depths of Retributio, he thought of the Steadfast Sage, and what it truly meant to have such a resolution.

To have a Steadfast Will does not mean being unbending in times of tribulation, he reasoned. Ever had he learned lessons to the contrary: it is better to bend in the breeze than to eventually break under its strain. He questioned it now in a way he never had before. *What does it really mean?*

Resolve
Devotion
Persistence
Perseverance
Determination
Commitment
Faithfulness
Dedication
Fortitude
Fidelity

It also meant Courage, he thought; but what exactly did that mean?

Daring
Bravery
Heroism
Gallantry
Audacity
Mettle
Valor

Strength-at-arms? he wondered. *Not necessarily.*

In the end, he arrived on what he deemed the best answer. Ultimately, to be steadfast meant fearlessness – the courage to go on, despite the immensity of the challenge.

"I do not fear Indignus," said Davis, speaking aloud again to the shaman.

He took a deep, calming breath. He loosened his grip on the hilt of his sword; and eventually, he let go of it altogether.

"Then you remember the Moon as it was outside the shadow," said the shaman. "But to be fearless is not the only thing you must accomplish. To grow beyond the danger of your foe, you must first come to understand it. You will not find Indignus on the surface of Limbus because you refuse to acknowledge that it is a part of You."

"What do you mean?" asked Davis, carrying on in his denial.

"You know the nature of Limbus; and still you expect to find Indignus here when you repress it?"

"I'm not repressing anything," argued Davis, "I've been actively searching for him, challenging him – demanding he confronts me!"

"And Indignus has not taken up the call. Why so?"

Davis didn't answer, only bristled and shook his head.

"Before you can confront Indignus, you must accept it as a part of you."

Frustrated by the inevitable truth in the Bush Doctor's words, the only option Davis had left was to question his credentials.

"And what makes you qualified to advise me on the matter?" he asked harshly. He stood up from beside the shaman, his hand once again reaching instinctively to the hilt of his sword.

At his own reaction, a sudden and unsettling perception rushed over Davis – a commanding sensation of déjà vu cast a fog throughout his mind; and when it cleared, for some inexplicable reason, his vision was sent back to an image from his insentience by the shore so long ago. He stood amid a vast field of purple flowers, the petals swaying gently in the breeze, looking out over waves of endless waves.

When he came back to his senses, he sat calmly again, on the ledge at the side of the shaman, although he had practically forgotten what they were talking about.

"Often, our people are afflicted by evil spirits of the bush," continued the Bush Doctor. "Most do not know that such things are not real, but it is far easier to drive the spirits out with the wave of a stick than it is to convince someone of that!"

The shaman laughed loudly as he let Davis in on this secret of his trade, but he soon returned to the serious point of his discussion.

"What we fail to see is that there are real causes for our problems, many of which are made by our own hands. If we can give them a name – if we can give them a form – we can banish them forth from our sight; and often, we find that the problem goes away. The hidden mind does the rest, from a desire to keep all the so-called Evil Spirits at bay."

"How do you know all this?" asked Davis.

This time, his question didn't come off as accusatory; rather, his full perspective had returned – after long ages of struggle – and he genuinely wanted to know more about the deep wisdom of his companion.

The Bush Doctor again lifted a prominent eyebrow, gazing at Davis in disbelief of his need to repeat himself so often.

"We told you," he said. "We are entrusted with the spiritual responsibilities of our people. If you fear not the ghosts of Talionis, there are many secrets it can teach you."

The shaman glanced far away, not outward over the ravine where Davis had been heading, but up the slope from where they sat. The night was now fully formed. The only light was that of a distant red glow, emanating from the crater at the pinnacle of the Great Volcano. If he took his time, it might provide just enough sight to fumble his way through the perilous landscape.

"You have climbed quite high," said the shaman. "Although from here, you seem to have been headed in the wrong direction. You must continue climbing, to the top of the mountain, until you can climb it no further. There, you will look into the core of Talionis itself – into its very essence, and the peak of its power. Take up your seat there and meditate upon your plight, until an omen comes to you at last."

Thunder rumbled from the menacing clouds that were now gathering at the peak. Davis jumped at the sound as it broke through the stillness of the night, rattled the sides of the mountain, and echoed through its chasms. The light grew progressively brighter as it reflected off the amassing storm, and the shaman continued.

"Then, and only then, may you be One with your Greater Self."

As the Bush Doctor spoke these words, Davis gazed along with him, straining his eyes upward at the deep, red glow reflecting off the clouds spiraling over the crater far above them. But when the words had ceased, and only silence remained, Davis turned back to begin his next set of pressing questions, only to find that the shaman was gone – vanished as enigmatically as he had appeared.

Davis shouted after the departed shaman, as loudly as he could.

"How will I know what this omen is?'"

The voice responded one last time from far away, bouncing around the boulders from no discernible direction.

"You will know," it echoed.

You will know.

Davis took the shaman's advice: he tried, in whatever way he could, to climb. From the ledge, he searched for a way up; and having taken the time, he came upon a narrow gap. He had missed it in his prior haste, and it was easy to do. The entrance was concealed by staggered sheets of vertical rock, and the way through could be seen only upon a close and careful inspection.

Rather than plummet into the ravine, as Davis had done, this path climbed upwards from the ledge. He squeezed through the hidden passage and scrambled along between its narrow walls, feeling his way along the rocks, and stumbling through the many shadows cast in the dim red darkness. The glow from the crater was faint, but it got brighter as he climbed; the air was cool, but it grew warmer with every passing step.

The going was slow, and tedious, and it went on long enough that Davis had little choice but to stew in his own musings. Why the Bush Doctor had been so noncommittal about his antagonist, he did not know, for his purpose was as clear as ever in his mind.

Nevertheless, the discrepancy troubled him.

Finally, the glow began to grow into far more suitable lighting, and the ground moved all the more quickly under his feet. He turned a final corner in the narrows, and the end of the long, winding path could be seen in the distance. The walls lessened in height and widened away from one another toward the end, but he couldn't see past the opening, as it was blinded by a bright red simmering, shining down the long passage.

The closer he got, the faster his heart was beating in this bodily form he had taken, and the stronger his sentiment of revenge. *I hate that man so much,* the memory replayed. Over and over again, it had echoed in his mind. And it lived within him still – in the rocks; in the lava; in the toxic ash of Talionis.

He stepped out from the passage onto a wide slope, and the last ragged peaks of the Great Volcano lay before him at its apex. The ridge formed a wide ring around a sunken crater, in which an enormous pool of magma boiled and bubbled. Overhead, the swirling cyclone had grown tenfold since Davis last saw it. Lightning darted back and forth among the clouds, though none struck downward at the land, nor did any rain yet fall. In its stead, flurries of ash drifted down; a thick layer coated the whole mountainside, as snow may have done on any less hazardous highlands.

And in the ash lay footprints.

Someone has been here before.

It was the only sign Davis needed to unleash his true desires. So quickly, having preemptively presumed the omen he was owed, he had forgotten his charge from the shaman.

"Indignus! Show yourself!" shouted Davis, reprising his challenge. "It's bad enough the man robbed me of my life," he mocked. "Now, he's come to haunt me in the afterlife too. Is there no justice in this place? Is there no vengeance for those who have wronged me? Show yourself, you coward!"

The sound bounced among the mountain features, as the voice of another had done before. As it lingered, so too did his anger. Long had his rage dwelt underneath the surface – stewing, festering, biding its time. But now, in concert with the molten rock of the Great Volcano itself, it was beginning to boil to the surface. The longer his demands were ignored, the closer he came to a breaking point, until eventually, he had reached it.

"Indignus–!" he screeched at the top of his lungs.

It would be devastating – tragic – for any to hear, should anyone else have been there to hear it; for it was that of a man utterly broken by grief and despair, but who had turned all of that infinite darkness into hatred.

There was no reply but his own echoes. He raced up the slope as quickly as he could, following the footsteps into the middle of the final ascent, kicking even more ash back up into the atmosphere. He began to cough uncontrollably, but he could not stop moving.

His present corporeal form had difficulty breathing, still bound – for now, and in its way – to the Laws of Limbus. His vision was becoming veiled, clouded by the increasing ashfall as he got closer to the peak, and from all he kicked up in his frenzy. The rim of the crater was not much farther, but it could barely be seen above him. He became light-headed and dizzy, but he could not stop moving.

"Show yourself!" he shrieked in madness. But when the echoes of his curses faded, it was clear that he was all alone.

His coughs grew more frequent, and more intense, until he could hardly stand at all. He hacked in the haze of the dust, stumbled, and collapsed. His knees sank into the soot. A large plume of ash rose around him, and he could see little other than a thick wall of gray on all sides.

At the last, within a short climb from the brink of the crater, he had fallen; and he had not the strength now to rise. He tried repeatedly, but each time, he fell back into the dust, stricken with fits of coughing – gasping in his need for fresh air. He tried again to rise, and again he fell forward on his forearms in the ash, his head hanging low between them.

Only now, almost defeated by the mountain, did a crack begin to form in his armor. He tried one last time to keep the floodgates shut, but he couldn't hold back the welling truth; for truth often has a means of coming out, one way or another. He knew with whom his anger lay.

"It's my fault," he said slowly, finally breaking through the barrier.

Tears poured out and fell to the ground. Each drop struck the ashes of Talionis, dissolving at least a small portion of its widespread Ashlands and carrying away the remains in tiny rivers of sorrow. Thunder bellowed again in the gathering storm; and soon, it too let loose its rainfall.

Down plummeted a heavy deluge from on high; but as it fell, so did it dispel much of the dense ash fog surrounding him. The droplets splashed the dust with great force, and the soiled water leapt every which way upon impact. The runoff began to mount, eroding the ash and carving far larger rivers in it; they careened recklessly downhill, growing wider and deeper as the rain persisted, swelling as they merged and combined forces.

Soon, the rainfall gouged great channels in the landscape, destabilizing the loose surface above the bedrock and setting off an unprecedented chain of events. Thus did a single tear unleash a landslide – a vicious mix of water and ash, pumice and soil, streaming down over the side of the mountain, sloughing off an era of volcanic dust like dead skin, and leaving only the barren foundations of the jagged mountain in its wake.

As if fighting back against the other elements, the Great Volcano responded: the lava began churning more fiercely, launching higher and higher into the air, but not yet breaking the rim of the crater. The storm mounted, and the lightning was set free, shooting down to the ground for the first time. Talionis had been challenged, and mayhem had commenced.

But Davis was not yet quite defeated.

"It's my fault," he sobbed again into the hillside, splayed out on all four limbs, his head still hanging between his arms as the forces of nature rebelled all around him.

By now, his heartache was pouring out of him like the rivers of ash flooding down the mountain. All the guilt for the role he had played in his own demise could finally come out; but it was so much more than that.

"I was so afraid," he confessed through the struggle for his breath. "I was so afraid – for me, for my family. I was only trying to protect us."

While true in every sense, he knew this wasn't the whole story. Surely, deep within him dwelt an unbridled fear that allowed him to justify his actions; but deep within him dwelt also the same possibility for hatred, jealousy, envy, and aggression as the worst of his foes – the same potential to do evil as any other human being. And he knew as well that all these things, deep within him, sometimes make their way out to the surface.

"He was nineteen years old," said another.
It was a familiar voice, but one which he had never heard from afar.

Davis raised his head to meet his enemy; and there he was, standing on the final ridge above him, at the crater's edge. He had shown himself at last.

In rising from his desolation, Davis learned of the changing conditions. The downpour had cleansed much of the suffocating ash from the air, and he was able to regain his lost breath. The light of the crater beamed past the newcomer, leaving only his silhouette, and it cast a long shadow down over Davis where he lay.

"Indignus!" he shouted up the slope at the shrouded figure.

His foe had arrived in perfect timing for him to have someone other than himself to blame. He rose from the ground and pulled the sword from its sheath. The blade rang out in its liberation, and it flashed in the light of the lava. *Finally, Validus the Mighty might fulfill its long-foretold destiny.*

From within the shadow below, he stepped forward on the attack, ready to finally rid himself of this great evil here before him. The aggression did not dismay the man on the ridge, who carried on calmly in his purpose.

"He was born into a broken family," he said. "They were impoverished in a way you could have never imagined."

"Lies!" he shouted from below in defiance.

"As a boy, his father beat his mother so badly that she needed stitches – not every time, but often enough."

"Stop!" he said as he took a step up the mountain.

"They couldn't afford a hospital visit, so he stitched her up himself after his father passed out in a drunken stupor."

"Stop changing the subject! Your tricks won't work on me."
Lightning struck below them.

"His father finally left when he was twelve, although that may have been for the better. His mother struggled to make ends meet on her own – among other ways."

"It's irrelevant! He was a criminal – creeping into my home in the middle of the night."
He took another step upward.

"Often, he would pass on eating, so that his little sisters would be able to. He would beg from time to time, or rummage in dumpsters, salvaging any bounty he could find – and yes, sometimes even steal to keep surviving."

"So you admit it! He was nothing but a criminal."
Thunder rumbled; the rain continued to pour.

"He had trouble finding honest work, or keeping it. So, he took whatever path he needed to provide for his family."

"How is any of this my problem?"
He took another step.

"He was in your house to take anything small enough that
he could carry, but still valuable enough to barter. The
police found only your wallet in his pocket once they
searched his lifeless body. It had forty-seven dollars."

"Stop stalling — stand and fight!"
Again, the lightning struck.

"He didn't even know what had happened when he felt that
sharp blow strike his head. He was dizzy and confused, and
he reached for the first defense he could find, to scare his
attacker away for long enough to run. He was shocked
and horrified when he saw what turn things took."

"He was a coward, just like you!"
Again, the thunder rumbled.

"He would have gladly left your house, but he received
no such pardon at the hands of his killer."

"He only got what he deserved."
He was nearing the top.

"His name was Joseph. He was terrified and all alone
when he died next to you in that ambulance."

"Enough!" he shouted from below.

He took a final step to the top of the ridge. The blade was cocked
backward and ready to thrust, but before the man could take his fateful
strike ... he faltered. Validus the Mighty was cast aside, and he fell once
again to his knees under the weight of an irrepressible grace, collapsing at
the feet of the one who was already upon the peak.

And through the furious denial of his own nature, he saw his mirror
image, and he knew at last what he was seeking. He looked up at his foe,
and whom he thought had been Indignus was now revealed to him as Davis;
and whom he thought had been Davis had now become what was Indignus.

Davis extended his hand to the man below, still shrouded in shadow. He
bowed his head in submission. Davis bowed to him in turn, but in empathy.
Ultimately, both sides of this soul bowed in recognition of the other.

The man kneeling in the shadow reached out into the ash, reclaimed the
lost blade, and began to raise it upward. Slowly, he placed the handle into
the outstretched hand before him, and Davis took the sword. He bowed a
final time, and the two became One. He turned his back to Indignus, and
once he did, the shadow was gone — but not vanquished.

Davis took the final few steps to the edge of the crater. There was a level spot on which to stand at the precipice, but only a single step beyond led straight down a ragged cliff into the scorching heart of Talionis. The lava still churned and bubbled, even more fiercely than before, and the mountain was clearly not entirely appeased. The rain had not stopped, nor had the lightning, and the spiraling storm clouds continued to gather.

Peering down into the magma, Davis gently tossed the sword over the ledge. And slowly did it tumble, end over end, to meet its proper doom. The moment it hit the boiling surface, the volcano settled into a brief hiatus, as if focusing all its might on the undoing of this mighty blade. When the work had been done, the turmoil resumed. Davis stepped back from the brink, sat down on the ledge, and crossed his legs to fulfill his final charge.

He closed his eyes, but he could still feel the warmth from the crater showering his face as he tried to clear his thoughts. Though no longer overrun with the lesser emotions that had blinded him, it was still difficult to abstain from reflecting on the turbulent events he had endured – or else those he suspected still awaited him.

When finally his mind was silent, and not a single thought entered into its void, only then did he receive what he'd been promised, though certainly not in a form that he could have predicted.

The mountain abruptly erupted in a violent explosion.

Davis opened his eyes at the heat and sound from the blast: a gigantic column of lava reached well into the sky, piercing through the storm and sending it surging outward like a great wave. The whole of Limbus quaked, and there would be few in all the land who would not witness this as an omen of the end times, whether or not they recognized its meaning.

Somehow, even at the very epicenter of these colossal events, Davis himself had been spared from harm – at least for now. The lava spouted straight upwards in a pillar, and as it reached its climax, the column slowed, paused at the top, and began to plunge back down towards the crater.

Davis knew when it was time to go. He closed his eyes and thought of somewhere else. A long way down below, he'd almost forgotten the rest of this world was still out there.

Watching the eruption from the safety of afar, he made a solemn vow.

This time I take watch, holding fast to my meaning
I cannot repeat the same fortunes this turn
When flesh has been placed in the path of the fire
Those who don't move will be those who are burned

The steadiest hand will awaken from losses
The firmest of wills will be yet reinforced
A chance to exert exponential potential
A chance to be deeply aligned with the course

SIX

6.1 \ A Ghost on the Wall

A Councilor of Inanimis walked along the top of a long wall, overlooking the desolate stretches leading up to Talionis in the south. The walls ran throughout much of the land at this point, and each one had a set of rails straddling its sides so that they formed an integrated system of antiparallel lines. Large chambers traveled along the rails, streamlined shuttles driven by magnetic gradients in an entirely efficient manner. The railwalls, as they were called, were the chief means of transportation from the inner city to the outer reaches of its sprawling civilization.

Out beyond the wall were the Ashlands of the mountain, and at the moment, the summit was engaged in a continuing series of violent explosions. Surges of lava erupted from the top of the crater, jumping by the dozens in an erratic yet graceful display of that most powerful danger lurking ever under the soil. The sky above was dark, though it wasn't yet midday, for the smog billowing out from the crater had created an impenetrable halo of gloom over the surrounding lands for many miles.

The Councilor turned back from the view and walked into the southern of two large towers. These stations were spaced evenly throughout the entire system, serving as both watchtowers and centers of operation. Each station had two symmetrical structures, one on either side of the railwall.

From the walkway atop the wall, there was an entrance to the central office of each tower. The lower level extended to the ground and housed a bunker which looked out from the side of the wall; the highest level consisted of an imposing turret, connected to the opposite tower by an enclosed bridge which spanned the walkway below.

As he reached the top level of the south-facing tower, the Councilor breathed an exasperated sigh, and he began a conversation with the two individuals there waiting for him.

"I have to admit, I do not like the look of it," started the Councilor.

"We have no choice but to inform the DMI," advocated the woman nearest him. She gave a look that suggested the enormity of the task for which she was about to advocate. "We must convince them to stop their actions at once, regardless of the risks."

"Do you have any idea what could happen if you're wrong, Fida?" asked the Councilor.

"Regardless of the risks," she repeated slowly.

"This is absurd," interjected the other, a man known as Credulus. "There is no purpose in turning back now. We agreed – in the usual fashion, through every formalized channel – that this was the action we would take."

"How do we know these events are not occurring precisely because of the activities of the DMI?" asked the Councilor. Fida nodded in agreement.

"Don't be ridiculous," said Credulus. "We have no empirical reason to think such a thing might be true. And even if it was, we knew there might be risks of this sort. But to undo what we've done, only to face a different set of risks altogether – only to get us back to the situation from which we began? It simply makes no sense."

The man had the slightest twinge of madness in his eye.

"The process has begun," he continued. "It is too late. We must stay the course until it's been run to completion."

"Until the track beneath us meets its quick demise?" asked Fida.

Had any of the three of them been looking out through the windows of their alleged watchtower as they engaged in this debate, they would have expressed a great deal of surprise, for a cloaked figure was making their way down from the heights of the very mountain they were discussing.

The three emerged to the top of the wall after a long meeting of this sort, going back and forth on the matter. Once outside, they turned to each other to conclude their remarks. Having said their rigid and ritualized farewells, the two Wardens returned to their posts inside the station, and the heavy metal door slammed shut behind them.

The Councilor was preparing to depart, but he was stopped dead in his tracks at the sight of a hooded stranger approaching along the wall. He walked with a hunched stature and his head bowed low, and the Councilor couldn't make out many details beyond those of a man of advancing years. He looked worn and tattered, as if he were well underway on a lifetime of wearisome traveling. The Councilor didn't notice much else about the old man as he approached, but as the stranger strolled past him, an odd sensation overcame the Councilor after the briefest meeting of their eyes.

"You there," he shouted after the stranger.

The mysterious figure turned slowly, but surely enough, and he lifted his cloak to reveal his face. The man didn't make a sound, but the Councilor fell immediately to his knees in disbelief.

"You..." he said in a stutter. "You can't possibly be, no – no, you can't possibly be ... the same."

"Indeed, I cannot," replied the stranger. "Nor would I want to be. Yet, that doesn't mean we haven't met before; quite the contrary, in fact. I know you; though when I did, you went by the name of Animulus." The old man stepped forward and stared deep into the Councilor's eyes. "In seeing you now, however, it seems to me that such a name is no longer borne."

The Councilor tried to speak, but his voice took a moment to recover from paralysis.

"You – you were laid upon the stone," he began again slowly. "I saw the stroke with my own eyes. Thirty-eight long years have passed since that day; and you come to me now, out of the mist, like a vision? Smarter men than me would have long since blamed such hallucinations on the noxious dusts of Talionis. The ash blows about in squalls even now, maddening my mind.

"I confess: many nights have I been haunted by the sight of your slaughter. But seldom has it bestowed upon me such unbearable oppression as the sight of you now." He moved back a step to keep his distance. "Speak, I command you ghost! Tell me what you have to say for yourself."

"I do not deny the resemblance," said the so-called specter. "But I assure you: I am not the same."

"Davis," said the Councilor, as if fearing the word. "Davis was his name."

"And so shall it remain," he replied, "wherever he may be."

"Then how can you explain yourself? Where have you come from? And what business do you have here?"

The old man didn't answer immediately. He looked instead over the side of the wall, towards the rolling Ashlands and the mountain far beyond.

"Who can ever really say?" answered Davis. "I had some business to attend to in the depths of Talionis. Wherever I was, I can assure you that it wasn't accounted for in the measure of years."

"There are none who survive an encounter with the mountain," protested Animulus. "You are clearly not of flesh and blood. So tell me: why have you come here to haunt me?"

"I commend your insight, my noble Councilor, for you have shattered the riddle. In truth, I am not of the flesh. Although, I would warn you that even the flesh may not be exactly as you imagine."

"Please," he pled. "Do not taunt me, phantom. Why have you come?"

"I come seeking your help — in the place where we still dwell, in the same form in which I came to you for aid in the first place. My purpose also has not changed. You once claimed to share that very same purpose; although, I wonder now what you desire."

"I will not be spoken to in this way," said the Councilor, mustering his courage. "I will not be chastised by the ghost of a traitor to his deity!"

"I do not seek your permission, nor your pardon for events you cannot understand," said Davis. "I have explained my long absence to the utmost extent of your comprehension; but now, I implore you to explain your own position. It seems that much has changed since I last walked these lands."

The Councilor didn't want to comply, for it had been far too long since he looked objectively upon his own actions. Nevertheless, he was subjected to the overwhelming imposition of a grander kind of will — one that demanded his allegiance, and one that he could not resist.

"I will tell my tale," said Animulus, "but then I insist, you must leave me in peace! You have haunted me too long as it is. I would be fully done with you, once and for all."

Davis looked empathetically upon his frightened old acquaintance, and he hoped with all his heart that he could do as he'd been asked.

"Should the tale you tell accomplish what I intend of it, peace is the very thing we may both yet find."

Having been granted an apparent agreement to his only request, the Councilor began a sad story from the beginning.

6.2 \ The Journey of Animulus

"On the last occasion that we met, the day was far from over when your eyes would last have seen. While I can't speak to the timeless halls to which you evidently traveled, it seems as though fate had a great deal more in store for each of us that day. But so soon in the story, I am getting ahead of myself. Allow me to clarify what happened following your death, and throughout the long years of toil into which that day has thrust me.

"There we stood – six of us to start – watching intently as you approached the altar, with bloodlust in our eyes. Showing hardly any hesitation, you laid down upon the stone, and the deed had been done. Your chest heaved under the force of the blow and your arms were flung wide, though that single motion is all of the sacrifice any of us would see. The instant the tip of that fateful blade struck stone, a violent explosion of light was released from the site of the puncture. It was as bright as a thousand bolts of lightning, emanating out from the center of your chest. It happened so fast that it veiled our sight of anything else for an insufferable moment.

"The force of the light struck us like a tidal wave, knocking us back to the ground in our blindness. The sound was equally overwhelming; it left room for nothing but a painful ringing in my ears as I flew through the air for a bewildering duration. It was strange – as if the world had slowed, and considered coming to a complete stop out of its sheer exhaustion. My head hit the ground hard when I eventually landed, and the white surrounding me faded suddenly to black.

"I have no sense of how long I was unconscious, but when I finally came around, my head was pounding, and the ringing in my ears persisted. I struggled through the wavering uncertainty of my legs as I rose, and I looked to see each of the others doing the same. I was the first to regain my composure, however vaguely, and I took a few steps towards the altar to assess what could have happened. No indications of any sort came from that direction, for there was nothing left but an unoccupied altar, the Blade of Entitlement sticking straight out of the stone.

"I could not believe my own eyes, and I walked to the altar for a closer inspection. I tried to remove the blade with every ounce of my might, but it was lodged far too deeply into the stone, and it would not budge. After finally giving up, I stepped back from the altar and looked out across the sea. The water was as still as glass, as if it might shatter were I to only throw a stone.

"This tranquility would not last long, however, as I know it now as the calm before an epic storm. As I stood gazing out over the sea, a worrisome rumbling began, ever so slowly, and I could tell it foreboded a great power.

"The water at the base of the cliff began to churn. I ran to the edge to see what I could make of the start of this turbulence, and I knew at once: a massive whirlpool had started at the base of the rocks. The rumbling grew stronger, and it soon began to ache in my already sensitive ears. By then, it looked like the whole sea was practically boiling, and I ran back from the ledge to the relative safety down the hill.

"I ran as far as I could, but as I fled, I turned my head to the sound of a great wave rising behind me. Surely enough, an enormous column of water had swelled from the sea so far below, and it towered over the cliff where the altar rested. The wave slowed as it peaked, came to a pause, and crashed down onto the bluff with an unspeakable power.

"As it crested, I thought we should all have been drowned – or at the very least, washed far away to fend for our lives in the flood. Rather, the wave bore straight down upon the area around the altar, ripping it from the cliffside and swallowing it effortlessly into the sea. When the turbulence ceased, and an eerie quietude set in once again, I stared in a daze at the craggy cavity where the altar once existed. As I lingered in this stupor, my trance was only broken by black ashes, falling all around me like a gentle winter snow.

"I snapped out of my bewilderment and turned immediately, knowing all too well what this portent implied. My brothers were staring back at me, their hands glowing red with rage, in the wake of the spiteful death of our adversaries. In the chaos of the torrent, they had fled for their lives just as I – stride for stride alongside the very Councilors they would soon slay. In the instant they realized the threat of a flood had passed, my brothers pounced upon their foes, exploiting their distraction, and setting each one aflame with their unrestrained malice.

"They looked up at me, in pride at first, as they knew not the change that had occurred in me. How could they? Even I did not understand what had transpired. All I knew was that the death of these men was an ill omen, and that it should have never happened.

"I do not know how I knew it," mused Animulus. "Perhaps it came over me at once, in that great flashing of light, or else it flooded into my heart with the onslaught of the waves. Whatever the case, my brothers noticed the change in my demeanor immediately, for I showed no joy at what they considered their most heroic efforts. The entire High Council of Inanimis dead; what more could have been asked for in the hopes of the Scrutatorus?

"It was almost foolish: little did any of us know just how dispensable the High Council of Inanimis really was. If we had known more about the true workings of the city, we would have despaired at the fact that they would merely be replaced by the next three aspirants waiting in line, and bestowed with the names that each position bears. At first, they would act solely from self-driven motivations; but each would inevitably become exactly as the former once the robes of their office grew heavy.

"And oddly, while history would have predicted such an outcome, that would not prove to be the fate of the High Council in the events that were to follow. But once again, I am getting ahead of myself."

The Councilor paused, having discovered his digression. He hesitated, struggling to regain the previous course of his narrative. *His thoughts are clearly taxing,* Davis knew, *and those of his brothers trouble him most of all.*

He began again slowly, as if he had waited years to speak this sentence.

"Instead of looking upon them with pride for their conduct, I chastised my brothers viciously for their act of sedition. And thus, they were lost to me forevermore. I cannot say what led me to react how I did. I held no allegiance to the High Council; they were my own avowed enemies. I shed not a single tear for their passing. But still, it troubled me. Perhaps it was out of sheer shock – the lingering anxiety after all that I had seen.

"I think, if I am to be truthful, that it was out of fear – a fear of the force that had arisen from the ocean. While my brothers were apparently focusing on their own opportunistic plans, I had been staring at the sea when it erupted into turmoil."

Even after all those many years, it was obvious upon the telling: the memory stirred an unparalleled unease in the spirit of the speaker. He continued cautiously, deliberately, still trying to figure it out even as he spoke aloud.

"Something in the force of that water – nay, something deep down in the very foundations of the world – spoke to me, as it slipped back through the cracks into its rightful abode. As I stared out upon the ensuing stillness of the aftermath, I heard a voice from beyond the Veil:

When your wisdom awakens within you, you may find me...

"...at a place I'd never heard of before. I cannot recall its name; and yet, it seemed so familiar somehow. I have sought for it ever since, but in all my travels, I have never again felt as close to it as when the voice from beyond first spoke to me in that moment."

You fear the voice, for you know to whom it belongs.

Animulus halted, as though knowing the mind of his observer. He'd practically forgotten there even was one, so greatly was he in touch with the needs of his heart. Terrified and burdened by the sight of Davis at first, he had confessed all that happened as if solely for the sake of his conscience.

"As I was saying," he continued awkwardly, "whatever drove me to do as I did, what I did was admonish my brothers with scorn. They turned defensive at the castigation, probably due to their own heightened anxiety after all that had happened. And something that can never be undone should never have been done to begin with."

The Councilor broke, dwelling on something terrible and troublesome, contending with the fact that he had not the nerve to speak of it aloud, but compelled by some greater will to move on with his story all the same.

"Cerebrus argued fervently against me; Manus sat idle for a time, but he was becoming more agitated with every passing rebuttal. My brother labeled me a traitor for indicting him in the deaths of our foes. He grew ever more aggressive, for he loathed my reproaches and the judgement they implied. I could feel the discomfort in the very air we were breathing — an unbearable tension in my chest. Unfortunately, it rose before it had ever been given the chance to wane.

"At one point, I stepped abruptly towards my brothers; I was attempting only to impose my will in argument, but they took the advance as a legitimate threat. Manus leapt out to intervene, but in the swiftness of the events, he placed his hand upon my shoulder and singed me out of instinct. The heat from his grasp seared my flesh, and it has left me badly scarred there to this day. The pain is surely no longer physical, but it burns me still. I suppose it always will.

"I myself escalated, though only out of self-defense, for I could not abide this assault at the hands of my own brother. I felt betrayed — forever wronged by one whom I had truly loved. At the pain, I threw my hands up to break his grip, and I pushed him backward forcefully. He reacted as I feared he might, and he sprang again to subdue me.

"I dove aside and circled around, evading his attack for the time. I tried to calm him down; my excitement had started to falter by then, and my greater will was returning. Despite my pleas, Manus could not be pacified. He continued to pursue me, and without ever attempting to do so, we worked our way gradually to the edge of the cliff.

"Cerebrus had also not cooled any in his disposition, and he followed us intently. As we neared the brink, he formed a flank around me, and together with his brother they had me pinned against the absence of ground. Where there once lay the soft grass at the foot of the altar, there was now only thin air that led to a perilous fall. With both brothers blocking any hope of access to solid ground, I had nowhere to go, nor any good options.

"Cerebrus and Manus continued to encroach, pressing me ever closer towards the edge. In retrospect, I suspect they were only attempting to coerce me back into their allegiance. I do not know that they would have preemptively caused me harm. Yet who can say? In that moment, with tensions as taut as they were, perhaps a momentary lapse in judgement was not so far from possible. I cannot know what would have happened. What did happen, however, was something I can scarcely explain.

"With no means of escape, and only terrible tragedy awaiting should I have attempted to fight for my freedom, I delayed any sort of decision for as long as I could, waiting in vain for some form of solution. As I hedged, my feet stepped slowly backward toward the ledge, in perfect synchrony with their own feet moving inward in their efforts to subjugate me. Having hesitated too long, I stepped a single step too many.

"The arch of my back foot set down upon the corner of the cliff, but the ground was unstable after the recent collapse, and the edge crumbled under my weight. I staggered temporarily, on the verge of utter ruin, but I could not recover my stability. I fell backwards through the nothingness and vanished into the black abyss of the sea below."

"But that cliff is extremely high," interjected Davis. He knew the answer to his own riddle, and his cajoling tone made that perfectly clear. "How could you have possibly survived such a fall?"

"I have asked myself that same question countless times," said Animulus. "I had seen the scale of that drop, and it was taller than I can even reasonably estimate."

He rubbed his forehead, still trying to justify it even now.

"I do not know; but by some bit of serendipity, I fell out far enough to avoid the rocks at the base. Even then, the impact from falling so far should have shattered my body. Without even meaning to, I must have landed at precisely the right angle to break the surface. I think about it almost every day, for it still strikes me as uncanny. It should not have ended well for me."

The Councilor raised his palms and shrugged his shoulders.

"I suppose even reprobates may earn the grace of good fortune now and then," he concluded. "Perhaps this world still needs me," he jested.

Indeed, knew Davis; and yet there was still much he could not see.

"It seems a long journey from the depths of the sea at the end of the world to the high walls of Inanimis in the robes of a ruler," said Davis. "Where did the tides direct you thereafter, to have ended up in so strange a circumstance?"

Animulus sighed, for the irony of his attire was not lost on him.

"What happened after that remains a mystery to me, until I woke up on the sands of a softer shore..."

6.3 \ A Heretic Revealed

"I lay face down on a warm beach, barely conscious. I heard an unknown voice speaking out to me. It took a while for the words to register, but eventually, I heard someone ask if I was alright. I was not sure what to say, for I did not know the answer. Sitting up, I inspected my condition before confirming – skeptically – that I seemed to be okay.

"Over me stood a wiry little man, rather ragged in appearance. He stretched out his hand, helped me from the ground, and told me his name was Avidus. He was a fisherman, so he said; and he certainly looked the part. Apparently, he had been trawling the length of the beach when he saw me passed out in the sand. When I didn't respond to his shouts, he reeled in his nets, anchored his vessel, and came ashore to my aid.

"As he helped me to my feet, I felt the name familiar, but I could not pinpoint why; that is, not until he noticed my scars. The shirt covering my shoulder had been scorched away by the fiery hands of Manus, and far more of it had become torn and tattered from my fall, and my ensuing struggle with the sea. The fisherman recognized my burns immediately, for he bore those of the same making, albeit of a different maker. I knew then and there: this was the same fisherman of whom Legatus spoke – the same fisherman burned by your own hands."

There is no such thing as coincidence, Davis recalled someone saying.

"Stunned to see them, he asked how I got my scars. 'The saddest way I can imagine,' I said, and little else. He pressed me for more details, but the pain was still too near to discuss. Evidently, he sought news of the perpetrator, suspecting it to be the same as his own. He still needed vengeance; I could see it in his eyes. He revealed his own scars, and he told me his tale – or at least the end of it.

"I was in such a state of shock, I did not reveal that I already knew of his incident. My hesitance must have been obvious, as he quickly steered the conversation to who I was and how I wound up on that beach. I granted him no further disclosures, but provided the only name I could – one imparted upon me instinctively in that moment. 'Fractus is my name,' I said. 'And I have come here through unknown waters.'

"All of it was entirely true – both the name and how I got there. Not knowing where I was, and having no clear directive since severing ties with my kin, Avidus convinced me to stay with him for a few days, or until I recovered my strength. He treated me with the utmost care and concern, and for that I will forever be indebted to him. For one with so callous an appearance, he displayed tremendous compassion and generosity to me. In the daytime, we fed on fish, fresh from his nets; in the night, we drank ales, played games, and sang songs of the sea. In a way, it was a wonderful time.

"What started as a few days turned into staying with the fisherman for many weeks and the remainder of his cruise. By the end, we had formed a fast friendship. It is one of the few I can recall, and even now it leaves me oddly nostalgic." Animulus paused at the onset of a melancholic smile. "Something tells me there are a great many more I have long since forgotten — faded friendships from the many phases of my life, which feel like different lifetimes entirely, now that they have so long since passed."

He snapped willingly out of his bittersweet attempts at reminiscence.

"On one of these nights, we somehow stumbled onto a more serious conversation. How it happened exactly, I do not recall; but eventually, Avidus confided in me a full accounting of the events that led up to his scarring. He told me about the confrontation with Providus — his own brother — and I knew then why he had omitted mention of it in the first recounting of his story. It pained him as much as my own altercation pained me. And yet, he had arguably even more guilt to live with, for in the fallout of those events, he had unwittingly driven his brother's family to the brink of starvation while trying to provide for his own needs.

"You see, his brother lived in isolation, and he was not formally affiliated with the city. Providus fished only for his family and a much smaller, local market near the coast. Avidus, on the other hand, fished for the city of Inanimis; he needed a far greater yield just to make the same meager profits. Even so, he admitted in hindsight that the accusations of his brother were true: his methods were destructive, but they were the only way he knew to make ends meet.

"His motivations were also not exclusively selfish. Each citizen of the city had need of provisions, he stressed, and someone needed to provide for them. Even if this was a secondary justification, its premise cannot be refuted. Moreover, if his sole motivation were to provide for himself, he could have enjoyed the simpler life of his brother. Rather, he took on a larger risk for the gamble of a larger reward, for himself and the city alike. He was not entirely altruistic, certainly; but neither was he entirely selfish. Therein is perhaps the most logical motive of all.

"Despite every moral validation, however, nothing could change what eventually happened; and it was this sad fact that ultimately led to the crippling guilt with which he will live out the rest of his days. Deserved or not, he blamed himself for the death of his niece.

"Her name was Immerens, and he adored her beyond words. Avidus had no children of his own, and he loved her without rival. From out of his angst, his face brightened as he told me of the happiest day of his life to date: the day she had been born. There was no way to describe it other than the insufficient use of the word miracle, he said. Holding her for the first time, he could imagine nothing more beautiful in the entire world. He was close with his brother then, before heading off in search of larger profits. They all spent many days with one another, confiding in each other with the incomparable trust and affection known only among family.

"Yet somehow, in the future, he would be cursed with the remorse of having shattered such a trust. Avidus cherishes those memories every day, he admitted – when alone on his deck, waiting for the nets to come in, overlooking the rolling of the endless gentle waves. He longed to return to those simpler times, though he knew there was no way of ever getting back.

"The brothers worked together in those distant days; but soon, Avidus was drawn to the prospect of starting his own business, selling fish to the rapidly expanding city. The years passed, as they always seem to do; and one day he found himself on a long dock, in a conflict over zoning with his own brother. He inevitably fled from that feud – burnt by your own hands, and frightened for his very life – but this did not stop him from fishing the areas surrounding the reserves left for Providus.

"Before long, the populations crashed; but as is the nature of these things, the tragedy was not limited to the regions where Avidus fished. With the overharvesting around its entire perimeter, soon the shoals upon which Providus relied were also bled dry. Despite this, Providus would not seek the aid of the brother who he knew had been responsible, nor anyone else for that matter. He was a noble man, said Avidus; but he was also proud.

"Disconnected from the city, and withdrawn from any who could help them, their entire small community became desperately impoverished. Providus and his wife gave almost all they had to Immerens, but she grew increasingly malnourished. Weakened as she was, she fell sick. Before long, her spirit had left them for good.

"Rumors of these events spread far and wide, for it was a turning point for much of the community. They knew they needed help, or else they would suffer the same fate. And so, many made their way to the city to seek refuge. It is only through these means that Avidus even heard news of it, for his brother would no longer speak to him. After a time, he stopped trying.

"The regretful recollections continued, and so did the ale; and while I could not yet bear to share my own story, by night's end, we were both stricken with grief for all we had lost. Avidus especially sank into a deep depression upon reliving these tragic events – misfortunes he helped bring about himself. I tried to rally all the optimism I could muster – to look forward to the future instead of dwelling on the wrongs of the past – but I had little left of my own, and nothing I said could console the poor man.

"The cruelty of the circumstances that led to Immerens' death weighed so heavily on his conscience that he broke down and cried before my very eyes. And something awoke within me in that moment. I might have called it insight; but in reality, it was just the realization of something I had known so long ago. I remembered my purpose: there has to be a better way."

"And yet here you stand as a Councilor of the very city you protested," pressed Davis again. "I sense there is more to this story. And still, it seems as though the city has only grown. How do you explain the apparent betrayal of your ideals, which you claimed even then to still hold?"

"Indeed, the city has grown," said the Councilor. "And I assure you: whatever ills it still possesses, they are not limited to its size. I shall arrive at my role in Inanimis in good time, but my status will only be poorly understood without the context of how I obtained it."

Carry on, nodded Davis, and the Councilor returned to his tale.

"Perhaps foolishly, I was moved by the fisherman's despair; and in trying to empathize with him, I professed more than I intended. I knew at least a part of his loss, I confided; for I, too, had suffered a confrontation with my kin. Caught in my own confession, I cast aside the shield of Fractus. I told him my rightful name and disclosed my allegiance to that infamous band of outlaws – the Scrutatorus – the Heretics of Inanimis.

"At my admission, Avidus leapt from anguish to anger. He felt understandably betrayed, for he associated me with the scars that still marred his flesh. He shouted at me, cursing my name and my implied association with yourself – for he considered you a Heretic, and each of us shared equal blame in his mind. I tried to calm him down and clarify, but nothing I said could dispel his rage.

"At last, I pulled my shirt aside and revealed my own scars. As the implication slowly crept in, his accusations slowed, until at last he was silenced, and his ire was replaced with confusion. In reacting to my true identity, he had forgotten that I confessed it in relation to his trauma. 'How did you come to receive your wounds?' he asked me again. 'At the hands of my brothers,' I replied, 'for I could not condone their killing of some unsuspecting men.'

"He demanded more details, and I had no choice but to reveal that these men were in fact the High Council of his city. He flew again into a frenzy, although at least this time it was not entirely directed at me. When the shock from these revelations had passed, we were able to regain a degree of productive exchange. As he calmed down, he came to eventually appreciate the gravity with which the situation bore on my being.

"While he detested my brothers, he could at least sympathize that it must have been difficult for me to part with them over matters of principle, and after all we had gone through together. He eventually even thanked me for siding with what he deemed the right side. I reminded Avidus that, while their latest actions were evil in their own right, my brothers and I had fought so long against Inanimis precisely because of its own set of evils – actions that harmed innocent people and their populations of fish.

"Avidus blamed himself for what befell Immerens, but I begged him to forgive himself, if he could. His nets may have been the mechanism, I told him, but it was the irresponsible ways of the city that truly bore this burden. And those were only the wounds he knew about; what about the suffering of all the others whom he did not know? I implored him: there must be a better solution – not only to his trade, but to all the many trades in which the city engages.

"We argued further, and harshly at times. But there were reasons the Heretics parted ways with Inanimis, I contended. We could no longer be a part of its devastation. And likewise, there were reasons I parted ways with the Heretics. I refused to fight evil with another of its forms.

"The fisherman had little more to say, for a time. He was lost in thought and still reeling in his pain. He was torn between the life he had chosen and the possibility that it may not have been the best of all roads. It had cost him what he cherished most of all. It had cost poor Immerens. After much deliberation, he had but a brief reply: 'I suppose we have to try.'

"In the late hours of that pivotal night, it was decided: I would come with Avidus when he returned to the city – to try as I may to steer the course of its fate. In the meantime, he continued to fish as was his custom; and so soon, it seemed that we had already failed. 'One last load can't hurt,' reasoned Avidus, although I wasn't entirely convinced this was true. When every container his ship could support had been filled, we returned to the land from which we had each, in our own ways, been hiding.

"By then, I had learned that we were fishing far to the north of where you and I last met. I must have traveled many miles after my fall, clinging witlessly to life in the surf. The beach on which I finally washed ashore was in the middle of a secluded bay, with a long stretch of fields that sloped upwards to a great forest in the distance. Avidus had found me in this place, and from there we fished together along the shore to the south. As the southern lands began to climb, I inferred these to be the highlands that formed the northern border of the Recordatio. I knew of the existence of more lands in the north, but as you know from the map we provided on our very first encounter, my brothers and I had never ventured that far.

"Between that northern bay and the canyon to the south, there was only one place to access the shore – the Port of Copia, as it was called in Inanimis. Avidus knew it well, for in this place was a dock frequented by the fishermen of the city. The cliffs were still tall, but it was possible to make the journey up to the highlands by a steep and winding road.

"A transporter was already waiting as we arrived. It was a huge wheeled container – as big as his hulking ship – into which the fish could be loaded. It was powered by fires, fueled by burning the earth before it in its path. The front was equipped with an adjustable plow, a wide blade that could be lowered to the ground. When the engines were in need of rekindling, the plow would drop as the vehicle trudged along, to scrape the upper surface of the road and feed the soil through a chute to the furnaces behind.

"Even I had to admit it: the transporter was an ingenious concoction. The soil made for prime fuel, and each scrape took only a small fraction of the road over a long distance. Even so, each was a fraction that would never be replaced – burned, instead, into the atmosphere.

"We transferred the fish and began on our way." Animulus took a deep breath. "And so did I return to Inanimis – to atone for my past, and to bring what they would surely view as ill news for their future."

$\infty\infty\infty\infty$ ∞∞∞

6.4 \ The Birth of Modicus

∞∞∞ ∞∞∞∞

"Upon arriving in the city, the fisherman and I parted ways, but in friendship. He had further business to attend to with his catch, and I had a mind to start in on my own task. It had only been a few months since I had last seen the city walls on a routine scouting foray with my brothers; but in comparing them to the landmarks, they had clearly expanded further into the west.

"There was only one way into the city, at least by the standard means of entry. In being ill-prepared for this visit, I had none of the climbing gear we Heretics were accustomed to using. Nor would such an entry likely have earned me a very warm welcome, I suspected. I entered a line outside the gates and waited patiently for my turn.

"The line was fortunately quite short, for it was labeled Political Inquiries. Most citizens were not concerned with these matters in the least, but were content to let the few that have such an interest take charge of the course they all would chart — for better, or for worse. Naturally, I couldn't help but question the motives of those few, though I knew most others never did.

"As I daydreamed at the front of the line, I was jolted to attention by a startling 'NEXT!' The man behind the window welcomed me to Political Inquiries and asked for my identification in an indolent monotone. 'I have no identification,' I replied. 'Not anymore anyway.'

"He huffed, and in turning his head over his shoulder, he shouted backward to the horde of important-looking people pacing around behind the clerks — something about a 'Non-ID.' He turned back to face me. 'The Registrar is twenty-eight aisles down to your left,' he said. 'This is Political Inquiries.' I did not hesitate: 'That is precisely why I am here,' I said, 'for I come bearing evil tidings. The entire High Council is dead.'

"A piercing alarm was immediately activated, and in a moment's notice, I was surrounded by guards. I placed my hands in the air, sank my knees to the ground, and volunteered for restraint. One of the guards came around from behind me, pulled his weapon from its resting place, and tweaked a knob on its side. He placed the needles in the center of my forehead, and everything I saw faded quickly away.

"I awoke in the middle of a dimly-lit room, surrounded by metal walls and a large group of officials. In this case, however, not all of them were guards. One man in particular approached me as I recovered, and he extended his hand in a surprising display of courtesy. 'I am sorry you had to be treated this way,' he said. He assured me that he meant no offense, but also that they must treat matters of security with the greatest precaution.

"His name was Sobrius, and he introduced himself as the acting Council Chair. The political rule of Inanimis at that time was made up of the High Council, but there was also the lesser Council, which ruled over the more mundane, daily matters of the city. The Council would elect a Chair to serve as their representative to the greater ruling body. Fortunes were in my favor on this day, for things could have easily gone far worse for me at the hands of a more typical Councilor. While I knew nothing of Sobrius at the time, I would come to know him as one of the only reasonable members of the lot.

"I would later learn that his decency was, against all likelihood, the only reason he had earned his position; and it was certainly not due to the moral desirability of such a trait among the other Councilors. It was a rather ironic affair, all things told. During the course of appointing the Chair, each of the others had spent every possible effort ensuring that none of their competitors were elected to the position. Due solely to his lack of adversaries, Sobrius had somehow managed to receive the majority vote.

"Those who had cast their votes in his favor no doubt meant them as a throwaway, intended only to detract from the totals of their opponents. They never expected that such a scrupulous victor could emerge from such an unscrupulous cohort. The Councilors were far from relieved at the news, however, for they could never trust someone so truthful. Whatever stroke of luck led to his appointment as their Chair, here he stood before me, the spokesperson for what was now the sole ruling body of the city.

"Sobrius may have been kind, but his colleagues underestimated him if they assumed that he was weak. He implored me to speak – to tell them my identity and all I knew of what I had claimed at the gate. I gladly obliged, for this was the very reason I came to the city in the first place.

"My motives were simple, but it made the Councilors all the more suspicious of them. They were also not entirely unfamiliar with the name of Animulus. While not privy to all the deepest secrets in the blackened hearts of the High Council, the lower Council was entrusted with a great deal of confidential information, especially when it posed a threat to the progress of the city – and the Heretics were certainly that.

"Despite all the skepticism about why I would make such a damning confession of my own volition, Sobrius alone gave me the benefit of a charitable ear. Quelling the uproars of his fellow Councilors, he allowed me to speak freely in my defense. While the others argued and speculated about my possible motivations, Sobrius simply addressed me directly, and he asked me for whatever proof I could yield to vouch for my story. No physical evidence would have swayed them entirely, but I did possess one possibility.

"I tore off the shirt Avidus had given me, revealing the blistering start of the scars on my shoulder. I chastised them for their paranoia and doubt. Whether they chose to trust me or not, their High Council was dead, I reminded them. I asked no ransom, reward, nor even pardon for my brothers. I came there solely to aid them in resolving their dilemma, but in a way that suited all our best interests.

"The Councilors immediately erupted back into accusations of treachery and treason. But Sobrius, for the moment, stood silent. When even the Chair could not yet make up his mind, I was officially arrested, and a trial was scheduled with the Court. The full account is a long and exasperating story in itself, and I will spare you all of its details. Ultimately, for the second instance in my life, my fate was entirely in the hands of the Court.

"This time, however, fate was more to my favor, for the Council Chair is afforded a special position among the jury in matters of state; and it is Sobrius alone whom I have to thank for my eventual freedom. The other Councilors protested his involvement, due to his tendency to engage in that most annoying trait called reason. But alas, it was written clearly in their laws and engrained in tradition; and even the Councilors of Inanimis hold law and tradition sacred, when their dealings are seen in the daylight.

"For reasons I cannot fully know or explain, the Chair saw past the most convenient explanations. He saw deep into my thoughts, and somehow, he trusted me. As difficult as even that must have been, he managed a far more miraculous task: he persuaded the remainder of the Court that, while not entirely innocent, I was not guilty of the death of the High Council. They could not prove my complicity, and against all odds, justice prevailed."

"Thus, I was a free man, and the Council was left to decide what to do about issues far larger than me. Though they called it by a different name, the standard practices of enmity, deceit, and corruption were commenced to find replacements for the High Council. The mightiest in cogency would be chosen as Exercitus; the one most soothing in speech as Politicus; lastly, Legatus would be they who most represented the will of the majority. The procedures began, and they were long in duration, for every Councilor vied with all their guile to earn one of the few coveted positions. As the competition continued, no clear leaders emerged from the avarice.

"In all this time, I continued to rise into a position of respect in the eyes of Sobrius. While the Councilors were distracted, focusing more on their possible promotion into greater power than even the affairs of governance, the Chair continued to visit with me after my trial. Curiosity implored him to find out why I had come through so much toil, only to tell the Council such dreadful news, and why I still lingered in the city after doing so. Unlike the others, he looked closely at my actions, and he saw in them something seldom seen in the city.

"In our many conversations, I spoke often – and passionately – about my desire to change Inanimis for the better. 'The status quo shall not sustain us,' I contended – and Sobrius understood, if not always saying so. Often, he would counter my claims with reasoned arguments, in the spirit of constructive debate; but never once did he protest my core thesis, nor deny his underlying agreement. He was of like mind, but he was also forthcoming about his predicament: he knew not what steps he could possibly take to break free of the city's longstanding conventions. On this, I had an idea; and it would only require the attention of the Council.

"And so it was that, at the behest of Sobrius, I came to speak once again before the Council. I played no games and spoke perfectly plainly: I had a proposition for them, I explained, and my fee was a modest one. Should they choose to adopt my proposal, I required only a seat as their peer.

"Such a bold suggestion garnered only hysterical laughter from the Councilors at first. I believe many only humored me out of curiosity, to hear what must have surely been an absurd and amusing proposition. Whatever the reason, I was given the floor. 'I have a plan,' I told the Councilors. 'And it should be of great interest to you, for it ensures that almost all of you will receive a greater share of power.' And thus, their attentions were immediately ensnared, for now I was finally speaking their language.

"By not electing a new High Council, I explained, only a few of them lost the chance to gain a great deal, but the vast majority were guaranteed to gain a little. That is, only three individuals, none of whom were yet elected, could become a High Councilor. In contrast, in the absence of a High Council, each of them would have a share of a far greater role in ruling the city. When faced with the math, there was only one logical choice.

"Many Councilors scoffed at the idea — at first. I suspect their derision was due to a principled disdain for the idea's progenitor, more so than the idea itself. Despite intense debate on the matter, eventually, the shared lust for their individual power won the day. The Council convinced itself, largely of their own accord, that mine was simply too good a suggestion to be ignored. They took up their pens, and reform had begun. For the first time in the history of Inanimis, a law had been rewritten, rather than simply supplemented; a tradition had been changed to adapt to a new era.

"Having accepted my proposal, the Council also begrudgingly agreed to my fee. Even this was not without attempts by a few of the most cunning Councilors to have things both their way. Sobrius protested any protest, however; and by the end, I was sworn into my role as Councilor — after all the proper forms had been completed of course.

"Once again, albeit in a very different way, I had become a visible figure in the public eye of Inanimis. The news of my principles spread, for I took a prominent role alongside Sobrius in the movement for meaningful reform. Given this reputation, I gradually become known to the people as Modicus, for the name of an infamous Heretic could no longer suit me. Nevertheless, I embraced my new moniker whole-heartedly, for it served as a testament to my purpose. After a time, the former was almost entirely forgotten — although perhaps not exclusively for good."

6.5 \ Schism in the City

"Thus have I answered your question as to how I came to be here, and so too does the last stage of my story begin. Once officially a member of the Council, I had a formal means by which to vocalize my opinions; and I had a great many of them. Every aspect of the city's business seemed rife with inefficiency, and I grew to be held in high esteem among some of the more equitable Councilors for calling it out. Eventually, I would rise to a high degree of favor among many of them, and my first suggestion for improvement played a large role in bringing this advancement about.

"One of the most glaring examples of the city's inefficiency was its linear progression to the west. The movement of Inanimis was fueled in part by its need for resources, but also by the need to escape its own poisonous waste. For ages, the city bore its way through the fertile forests of the highlands, leaving a wake of destruction behind it, in the form of the Inviocassus. Upon reflecting on the problem, I realized the simplicity of the solution: the expansion could be slowed if we could consolidate the disposal of waste. I devised a system to utilize the existing Inviocassus; and in collaboration with the Department of Engineering, the system came to be.

"As you may recall, the previous system for expansion required two walls on each side. To the east, the space between the inner and outer walls was filled with waste. When it was full, it was time for the city to move once again; on each side, a new western wall was built, and the previous eastern wall was destroyed. In this way, the city advanced one step to the west. My idea was to eliminate the two-wall system for waste deposition, and replace it with one that sent the waste outward, over the vast area that was already the Inviocassus. The city's progress to date had left uncounted miles of wasteland behind it, and utilizing this existing space would eliminate the need for continued westward advancements.

"The system I envisioned consisted of two walls, running far along the Inviocassus, each with a single rail on the inner side. Between them would sit a device for traveling down the rails and depositing the material at the furthest side. Because of the great distance, it would take many years to reach the wall closest to the city again; by that time, the distant waste would have broken down enough to allow for the addition of more.

"Over the years, my reputation and authority in the city had grown tremendously, and it was thanks to simple insights such as this. Even those Councilors who disagreed with my principles could not help but concede the usefulness of my innovations. For practically every new aspect of city life to which I turned my attention, I found flagrant faults that could be easily improved with a bit of ingenuity. Ever as I advocated against a wrong approach, ever too was Sobrius strengthened in his own resolve.

"One of our most important reforms involved questioning the structure of the Council itself. Although the disagreement was long and wearisome, we were eventually victorious in enacting our revisions. The first proposition was to expand the Council, for its current state tended to result only in an impasse to any progress. When confronted with dilemmas that would benefit our people, the Council would refuse every meaningful solution. It became ever more apparent that the motivations of the Council were not in alignment with the wishes of the citizens, whom it claimed to represent.

"At first, the majority of Councilors were concerned solely with the depletion of their power – the very thing by which they had been swayed to dissolve the High Council. As time passed, however, and the Council dove more and more into the details of countless issues, an early quorum came to acknowledge how many things needed urgent improvement.

"Having amassed an assembly of reformists, we greatly increased the size of the Council. In doing so, we opened the Council for the first time to women, who have ever proven less rash than their counterparts. Over many long years, the Council has ultimately expanded more than tenfold, and thus does it reach a finer consensus concerning the true will of the citizens.

"As opposed to the selfish and short-sighted actions of the old Council, this broader perspective revealed a city that was at least as concerned with the problems of tomorrow as it was with the rewards of today. Together, Sobrius and I had a vision for a more efficient, yet more far-sighted, future for Inanimis; and we negotiated tirelessly with the full Council to ensure that our vision came to pass.

"Alas, our fates would not allow our vision to be, as time began to gradually reveal. Despite this increasing concern for the will of the populace, there was still much to overcome before sufficient change could occur – an immovable inertia, against which we were pushing to little avail. In each area for which I would advocate simplicity, there was an equally compelling drive among the more industrious to put my efficiency to use for expansion – a desire they concealed in the form of the word Progress. And as a twist of cruel humor, in my early efforts to halt the city's expansion, I myself had conceived of the very invention that would allow it to spread on a scale that would have been previously unfathomable.

"While the city was no longer obligated to move westward to escape the Inviocassus, it still had need of many resources from beyond its borders. It took only a slight modification of my rail system to employ it for the transportation of goods and people, from the heart of the city to the outer reaches of the world and back again, as often as needed. Over the years, the railwalls gradually reached outward – groping their way across the land in all directions; engulfing everything in their paths; shipping it back to the center for consumption; slowly bleeding dry the bounties of nature.

"Sobrius and I vehemently opposed the application of the railwalls for this purpose, having foreseen the inevitable depletion of our surroundings. Some inventions are perhaps of best use when used only in moderation. Yet

241

a crucial fact remained: the people of the city needed to be fed. Likewise, as leaders of the city, we were ethically bound to respect the will of the Council majority. Deceit would not befit our purpose, for we could never eliminate such a malignance by endorsing it ourselves.

"And so, we watched the development unfold. It seemed to happen slowly at first, with each acquisition of the frontier being justified as both necessary and judicious. Nevertheless, this eventually led to the state of the city as it is: the tentacles of Inanimis cover the whole of Limbus, but for two last remnants of uncharted wilderness at the edges of the world."

But not entirely unknown, thought Davis.

"As the years passed, the citizens continued their constant struggle between the forces of heedlessness and foresight. There were those that followed Sobrius and me, and our promotion of simplicity; yet so many others were drawn by the allure of expansion in the name of Progress. After all, it had been a precedent set from as far back through the ages as our histories could recall.

"Initially, these outlooks were no more than the common tendencies of individual Councilors; but over time, they became fully manifested as official parties of the Council. Thus, the cohesion of our legislature was fractured; what was one became severed in two. The division began with the formation of the first official faction, led by those of the Council who were indignant at our hindrance of their industrial advances. They called themselves the Interritus – the Undismayed – in defiance of those whom they claimed were merely afraid of Progress. They labeled these members of the Council the Trepidus, in spite; but it was a name the party embraced, as a testament to their reservations regarding the deeds of the Interritus.

"The Interritus accused the Trepidus of personal cowardice, but also of willingly instilling fear in the hearts of the citizens, for catastrophes the Interritus claimed would never come. The Trepidus responded in turn, accusing the Interritus of favoring only those pieces of legislation that supported their own economic benefit. Despite the inclination of the Council Chair, the Interritus held a clear majority in the early days of these new parties. While other issues were still debated, it was this fundamental question – expansion – that was at the core of the divide.

"Foremost in forming the Interritus as an official political party was their most outspoken and persuasive advocate: a man by the name of Prodigus. Ever did Prodigus long for anything that would bolster his own bank ledger, even far beyond the days when there was any need to worry for its welfare.

"I speak of him as if a relic of our past, but he may be found this very minute, behind closed doors in the city center, no doubt plotting ever grander visions of our future. Or perhaps, he may be found circling the stairs of the Council Chamber, like a vulture does the sky at the slightest scent of carrion – bartering, bribing, blackmailing, even begging for votes in support of his most recent schemes.

"As Council Chair, Sobrius decided that he would not officially endorse either party once they became formal entities, although he always made it clear to whom his allegiance belonged when it came time for a vote or debate. While not quite Chair, I was also in an unofficial position of greater authority, by way of my reputation among the Councilors. And yet officially, I was no more than a standard member. I could have publicly joined one side or the other, should I have so desired; and as such, I was lobbied intensely by both for espousal of their party.

"The Trepidus knew of my hesitations when it came to the industrial applications proposed time and again by the Interritus. The Interritus, on the other hand, respected me as a forward-thinking individual with admittedly good ideas, many of which they had already co-opted for their own desires. They knew of my ethical objections to their actions, but they viewed me as an indispensable ally, should they be able to somehow sway me into condoning their designs.

"To most, it was obvious with whom my allegiance fell, although I felt it best to stand in solidarity with Sobrius. Thus, I was the only other independent Councilor, formally endorsing neither party. The unity of the citizenship was more important, I reasoned. Unfortunately, the division of the Council had the opposite effect in the years that were to come, as I had rightly foreseen.

"Council sessions began to revolve more around vicious battles of slander and deception than honest discourse over the appropriate mode of action. These tendencies were not limited to the Council either. As the brain thinks, so acts the body. The citizens became as polarized as the Council itself. Depending on their own political propensity, they either claimed the Trepidus were foolish and obsolete, or the Interritus were foolhardy and oblivious. Civil life devolved into quarrels between neighbors who had otherwise been perfectly content to leave policy to others."

Animulus sighed a heavy breath of regret. The thought of the public plagued him most of all. *They are the people the Council has sworn to serve, and yet so many Councilors care to serve only themselves.*

"Despite our ample resistance, the longstanding tradition of Progress has managed to prevail at the hands of the Interritus. To say that it led to no good would be unfair; but there were certainly consequences to be found. Even after these few decades, we are beginning to feel them.

"Over time, as the city grew to cover most of the land, resources have become increasingly harder to come by. As with poor Immerens, the hardihood of the people has begun to wane. All the while, any goods the city can procure are used for increasingly industrial applications. Our food, air, and water have grown even more repugnant than afore; they weaken us, rather than nourish. Many grow sick at earlier and earlier ages; their minds fail them before they become old, or their bodies fail them and will never allow it. Even the cells within us have succumbed to the same ravenous greed as the city – to expand and conquer their neighbors at any cost.

"The vitality once possessed by the youth is giving way to a decrepit crawl into senescence. Meanwhile, the longevity of these frail bodies has continued to extend, so that the city is faced with the melancholic challenge of how to deal with its members who can no longer function as necessary. As ever, our creative adaptability has led to technological solutions to diagnose and address these problems as they develop. The key to doing so is to detect the issues early – to find them before they grew incurable. But these solutions are extremely expensive, and they are not available as a realistic option for a large proportion of the citizenship.

"The city's poor have become increasingly aware of the great disparity of wealth, along with access to the essential commodities it affords. Some of the more desperate and radical are convinced the situation is intentional – a calculated ploy to eradicate the poor. Even the more conventional members of the public deem it unjust; and rightly so. In their eyes, the Council looks upon their woes and does nothing, and that is as bad as if the cruel scheme had truly been purposeful. Thus, there is a great outcry by the sick and needy, and we are currently cast toward the brink of rebellion.

"As we gradually began to feel the effects of our improvidence, some of the more moderate members of the Interritus have become increasingly aware of the costs of their actions. And so, the balance of the Council is beginning to tip back into parity between parties. Still, it has not tipped far enough in favor of the Trepidus, as it surely must. At present, the Council is divided almost exactly in half – frozen in a stalemate between any actions at all, be they for good or for ill."

Animulus looked tensely toward the two opposing towers of the railwall.

"Several recent events stand out as a testament to the Council's polarization, and they pose perhaps the gravest danger we have ever known. One group in particular, the DMI – the Department of Metageophysical Inquiries – has been on the verge of what they claim to be a remarkable breakthrough. The department was initially developed by the Interritus as a means of investigating matters relating to the physical world, and everything beyond it. Its intention, of course, was geared toward technological applications that might aid in development.

"Over time, however, more theoretical research began to take hold, and numerous unsettling experiments led them to conclude that the physical world may not be exactly as we had imagined. None of their observations were lining up with their predictions, and soon a new consensus model of reality was favored. Ultimately, they concluded that the world as we know it consists of simultaneous dimensions – layers of reality, occupying the same space, but in ways that are inaccessible to our normal waking consciousness.

"The DMI claims that our current dimension is pressing upon the threshold of another, grander reality. Becoming more convinced of their theory and more enamored with its prospects, the Interritus, and Prodigus chiefly among them, proposed a study to investigate the possibility of breaking through this barrier – to break the Veil, as they call it.

"The Interritus promised a solution to all the city's problems, and despite the fervent protests of the Trepidus, much of the Council was seduced by the allure that this one final action might heal all our worldly hurts. After a long and livid debate, the Interritus leveraged their majority, and the Council approved the proposal.

"Having been granted authorization, the DMI began enacting their plan to study the Great Volcano as a mechanism. They seek to harness its great power, as a means to dislodge us from this dimension and enable passage to the next. This activity has only begun in the last few days, but I fear we are already beginning to witness the ill effects."

True to his allegiance, Animulus stared in trepidation at the violently erupting volcano. He needed to say no more, for his point was understood. Turning back to Davis, something drove him to confide in the ghost of this sorely remembered acquaintance.

"I know not what to do," said Animulus. "I fear we may have grappled with forces far beyond our understanding, and I fear it will not end well."

Knowing the true nature of the eruption, Davis tried to steer Animulus to matters that were much more pressing than the feeble attempts of his people to tinker with time and space.

"It is surely a mighty omen," said Davis. "But you are not the one who should be frightened of it."

6.6 \ Putting Pieces Into Motion

It was a total lack of consolation, and Animulus was appropriately exasperated. There were practical issues to deal with on this matter: an entire city would be looking to him should the world start collapsing out from under them, or should fire rain down from on high.

At the start of his tale, the Councilor had scarcely recognized how badly he needed the counsel of this long-dead ghost from his ill-repressed past. Upon first sight of the specter, the terror that filled his heart bade him only to escape as quickly as he could from the guilt that was unleashed from ever having to cross paths with him again.

But now, having recounted his journey through so many years and so many tribulations, Animulus detected something else. Somewhere past the panic, he sensed grander reasons for the appearance of this apparent apparition, motives subtler than vengeance for a deed long passed. Having finally arrived back at the present after so long a story, he cast off any remaining apprehension and sought his much-needed advice from this, the least expected source of wisdom.

"What am I to do then?" he asked desperately. "What am I to tell my people? Whatever it takes to stop the actions of the DMI, I will do it — the Interritus be damned."

Davis stood with his back to the mountain, and seeing that the ominous chaos emanating out from the volcano was clouding any hope of rational thought, he raised his palms toward the Councilor as to calm his nerves. He then turned them to the ground and gently waved them downward in a single sweeping gesture, as if convincing the earth itself to settle. Whether cause or coincidence, the violent explosions in the distance came to a gradual quiescence that mirrored the motion of his hands. At last, he spoke.

"You have come a long way, my friend," said Davis. "From the halls of the Heretics, where you first helped steer me on the path of my destiny; to the shores of the sea, where you first heard the voice of redemption; to the high walls of the city, which you have tried to save from fulfilling its own damnation. In all these places, you have followed your heart. And yet at times, as we know, it can lead us astray. But if it is pure — if it is determined to find the salvation that lies somewhere deep within — then it will always make its way back to the path on which it belongs."

Animulus was clearly shaken, but Davis pressed the issue without pause.

"So do I stand here before you, and I ask you to trust me as I once trusted you, when so long ago we learned of each other that we share the same purpose. Your story has taken you far already, but you must ask yourself in earnest: what do you want of its ending? What do you seek? What will you be? A savior, or a scoundrel; a knight, or a knave?"

Animulus by now had fallen to his knees in self-pity, tears streaming silently down the length of his cheeks at the mention of his many trials. For a moment, Davis was gone, and the Councilor was all alone atop the wall. He stared out over the Ashlands in disbelief. Talionis looked as peaceful as a sleeping child. The menacing clouds that had filled the midnight sky around it had entirely dissolved, giving way to the bright and waxing moon.

"I beg of you: fear not the mountain," said Davis from behind him now. "Change must ever come, and the way is often turbulent; but so too can it herald an evolution that is in the interest of us all."

Animulus rose from the concrete of the wall where he had fallen, gathered his composure, and arrived at a place where he was once again concerned with making logical sense of what was happening around him.

"I trust you," he confessed, "though I cannot justify why. I will tell my people not to hinder the plans of the DMI if you deem their work prudent."

Davis laughed heartily, and confusion returned to the Councilor's face.

"Prudent?" said Davis. "Far from it. The actions of the DMI are mere scratches at the surface of a door they could hardly nudge. Even so, they are correct in their assertions: we are indeed pressed upon the edge of a far grander reality. Yet there is but one way through the door, and they have not the key. Nevertheless, you should stop them if you can, as such meddling may slow us down just long enough to prove fatal."

Animulus nodded in acceptance of the task. Old grudges die slowly, and it suited a desire for reprisal he would not have easily admitted.

"And this door?" asked Animulus. "How are we to enter?" A nascent optimism began to grow — a vital grace for surviving trying times, and one that he had long desired, but almost abandoned hope of ever finding.

"I can only hope that we shall know when the time arrives," said Davis. "In the meantime, there is still much to do on this side of the door before we can trouble with trying to open it."

Davis turned from the Councilor, and stepping to the northern edge of the wall, he cast his attention to an even bigger threat than Talionis. Far off in the distance, there radiated a distasteful glow from the lights at the heart of Inanimis.

"The city has sprawled across almost every corner of Limbus," said Davis. "It is voracious, consuming everything in its path, while perpetually discontented with the harvest. And yet, there are but two regions of the wild that even the avarice of Inanimis has not been able to exploit. What do you know of these last remnants of wilderness?"

The Councilor joined Davis on the wall, and for now both the sight and the fear of the mountain were behind him.

"If they have any proper names, I do not know them," said Animulus. "None have ever ventured their way. The first is far to the north, and so overgrown with an impenetrable wall of deadly thorns that it has not yet been worth the effort it would take to invade it."

Davis smirked, but the Councilor didn't notice, and he carried on ahead.

"The second is far to the south, and no more than a barren desert. It is the very same region as that of the map I gave you so long ago, in which there dwelt only blank space."

This time, Animulus paused – and unexpectedly, it would seem. The thought of this place dazed him at once, and he lost his train of thought altogether. Davis interjected and roused him from his stupor.

"Two poles," said Davis. "And though they are separated by the whole width of the world, they are intimately related in a way you have yet to understand. You are also wrong to think that none have ever ventured their way. In the north lies the Guardian's Glade, though to call it by such a name in this age of the world is both inaccurate and irreverent. In this realm, the will of the Lord of the Land prevents any uninvited from venturing that way." *Or almost any*, he tacitly corrected.

Animulus gazed at him, perplexed. As neither Prospector, Heretic, nor Councilor had he ever heard rumor of this so-called Lord in the North.

"The Lord of the Land?" he asked.

Davis answered with as little context as he could, with what he hoped would suffice as a warning that Animulus was not to trifle with this power.

"The Lord is treacherous, and covetous, seeking nothing less than dominion over all of Limbus. In fact, it proclaims indefinitely to have obtained this feat already. Despite its declarations of ultimate authority, the Lord fears losing power even more than it desires gaining it. It is fearful and paranoid, dreading more than anything the upheaval of its tyrannical claim over the whole of Limbus. It has valid reason for this paranoia, of course: there are always others who vie in secret for the authority which the presiding Lord possesses, and the title is continually being seized by mutinous acts of duplicity.

"Long before the arrival of the city in the west, the Lord did possess an active ownership over a great expanse of the world. Upon the intrusion of Inanimis, however, the realm of the Lord began to shrink, but willfully, in fear of having to actually contend for what it deemed its sole birthright. The Lord justified this in its mind with one denial or another – a show of its unmatched generosity, or the simplification of the demands of its rule. But do not mistake this retreat for weakness; a desperate despot is all the more deadly. The small extent of its territory at this point in the world is in no way an indication that the Lord is any less dangerous, for the evils it embodies have their foundations deep in the making of the world."

"Interesting," said Animulus, clearly intrigued. *And what of the south?* He almost brought himself to ask, but he had neither the will nor the need.

"In the south, another power altogether bars your entry to its realm."

"Another power altogether?" asked the Councilor. He was no less shocked by the existence of anything far across the exhaustive expanse of desert. "Who could dwell in such an inhospitable place?"

There was no immediate answer. Davis cracked a wry smile and began reciting a meandering rhyme – evasive, but not entirely incomprehensible.

The ground likely seemed rather arid to you
And unable to offer much more than a view
Yet deep in the soil dwell roots that could grow
The most splendid garden you ever could know

Much have you questioned and far have you roamed
Little was owed you, but much has been shown
Low have you fallen and high have you climbed
Yet one thing there is that you have yet to find

I remind you of this in this most pressing hour
As the desert for me once put forth one first flower
High up on the cliff where the waves called your name
May you meet the great spirit you sought long in vain

Animulus retreated a single step at the implication, shaking his head to the side in bewilderment.

"No," he muttered. "How could it possibly be true? I sought long in secret for any news I could gather of the Guardian, for such an allegiance was a subject I could never bear to broach with my kinsfolk in the city. Despite all my efforts searching beyond its walls, none anywhere in Limbus had any more news than me. The last I knew, Praestes had been slain by your own hands; and yet here is the very same perpetrator, standing before me, after having himself been sacrificed by the hands of another."

The hands of another... he repeated to himself, cast deep into thought.

"The hands of another," he said aloud, snapping out of the daze. "That explains it, at least in part. In the fury of our debate, we hardly remembered the creature was present, but it was not the first we saw of it. On that same day of your doom, my brothers and I were approached in the wilderness by this being, the likes of which we had never before seen. It named itself Hortulanus, and against our better judgement, we trusted it somehow.

"It was a simple creature, childish even, and it implored us to follow — somewhere important, it said, and somewhere we could otherwise never hope to go. It spoke no direct word of our destination, but when I asked it to show us the way, it simply waved its hand before my eyes, and an irrefutable, dreamlike trance overtook me. I fell backwards in delirium, and before I could even hit the ground, I was lost in a euphoric void.

"When I awoke, I felt the hot sun on my face, and in opening my eyes I found that I was lying in the dry, sparse grass atop a bluff by the sea. I had never seen nor heard of this place before, but it was the very place where you would soon meet your swift demise. As we awoke, we soon learned that we were not alone: the High Council of Inanimis was also present. We became so overtaken with quarrelling that we never gave ourselves the chance to ask for any explanation before your outline appeared over the edge of the nearest dune, and events so quickly slipped out of our control."

Davis nodded, for none of this was news.

"You were wise to trust Hortulanus," he said, "and yet so foolish when you arrived at the place where you were led. But despite all our subsequent struggle, we would not be where we are now without the actions of that day. It is but a small comfort, I know; but such is the way of fate. As for the day itself, you are accountable for much, but you are not to be blamed for the reason I was laid upon the altar of Expiatio. I am sorry if those images have haunted your dreams. My own choices led me to that end, and a power far greater than either of us would not have had it any other way."

"My journey since that day has indeed been arduous," said Animulus. "But still you have not told me what happened to you in the moment that blade struck stone. You vanished into thin air, only to arise from the ashes of the mountain, on this day, of all days, so far into the future. There is much to explain of your long absence."

"And there is no way I could adequately explain it," said Davis. "For now, a ghost I shall remain. I bite my tongue not in derision, my friend, but because you literally cannot understand. In due time, all will be made clear. In the meantime, there is dire work that is in dire need of attention."

"Then what must I do?" asked Animulus again.

He stood now straight and tall, shaking off the weight that was cast upon him at the first oppressing sight of this ghoul. He longed for clearer answers, surely; but against all odds, his faith had been reborn from the ashes along with the hooded stranger who descended the slopes of Talionis. Above all else, he understood that there were urgent issues at hand. While the answers to his many inquiries would have to wait a while still, this most recent one was exactly the kind of question that Davis could now answer.

"First, there is much to be done on the surface where we stand. Your arrival in Inanimis has brought about the liberation of the minds of many of your people. It has also acted as a catalyst for the disingenuous motives of those who strive only for greater power. Their treachery runs far deeper than you know. Your people have been divided in two, and what little harmony existed in the city at first has now been all but lost. Inanimis is barreling rapidly down the path of its own destruction, and with it will go the whole of the world. I charge you with the task of uniting your people, to steer them from this course and into a new era of prudence.

"Second is a task that runs much deeper. You have turned your eyes to worldly matters, but in doing so, lost sight of the one whom you sought above all. The voice from beyond calls to you still, though you have not heard it for a great many years. 'When your wisdom awakens within you, you may find me...' spoke the voice, and still it goes unanswered.

"Through much abasement, the truly wise will come to know how much they have yet to learn. In that sense, perhaps wisdom may never be fully attained; and still, I bear witness that it has awoken within you. And so do I charge you also with this task: fulfill the prophecy you heard in your heart on that day by the sea so long ago."

Animulus was struck silent, but he nodded subtly in acceptance.

"So must you labor, both outward and inward. These domains are more connected than you appreciate, so much so that you will not achieve success in one in the absence of the other. In both cases, you must right the wrongs of your kin. But as you go forth, you must also remember something crucial that you have too long forgotten."

Davis placed a gentle hand on the shoulder of Animulus, and only then was the Councilor finally convinced that he was real.

"You are not alone," said Davis.

It was a comfort, but as with all words that touch too near to those one needs most, they brought forth all the pain they were intended to alleviate. The Councilor's throat had tightened completely, a last floodgate for sentiments he could barely hold back.

"Like the people of your city, your own being has been divided, fractured into separate pieces where there had once been only unity. Before you can hope to heal your people, you must first heal yourself. The parts of the whole must come back together, for together they equal far more than their sum."

Animulus could hardly get the words out, though he longed desperately to speak them. He knew exactly what he needed to find.

"Where do I begin?" he asked.

Davis reached his other hand out from underneath his cloak, and he stretched it outward to offer over an old and folded piece of paper.

"There is a glaring void in the map you once gave me..." said Davis.

The moment the Councilor's grip clutched the paper, the apparition was gone. Lightning struck the mountainside, and the storm was renewed with full force. The man's image had vanished, but his voice had remained — though only long enough to utter three remaining words.

"Fill it in."

6.7 \ The Sapient Sage

Davis closed his eyes, and when he opened them again, he was standing in the middle of a lush garden of indescribable beauty. He strolled leisurely through the flora, surrounded on all sides by forms both distinctive and diverse. He brushed his hands gently against their leaves, admired the great height of their stems, and imagined the vast network of roots spreading through the ground beneath him. There were innumerable different designs, each with its own special splendor; each with its own special role in Elisium.

Long did he wander in awe, appreciating delights both obvious and subtle, and not once did he wish to arrive at his destination prematurely. Eventually, he did come to a small pool, under the crown of an immense tree growing by its side; and he knew that he had found it at last − or that it had found him. Here by this spring, in the heart of Elisium, dwelt the Proavia Tree, the most ancient of all forms of Life in this realm.

A beautiful woman was awaiting him at the water's edge, basking in the faint streams of moonlight filtering down through the leaves. Davis held a small piece of paper in his hand, but he set it softly on a rock beside the pool, for he needed it no more. He had arrived in Elisium, and only further patience was now required of him. And the words he knew well, for he had read them carefully, and much of their meaning was evident from the first.

To Our Greater Self,

> *The wisdom of Life is hidden in plants*
> *They've no need to wander, to weep, or to dance*
> *The leaves that they shed have no sense of their roots*
> *Yet in time they arrive and rise back through the shoots*
>
> *It seems that their death was a sad lot indeed*
> *When one cannot see the whole truth of the need*
> *For most of the tree will survive through the cold*
> *Thanks in part to their kin who will never grow old*
>
> *We find as we wind our way back to the stem*
> *Through the function of branches connecting again*
> *What seemed like so many parts largely divided*
> *All share the same roots and are clearly united*

To our leaves as they fall,

The Sapient Sage

Davis did not look back — to the note, or indeed to anything before it. By now, he assumed he had fully shed his past — that deciduous part of him which, though it demands so much of our time in its brief moments of supremacy, was not all that we are, or all that we'll be.

"I see that you have set well in motion the steps you must take," said the woman. She smiled, but her tone was solely pragmatic. She did not yet pull her attention from the rays of moonlight diffusing down to the ground.

"I hope so, my lady," answered Davis with respect. "And while I do not know the full extent of the ending to which they may lead, I should like to think I am beginning to see things more clearly."

The woman turned to greet him properly; and though her demeanor was kind and her sight brought him joy, so too was she onerous to behold.

"It is good to see you, Sophias," said Davis as their eyes finally met.

"It is good to see you too, Davis," she said in response. "Though such a name hardly suits you any longer."

She was a gentle soul, not at all like the occasionally gruff Sages of the lower levels. She was tall, and slender, and looked as if she sprouted straight out of the ground where she stood in the grass. She fit perfectly with her time and place, and Davis knew that there was more to her beauty than her regal but humble appearance would ever dare to suggest.

"You have managed to discover so much about yourself," said Sophias. "And yet, there is ever more to learn as we explore the uncharted regions of our nature. We are but one part of something much larger than ourselves — a fact which most of the natural world implicitly accepts, but which the waking mind often fears as an obstacle in its quest for everlasting glory."

"This I know, my lady," said Davis.

"You are no doubt familiar," she said, "but if you were to truly know this, in every facet of your mind, then there would be no need for your visit, and the troubles of our world would be over."

Davis bowed meekly, and only then did the Sage continue.

"Even a fool can easily accept that they are a part of something bigger than themselves alone; for everywhere we look, there are various other entities, navigating their way just the same as ourselves. But it is less easy to understand what it really means to be a part of something so large. Despite all your great progress, you are still barely making your way back from the outermost branches of your being."

"I don't understand," said Davis. He thought, for some foolish reason, that this visit with the Sage would be simpler than those that came before.

Sophias turned her back to Davis once again, resuming her gaze at the leaves of the giant tree above them and the moonlight shining through it. And as she did so, the outline of the Proavia itself began to glow. The leaves radiated with a beautiful iridescence all their own, but one that had been hidden from his sight until now.

Sophias walked around the side of the tree, and she pointed to a single meager light, blossoming on the tip of a minuscule part of its great crown.

"A tree may be a metaphor for a great many things," said Sophias. "For now, you may think of it as a symbol for the evolution of your kind. We are all descended from one root – all separate branches on one Tree of Life. We are here," she gestured, "but the many other branches represent the many other forms of Life, which time and the struggle for existence have crafted."

Tiny flickers of light glimmered across the surface of the crown as she spoke these words. From far enough away, the Proavia might look like a single shape; but from this close, and with each leaf emitting its own light, Davis realized just how many countless leaves made up this one body. The lights reflected off the pool below it, just as it shined in the moonlight from above; and its own brightness was enhanced so that the entire garden shone with an overwhelming and ineffable aura.

But as quickly as she revealed them to him, Sophias dimmed these other lights, and the glow in Elisium was greatly lessened. She brought his attention back to the original blossom in question; and on its own, it now seemed forlorn and insufficient. In a sudden contrast, the garden fell dark and felt dreary, compared to the fleeting brilliance he had just witnessed.

"Your perceptions of the realm in which we dwell are entirely biased by your position in the tree, as you try in vain to grasp an understanding of its grander structure. You have come to know the forces at work in the world, but you perceive them through an anthropomorphic lens: they manifest in human symbols, and you label them in human terms. And even humans cannot agree upon these perceptions, for as closely related as all people may be, they have nevertheless wandered far and wide down different pathways. Humans are but one race, on one tiny branch in the furthest reaches of the tree; even so, there are yet many leaves on its many constituent branches.

"Other people come from different branches than yourself; and thus, they would know these forces by different names entirely. And should the words mean much the same, you might have no way of knowing it. On the contrary, different words from different tongues may have slightly different meanings, for they carry with them the weight of their use through the years. It is for precisely this reason that words fall so short as a satisfying means of communication. What you call one thing, someone else may call something else – and though you should look upon the very same thing, your perceptions of it shall differ, due to the words with which you label it."

She walked around the perimeter to a different section of the tree.

"Other beings come from even more distant branches, and so they do not commune in a language of your sort at all. This does not mean that they do not communicate, of course. Every part of the tree is a part of the whole; and while life-forms surely differ in a great many ways, so too are there rules of the game by which all must abide."

"So it seems," said Davis. "And yet the differences are all too evident."

"If you only ever look for divergence, it is all you will find, and all will seem separate. But if you look as well for unity, you will find it in spades."

"Is this why I'm here?" asked Davis. He did not mean to rush the wisdom of Sophias, but he was also not sure that he could put all these pieces into their proper place on his own.

"In part," said the Sage. "What you once saw as separate, you must now see as one. Of course, logic also tells us that life-forms are separate indeed. How else could they interact as they do? But, on another scale, they are a part of the same whole. They are all tips of the same Tree of Life – all cells in the same Being."

They can't be both separate and together, he felt instinctively, and Sophias knew his mind.

"Why of course they can," she laughed. "We simply need to consider both truths from the proper perspective. And this perspective takes the form of another Great Paradox: The Inseparability of Separate Entities."

Davis didn't answer, and seeing that the revelation did little to comfort him, the Sage took a step back to try another approach.

"When you would catch a fish by your home on the shore, how could you have caught the creature if it was a part of you?"

Now that is a ridiculous question. It seemed to make his point precisely.

"You obviously couldn't," he answered. "We are separate beings. I was not a part of the fish, and the fish was not a part of me."

"Correct," said Sophias. "You can't catch a fish if it is not there. If there were no such different things as you or the fish, then we would have no need to have named them accordingly." The Sage smirked, for she couldn't resist a brief tangent to make her point twofold. It was no paradox, but rather a truth that was entirely logical. "And yet," she continued, "you would surely be startled to know that humans are in fact a kind of fish."

The notion clearly offended the man, for he had never considered it; and while he had no quarrel with the fish, it still seemed such a lowly creature.

"How so?" he asked dubiously.

"You are descended from fishes, and though you have adapted for land and have thus changed greatly in form, a fish you will ever remain."

"I'm not so sure I understand," he said. The man was still skeptical, due in no small part to the blow to his ample primate pride. "There are plenty of fishes living alongside humans. How can a human be a fish?"

Sophias waved her hand, and the light far out at the tip of the tree expanded, illuminating more branches, reaching further back in the tree and encompassing a larger portion of the total crown.

"What we call the 'fishes' of today are merely some of the descendants of the fishes of long ago. Some of these ancestors gave rise to the first vertebrates to make a bold and momentous transition: to transcend the Sea and take to the Land."

She gestured to the glowing branches as she spoke. Two small lights flickered from opposite ends of the glowing region of the crown; they traveled back along the branches, winding and weaving, until they collided at the very same node where the light first began.

"Today's 'fishes' have retained many of the traits of their ancestors, whereas many other descendants have diverged more noticeably from that ancient form; but the 'fishes' of today are no more a fish because of it. All the descendants of that ancestor are equally related to it, regardless of their superficial composition. And thus, all descendants are, in equal parts, a fish."

Davis scratched his head. *I am literally a fish?* This was not the least surprising revelation he'd encountered in all his time in Limbus.

"And that is far from the only way you are united," continued Sophias. "When you cooked the fish over the fire and ate of its flesh, what then? Where was the fish then?"

This was another deceptively simple question, and he felt it a trick.

"Part of it I ate, and the remains I would bury in the ground."

"And what would occur when you filled in the dirt?" asked the Sage.

"A flower sprang forth." *And a new life was formed,* he realized.

"And what of the part that you could in fact consume?" she asked again.

"It would satisfy my need for the flesh of another."

"For a time," she said. "But why did you have need of the fish at all?"

Davis was surprisingly reluctant to answer. It was such a fundamental experience, but it was one that he was incapable of questioning at the time; and in all the time since then, he had somehow never thought to do so.

"It provided me nourishment," he said eventually. "It gave me energy."

"And what does that actually mean?" *Consider how you are made.*

Again, he found it hard to answer. But just as she suggested, he thought about what comprised him, and what comprised the fish.

"I took what was a part of the fish and turned it into a part of me."

"And there you have it," said the Sage in a familiar tone. "You are both separate and together. The fish lives in you now, for a time, until even those parts of you turn into other forms. And so will you both eventually become a part of something else entirely."

She paused, hoping there was no need to elaborate. Davis stood still and did not speak. As perplexed as he was, the Sage was equally persistent.

"What once belonged to others become the parts of you, just as those parts of you will in time belong again to others. Separate as we may be, we all depend entirely on one another."

Davis insisted the Sage had not caught him in her ruse. His tone had turned from that of a discerning spiritual scholar upon arrival in Elisium, to that of a spoiled child – resilient noncompliance in the face of proven error.

"Just because I ate it doesn't mean it's the same as me," he said. He tried to rationalize it however he could, in sheer defiance of what it might mean to accept it. "I don't see a need to invoke any deeper meaning in the process at all. The fish is separate from me, and therefore I can eat it."

"And where does that energy go when you're done?" asked the Sage. Her voice seemed to grow, developing into the closest she could come to being forcefully assertive. Even now, it was far too simple for Davis, and yet too complicated, as if the weight of her knowledge was a tiresome burden.

Sophias continued in a firm but gentle tone:

Why must you eat if you need not the energy?
As you have such a need, how then does it flow?
How could the ground afford those new flowers,
From the fish in the earth that you put to rest so?

Davis could not admit an answer to these questions. His primal urges were clouding his vision once again, demanding that he pay them their due. He turned from the Sage in anguish. With every insistence made by the Sapient Sage, the impulse of individuality within him fought equally hard in stride. It yearned for recognition, battling with an unruly desperation that only one on the verge of imminent defeat can muster.

Another part of him looked to Sophias, waiting for her to put an end to this lowly insurgence for him – to ease the unrest escaping from deep in the dungeons of his mind. Sadly, like all those before her, the Sage could not conquer it for him. But she could help as she may, for she could not bear to lose him, and neither could the rest of Limbus.

It was as though he were a leaf on a wave, crashing against the shore and struggling to stay on dry land. He would try to hold on to his progress, so sure he had finally made it, only to be swept back into the water at the arrival of another wave. Only at the highest tide did he stand any chance of remaining, when the furthest inward surge is followed at last by the lesser waves of an outgoing current.

Sophias understood both causes – resistance and persistence – and she would not yield. The Sapient Sage was not about to let him give up now, when momentum seemed so firmly on his side this turn through the cycle. She knew that she need only wait out the tide, and continue pushing him closer to solid ground. Seeing his strife, she spoke softly in a pacifying tone.

"The energy never leaves the system; it only moves about, flowing from one form to another. And thus have we arrived at another Great Paradox: The Permanent Impermanence.

"Nothing exists forever; but neither does it truly end. Things perpetually change forms, exchanging the gifts of creation with one another for eternity. Some hoard these blessings for as long as they can; but in the end, we all must give, as we've been given."

Davis looked again to the Proavia Tree, for as Sophias spoke its light began darting back and forth excitedly between the branches. The energy flowed throughout the tree, swirling around in a brilliant display, like white lightning, leaping among the millions of leaves.

Individual blossoms sputtered on and off as the lights arrived, and then fled; but despite all this dynamic wavering, the total brightness casting down on their faces never so much as flickered.

Davis stared intently at the dancing lights. He saw each and every one of them, flashing about from one twig to the next — millions of separate chemical reactions, repeating endlessly in all directions, in this stochastic yet systematic manner.

Looking up at the Proavia Tree and basking in its glow, Davis felt the surge of the furthest incoming wave. He longed now for nothing more than to surrender — to simply be a part of it, whatever it was.

As these thoughts floated away into the clear night sky, the millions of separate lights before him appeared to fuse together. The furious uproar from the dungeons of his mind was washed away in a sea of serenity behind him, as he lay in peace on the shore.

Whereas before he saw millions of separate processes, he now saw only a single magnificent aura of the purest and most beautiful light. The sphere expanded, passing over his body in an explosive burst, and then it waned, leaving behind only the dim natural beauty of the humble Proavia, shining softly in the moonlight.

I don't have to long to be a part of it anymore, he understood.

I already am.

"I'm sorry, my lady," confessed Davis as he hung his head low.

"I know, my child," said Sophias. A proud smile had come to her face.

He thought about explaining all the conflicting emotions that had biased his thoughts, but in looking upon her, he realized there was nothing more that need be said. Sophias knew, and Davis himself suspected, that he was almost to a place where such emotion would matter no longer.

"I think I understand the Paradoxes," said Davis, "and I see how they could trouble my lesser mind."

"You see pieces of them," said Sophias. "And the truth is that they are hardly paradoxical at all. They seem that way, when our mortal perceptions shroud our better judgement; but in reality, they are purely the laws by which Nature exists."

Davis stood idle, still mesmerized by the blissful sensation that had overtaken him at the moment of his epiphany. Yet this was not an epiphany in the sense that he acquired some new and esoteric information; but rather, that he was finally able to unchain himself from the denial of things he knew already. The Sage could tell that he had done so, but time was of the essence if he was to fully evolve beyond his biases.

Sophias continued, not wanting to break him of his rapture, but needing to bring his attention back to the tasks still ahead of him.

"Yet in spite of all your latent wisdom, it will mean nothing if you do not use it toward its proper end. Formidable forces are on the move: forces more powerful than you can imagine; forces that strive, among other things, to undo all your great progress and unweave the fabric of your world."

Thinking he knew vaguely of whom the Sage implied, his disposition turned serious. He tried to regain both his composure and humility, and to remember his role at this point as the Steadfast Sage. In time, he hoped that he too would become Sapient, but even all the wisdom in the world may not prevent an impure heart from faltering, when faced with choices on the verge of a great cataclysm.

"As of now, we have focused mostly on the sanguine side of Nature. We have emphasized beauty and harmony in Life, for there is much to be seen therein, if one is so inclined to examine it. Yet, everything in Nature exists in the balance of opposites. In this realm, as in the Universe at large, there exist the complementary forces of Order and Disorder."

"I understand," said Davis, for this aspect of his mission was perfectly clear to him. "I will do what I can to conquer the forces of Disorder."

"Say not such wicked words, my apprentice!" said the Sage, and her expression turned grave. "You do not understand. The forces of Nature are forever swaying in balance – ebbing and flowing in response to each other.

While our own penchants may lead us to favor one form or another, it is not so simple as one being Good while the other is Evil. These words are often used, but it is a much more difficult matter to define them."

She pointed again to the wide crown of leaves over their heads.

"Even the grandiose splendor of the noble Proavia exists as a function of its own self-interest. It reaches this impressive height and breadth solely because of the need to rob its competitors of the rays of the sun. Are these deeds Evil? I am not so rash as to say, for the truth is complex."

"I'm sorry," said Davis. *Perhaps it's best if I just listen for a time.*

"Every aspect of Nature exists because it can fulfill a particular purpose – a niche in its environment. Things may seem unsightly, without value, or even downright evil by our own calculations; but this does not mean that they have no part to play in the whole of creation. But if one force tries to conquer its counterpart, or achieve more for itself than what it is due, the world is thrown out of balance, and it is left with only the challenge of restoring it."

"I don't understand," said Davis, giving in so soon after resolving to be patient. "It sounds as though you're saying that everything in nature is exactly as it should be, and that by attempting to control it, I only risk disturbing the delicate balance. Do we have no role to play in the world? Are we to merely drift with the currents that pull us through life? And if so, then what am I even here to do? For a time, I thought that answer clear to me, but now I'm not so sure that anything matters at all."

Sophias looked at him kindly, partly pleased by his apparent motivation for the tasks that lay ahead, but partly invoking her own ample patience.

"You are certainly not here to conquer Limbus," she stressed. "No more than Inanimis or the Lord of the Land. You are here instead to achieve the very balance I have been describing. Things in Limbus are most certainly not all as they should be – and even Limbus is a tiny sliver of all that there is. And so, as in any small system, things may be far outside the equilibrium of the greater realm. In that sense, your psyche is riddled with the human prejudices it has acquired since its inception, and these will fight viciously to stop you from transcending your limited perception."

"What prejudice?" asked Davis, but earnestly. Even so, he slipped back into the very human state of desperation, as a man sick of living with his longstanding problems might speak. "I feel that I have overcome so many of my preconceptions, and at this point I want nothing more. I'm ready to let them all go," he griped. "I want to be free of them."

"Preconceptions are not themselves a disservice, so long as they are not misconceptions. For one: your use of the word 'I' is an interesting choice. It is not intrinsically wrong, although I wonder if you know what it means."

"Of course I do," said Davis. "How could I not? It refers to me."

"And what are You?" she asked, calling out his misplaced confidence.

"As I am now, I have only a guess," he said. "But as for what I was, I am quite sure of it."

"And what was that?" asked the Sage.

"I was human," said Davis with pride.

"Truly," said Sophias. "And an ape, and a mammal, and a fish, and a vertebrate besides, as we have already established. And even those are only the outer edges of your family tree, for your genealogy runs far deeper than that. More to the point, why is there a need for the word 'I' in the language of humans?"

"To distinguish me from others as a distinct individual," he said.

Sophias grinned and spread her hands out widely before her, as if Davis were to see the same invisible truth that lay in front of them. He didn't.

"I assume we've arrived at another Paradox," he teased.

"One of utmost importance," responded the Sapient Sage.

When are they not? thought Davis with the same sardonic air.

"Precisely," said Sophias. The sarcasm didn't escape her attention; it just wasn't warranted. "The Paradoxes are all of great importance, but few will be more instrumental to your success than this."

"And what is the name of this Great Paradox?" asked Davis.

At the mention of relevance, he was once again genuinely intrigued. While at times he lost heart from the weight of all the requisite wisdom, he had never lost sight of his purpose.

"The Illusion of Individuals," she answered.

"The Illusion of Individuals?" he said, while doing a poor job hiding the offense he took at the implication. "What's illusory about it? Have we not covered this ground before? We already agreed that I was dependent upon others, and that we are all descended from a common root; but we also agreed that I was clearly different than others."

"Your cynicism betrays your weakness," said Sophias. "It is clear that such an issue touches too near to your latent human need for validation. Need I remind you of the grave misconceptions with which you entered into our conversation? Should I allow you to carry on in your journey, blind to the trouble that troubles you most?"

The Sage spoke frankly but maintained an amiable tone, like a patient and loving mother trying to lead a stubborn child to comply with her wishes and their own best interests. Davis bowed his head in deference.

"Though neglecting the broader perspective, you are not incorrect in your assertion. Quite obviously, there are many differences between people. You are separate from them as you are separate from the fish. In much the same way, you are also not as independent of them as you may think. But as you noted, we have established that, and it is not the focus of this Paradox."

"Then what is the Illusion of Individuals?" asked Davis.

"The Illusion lies in how we define an individual in the first place," said Sophias. "You were no doubt different from your fellow humans, and thus you were an individual in one sense; but to think of yourself as such would be to ignore the numerous parts that compose you. This truth permeates every aspect of Life, but let us focus for now on your body as an example.

"The human body is a collective comprised of trillions of cells — a number far greater than the number of stars in the galaxy they inhabit. And each of these cells is very much alive in its own right; although, they would not survive long on their own, without the help of their kin. Furthermore, each cell is itself a collective of smaller constituents. Thus, the body is a collective of smaller collectives.

"Yet, on each level of scale at which a collective is formed, that collective obtains properties unlike those of its components. It takes on emergent properties, and it becomes an entity all its own, unlike any below it on the lower levels. In any case, how can we consider the collective a single entity when it is so clear that it is not singular? Conversely, as the collective acquires characteristics unique to that level of organization, how could we not consider it an entity on its own?"

The questions were rhetorical, but still the Sage gave Davis a moment to process all he heard. He didn't respond, and it wasn't clear that any extra time was helping.

"Let me explain by extending our example further downward in scale," said Sophias. "Long ago in the history of the world, the largest forms of life that existed were the ancestors of modern-day bacteria — and they have far more descendants besides, when you consider what I am about to tell you. These ancestors were examples of what some might call a 'prokaryotic' cell. Countless species of this kind still exist as individuals in the environment, each striving on its own for survival and competing with its neighbors. But these species have simply retained one ancient form of individuality.

"Other prokaryotes took a different approach, however: some of these organisms joined forces over evolutionary time, when the benefits of their cooperation outweighed those of competition. These prokaryotes grouped together, dividing up the labors of Life to form a different kind of cell altogether — a 'eukaryotic' cell — and it is this type of cell that eventually gave rise to you and the Proavia Tree alike. The tree's body, like your own, is in truth an enormous civilization of cells. Again: the body is a collective of smaller collectives — a social group of smaller social groups.

"Despite all this, it would not be improper to label one of your cells as an individual entity, any more than it would be improper to call your body an individual person. At the same time, we would be equally correct to call you a collective of many little collectives. The Illusion of Individuality does not imply that individuals do not exist; but rather, that they are not actually individuals at all, and that the concept of an individual is relative.

"A single prokaryotic cell and a single eukaryotic cell could equally be called individuals; but the latter is actually a group of the former, existing on a different level of organization. Likewise, we would call both the human body and a single prokaryotic cell an individual organism, but the former is a collective of a collective of the latter. And remember: a collective acquires properties that do not exist for its components. In uniting, they transcend the limitations of their ancient form and arrive at a higher existence.

"There is more to this story, however. The cells of the body are obviously related closely to one another; it would be easy to see how they could get along so well. As such, you might be inclined to make light of their feat of cooperation. But the same cannot be said for the group of prokaryotes that evolved to exist as a single eukaryote.

"It also calls us back to the Inseparability of Separate Entities, for to survive as a human requires more than even the countless cells of your own composition. Human life as we know it also requires the presence of tiny symbiotic bacteria, such as those that live in the gut and aid in digestion, or those that live on the surfaces of the body and protect against invasion. Without the aid of these distant relatives, a single human body would not be able to exist. And as we have noted, neither can an individual human survive long without other members of its species.

"In short, close kinship is not required for these transitions to occur; even highly different entities can unite under common purpose when the circumstances require it. And second, humans are utterly dependent upon cooperation, on both the microscopic and macroscopic scales."

Davis had never really thought of his existence in this way; but now that the Sage walked him through these basic facts, he had to admit that it provided a new perspective on what it meant to be alive.

"It's a lot to process," he said. He was not unwilling, but he needed to contemplate these concepts far longer for their full significance to sink in.

"Then let me help you expedite the process," said the Sage. "What we think of as an individual entity is in reality an entire ecosystem, itself made of smaller ecosystems, existing as one entity across many levels of scale. Life consists of groups, made of groups, made of groups. And this great ladder has been ascended through the triumph of cooperation over conflict at each respective level. But for humanity, the picture is not yet complete.

"Despite this pattern being written into the very nature of our being, we fail to see these truths and apply them to our own existence. Humans long for independence so greatly that they ignore their interdependence – to each other, and to the countless other forms of creation. Even if they acknowledge that their own body is a collective of collectives, they will resist vehemently against the notion that they form a collective just the same. But this ancient pattern does not stop with you, for you are but one cell in a much larger form of creation."

The Sage waited to assess if her message would get through. A genuine look of modest acceptance from Davis made it clear that her numerous efforts were not squandered on one who was still unready to move on.

"Come with me," she said softly, and she reached out her hand.

Davis slowly placed his palm in her grasp. She closed her eyes, and for a second time, he echoed her action. When he opened his eyes again, the two stood hand in hand atop the cliffs of Immolatio, gazing out upon the unending waves of an unnamed ocean.

6.9 \ The Tyrant of Amadea

"Why have you brought me here?" Davis asked the Sage quietly.

"For a similar reason you sent your own disciple this way," she answered. "He has yet to arrive, for he knows not the way, and the walk is long and strenuous. I fear his path may be even more arduous than usual."

"But I have fulfilled my own purpose here," said Davis.

He knew perfectly well that Animulus was beyond his aid.

"His purpose is your own, and your success dependent upon his," the Sage assured him. "But I did not say that I brought you here for the same exact reason. He comes in search of the one whom you already know, and yet here we arrive at the similarity. You know the mind of the Guardian, but you know not what it guards."

Davis paused, for the name of this place was still unsettling to speak.

"Amadea," he said in a slow and somber tone.

"Amadea," repeated Sophias. "Long ago, when the purple flowers on the shore of a bay far to the north numbered far fewer than today, there was once a great civilization that came very close to discovering it."

Raising her arm, Sophias pointed out across the rolling waves of the ocean. The sea was lit by the moon alone, but it provided enough light to see the place to which she was pointing. Far off in the distance, a single feature broke the conformity of the horizon as it rose, the only island in the Infinite Sea. Davis said nothing, for he was too perplexed to gather his thoughts before the Sage continued.

"These people inhabited the island you now see: the island of Amadea. Through the ages, they had heard whispers and rumors of its name, and their leader had gained so much wisdom in his time here that he knew, beyond any doubt, that their entire purpose in Limbus was to find it."

"Wait a moment," said Davis, having stumbled upon an inexplicable inconsistency. "You said these people 'almost' discovered Amadea. If they inhabited the island, how did they not discover it?"

The Sage answered him succinctly.

Because it isn't a place.

"What is it then?" asked Davis uneasily, having considered her thought for a moment on his own.

The Sage didn't answer. She simply stared out at the see in solace. And in the absence of an answer, Davis was bombarded by even more questions.

"What happened?" he asked anxiously. "And how have I never seen this before? I gazed out at the sea intently on my last visit to Immolatio. Surely I would have noticed such an obvious structure."

"Because it doesn't exist," answered Sophias just as briefly.

"What do you mean it doesn't exist? I'm looking at it right now!"

The Sage cleared her throat and amended her reply.

"Excuse me: because it doesn't exist anymore. Their leader was a wise man; but he was also proud, and stubborn, and quick to assume he'd arrived at the ultimate answer once he found the first available. When he eventually learned that his purpose was the Quest for Amadea, he searched long and fruitlessly for any news he could gather of it. When an age of the world had passed, and still his people were no closer to finding it, he insisted that his purpose was not to find Amadea – but to build it.

"To achieve this vision, he enlisted the labor of people from all over Limbus. Some volunteered willfully, either out of dedication to their leader, or a farsighted fear of what he might become should they resist. Others did not comply, but they were enslaved for this undertaking by force all the same. His rule over Limbus became tyrannical, longing above all to succeed in his ambitions, at any cost. Over many years, thanks to technical ingenuity and a merciless domination over the peoples of the world, the island was constructed. The Tyrant named it Amadea."

"What happened?" he asked. "Why doesn't the island exist any longer?"

Sophias sighed, for the memory was hard to recall.

"It was swallowed by the ocean in a torrent more powerful than the world has ever since known," said the Sage.

"And what of its maker?" asked Davis with a tinge of unease.

The Sage hesitated a second time, for these answers clearly brought her so much sadness. But he needed to know, and so was she obliged to say.

"He awoke in a mindless stupor, on the shore of a bay far to the north, and its field sprouted forth one more flower at the end of the day."

"You mean..." murmured Davis, but he was left in speechless disbelief.

The Sage confirmed his suspicions with a nod.

"Like the fell Tyrant of Amadea – this poor soul who came so long before you, and who has come so many times since – you have the chance to fulfill your destiny, and put an end to this long purgatory. And so has your purpose also not changed: you are here to discover Amadea, and its secrets are guarded by one dear to your heart."

Sophias stared out upon the distant landmass one last time in sorrow, and she breathed a long and thoughtful exhalation. She waved her hand, and the next time Davis looked out toward the island, it was gone.

"There is more you must know before continuing this quest," she said.

Though hardly surprised, Davis yielded again for the time to humility. The thought of the Tyrant being swallowed by the sea had scared any sense of infallibility clear out of his mind. His resolve was only strengthened for it.

This time, all this progress must not be in vain.

The Sage turned from the cliff and led Davis down to the place where Animulus once watched as the altar of Expiatio was swept into the ocean. She bent down and traced a symbol in the sand between patches of grass.

"How many lines make up this shape?" the Sapient Sage asked Davis.

He thought for a moment and responded in turn.

"Just one," he suggested, unsure about the nature of the exercise.

"I see," replied the Sage. She looked back down to the sand, and in a single swift motion, she drew another line through the length of the original shape, bisecting it in two longitudinally.

"Ignoring the line I just drew, what do you think now? How many lines make up the same shape?"

Davis thought again, rubbed his neck, and answered as best he could.

"I don't know."

"Very good," said Sophias with a smile. "Intellectual honesty is ever the best policy in matters of philosophy. You don't know because there is no way to discern between suitable options; the answer depends on the mind of the observer.

"If you had not seen me make the shape in one single circling motion, it would be impossible for you to know whether I drew it as one line or two, or perhaps even more. At first glance, we can easily see them as a single circular line, for they are intimately connected. If we look a bit closer, however, we can also easily see how they could be two separate lines oscillating around the center, each crossing the other when traversing it."

The Inseparability of Separate Entities... said Davis to himself.

"And as we have noted, what we may see as one shape may also be comprised of many smaller pieces."

The Illusion of Individuals... he thought again in awe.

"For the time, let us think of them as two lines. They complement each other completely, so that as one is at its maximum, the other is at its minimum. The lower will then rise by the same degree in which the upper will fall, until they cross each other over and their roles become reversed."

She pointed with her hand at the relevant features of the symbol as she highlighted them. Having finished one cycle, she continued circling her hand along the shape in an infinite progression.

"Now let us think of two again as one," said Sophias. "My finger never stops moving, but it never leaves the shape; it crosses back and forth from one line to the other, but it never leaves the shape."

The Permanent Impermanence... he conceded optimistically.

The Sage rose from the ground, and with a gentle wave of her hand, a calm breeze swept away all traces of the image.

"You have learned quickly, Davis; although I have no doubt that you will have much to ponder between now and your final machinations, as you seek to bring about an end to this long game. I leave you with these last words of wisdom, for in them lies the key to your transcendence."

The Sage bent down a second time and waved her palm in a horizontal motion over the sand. And in its wake were left three inscrutable words.

Embrace Inverse Vibrations

"When at last you know their significance, you will have indeed found Amadea, and your journey will be complete."

Rising, Sophias smiled one last time at Davis. She waved a hand in front of her disciple's eyes, and in an instant, both of them were gone. A warm wind began to blow from the west, soaring over the sea, rising up and pouring over the high cliffs of Immolatio – and the words faded away as the sand tumbled down the bluff.

SEVEN

7.1 \ A Growing Storm

Animulus stood before a ghost long dreaded, atop one of the many sprawling railwalls of Inanimis. While he could not say exactly, the two had spoken for a long time – as if a whole lifetime of memories had flooded out of him, while hardly needing any words to convey them. In the distance, a dense black smoke rose from the crater of Talionis, though for now its violent eruptions had subsided.

The specter spoke a few last portentous words, and as he finished, a great bolt of lightning struck the mountainside behind him. Animulus winced, averting his eyes from the unbearable brightness; and upon opening them, he found that the phantom had vanished into thin air.

"By the power of Praestes!" he cried at the ghastly exit of this ghoul.

And he was right.

Having been subjected to so strange an occurrence, Animulus knew not whether to trust his senses any longer. The rational explanation begged him not to believe what he'd beheld. And he held no proof – not even a folded piece of paper. He knew well that the dusts of the mountain had caused many a lesser man to go mad. Long ago he had warned the body belonging to this very same ghost to avoid even the foothills of Talionis for that exact reason. Yet, something else implored him to consider the alternative, albeit unlikely possibilities. This same urge did not need a rational explanation, only an impetus sufficient to stir the rest of him to action.

Whether he understood it yet or not, it had already succeeded.

"Davis!" he shouted in vain at the top of the wall, partly surprised to find the courage to call this name aloud.

His eyes scanned all directions but found no trace of the apparition so recently departed. The Councilor continued to shout in desperation, eager to call back his tormentor in the futile hope of achieving validation that he hadn't lost his mind. He hoped as much for even clearer directions as to exactly what he needed to do, should he give in and believe against all reason. Prior to the departure of Davis, Animulus had been rallied to imminent action for the good of all Limbus. But now, he found himself only confused, distraught, and frightfully alone.

"Davis!" he howled again. "I can't do this on my own!"

Animulus fell to his knees in grief where he stood. The full meaning of his visitor's final advice had clearly not yet registered.

Lifting his head from his anguish, the Councilor faced the terrible storm gathering around the summit of the mountain. It was in that moment that he realized the magnitude of the impending tempest, brooding about the crater in the distance.

While the eruption itself had yielded, the encircling clouds had grown taller, wider, and darker than only a short time before. Lightning danced about through the noxious exhausts and stabbed downward at the surface in fits of spiteful destruction. Whatever violent distress had been brewing in the bowels of Limbus, it had not ceased after all, as he'd hoped when Davis had held the chaos at bay and coaxed it back into the earth. Rather, the turmoil had merely given in to the will of its master. But that master was gone now, and the world was on its own. Unleashed from its fetters, the chaos made its way back to the surface, whence it could finally spread.

Upon hearing the frantic cries from outside, the great metal door of the southerly watchtower swung open, and the two Wardens with whom the Councilor had recently been conversing spilled out onto the wall, both appropriately alarmed and confused.

"What is it Modicus? Are you alright?" said Fida with genuine concern. "Who are you shouting for?"

Lost in his own internal strife, Animulus hadn't yet noticed their return, and he was equally startled by the sound of them. He jolted backward, as one waking suddenly from a traumatic shock. He climbed to his feet, dusted off the front of his robes, and feigned equanimity to the best of his ability.

"Yes..." he said shakily. "Yes – I am fine. And I am sorry to startle you, but I was startled myself by ... the sudden change in the weather."

"Who were you shouting for?" asked Credulus. He was audibly skeptical, and more intrigued by the question that went unanswered than concerned for the Councilor's well-being.

"It was no one," said Animulus. "I mean: I was not shouting for anyone."

He quickly tried to cover any conflicting indications, but Credulus stared at him in suspicion, not entirely unaware of the potential contradiction. Regardless, he had no time, nor the authority – though that may not have stopped him – to press the issue before Fida spoke again.

"I see," she said. "I was just as surprised by the change. When we entered the tower, the volcano was completely consumed in fire. The whole earth was shaking, and lava leapt forth from the crater constantly. We were inside for barely a moment when the mountain stopped erupting altogether. Feeling the momentary peace, we ran to the window to see what had changed, and it was then that we heard you shouting from outside."

Every ounce of color drained from the face of Animulus. Here was further evidence that the inexplicable event had been entirely in his mind, and he didn't know if it could be refuted.

"What do you mean?" he asked anxiously. "Surely your sense of time is mistaken. I was outside for long after we parted."

"I think your mind is broken old man," sneered Credulus. "We last spoke not more than a minute ago."

Fida didn't respond; she only looked upon Animulus with confusion and compassion. He had no means to reply. He couldn't explain the disparity to himself, let alone to anyone else.

He rubbed his head and tried to make light of his misunderstanding, thinking as quickly on his feet as he could. He needed time to think these things over, and it would be far more difficult in the company of others. All the while, the storm clouds continued to gather.

"I apologize for my madness," he laughed in false disclosure. "I confess: I have been greatly troubled by the ill winds from Talionis. I am afraid the stress is finally playing tricks on my mind – or indeed the toxic dust."

He glanced briefly at the mounting storm dispersing outward from the peak of Talionis. *I need time,* he knew, *and time is swiftly running short.*

"I am fine," he said, sounding a bit more like himself. "I have no doubt that the trouble is passing. Thank you both for your concern. But for now, we should again be on our separate ways. There is much to do."

The others paused, unsure for different reasons if they should truly leave him be. Eventually, they each gave their own reluctant nod and left the conversation even more confused than when they emerged from the bunker. They said their farewells a second time and returned inside to their posts. As the door slammed shut again, Animulus racked his mind for a better account than he had given them.

"Surely I am in need of rest," he said aloud to himself. "And then again, it appears as if I have already been dreaming."

But what was the significance of such a dream? Seldom have they been so profound that they should ambush me in the waking world.

He walked to the edge of the wall, placed his hands on the ledge, and stared out at the coming storm in contemplation. The clouds had reached the northern edge of the Ashlands where the railwall dwelt, but no rain yet fell – only an undeniable foreboding.

And still, the same ghost haunted him.

"What is the meaning of it all?" he asked the mountain.

At that very moment, a bolt of lightning pierced through the sky from its abode in the clouds and struck the ground directly below where he stood on the wall. White light emanated out in all directions; dust and sparks shot outward from the impact in a monstrous plume of ruin.

The explosion threw Animulus back violently, and his ears felt as though they had been shattered. The sound was literally deafening, and it left no room for anything other than a painful ringing. He flew through the air for what seemed like eternity – as if the world had slowed, and considered coming to a complete stop out of its sheer exhaustion. His head struck the concrete with great force when he landed, and the white all around him faded suddenly to black.

He had no sense of how long he was unconscious, but when he finally came around his head was pounding, and the ringing in his ears persisted. Struggling and shaky, he rose to his feet; and although he had experienced something similar before, this time, the world that he found was not at all as he expected.

He stood alone on a sandy bluff, looking over the calm of the Endless Ocean. A gentle breeze blew his hair backward as it rose over the cliff. The warm rays of the setting sun graced his face as it descended over the horizon far away, to visit once again whatever lay beyond in the uncharted realm of the west. Slowly his ailments faded entirely away, and he was left with only the feeling of euphoric weightlessness. For this one moment, he thought that the world might finally consist of only stillness and serenity.

The tranquility of his surroundings was broken only by the faintest sound of a voice calling his name from behind him. He turned around slowly, and with surprising difficulty, as if the air all around him was thick and viscous. He walked down eastward from the edge of the cliff, in search of whoever was beckoning him. He scanned the hills as far as he could see, but he found no one. And again, the voice called out his name from behind. He turned around a second time to see the place where he had first awoken; only now, he knew it for exactly what it was.

Before him stood the place where there long ago had been an altar, with only sea and sunset beyond it. Before him stood the place where he had witnessed the death of the one who had haunted him. Before him stood the place where he had last laid eyes on his brothers. Before him stood the place where he had first heard the voice from the waves.

In walking back up to the edge, he realized that it was the very same voice that was calling to him now, emanating out from the sea all along. It had never really stopped, he supposed. Perhaps it was he who had merely drowned it out with so many other senses. He stood again on the edge of the cliff, and he tried as hard as he could to answer it, but his voice could not be found. Having no means with which to speak, he reached out to the sound of this stranger.

His feet inched closer to the ledge. His hands stretched further outward. The ground below him began to crack, and before he knew what had happened, he was plummeting rapidly down toward the sea. The voice grew louder as he tumbled, and soon it could be heard quite clearly.

Animulus... it said. *Animulus...* it said again louder. *Animulus...*

He opened his eyes. His head again ached in horrible pain; his ears again rang. He could hear only faint and fuzzy words from the people above him.

"Modicus..." said Fida as she gently slapped his face. "Modicus..." He was beginning to slowly come around, but still he was unsure if they were speaking to him, or to some other person with some other name. "Modicus, wake up!" she shouted. "We have to get you inside."

The rain was pouring down now, and lightning struck rapidly across the mountainside. The two Wardens lifted the Councilor to his feet, held him between their shoulders, and together they scrambled to the door of the southerly watchtower. When they got Animulus inside, they hobbled him over to the nearest chair and he fell forward into it in agony.

"Are you alright?" asked Fida. She was terrified for him, but also of what it might mean should he, of all people, be taken from them by some cruel stroke of fate.

Animulus didn't answer at first, only held his head in his hands and tried to wait out the resounding ringing in his ears.

"Well don't just stand there," she shouted, turning to Credulus. "Run and get the poor man a towel!"

He shuffled away grudgingly and disappeared into an adjoining room.

"Are you alright?" she asked him again.

"Yes," he answered at last. "Yes, I think I will be alright in time. My head aches, but the ringing in my ears is starting to fade."

Animulus looked up and saw the relief on her face. It was a kind face, and one that he had come to trust more than many. He doubted whether he should speak of such strange experiences, but something urged him onward.

"I had the strangest dream," he said. "It was eerie, and yet somehow reassuring. I stood alone by the sea, in a beautiful place I have seen only one time before. A gentle breeze cooled my face, and the rays of the setting sun warmed it again. The ocean lay below, and I was high on a cliff, far above it. But I felt no fear."

He smiled and looked Fida straight in the eyes.

"For a moment, I was completely at peace."

A loud crack of thunder shook the watchtower, and the rain continued to assault its walls. Fida flinched – she who could not easily be shaken.

"It sounds like a better place than here right about now," she said.

Animulus smiled an earnest smile, and he laughed heartily for the first time in a great long while.

"Yes," he said, as he slipped through the mirth to a somber reality.

"Yes, I suppose it does."

7.2 \ High Treason

The central door of the Council Chamber in the heart of the city swung open abruptly. Animulus rushed through the threshold to find a much-needed comfort in the sight of Sobrius, sitting alone at a desk in the center of the chamber floor below. He saw Animulus arrive, but Sobrius did not speak. Instead, he merely looked up from heavy contemplation with an inconsolable expression. His eyes spoke of greater regret than his words could have ever conveyed.

Overwhelmed with urgency, Animulus didn't immediately register the disturbed state of the Council Chair. Without delay, he descended the steps toward the middle of the room, speaking frantically with each bound.

"Sobrius," he said, gasping for breath. "I am glad to find you at last."

"Modicus–" started Sobrius, but Animulus took no heed.

"I have little time, but we greatly need to speak. Things are far worse than either of us feared."

"Modicus–" said Sobrius again, this time slightly louder than the last.

Blinded by fear, Animulus still took no notice, but continued barreling onward in his hectic plea for help.

"Listen closely to me my friend, and I am afraid I must call on every ounce of your trust. I have to leave for a time, to deal with a matter of tremendous importance. I know what I seek, but not what to expect if I should find it. I can spare few details, for I hardly understand them; but while I am gone, I need you to garner all the support you can from the Council to stop the actions of the DMI at any cost."

Reaching the end of his appeal, Animulus arrived at the center of the Council Chamber where Sobrius sat brooding on a vital but stifled reply.

"Modicus!" said Sobrius. He spoke louder and firmer than either of his previous attempts, and this alone captured the attention of Animulus. An eerie silence filled the chamber hall as the sound of this name echoed through the vast expanses of the large and empty dome. Sobrius waited a moment, unsure of how to proceed, and then spoke softly in a solemn tone.

"You should have never come back," he said.

As the words left his lips, a series of loud crashes broke out from the top of the stairs. Doors lined the room's perimeter, and each set was thrust open in forceful synchrony. Guards poured in from all directions, weapons in hand, and they began to block the exits of the aisles leading down to the chamber floor. When the first wave arrived at the bottom, they stood still at their posts, waiting for the others to fill in their positions. When every exit had been blocked, they glanced back to the chamber's main entrance.

The Commander of the Guard stepped slowly into view through the main doorway far above. With a single tilt of his head, the forces began a slow advance toward the center of the room, constricting all hope of escape.

A torrential rain beat against the domed roof of the chamber ceiling.

Surrounded on all sides and greatly outnumbered, Animulus had no plans come quickly to mind. It was unexpected, to say the least, and he was dumbstruck – caught entirely unsuspecting of the possibility of a sudden assault by the guards of his own city, a city for which he still served as an honored and distinguished member of government. While his mind tried to grasp the significance of such a puzzling event, his body had already begun to decide how he should act.

The guards continued in their steady advance, and it was not long before Animulus snapped out of his stupor. He circled rapidly around Sobrius, facing outward as to form a barrier in a sacrificial defense of the head of his Council. An incurable rage began brewing in his chest, and he tried to calm his growing animosity before it slipped from all control. Despite his efforts, his hands began to glow, burning with a searing anticipation of aggression. Countless questions raced through his head, the inevitable answers of which only led him further down the vortex – toward justice, as he deemed it, and the need for vengeance upon his transgressors.

He raised his hands in expectation of a fight, an unbearable bright red vehemence emanating outward from the center of his palms. He was not the only one to notice. He stepped forward in a show of force, and the guards in all directions retreated backward by equal measure. He may have been a Councilor, but the infamy of the Scrutatorus lived long in the memory of the city. They knew what this man had been, and what he was surely capable of becoming again if forced by desperation. Skeptical at first, they were bolstered by an overwhelming strength in numbers. They looked at one another to confirm their solidarity, and resumed their advance, flooding into the bowl of the chamber as an avalanche might fill a valley.

And in that moment, something changed within Animulus. Or rather, something that had changed long ago was remembered yet again.

Despite the wrath encircling his every emotion, his thoughts were cast back to the lesson he'd learned the hardest way, long ago, upon the high cliffs of Immolatio. Even in the face of such unwarranted provocation, somehow, he found a light, shining through the fog of fear that shrouded his judgement – that loathsome haze of paranoid self-preservation which provokes an instinctual call to arms.

Animulus looked down at his hands, hatred literally bursting out of them, and he realized what such a confrontation really meant. Striking now in the name of justice was the entirely wrong means and the entirely wrong mark. These guards were not responsible for their orders, nor did they have any recourse to question their validity. They followed their directives blindly, for it was exactly that kind of devotion their city demanded of them.

Here he was, a Councilor, face to face with the people of his city — the same people for whom he had sworn to advocate; the same people he had sworn to serve. Lashing out at them would lead only to an even greater schism in an already fractured city. The fire in his heart began to quell. His hands ceased their radiant rage. He hung his head low.

The guards hastened their advance, but Animulus once again halted their assault. This time, it was with words — not displays of destruction — that he had gotten their attention. He turned to the Commander waiting safely at the top of the steps and spoke over the heads of his assailants.

"Enough!" he shouted, and a stillness set in. "The Council Chair may do as he pleases; and I regret to inform you that I will defend him if I must. But if he likewise deems it wise, we will surrender ourselves — under this condition: you must tell us the meaning of this insult, and the justification for this unprovoked assault on two members of the Council."

Animulus shot a sidelong glance at Sobrius, and the Chair confirmed support of his plan with a decisive nod. The Commander broke through the rank and file, and made his way down the steps to the chamber floor.

"I am in no position to answer your questions," he said. "I assure you, however: they will be answered by one with the proper clearance upon your immediate surrender."

The two Councilors conferred again with a glance. Seeing few other acceptable options, they bowed their heads and placed their hands out before them. The Commander signaled to two of his guards and they quickly attended to the binding of the prisoners. They forced the men to their knees and pulled their arms behind their backs. Their wrists and ankles were bound effortlessly with the help of a small black device, which shot forth long lengths of wire in a rapid circular motion. The wire surrounded their limbs many times over in a matter of seconds, ensuring that escape from their bonds would not be possible.

Once the prisoners were properly subdued, the guards returned to their posts at the border of the chamber floor. In seeing that the task was done to his liking, the Commander nodded in approval, pulled a whistle from his waist, and blew upon it loudly. Upon receipt of the signal, one last figure appeared in the main doorway at the top of the hall. A dark silhouette stepped out from the shadows, and the events of that afternoon were no longer quite so shocking to the two men bound in wire.

"And so have the Interritus revealed their true treachery," scoffed Sobrius. "Why am I not surprised to find you at the helm of this mutiny, Prodigus? Long have your words been as venomous as a viper; but your deeds reveal a cowardice that would shame so proud a creature. For where a noble foe would reveal itself clearly, you lay secretly in wait, striking only the unsuspecting and indefensible."

Prodigus sauntered boastfully along the chamber's upper level, basking in the chastisement he had worked so hard to earn. Sobrius was happy to humor him, and could have continued even longer than he ultimately did.

"You are a disgraceful leader of a reprehensible lot," he scorned. "Long ago should I have advocated openly against the venom you would inject into the unsuspecting ears of the easily-deceived. Alas, I bided my time, hoping in vain that my composure would provide room for the righteous to flourish on their own. Curse my patience! I feared forcing my own will upon that of the people, only to allow it to be strangled by the wanton will of a villain. I command you, as Chair of the Council of Inanimis: by what authority do you detain the two of us, and hold us against our will?"

Prodigus simply strolled down the stairs of the chamber in the same casual and arrogant manner. The head of the Interritus soon arrived at the chamber floor, but before addressing the captives questioning him, Prodigus took a deep breath, to savor the moment for as long as he may. Having waited so long to speak these words, he set out to deliver them exactly as he had envisioned in the frequent reruns of his darkest fantasies.

"Troubling evidence has been presented to the Council," he said. "You have been charged with High Treason for your crimes against the very city you swore to serve. An emergency Council meeting was called to order, to address the allegations. By the will of the Council, I have been instated as the interim Chair. You are hereby divested of your titles, and so do you forfeit any authority concerning the affairs of the city. You are to be brought before the Council to state your defense, whereupon their judgement will decide your fate. You speak of the will of the people, Sobrius, and the will of the people shall be spoken indeed."

He turned to the Commander of the Guard and ordered them to leave the chamber, close the doors, and stand watch. When the last door slammed shut, Prodigus let out a laugh that was both shrill and snide. Only then did he elaborate, though he was clearly still mindful of who might hear what, and how much of it.

"Speak all the ineffectual words you wish, Sobrius, as you have ever done. You speak to me of patience? Long too have I waited, enduring the folly of your hesitation, while as Council Chair of our fine city you aimed to halt every effort to improve it. You hide behind the guise of your self-proclaimed composure, claiming to serve the best interest of Inanimis, all while preventing the means necessary to bring about an advantageous end for its people. You speak of cowardice? It has always been the Trepidus who are afraid, and you chiefly among them. You fear the promise of Progress, and cower in the face of true achievement."

Sobrius did not sully himself with a reply, for it would do no good and he knew it. Prodigus turned his attention next to perhaps the only foe he feared and detested more, and for whom he had as many spiteful words.

"And I forget not the man who served as the spark for the fires that first scorched the well-being of our fair city." His innuendo was perfectly deliberate. "You have not fooled me – as you have so many others – with your soothsaying ways, Modicus. Or should I call you by your true name? For once you are branded a Heretic, forever so shall you remain."

It struck near enough to sting, but the captive took it silently in stride.

"I see through your ruse – *Animulus* – for whether in the tattered cloaks of the Scrutatorus or in the robes of a Councilor, ever have you strived to sabotage the progress of the city, waging war against the innocent people within it, who try only to provide for their own."

Prodigus stepped forward to where the prisoners rested on their knees, barred from movement by the binding of their limbs. He leaned between the two men and spoke softly, almost sweetly, in a mellifluous but maniacal taunt. And hidden in whispers, he revealed his true intent – at least in part.

"With the two of you removed, the Interritus will control the Council by a two-vote majority. Long have I dreamed of the day when I would be rid of each of you; and now it is only a matter of abiding the inevitable formalities. No longer shall you sit idle in my way. Soon all of Limbus – and Beyond – will bow before me."

Prodigus pulled his own whistle from his waist and blew it loudly. The main chamber door swung open again and the Commander returned with two guards following closely behind. In seeing that further patience was all that would save them, Sobrius spoke, but only in an effort to maintain what he clearly saw as the failing spirit of his most trusted ally.

"Then take us there at once," he said sternly. "I have faith in the Council. Your sedition shall not stand. We will make our case and refute whatever heinous allegations you have no doubt concocted in the dark. The Council will see through this deception, for deceit will never conquer truth."

Animulus wished more than many things to share the same sense of unwavering political optimism, but his own experience with the Council had jaded his view that they would do the right thing when the time came for action. Half-heartedly, he set aside his doubt for the sake of the faith of his friend – and because he had no choice left but to hope.

"That may come to be," said Prodigus. He spoke now loudly for all to hear who may. "And I wish very much that these allegations will prove untrue. For the Council to lose two of its most valuable members to corruption – it would be a blow too painful to bear. But you will have to be patient my friends: the Council will unfortunately not be able to hear your case for some time due to other urgent matters."

He leaned in closely one last time and whispered even more softly than before, and in an even more malignant tone.

"But by then it will be far too late."

Prodigus turned and walked back to the main aisle, gesturing to the Commander as he passed him on his way out. In turn, the Commander signaled to the same two guards who had bound the captives; they each pulled the weapon from their side and flicked the dial with their thumb as they walked forward. On arriving in front of the prisoners, the guards placed the sharp prongs deep into the flesh of their foreheads and pulled the trigger without a moment's hesitation.

7.3 \ The Lord of the Land

Davis stood alone in front of a massive wall of thorns, in what would have been total darkness but for the faint glow of the moon, barely breaking through the dense layer of clouds overhead. White flashes danced about the sky in the distance far to the south, and the rumbling of thunder could be felt across the long miles that separated him from the source.

The thorns that lived in the understory of this region were of a single sort, for all other species had long since been choked out of existence. They produced but a single large and swollen berry at the tip of a central stalk, having ever been encouraged to yield those that were bigger and brighter. While impressive in stature, the taste therein was foul – the absolute minimum amount of satisfaction the plant dare provide without entirely discouraging the endorsement of its caretaker. The vines fruited solely in spiteful compliance to the will of their master.

Menacing sounds darted out from the spaces between the thick and thorny stems, and the shine of numerous sets of malevolent eyes glared inward from them. Each flickered for only a moment before slinking back into the thicket and disappearing, no doubt to warn their master of the presence of this unwelcome guest.

Davis leaned upon a sturdy oaken staff, the only possession he had brought with him to this foul and treacherous territory. He rose to his full stature to confront the barricade; and with a gentle wave of his hand, the thorns had no choice but to part before him. The sight and sound of their retreat was like a thousand hissing snakes, as the vines writhed against each other, competing with their own kin to be the first to escape.

The tunnel through the thorns was long and confining, and the glow of the moonlight was entirely impeded. Davis was not lost in darkness, however, for a bright light of all colors shined forth from within him. The thorns recoiled at the burning sensation from the rays of this light, and the eyes tracking his movements could only bear to look upon him from well behind after he had passed.

He walked forward at a slow but constant pace. As the thorns before him would recoil, so too would those behind close in again after the threat of their foe had lapsed. In this way did Davis advance, enclosed by a moving sphere of air in the midst of a sea of spines, strolling calmly through an otherwise impenetrable barrier guarding the realm of the Lord of the Land.

After a great while moving onward in this manner, Davis began to again detect a faint glimmer of moonlight, trickling in through the thorns ahead. As he hastened, the glow began to brighten, until at last the vines unfurled one final time and were no longer followed by any more beyond. Davis stepped freely into a familiar clearing in the far northern reaches of Limbus.

The clouds were just as thick on this side of the thorns, and the moon was equally shrouded by the dense blanket of gray up above. But as Davis entered the opening, the moonlight mingled with that of his being, and the glade shone all the clearer for it. Even in this dim light, Davis could see the large rock below in the center of the clearing, jet black as a starless night. There was an empty basin all around the boulder, where a virtuous spring had once dwelt. But at present, the earth there was only hard and arid — parched and cracked, as clay scarred by an era of drought. There was no sign of life anywhere to be seen, and the night was cold and silent.

Davis stepped further out from the wall of thorns at the edge of the clearing. He stopped, closed his eyes, and took a deep breath through his nose, as before a plunge into cold, dark waters. He grasped the oaken staff with both hands and raised it straight overhead; he halted for a moment, holding his breath, then drove it firmly into the ground in a blinding flash.

The staff hit the ground with a force as potent as any lightning strike from the Tempest of Talionis, and the earth trembled accordingly. A column of pure white light shot out from the epicenter and climbed through the air in a spiral that pierced the full height of the sky. The light swirled as it rose, causing a cyclone to spread out from it in all directions. The furious winds ripped apart the clouds that were suffocating the clearing and sent them scurrying away, far beyond the trees, never to return.

The bright light of a full moon shone down through the clear night sky above, and a powerful stirring commenced in the depths of the earth.

Having provided more light by which to inspect his surroundings, Davis approached the rock in the center of the glade. As he walked towards it, he noticed a small pile of remains lying to his left, in the very place where he had once left the body of the Guardian to rot. He went over to examine the bones more closely and recognized them immediately.

They were the bones of a weasel.

"Here rests Callidus the Cunning," said Davis sadly. "So has the usurper become the usurped: slain, like so many before, by the cycle of deceit."

Davis waved his hand over the forlorn pile of bones.

The corpse turned to ash and settled down into the soil.

As he stared down at what was left of the poor creature, the rumbling deep in the earth grew louder. The ground shook violently. Davis stepped back in surprise and raised his staff in defense. Steam began to spew forth from cracks in the arid basin at the center of the dell, whistling loudly in an increasingly high-pitched shriek.

When the squealing reached the peak of its crescendo, the pressure forced the cracks to radiate outward. Winding their way out into the rest of the glade, they sliced the ground into a maze of abyssal ravines. Davis stumbled as the ground below him shifted, and out of the expanding chasms seeped a spine-chilling hiss that came from all directions at once.

"Sss-o," hissed the voice that filled the glade. "You dare sss-how your-sss-elf here again, Davi-sss!"

Davis circled in the hope of spotting the source of these evil tidings, but it couldn't be found.

"Yes, your eminence," said Davis loudly. "I come to pay my respects to the Lord of the Land."

"Be sss-ilent!" it shrieked. "I know an a-sss-a-sss-in when I sss-ee one."

"You misunderstand my intention, my liege," said Davis calmly. "I am no assassin. Come out, so that we might enjoy this beautiful evening air. The storm seems to be passing. Come out, and discuss what ails your mind."

There was no reply, but an odious rattling clattered out from deep within the cracks in the earth. It unsettled and distracted the man, but he held fast to his purpose.

"Will you not join me, my lord?" asked Davis again loudly, still circling about to watch all directions at once.

There came no reply. Neither did Davis speak again, but rather listened as the rattling from below mingled with the incessant, sickening hiss. The warnings wove together, dancing unpredictably as they echoed through the glade. Many moments passed, and Davis could see that the Lord was reluctant to reveal itself. Thus was he compelled to entice the beast to the surface more convincingly.

"Will you not join me?" asked Davis firmly. "Perhaps I was mistaken, for I sought the company of the Lord of the Land. It claims to be the supreme ruler of all, though it has only just arrived here and knows not the Way. Its true name is Excidium, though I doubt it would admit it. I gather it goes by a new name of late."

It was an inexcusable insolence; the echoing threats grew louder, and they circled more quickly. The earth again began to quake, and steam again spewed from the cracks. Many waves of devastation overcame the glade, each louder than the former, until the turbulence reached a dreadful climax.

The ground exploded as an enormous serpent shot straight into the air.

From behind the blackened boulder, the snake emerged from its lair and rose to a terrifying height. When the first half of its gargantuan body reached the tip of its trajectory, it crashed to the earth with a thunderous shudder. The ground where it landed was rent under the incredible weight, crumbling inward from the blow. The beast's front half slithered out of the crevice so formed, while the second half made its way to the surface.

"You FOOL!" it hissed, skidding rapidly toward Davis. "How dare you challenge my sss-upremacy? I am older than the earth it-sss-elf. It bend-sss to my will and beg-sss for my mercy, and now you sss-hall do the sss-ame!"

The snake reared up to poise for a strike and towered far above the tiny figure of the man – above even the height of the trees. It cocked its head back, and in a single sweeping motion, the serpent plunged downward at Davis to prove once and for all who was Lord of this Land. It lashed out like a whip, intending to deliver a single lethal strike to this impudent intruder.

As the snake lunged toward Davis, he spun his staff through the air in the last possible moment and dealt a powerful blow to the side of its head. The force sent the creature reeling to the right of where it aimed, but its momentum was not lost. In one continuous motion, the snake recovered from the redirection and began to encircle Davis with its giant body. The creature was as committed as ever to victory, but so was it wise enough to be more cautious about the manner of its next attack.

The snake slithered wide in a wild fury of rage, flanking its enemy. Its body was so huge that it formed a tall circle around Davis multiple times. It moved constantly, but did so in a circular motion so as to entrap his foe. The oscillating contractions of its long body created a spellbinding illusion in the mind of the minuscule man trapped within its center. The motions rippled down the length of its body, and it looked as though there were dozens of separate, staggered threats, lunging in toward him and then immediately retreating.

In and out the scales pulsed, rhythmic and yet unpredictable. They instilled in him a great fear, and yet lulled him to complacency. The pattern dazed him, enthralling him long enough that he lost track of the snake's head. From outside the circle, the serpent taunted him with its disquieting hisses, biding its time until the prey had been sufficiently bewitched to deliver the venomous blow.

Davis shook his head, trying to break the spell – trying desperately to identify from which direction the imminent assault would finally come. From time to time, he would see a bulbous rattle slink by at the top of the pulsating wall of scales, shaking sporadically to add yet another layer of confusion to his already overpowered senses.

At last, the serpent deemed its time had come. Beyond the great wall of scales, it cocked its head back as if compressing a spring; its jaws exploded inward, opening wide in midflight to reveal a deadly set of venomous daggers, each the size of Davis himself. As the fangs stabbed in at the man, he gathered barely enough of his wits to detect the assault. Davis turned toward the snake at the last possible moment and strode forward. A stream of bright green fire shot out from the center of the man's palms in defiance.

At the sight of the flames, the Lord instantly withdrew. It recoiled backwards in terror, for there was little in creation that this snake hated more than fire. Of all the forms of death and destruction that the vile serpent would weave into the workings of the world, fire was one force it could never control, and for this reason did it fear it most of all. And this was a different sort than it had ever seen before.

The snake may have retreated, but it had not lost its patience. It circled Davis in the same bewildering fashion, striking inward now and then, but each time being bested by the incorruptible flames. Between strikes, the snake tried every trick that it could think of to distract its opponent long enough to bypass his defenses.

The Lord tried breaking his will with threats of inevitable defeat; it tried bribing him with the chance of serving as a vassal to its rule. It tried perfidious lies, as to shatter his beliefs; it tried promises of great wealth, power, and dominion. Each time that its tactic failed, the snake would lunge inward again in an effort to cripple its rival; and each time, it was foiled by a wall of green flame.

When at last the serpent had run out of schemes, it spoke bluntly to Davis, as the wall of scales slowly constricted inward toward the center of the circle.

"You sss-ee, Davi-sss, we are one and the sss-ame," hissed the snake. "I know of your weakne-sss, for we have met on one occa-sss-ion before."

> You de-sss-ire to sss-lay me, a-sss I would sss-lay thee
> What it i-ss I po-sss-e-sss, you are sss-eeking to sss-eize
> Ju-sss-t admit that you lu-sss-t for the sss-ame thing a-sss I
> And at la-sss-t you'll be free of thi-sss sss-hameful di-sss-gui-sss-e

The snake whispered to Davis in a perilous rhythm, synchronized to the pulsing waves of its scales – a final effort to enchant its prey and inject its fatal venom without ever having to strike.

"Save your shallow threats and feeble bribes," said Davis. "We may have met before, but you have never yet been faced with a foe the likes of me."

The thought of the flames protecting its prey sent a chill down the serpent's long spine, and it knew the boast was at least partially proven.

"I know the weakness of which you speak," said the man, "but it is not one that we share any longer. Nor do I desire to usurp your cruel throne. There is a vast world beyond your barbed walls – one you do not control – and still have I come here to liberate it from you further."

Davis breathed deeply, and his perilous light seemed to swell.

"I have battled the demon within; now do I battle the demon without. I have passed through death, rebirth, and death once again; and I prepare now for a final rebirth. I fear you not, snake, for I know your true name."

"You know nothing!" it hissed in a maniacal squeal. "I am Imperator the Sss-upreme, Sss-erpent of Sss-plendor and Lord of the Land!"

The circle formed by the snake began to loosen. Its body flailed erratically in a psychotic wrath, boasting in distress, demanding recognition of the honor it deserved.

"I know what you are," said Davis, "and I know that's not your name."

The snake roared in agitation. It lunged inward at Davis, but it was thwarted yet again by bright green flames.

"Tell me, Excidium: why the need for the change?"

The snake writhed in woe, tormented by the sound of this abhorrent name once again. Its coils continued to loosen, though it only quickened the pace of its circling. It let out a dreadful screech and prepared for a final assault, to end this insubordination and squash all hope of rebellion forever.

The lunacy of the serpent spiraled out of its control, furious at the implication that another dare to impose their will. It revolved around itself uncontrollably, thrashing from head to tail, its scales now forming only a pitiful attempt at a blockade. In such a state of vexation, it was easy for Davis to track the movements of the snake. He followed it carefully with his eyes, while looking deep within himself to confess his true purpose.

"I am not here to slay you," he said gently. "I am here to set you free."

With these final words, the snake sprang again toward Davis, its jaws stretched wide, yearning more than ever to taste flesh. Davis was keenly aware of the assault. He moved one step to the side, and with both hands gripping firmly onto oak, he swung with all his might and dealt the serpent a final blow to the side of its skull.

Exactly as before, the snake's momentum was not stopped, but rather redirected. In its unyielding lust for blood, the serpent clamped down on the first contact it made – and plunged its fangs deep into its own tail.

The snake had struck the target so hard that its fangs were entangled in the meat of its own body. It squirmed, twisted, and whipped its head around to dislodge from its victim. By the time it was freed, however, the venom had already firmly taken hold.

Even the serpent was not immune to such a dose of its own poison.

The beast became dizzy, and its motions erratic. Turning, it found Davis and tried in vain to attack, but its addled mind saw so many duplicates of its adversary that it knew not which to strike. At last, the snake fell subject to its own toxic decay; its head reared upward for a final threat – but gave way to enervation, and smote the earth with a terrible crash.

While its motions were stifled, the creature still drew air, though it had barely enough left to offer a malicious farewell.

"It matter-sss not whether you think that you have sss-lain me," said the foul thing, gasping piteously for its departing breath. "I am a-sss old a-sss the world it-sss-elf; and like the venom that now cour-sss-e-sss through my blood, sss-o too have I poi-sss-oned the whole fabric of Limbu-sss."

Greed will alway-sss conquer when it ha-sss the chance to grow
The venom offer-sss great reward, sss-o ea-sss-y to be sss-own
Avarice sss-hall take you all, and then at la-sss-t you'll know
Harmony and beauty have no place in human sss-oul-sss

"Your boast is perhaps the only thing you have said worth believing," said Davis. "Yet when such is the case, one must but draw out the poison."

"Sss-ilence you fool!" hissed the serpent. "And li-sss-ten, if you know what i-sss good for you. When the young one die-sss at the hand-sss of the covetou-sss, then will you sss-urely know the truth in my word-sss."

The wretched snake heaved as its concluding breath expired, and the Lord wilted under its own weight. It looked peaceful for the first time in existence as its enormous eyelids slowly sank to a close.

Davis likewise took a deep breath, and he stepped away from the lifeless body. He sat in silence for a moment, pondering the monster's dying words. When he was roused from his contemplations, he brushed the dust from his clothes and gazed around the Guardian's Glade — reclaimed from the Lord by the very man who so long ago had conquered the place in its name.

The thorns at the perimeter began to wilt with a sigh of relief that their bonds had been broken. Each slinked away timidly and dissolved into the darkness of the woods. Davis waved his hand over the body of Excidium, and like its predecessor, it fell to ashes in the dirt.

The boulder in the center of the glade shone brightly in the light of the full moon. Davis walked down to it in reverence and climbed atop the stone. He wedged his staff onto the surface and the wind again began to stir. The cyclone slowly surged, eventually filling the whole clearing; the ashes of Excidium drifted up into its currents and diffused outward from the glade until they were all but undetectable.

And so did the Lord's words prove partially true, for it would now forever become a part of everything else there ever was.

7.4 \ Brothers in Arms

Animulus awoke to the cold sensation of rain on his face; the sky was slowly sliding by in front of him. It was daytime, though it was difficult to tell, for storm clouds filled the air and blocked much of the light of the sun.

His body ached, and his mind was still hazy from however long he'd been unconscious. The ground below his back slid along at the same pace as the sky, scraping against the length of his body and bouncing the heels of his boots last of all. His hands were over his head, and he pulled them against the force dragging him once he discovered his condition. The guard, slow to realize the cause of the resistance, finally stopped when he noticed his captive had awoken.

"Good," said the guard. "Now get up, would you? I'm sick of hauling your dead weight. It's about time you walk on your own."

Animulus rolled over to his stomach and pushed against the concrete with tethered hands. He rose wearily to his feet, for the wire around his ankles had been removed in the event that the prisoners should awaken and could walk for themselves. As he stood, he saw that Sobrius had already been roused, for he was marching onward at the prods of the guards in the front of the small procession.

The instant he stood, Animulus instinctively counted the guards and took in his surroundings — six of them in all, leading the captives along the top of the main westerly railwall, on the outskirts of the inner city. There were no other people to be seen, for Inanimis had been put on total lockdown, allegedly on the basis of the eruption of Talionis and the ensuing Tempest, as the people would come to call it.

At the sound of the guard speaking behind him, Sobrius wrenched his neck backward to catch sight of Animulus. The guard leading him on poked at his spine with the prongs of his weapon. The deposed leader dared say no word, but his countenance revealed that his earlier optimism had since been supplanted by dread.

They were nearing the first set of towers, marking the beginning of the outer system to the west. For miles on end, the railwalls would be stationed in regular intervals, with tower crews led by Wardens in charge of the local district. The guard who had been dragging Animulus felt it ample time for his captive to catch his breath, and he likewise took to jabbing him onward.

"Where are you taking us?" Animulus asked him calmly.

"You're being moved," he said, and little more.

"Yes, I see," said Animulus, still maintaining the etiquette expected of a Councilor. "But where are we going?"

"I don't have clearance to answer your questions," said the guard with another jab. "Just keep quiet and walk."

His feet complied with the tedious trudging, but his mind was not without thought of escape. The facts were not in his favor, however: his hands were still bound, they were greatly outnumbered by armed guards, and his companion had no experience in hostile dealings of this sort. Most importantly, very little had changed since the assault in the Council Chamber. Even should he have the desire to rebel, Animulus still faced the same dilemma of how to deal with the guards without betraying his ideals.

He had only just resolved to rely on patience once again when they finally arrived at the towers. Fate was on his side in that moment, however, for it provided him an answer he would have never anticipated. As the convoy arrived on the wall between the towers, the guards called up to the operators to send for the outgoing car. The only reply was the beating of heavy rain against the glass panes of the lookout.

The silence set the lead guard on alert, and he signaled to two of his men to enter the northern tower and assess the situation. The guards swung open the large metal door and began to search the building. It did not go well for them, but the only sign the men outside received was the sound of a brief scuffle and the discharging of weapons. It lasted only a few seconds, and just as abruptly as the noises had started, all was silent again.

By now, the guards outside were prepared for the confrontation. Two of them ran closer to block the doorway, while the other two shuffled the captives toward the southern tower. Before either group had a chance to think much further, there came a loud shattering of glass. Shards rained down from the crossbridge above. With the glass came two thick, black ropes, landing with a thud. A cloaked figure slid down each of the two ropes and settled gently, with one hand planted firmly on the ground. In a blur, they rolled forward and sprang up into a streak of shadows, darting between the raindrops.

The guards sent blasts of electricity through the damp air, unsure of where to aim but firing anyway as a matter of necessity. The shadows circled one another, back to back while facing outward; and one by one, the guards fell to the ground in convulsions. When the only men left standing were the captives, the figures approached and threw their weapons to the ground. The metallic devices clanged as they slid away from their wielders.

"Fear not, brother: they were tuned to the lowest setting," said Cerebrus. He remembered well the manner in which they had parted ways. "They will wake in a while and feel as miserable as you do at present, if the markings on your forehead suggest what I suspect."

Animulus didn't know how to respond, and for a time he simply couldn't bring himself to do so. It felt as though he had lived an entire lifetime since parting with his brothers, and that parting was of the bitterest sort. His blood boiled – an intractable whirlwind of sorrow and rapture; anger and elation; guilt and scorn; confession and forgiveness. His brothers gave him the space he needed to cope with the shock, and it was Sobrius who first broke the uneasy silence.

"Thank you for your aid," he said.

Cerebrus would have acknowledged his appreciation were it not for the unexpected onset of his brother's swift embrace. The moment the silence was shattered, all conflicting emotions were cast entirely out of the mind of Animulus; the only one left standing was gratitude — gratitude for the sight of his kin at last, after what felt like an age of the earth without them. All three brothers huddled deeply, each with his arm around one of the others, reunited again as an immovable triad, the strongest of shapes.

When the excitement of their meeting began to give way to an awareness of their dilemma, the conversation quickly returned to practical matters. His mind overflowing with equally perplexing questions, Animulus didn't know where to begin.

"What are you doing here?" he asked, but he gave no chance for reply. "Did you know we would be here? How could you have? Where have you been all these long years? Why show yourselves now?"

"There's no time," said Cerebrus quickly, scanning the wall to the east for signs of anyone who might have seen them. "The danger hasn't passed. We need to get away from the inner city for a time, and then may we fully bring our histories up to date."

Just as he spoke these words of warning, the lights of a railcar broke through the mist and downpour far away in the west, speeding towards them on the southern wall. Normally, outbound cars would arrive from the east; but because this was the innermost station, the car had to return and cross over to the northern wall before they could depart. The fugitives were clearly anxious at the sight of the car, and Manus tried to ease their nerves.

"It should be fine," he said. "We called for an outbound car right before we attacked the guards. As long as no one got in when it departed the previous station, it should be vacant. Quickly: let's get the guards inside the tower and we can wait there to confirm the train is empty."

The four men each dragged an unconscious guard into the tower as the car raced towards them. Running back to the center of the wall a second time, Animulus and Sobrius each grabbed one of the two remaining guards while the brothers picked up weapons in both hands. Once the last two guards were in the tower, the brothers handed a device to each of the former Councilors.

"In the sad event that you need it," said Manus.

"Make sure it is set to incapacitate," said Cerebrus. "I doubt the guards were dealing us the same courtesy."

The men made their way up the stairs of the tower just as the incoming car arrived and began rounding the rail to cross over to the northern track. In some ways, the lockdown ordered by the Interritus was working in the favor of the fugitives, for there were very few people about, and all the fewer the nearer they came to Talionis. On finding the car empty, they ran through the crossbridge to the northern tower to find the operators of the station still unconscious on the floor.

"You three: get down the stairs and into the car," said Manus. "Someone needs to flip the switch. I'll stay behind and catch up if I can."

"You cannot make it in time," said Animulus, knowing well how quickly the railcars moved. "There has to be another way."

"There is no other way," said Manus. "You need to get out of the city, and someone needs to start the car. I'll find you in due time."

"We may not have the time we are due," said Animulus quickly. "I am not sure what exactly, but the Interritus are planning something treacherous that I fear cannot be undone, and yet may undo all."

The brothers stared at each other without speaking, defeated by the impasse for a time. All the while, Sobrius stared in solemn silence out the window — not to the west, but to the center of the city.

"Besides, we have somewhere to be," started Animulus again. "And while I do not know why, I am certain we may only go together."

His brothers looked at each other gravely, but they made no protest, nor questioned the suggestion of Animulus. It was as if they already had some sense of the plan he had in mind, but it was not one they took lightly.

"We'll walk then," said Cerebrus staunchly. "There is no other way."

"We must walk most of the way as it is," said Animulus. "We need every advantage of speed we can find."

"Well, what do you suggest then?" said Manus in frustration.

His brother stumbled, trying to find an answer, but he didn't have the chance to provide one.

"I will stay behind," said Sobrius, still somber from his own ruminations.

Animulus said nothing, but wished no more to part with Sobrius than with his other brothers, for that is what Sobrius was to him now.

"Though my curiosity implores me to follow you into whatever darkness you presently seek, my heart will not allow me to abandon my kin," continued Sobrius. "Whether they hear my words as a free man and their equal, or in the bonds of a prisoner, it matters not. What matters is that they hear my words. I will not forsake them; to whatever end their malice may lead, they are nevertheless my people. I will not abandon them. I must do whatever I can to pull them out of their path to inevitable ruin."

Sobrius paused, himself unable to bear parting with Modicus, his most trusted ally. All the same, he was unsure of where this ally was headed, and whether he could be of any help there.

"We are together in purpose," he said. "And yet, I sense that we are on separate journeys." He sighed in one last deliberation. "Farewell, Modicus."

Seeing that Sobrius was not of the mood to speak rashly after all he had been through, Animulus made no attempt to dissuade him.

"Farewell, Sobrius," he said unhappily. Animulus was still pained to part ways with his staunchest advocate, but he knew the man's insights were correct. A trip to the sea was not something Sobrius could understand when his city lay behind him, foundering. "It is not the darkness we seek, my old friend; but rather, the one who may release us from its long reign."

The voice from beyond grew a little in volume, like a whisper on the wind, trying not to drown in the sound of pouring rain. Lightning continued to flash above the mountainside, and still the clouds spread ever outward.

"If you are to return, you at least need a plan," said Animulus. "What will you do, brother?"

"What you asked of me when you returned to the city," said Sobrius. "We must stop the actions of the DMI. Even more importantly, we need to learn what Prodigus is planning. I suspect the latter is related to the former, so perhaps I may achieve both goals with one venture."

"I agree," said Animulus. "The two must be connected. But the guards will be watching for you everywhere – and the whole city knows your face like their own."

"Then I shall use this weakness instead to our advantage," said Sobrius. "The Interritus may despise the two of us, but surely you and I are not alone in our fight. I will reveal what news I can gather of their plans, to gather our allies about us to defy it. I will shed light on that which our foes no doubt wish to keep in the shadows. We shall expose their coup to the open air for all to breathe its foul stench, and trust the people to be revolted by it enough to revolt."

Animulus smiled an inspired approval, thankful for the man to whom fate had delivered him, so long ago, after washing ashore from the sea.

Sobrius gestured to the west and bid his friend an ominous adieu.

"When you find whatever it is you seek in the sunset, I pray that you find me again – and that you find me well."

The two men locked forearms in camaraderie; and in sensing it an insufficient means of departure from a friendship so valued, they clasped one another tightly in a bitter farewell.

7.5 \ A Final Summons

Davis sat on the edge of a beautiful spring, shimmering ever so gently under the light of the bright full moon. The air was cool and crisp, and filled with the calming sounds of the gentle creatures of the wood. His surroundings looked as if an epoch of restoration had taken place, and that whatever insults the clearing had been dealt, so too had they been healed by the nurturing passage of time. The glade was now very much as it had been the first time he set his sight upon it, excepting that the extraordinary being which had occupied it was nowhere to be seen.

Despite the consummate peacefulness that existed around him, his thoughts were plagued by a dreadful doubt, injected into his veins by the dying words of the snake. He was fairly certain he had a sense of the covetous, but the young one was someone he hadn't considered.

While it was a problem that thankfully proved less frequent than afore, Davis was once again entirely unsure of the next move he should make. He searched long and hard, asking himself question after eager question, none of which could he ever adequately answer.

When frustration and exhaustion had led his thoughts to finally quiet, the internal clamor was slowly replaced by an awareness of little more than the tranquil sounds of the night around him. The water rippled softly; the grass bent in the breeze; the birds chattered meekly in the trees. His breath cooled his disposition as it moved slowly inward through his sinuses, paused in the furthest reaches of his lungs, and moved slowly outward again, returning to mingle with the rest of the atmosphere.

His demanding dialogues were no longer to be found, replaced instead by only a trancelike awareness of everything and nothing at once. And then, like a solitary candle lit in the midst of a large cave, a small part of the answer revealed itself, providing just enough light to go on.

After long hours of meditation, Davis felt foolish in the face of the solution's simplicity, for the plan now was the same as it had been all along: he needed to find the Sage. Yet within this answer there dwelt only a second question. While he knew to seek the Sage, he didn't know how to find them, whoever they may be. And as he asked himself a second question, so too did he return to the darkness and light a second candle.

He closed his eyes and sought out the Sage, calling them forth from somewhere deep within himself. When he awoke from the cave, far across the glade hung a meager piece of paper, pinned to the very same tree on which he had received one once before. He sprang from the site of his soul-searching and ran for the note, like a child having just been presented a present – a stark contrast to the calm, detached mystic of a moment before.

To the Savior-to-be,

> *You know where you are and where our endings lie*
> *Yet all wisdom is useless if never applied*
> *And so, I applaud you for learning at last*
> *The answers you seek are right here in your grasp*
>
> *You are the dreamer, and this is the dream*
> *There is nothing that happens that cannot be seen*
> *This place has been peopled by parts of your mind*
> *Look deep in yourself and their secrets you'll find*
>
> *Take charge of the Will and the world shall so be*
> *If your motives are true may you soon become me*
> *Take control of the Will and the world shall so be*
> *If your spirit is pure may 'I' soon become 'We'*

> *As the one is Many, so are the many One,*

> *The Sage of Salvation*

Davis, rather pleased with himself so far, applied his introspection even further in response to the provocation of the Sage. Perhaps there was yet more he could gain in this manner. While he longed to speak with the Sage, the chronicles of Limbus were spinning wildly out of his control, and it was time he took charge of it once again.

He walked back by the edge of the pool and crossed his legs as he sat by its clear waters. Closing his eyes, he silenced his mind, and searched within for the secrets dwelling just outside of his sight.

∞∞∞∞∞ ∞∞∞∞∞∞∞

7.6 \ Maleficent Intent

∞∞∞∞∞ ∞∞∞∞∞∞

Prodigus stood alone in front of a massive wall of thorns, in what would have been total darkness but for the faint glow of the half-moon above. He had come seeking an answer to the mystery of the small remaining sliver of Limbus that did not surrender to the will of Inanimis.

Over the years as the city spread, often he would set out in secret to scout the land at its periphery, pressing ever onward in his selfish quest for glory outside the walls of the city, and discreetly driving its people to follow his vision upon returning within them.

In recent times, the tendrils of Inanimis had butted up against suspiciously firm boundaries, and Prodigus feared that it may one day be prevented from acquiring the necessary resources to keep growing. It was this need, among others, that drove the city to creep forever outward. Driven by an inexplicable urge of his own, Prodigus had departed again to test the rigidity of these barriers — first to the south, and then to the north.

In the south, he found little more than a desert that stretched to the distant horizon, at least. His desperation implored him to explore, but he dared not begin the long walk. He didn't know how far the desert extended, nor was he prepared for the cruel conditions he rightly suspected it would present. A suspicious voice within him whispered that he would never return, should he decide to head that way. Though he seldom backed down from a challenge, he knew this time that such an intuition was correct.

The north offered him a much more realistic curiosity; and it was by no means less intriguing, for he had never seen vines the likes of these before. They were tall and dense, and rose from the ground to the canopy in an almost perfectly formed fence, spanning well beyond his field of vision. More to the matter, rather than dissuading him, it seemed to Prodigus that something in this direction beckoned him to come thither. A different voice from within assured him: all of the fanciful desires that had driven him there would be fulfilled. And again, he believed it.

Unsure of how to penetrate the barrier, Prodigus walked along the thorns for a long while. The voice continued to urge him on, its enticements growing louder and more convincing with every step he took. Eventually his wish for a way in was granted; he found a small gap in the thorns, just large enough to weave his way through, and he entered without any reluctance.

As he progressed through the gap with great difficulty, he was surprised by the thickness of the wall and the extent of the thorns' domain. Slowly, the route became narrower and narrower. His clothes were snagged and shredded; his body was scratched on every surface. But still he went on.

When he came to find the last hope of his passage closed off by the vines, Prodigus thrust himself upon them with his full weight. He had come too far, and the rewards he envisioned were too great to turn back now. Spines delved into his arms and chest, but the vines did begin to give, swaying backward under the pressure. By the end of the great struggle, his will proved even more stubborn than theirs; the last vines holding him back finally yielded – and then snapped. Prodigus broke through the barrier with a jolt as they gave way. He fell, rolling forward at the sudden release, and came to rest upon the dusty clay ground at the edge of a dreary clearing.

Bloodied and bothered, he looked out from the ground to see at last what lay beyond this vexing barrier. The dell was mostly desolate, and for a time he thought all his arduous efforts might have been wasted. In the center was a great black boulder, and being the only landmark in the otherwise lifeless circle amidst the thorns, he got up, briefly nursed his bleeding wounds, and walked down to investigate.

As he approached the stone, he saw a small hole in the cracked basin at its base. He bent over to inspect the hole closer, and just as he did so, something deep in the darkness within began to stir. Prodigus leapt back at the surprise, when out of the hole slithered a magnificent serpent. Emerging from its den, the snake nodded its head in a courteous gesture, and circled its way upward around the boulder. Upon reaching the top of the great rock, it lifted its front into the proud stature expected of royalty, and spoke to the man on the ground down below it.

"I'm sss-orry to have sss-tartled you, my good sss-ir," said the snake.

The serpent was arrayed with wondrous coloration: beautiful patterns of red, orange, and yellow speckled its scales. It was a large snake, and it would come to be far larger yet; but for now, it was no more than the length of the man. Once he had seen what it was, for some reason, Prodigus did not fear the snake at all. It spoke kindly to him – kingly, even – with a grace and nobility the man had never before encountered in Limbus.

"Oh," said Prodigus, still surprised if no longer frightened. "Why, thank you," he said awkwardly. "My name is Prodigus, and I come from Inanimis."

"I know of Inanimi-sss," replied the snake. "And I know who you are. New-sss of your valor ha-sss traveled far to reach my ear-sss."

Prodigus formed a flattered smile, but only as a show of false humility; he was never surprised to hear how fondly others thought of him, even when it preceded his acquaintance.

"I am Imperator the Sss-upreme," it said, "Sss-erpent of Sss-plendor and Lord of the Land."

The snake rose further off the rock and puffed its chest at the proclamation of its name.

"I am honored to make your acquaintance," replied Prodigus. "It is a privilege to meet someone of such worth." *Finally: a fitting ally,* he schemed.

"Ye-sss," whispered the snake slowly. "Perhap-sss we may both be of worth to each other."

The serpent stretched its neck downward, reaching closer to the man. Its eyes widened and protruded outward, staring deep into his soul, whether he approved of it or not. Prodigus leaned backward, his own eyelids widening as the serpent locked firmly upon his gaze. Any arrogant delusion that he could contend with the will of this creature fled at once like a feather on a stiff wind.

"You sss-ee," said the snake, "I know what you sss-eek. I may be able to aid you, for I have lived in thi-sss place longer than even the mo-sss-t ancient chronicle-sss of your city can recall."

"Go on," said Prodigus, mustering his best attempt to feign autonomy in the conversation.

Imperator leaned back slightly and relaxed its constriction on his mind. The man was intrigued, and so was it best to let him breathe for a time.

"It ha-sss come to my attention that your kind ha-sss been exploring the nature of our sss-urrounding-sss. I worry, de-sss-pite the progre-sss you have made, that you lack the context with which to under-sss-tand your revelation-sss."

Prodigus looked confused, and he thought it his own idea to try to clarify. In actuality, it mattered little whether he spoke any longer at all. The snake knew his thoughts in full. Excidium had discovered long before Davis that it could see what it wished of the world. And these were hardly novel ambitions; the Lord had known each and every one of them before.

"You refer to our Metageophysical Inquiries?"

"Preci-sss-ely," replied Imperator. "If you are not aver-sss-e to an out-sss-ide per-sss-pective, I would be glad to offer sss-ome of the in-sss-ight my old age ha-sss afforded."

"By all means," he said eagerly. The man's interest was fully piqued, and his eyes widened even more at the prospect of any advantages he might gain from such privileged information. Perhaps the rewards he was promised by the voice which drove him hither would prove even greater than those he had envisioned.

"The world that we sss-ee is only a sss-liver of all that there i-sss. That much you know; what you do not know, however, i-sss that, if you li-sss-ten carefully to my unfaltering wi-sss-dom, you may tran-sss-cend thi-sss realm to find the one which lie-sss Beyond — a land of greater glory than you could ever imagine. You have claimed practically all there i-sss to claim in thi-sss realm; but in the next, your lu-sss-t sss-hall know no limit-sss."

The snake paused, leaned in closely a second time, and again constricted around the man's will. Prodigus never broke his stare into the enchanting eyes of the Emperor.

"But a-sss alway-sss," hissed the snake, "there i-sss a catch."

"I'm listening," said Prodigus impassively.

"There i-sss but one door that lead-sss out of thi-sss realm, and only one may enter. You mu-sss-t ha-sss-ten your plan-sss, for even a-sss we sss-peak there i-sss one who sss-eek-sss to do the sss-ame."

"How do I stop him?" he asked quickly.

Having fully ensnared its prey at last, the snake leaned back and loosened its grip a second time. It gave a seductive grin, or as much of one as a snake can manage without revealing its fangs.

Rather than answer, the serpent turned and circled down the boulder. It had just disappeared behind the rock when it reached the bottom; and without pause, it came around the front and began ascending it again, its jaws clamping down upon a glistening dagger. When it reached the top, it stretched out its neck and opened its mouth.

The blade lodged straight into the ground at the feet of the man.

"It i-sss the Blade of Entitlement," said Imperator. "It ha-sss a long and sss-ordid hi-sss-tory, and it took me con-sss-iderable effort to obtain it again. With it, you will find your de-sss-tiny."

The man bent over and plucked the dagger from the ground. Set free from his hypnosis, Prodigus discovered a skepticism that for a time had eluded him. This was no folly on behalf of the serpent, however; it knew full well that the man's own wishes would be sufficient to fulfill every aspect of its maleficent intent.

"Wait a moment," said Prodigus. His cynical nature warned him never to trust another fully, and he had found a crucial discrepancy deep in the details. "If only one can enter, why would you tell me all this? If the realm Beyond is as glorious as you claim, surely you would desire this privilege for yourself. Why should I believe you?"

"I have no de-sss-ire to leave," said the snake coyly. "I've lived here far too long, and I couldn't bear to part from thi-sss place. Be-sss-ide-sss, when you have left for the realm Beyond, it will leave thi-sss one entirely for me. In thi-sss way, we sss-hall both get exactly what we de-sss-ire above all."

Prodigus turned his attention from the snake and stared deeply into the shining glow of the blade. He was lost in thought for a moment, but there was little chance now of escaping his fate. He squinted at his reflection in the dagger.

"What must I do?" he asked cruelly.

The snake grinned, but was careful not to reveal too much of its malice.

"The one who threaten-sss to beat you through the doorway i-sss weak, and will not be able to enter it without the aid of another. End the life of the Sss-age, and you sss-hall have your liberation."

And suddenly, the snake halted its instructions, for it was overcome at once with a terrifying sensation. It had suspected the unwelcome eyes of another. It scanned the clearing frantically, looking in all directions for the sight of the intruder. Finally, it called upon the full prowess of its wit.

The serpent strained as hard as it could, trying to peer through the shrouded veil covering its perception. There, in the hazy darkness, it locked its eyes upon its most hated adversary, sitting cross-legged in peace, on the bank of the empty basin surrounding the boulder.

The snake was thrust into a fit of terrifying rage at the detection of its observer. It cast off all previous pretexts of civility, overtaken by a savage bloodlust — and this fueled the Lord, and it grew. The body of the serpent soon surrounded the entire boulder, and it was growing at an alarming rate, catching up quickly to the monstrous form in which it met Davis — or rather, in which it would meet him in the future.

Excidium shrieked at its enemy in a bloodcurdling wail and plunged down at him with outstretched fangs.

Davis was thrust from his deep meditation, as if waking in a shudder from the most horrifying of nightmares. He lurched backwards from where he sat by the pool, panting heavily in dread. Sweat beaded on his brow and fell like rain upon the grass of the glade. He knew that this was no nightmare, however: somehow, his plan had worked. He had divined the very secrets he sought — secrets that had taken place only a short time before, in the very same place he now sat.

If it was mere fear that he felt at the snake's dying words, Davis was now overcome with utter terror. Its venom had indeed been sown deeply.

7.7 \ To Break the Veil

A car approached the outermost station in the southwest quadrant of the city's meandering railwall system. This distant station adjoined the foothills of Talionis, and only two days prior Animulus had visited there as a trusted city Councilor. Now, he approached the same station in an entirely different manner: an outlaw in the company of his long-lost brothers — a Heretic, as so many decades before.

The Scrutatorus had not passed by the other stations uneventfully. In fact, since they parted ways with Sobrius their journey could well have been characterized as disastrous, had the brothers not made it as far as they had.

The city and its territories were on total lockdown, and the unexpected rail travel was highly suspicious to the station operators. The brothers knew this would be the case, but they couldn't afford the delay. The shuttles were risky, but they were fast, and they all agreed it was a necessary gamble. Had their luck proven even kinder than it was, they may have been able to sneak by without detection; but this was not the way things transpired.

The towers were given prior notice of the small party conveying Animulus and Sobrius to an undisclosed location. So too did they know that the Councilors had been convicted of High Treason and detained until they could be held accountable for their crimes. The operators of the first station to the west were indeed anticipating the arrival of the prisoners, but no call had come through indicating their departure.

On spotting the car, they immediately found it odd. One of the two operators came down to inspect the unexpected arrival, while the other had the presence of mind to stay behind in the tower, should anything be amiss. Luck was in favor of the fugitives even more than they realized, however, for the Wardens of this tower were for the moment nowhere to be found. Most likely, they attended other matters in the bunkers until official word came through; in any case, it made for two fewer people to manage.

The brothers attempted to disguise their intentions as best they could, conversing with the operator naturally when the doors slid open. Cerebrus took the lead while Animulus stood behind his brothers, trying to stay as inconspicuous as possible. The operator soon pressed the men for further identification, and upon inspecting the third passenger directly, recognized him at once for who he was.

The station operator shouted to his partner, but he got hardly a syllable into the air before he struck the wall in convulsions. On hearing the shout and assault on his partner, the second operator immediately got ahold of headquarters. Like the former, he'd barely spoken before Manus climbed the stairs to stun him; but the few words he managed to speak were enough.

Had the Interritus been more prepared for this possibility, the Heretics would have surely faced an unending swarm of guards at each station, or have been otherwise thwarted somehow. As it was, however, the mutiny had been far too silent and sure of itself to anticipate its plans going awry. The Interritus had failed to allocate more guards to the periphery; and in reality, there were few to spare. Eyes and arms were needed in great numbers in the inner city to help enforce the lockdown – and while they knew it not, to help carry out the plans of Prodigus.

Thus, there were fewer guards to contend with, but each movement was scrutinized far more carefully. In this way, the lockdown had both hindered and aided their escape to the outlands. Nonetheless, at each subsequent station the brothers had to grapple with the modest resistance awaiting them on the platform, and continue to outrun the much more substantial resistance scrambling toward them from the east.

Guards or not, there was little in Limbus that could stand in the way of the Scrutatorus when united as one in a common purpose. As the railcar sped along the track toward its ultimate destination, the Heretics hoped that both their luck and skill would continue to prove just barely adequate.

The car pulled into the last station; but to their great surprise, there were no anxious operators or Wardens awaiting them with zealous weapons. The brothers stepped out cautiously onto the platform and observed their surroundings. The downpour had not abated; it had only gotten worse and more widespread the nearer they came to the mountain.

Lightning hewed at the foothills and spread far to the north among the sprawling clouds. Thunder boomed through the Recordatio past the northern side of the wall; the clouds slowly climbed the highlands beyond it, grasping their way to a bay by the sea that dwelt in that direction. To their surprise and excitement, the Tempest didn't venture far in the direction the Heretics themselves were headed. It was the only refuge in all of Limbus.

As the fugitives took in the grim conditions in all bearings but one, they spotted a figure in the watchtower, standing perfectly still and looking down at them directly. Oddly, rather than raise the alarm, the figure slowly raised a hand and began to wave. The silhouette turned for the closest door and descended the stairs. The large metal hatch creaked as it opened, and one of the Wardens with whom Animulus had interacted two days prior – and to whom he had acted so strangely – stepped out into the heavy rain.

"A message came through yesterday informing all the stations of your crimes," said Fida. She paused. "I didn't believe it."

Fida was one of the few members of the Trepidus serving with the DMI, and she had been with them from their inception as a critical player in the intricate scientific analyses involved in the work. It was no doubt for this reason alone that they tolerated her presence at all. Fida had recently been stationed as a Warden for this locale, to assess the signs of the volcano when they put their proposals into practice.

It was for this purpose also that Animulus had been present here. The eruption of Talionis had garnered the Councilor's full attention before the abrupt appearance of a ghost from his past had rattled his foundations. Despite his engagement with the escalating situation over the last several days, Animulus was now vexed over how little he actually knew about the details of the DMI's endeavor.

In fairness, it was precisely for this reason that Animulus had arrived at the outer station in the first place. Much to his dismay in some regards – and to his great fortune in others – the Councilor had not had time to acquire all the information he sought before other events upon that same wall sent him hurtling down his present path.

The second Warden assigned with Fida was a man by the name of Credulus. He was a staunch member of the Interritus, though every bit as instrumental in the work of the DMI. Credulus was vehemently in favor of their recent proposal, to the point of arousing suspicion. Like Fida, he had been assigned to his post once their plans for the mountain were put into motion. At the moment, however, he was nowhere to be seen.

"Come inside – and quickly!" shouted Fida.

Cerebrus and Manus looked to their brother, to see if he trusted the woman they knew only as a stranger. Animulus paid them no mind and ran straight for the tower. They locked eyes, shrugged their shoulders, and followed promptly behind. Once safely inside, the fugitives wasted no time.

"What more can you tell me about what the DMI is planning?" asked Animulus. "I know mostly broad strokes only, as shared with the Council."

"It's far beyond planning," said Fida. "Besides, I fear that it's too late."

"What do you mean it's too late?" asked Cerebrus.

Animulus had brought his brothers up to speed on the situation when in transit, between bouts of self-defense at the stations. There had not yet been time for his brothers to return the favor.

"I mean it's too late," repeated Fida. "They've already made contact."

"Made contact with what?" asked Animulus tensely. "The proposal I received in the official session on the matter stated that the DMI were to study the properties of the volcano before any future applications were discussed – to study it, not make contact with anything."

"That's because the Council briefing didn't contain the material the DMI subcommittee deemed classified. Even now, I'm sworn not to disclose any of this to you."

Fida laughed uncomfortably in appreciation of the circumstance.

"Then again," she said, "I suppose that's irrelevant, considering you're a wanted fugitive. Oh – and that this happened."

She gave the men a dubious look and pushed against the door to the room adjoining the entryway. The door pivoted open and the light from the foyer slowly revealed the furious faces of three bound men. Credulus was tied together with the two station operators, their mouths taped shut and their backs propped against one another on the floor.

The mystery of Fida's missing partner would have been solved, if it had only occurred to Animulus to even wonder about it amidst everything else that was happening. Fida leaned her shoulder into the room, grabbed the handle, and leisurely pulled the door shut again.

"Let's just say they didn't share my skepticism over the official story."

"I see," said Animulus briefly, before turning his attention back to the puzzle at hand. The Heretics were not in the sanctimonious position to judge the methods of this unanticipated ally. With guards surely speeding towards them in pursuit, however, they did need information quickly. "What was classified?" he asked. "What did they make contact with?"

"The purpose, in the political sense, was to study the volcano. Their true objective was to tap into it — to use its power to break through the Veil."

"And the members of the DMI let this happen?" asked Animulus. "How could you let the Council be actively deceived?"

"The DMI was torn, just as the Council would have been," said Fida. "In the end, it came down to majority rule all the same. The Interritus held a huge majority in the DMI; thus, we were obliged to maintain our secrecy under threat of High Treason — a crime punishable by death, as you know."

His brothers smirked at the quip, but Animulus was unmoved.

"Needless to say," she defended, "not many of the Trepidus ever thought very seriously about speaking out, or for very long."

Animulus placed his hands on his forehead to ease a growing ache, and to catch hold of his rising temper.

"I apologize," he said calmly. "It is no deliberate fault of the DMI, and it is certainly not yours, Fida. This campaign was put forth by Prodigus. My latest dealings with him — and my intuition — tell me that he is plotting far more than even the classified plans of the DMI could reveal. I may not have been privy to the science, but something as irrational as my behavior a few days ago has instilled in me a great fear — a fear that if we fail to stop Prodigus, the world as we know it shall fall into ruin."

He thought back to the unspeakable power in the torrent that had washed away the Expiatio, on the same cliff presently awaiting his arrival.

"I'm afraid to say that even the science leads me to conclude you might be right," said Fida. "And my own intuition feels just as off. When I saw you on the wall after the eruption ceased, you looked as if you'd seen a ghost."

Cerebrus and Manus gave each other a nervous and knowing look.

"Something didn't sit right with me," continued Fida. "When you left in such haste, I pleaded again with Credulus to rethink our plans. He wrote me off in typical fashion. That's when I delved back into the math. I pined over the figures, recalculating dozens of equations. I was paranoid, admittedly, but things weren't adding up as I expected.

"I was certain my work was correct, so I contacted some other stations to verify the data. I asked them to resample, and they had little cause to suspect anything of me. Sure enough, the numbers they obtained weren't the same as those we'd been provided in our briefings.

"I tried to contact headquarters after uncovering the inconsistency, but I could never get through. It furthered my suspicion, but it was also a stroke of great luck. When I couldn't contact the DMI office, I called each of the outer stations directly for the values from their sampling, telling the crews that leadership had asked me to confirm the analyses for them, in light of their recent communication failure."

"The outer stations?" interrupted Animulus. "What stations? Where is all of this happening?"

"All over Limbus really," she answered. "We sent teams to sample throughout the outer reaches, in search of the places that were closest to the nerves of the mountain. We looked practically anywhere the logistics would permit. Since then, large emitters have been brought to any sites that the sampling had deemed suitable."

"To do what?" asked Animulus.

"To begin poking at the nerves," she said.

"And what will that do?" asked Cerebrus.

"I was trying to answer that question all day. With the true numbers in hand, I reran the calculations. And the results were..." She trailed off. Finally, she brought herself to use the only fitting word. "They were terrifying," she said, and Animulus knew the feeling well.

"Meaning what exactly?" he asked.

"We would be able to break through the Veil, as the original models suggested. But, the resultant energy from the reaction was far greater than the fabricated data suggested. It would be enough to obliterate the whole of Limbus, probably many times over.

"In the folly of my unease, I told Credulus all I discovered, but he again turned belligerent at my meddling. He seemed to know more than he was saying, and he also didn't seem surprised to find me asking questions. Something told me there was an evil conspiracy afoot, and I was inspired, against my character, to take some wicked action of my own."

She tilted her head toward the closed door to the adjoining room.

There was hardly an answer Fida could give that Animulus would not have found useful, but his urgency continued to drive him on. He glanced back at his brothers, and they knew it to mean they should make ready to depart. Animulus turned again to Fida and spoke briskly to her as the Scrutatorus rallied to leave.

"I cannot thank you enough, Fida. Nor should I ask you to do more than you have already done, but it pains me to say that we need your help again. First and foremost: return to the city and find Sobrius. The last I knew, he was trying to sneak his way into the office of the DMI to gather what news he could of these affairs. It was always a fool's errand, but in light of your experiences, I now fear for his safety more than I already did. With your status and clearance, hopefully you can make your way back to the inner city without too much trouble. Considering the contents of the next room, I suggest you take a weapon from upstairs. Just in case.

"Find Sobrius, if you can, and aid him in his task. If you are able to do neither, find whatever you can about the motives of Prodigus. He is clearly the snake behind this evil tide. If you are correct in your assertion, and it is too late to stop the DMI from making contact, we will at least need to focus our efforts on stopping whatever else Prodigus has planned – at any cost."

Fida looked as though the weight of the world had been placed on her shoulders. Unprepared for the charge laid upon her, at the very least, she would rise to accept it. Everything after that was uncertain.

"Goodbye and Godspeed," said Animulus.

And in a flash, the Heretics had disappeared out the door.

Outside on the wall, the men ran around the side of the southern tower, leapt onto a metal ladder leading to the ground, and slid down the sides of it hastily. As he gathered the impetus for a journey to Immolatio, Animulus stood still for a moment, staring in silence as his brothers rushed onward.

"What's the matter?" asked Cerebrus as he turned back and noticed his brother's hesitation. "Let's finally get out of this cursed rain."

Animulus looked up from his solace to find the brothers he had missed for so long; and it was only in that moment that he finally appreciated the full significance of their reunion. In doing so, however, he realized that he still had every question as to how it came about.

He stared at them, unable to ask, and unable to step a single foot in the direction of the desert. His voice shook, as though a great offense had been done unto him. In truth, he feared the answers they might give.

"How did you find me?" he asked. "And why then, after all this time?"

Manus deferred to Cerebrus with a look. Cerebrus just shook his head, as if he were not exactly sure of the answers himself. He walked slowly back to the base of the ladder where Animulus lingered.

Cerebrus started timidly, for as much as Animulus fretted over their answers, he detested the prospect of reliving their experiences all the more.

"The years that passed after we parted ways on that inauspicious day were longer and darker than an unending abyss. When you fell from the cliff, we turned from the sea and sought our desperate escape through the desert. We wandered for days, but at the height of every dune, all we ever found was sand for as far as we could see. One day, we discovered a small oasis, a single tree rising out of the sand by the edge of a pool. No matter how far we ventured, our journeys only ever led us in circles back to this place. In one sense, we were lucky to find it, for this haven provided just enough nourishment to keep us alive over all these long years.

"The affliction we suffered was prolonged and persistent. I am ashamed to say we did not rectify it quickly, or entirely on our own. Long did we wander the desert in a bitter resentment, one that we swore was caused by the actions of others. But eventually, the spell began to loosen its grip. In all that time, we had little else to do but reflect upon our deeds, and our acrimony turned from outward to inward.

"We were still unable to comprehend the change that overtook you so many years ago by the sea; but nevertheless, we came to know that our own actions were the reason we had lost you. After long ages of decay and renewal, nourished by the only source of water available, we eventually did come to understand your transformation.

"Not only did we lose you that day; we lost the one whom we sought with you, as one together. Having shrouded the sight of our two greatest beacons, we lost all hope, and our spirits fell further into anguish."

"But how did you come to find me?" asked Animulus again, still greatly aware of the need for haste.

"Only two days ago, we were haunted by an apparition of the same man who was laid upon the stone of Expiatio – or rather, the same man, but different. We had wandered high atop a dune, far from our oasis, and at last we saw the only other landmark we had ever seen in all our years trapped in the desert. Talionis towered over the dunes, far away in the distance. Lava erupted violently from its summit. The sky went gray, and horror overtook us at the sight of the ghost before us.

"We knew that the day of our judgement had finally come, but we quivered most of all out of the knowledge that we deserved whatever vengeance this shade might impose upon us. Yet, to our surprise, the spirit showed us mercy. He turned to face Talionis, and with the gentle waving of his hands, the violent explosions calmed in an instant before our very eyes."

Animulus balked at the resemblance to his own experience, but this was a part of his story he'd conveniently left out in recounting it to his brothers. Cerebrus noticed his reaction but continued without pause.

"He told us that all hope was not lost, and that the one we sought so long ago still longed to make our acquaintance. He spoke in cryptic words and verse, but we gathered that our path to redemption lay in the same place by the sea that we had left so long ago.

"We would not be able to make the journey alone, he said. So too did he tell us how we might escape the desert and find you again at last. And so here we are, standing in the rain on the dusty Ashlands of Talionis, while the sky shines blue over our destination to the south."

Truly, the Tempest beat down on them; but rather than driving Animulus onward, the unending storm had finally chilled him to the core.

"Are you not ready, brother?" asked Cerebrus.

Time passed. Animulus didn't answer directly, for he debated the very same question. He was stuck on the irony of their ill-fated journey. At last, he spoke slowly of the place they had left.

"We were already there, so long ago, though we knew it not," he said. "Surely you remember how we came to that place. We awoke from a strange enchantment on the far side of these desolate reaches, arriving effortlessly – yet against our will – at the place where we now need above all to go. And yet, it's not clear that we even know the way."

His brothers tried to urge him to embark a second time; but for a second time, Animulus did not budge. His expression was grave, and he had not finished his piece. Finding their destination was no trivial matter, but it was not the root of their problems.

"None of us truly know what awaits us at the far end of this desert," he said. "But I do know that it is not to be taken lightly. The last time we visited this place, it led to a schism that took many years and the workings of some untold serendipity to amend. We cannot falter this time, brothers. I am certain it would prove to be to our final ruin."

Without speaking a word, both of his brothers fell to one knee, in deference and fealty to the guidance of Animulus. He smiled, but he shook his head, and he motioned to his brothers to rise from where they knelt. The grave expression on his face had transformed into firm conviction.

Animulus grasped each brother by the shoulder. And in understanding this gesture, each brother did the same, as before when they were first so joyfully reconciled. There stood the Heretics of Inanimis, united in a trinity at the entrance to Immolatio. Yet even in the face of their rising morale, the sea was a long way away, and it would prove to be a tedious walk.

7.8 \ Proof of Perfidy

Sobrius crept along the side of the building to avoid being seen. After a long journey, he had finally arrived at the headquarters of the Department of Metageophysical Inquiries.

It must be here, he assured himself. *I need to find whatever proof I can.*

How he had escaped detection for so long, he did not know; for Sobrius was a man of diplomacy, not espionage. Guards filled the streets, passing from one block to the next, constantly circling through the frigid rain like sharks that have tasted a faint whiff of blood.

Still, he knew the streets of the city well, for unlike other members of the Council, Sobrius had always been keen to leave the Council Chamber and mingle with the "lesser" peoples of the city. There, he would do something unpleasant and unthinkable to most: he would speak to the people directly, to survey their needs and desires. Others were content to sit in the comfort of the chamber and speculate about what they assumed — perhaps wished — the wishes of the people were.

While never trained in the art of secrecy, Sobrius had a sharp mind and perceptive intuition. From the innermost station where the captives had escaped, he descended the stairs to the ground level for his return to the inner city. An aristocrat of Inanimis would never dream of stooping to such unsightly means, even in dire circumstances, and he hoped to use this preconception to travel unseen.

When he reached the great walls of the inner city, he knew there would be no chance of entering it by gate. At the base of the wall, however, there was an opening to a maintenance tunnel, which allowed access to the wall's infrastructure and the bowels of the city beyond them. In actuality, Sobrius knew the underbelly of the city well; having served so long on the Council, he had been privileged to countless details of city functioning that most ignored gladly. He squeezed between the bars of the grate and made his way through the darkness toward the heart of the city.

On arriving there, he navigated the maze of tunnels to an exit point as near to the DMI as he could estimate. It was not easy to do so from memory, having only his crude approximation of distances to guide him through the unvarying shafts. When he got as close as he could guess, he lifted the lid of an access porthole just enough to peek his eyes out.

Sobrius waited, scanning the streets and eager for them to clear. He had little time, but he exercised restraint — patiently watching the rhythm of countless cycles of guards, even calculating the average duration between them. At last, there came another lull, and he took his chance. Popping out at street level, he navigated the lesser-traveled side streets and alleys, staying close to the buildings and keeping a keen eye on all directions.

He moved slowly, and only when he was completely convinced that all was clear. In such a way did he inhibit the sharks from catching his scent. And now, he was finally closing in on the door to the answers he sought. Knowing that there would be no means of concealing himself any longer, he swung open the door and burst into the office like a powerful breeze.

His plan had gone surprisingly well so far, but to his great chagrin, the office was completely abandoned – the inside burned to a crisp, to avoid anyone such as him from snooping around too closely. He rummaged briefly through the disorder but found nothing of any value. The hope that had sprouted from making it this far now wilted again with a sad realization.

Prodigus had beaten him to the punch.

He cracked the door to assess the streets for his exit, but in doing so, he noticed the steady flashing of a red light casting down upon his arms. The alarm shining on him from above, he inspected the doorway closer; it was then that he noticed the magnetic detector on the frame, which in his haste had escaped his own detection.

He tried to think on the fly. The sharks would no doubt be arriving any instant, and there was no hope of escape should he choose to hide out in the office. Sobrius took to the streets and tried to sneak away via the same clandestine route by which he had come. As he rounded the corner, guards were already closing in on him from that direction, and quickly.

Far from inconspicuous, the instant he turned the corner, he reeled around again in the other direction. And in that brief moment, more guards had now made their way onto the street in front of the office. They were closing in just as quickly. Before he had even one more moment to think, the guards had converged on him from both directions.

He had no choice.

He pulled the weapon from his side and aimed to discharge it at the first guard in his way. The device clicked, but nothing happened. The guard leapt at him, but somehow, he managed to slide out of the way. He tried for a second shot, but the device only clicked with resistance a second time.

The guards slowly stepped inward as Sobrius stared at the device, in the feeble hope of discerning the problem in too short a time. At last, one reached in, grabbed the side of the weapon, wrenched it over both of their heads, and laughed at the fugitive's pathetic attempts at heroism.

"You have to hold here – and here – at the same time with these two fingers," mocked the guard. He pointed as he spoke, and showed the former Councilor how to discharge the weapon while they grasped it together in a stalemate, the tip aiming safely up and away from any guards.

A bolt of electricity fired back upward at the lightning flashing in the clouds. The guard ripped the weapon from his hands, made sure the dial was where he wanted it, and immobilized his prisoner.

After all, Sobrius was a man of diplomacy, not espionage.

7.9 \ Sabotage and Subterfuge

"What do you mean it isn't working?" asked Prodigus frantically.

He may have forged the numbers to underestimate its consequences, but he had been unequivocally confident in his ability to shatter the Veil.

"I'm sorry, sir," said his most trusted deputy, a man by the name of Stultus. "Our readings have leveled off. The mountain isn't responding."

Davis smiled wherever he sat, watching from afar as the tension mounted in the office of the DMI the day before.

"Well try again!" shouted Prodigus.

His patience was wearing thin at the unexpected unraveling of so many facets of his plan, and he was no longer always able to disguise his contemptible disposition. There were only a few key members of the DMI with him in their headquarters, for he had arranged it that anyone who could serve as an obstacle was stationed at the outer posts, where he could be certain they would not interfere with his plans.

"I've checked dozens of times already, sir," said Stultus as he stared into the control center. "The emitters are all operating at maximum capacity. The detectors appear to be working just fine. We were making steady progress for days, so the system had clearly been working."

"Then why the sudden change?" Prodigus snapped back.

"I can't say, sir. The mountain simply isn't responding anymore."

Prodigus turned away from the console and paced the floor of the office, his face cast into scorn. Panic brewed beneath the surface, but for now it was masked to his compatriots as only the disdain for the failure of their plan. The other members of the DMI looked around at one another doubtfully, but none said any word, as none had any idea what to do.

The silence was quickly broken by the door of the office swinging open; a courier stepped inside and held forth a folded piece of paper, its crease sealed in green wax.

"Prodigus, sir: this came for you," said the courier. "It arrived at the gate and we brought it as quickly as we could."

"Delivered by whom?" he asked dubiously, for he was not expecting any such form of communication.

"I do not know, sir."

"Then you are of no more use to me," he sneered. "That will be all."

He grabbed the paper forcefully, still frustrated at the situation slipping out of his control. The courier bowed, turned, and left the office at once. Prodigus cast a sideways glance at Stultus and the others, and turned his back to them all as he opened the note.

Prodigus,

> *Try as you may, you shall never succeed*
> *Your work is in vain, as there is no such need*
> *While the freedom you seek will be justly achieved*
> *Freedom cannot be gained how you envisioned the deed*

> *You may find me at the Grove of the Sentient Sage.*

> *As the one is Many, so are the many One,*

> *The Sage of Salvation*

"At last!" shouted Prodigus as he crumpled the note in his hand. *Perhaps all this time has not been in vain,* he brooded silently.

As he came to his senses, he realized just how loudly he had exclaimed in exultation. He looked back over his shoulder to find his aides curious and confused. He turned back to the men at the console and adapted quickly to the changing scenario.

"I regret to inform you that our plan has fallen victim to sabotage, by others of the Trepidus in league with the traitors we already captured."

"That's terrible news," said Stultus earnestly. "What was so amusing?"

"Did you not hear me?" he said, his voice dripping with ire. He would not suffer to be questioned now. "We have uncovered this plot; and so have I found a way to sway the momentum back in our favor."

Prodigus scanned his eyes around the DMI office to give the impression that he was thinking long and hard about his situation. In fact, he knew perfectly well what he was about to ask the men to do.

"Burn everything," he said methodically. "We cannot let any more information fall into the hands of the enemy. When you've finished, return to your normal duties until you hear from me again. These events are to be considered fully classified: you are not to speak about them to anyone – not even your fellow members of the DMI – until our work is resolved and we have a final briefing together. If anyone asks about the office, you will deny any knowledge of its condition. Know that, as always, a breach of classified information is considered an act of High Treason, and you will be held accountable to the full extent of the punishment. Is that understood?"

The men each timidly agreed to the terms of their orders and began nervously destroying every aspect of the office as instructed. Prodigus bid them farewell and left the room in a manic dash.

Davis opened his eyes and grinned widely.
Now it is only a matter of patience.

7.10 \ The Sage of Salvation

When three whole days had passed since the eruption of the Great Volcano came to an unexpected standstill, Prodigus closed in on the Grove of the Sentient Sage. Unbeknownst to him, however, so did many others.

In this age of the world, the grove was little more than a gaunt buffer of trees surrounding a desolate clearing. The high railwalls of Inanimis enclosed the area on all sides as they stretched westward. This was a key routing point and a highly traveled area, and the colossal structures parted only temporarily in avoidance of this small and lifeless space.

The grove was one of the few places spared from the concrete so recklessly applied in the outer reaches, for it had been zoned as an archeological site of significance by the Department of Anthropology. When surveying the area many years beforehand, they uncovered a fire pit in the center. This would have mattered little on its own, but the team had also unearthed an ancient stone tablet with an incoherent verse, signed by the mysterious figure for whom the grove was named. At the time, the grove was the frontier of city expansion; but here it was now, consumed on all sides in the midst of the monster.

The brutal Tempest still raged in the lands around the grove, though oddly it no longer did so here. Somehow, the storm directly overhead had cleared. The moon beamed brightly through the ring of clouds; and to the great perplexity of the Department of Astral Studies, it was still full. Having waxed completely as expected, for the first time ever, it had failed to wane.

In the ancient pit in the center of the grove roared a fire. A single boulder sat by its side, and atop the boulder sat a small boy. He was young, and pure; and while he was not the same, he bore a striking resemblance to the Sage whom Davis had met so long ago in this very same place. For now, the scene was serene, for the lockdown had ceased almost all travel along the walls. In the absence of the madness, it was almost like in ancient times, when there was naught to hear but the gentle sounds of the night, and naught to see but the flicker of a fire and the moonlit sky above.

But this peace was not to last. Out from the trees at the edge of the clearing stepped Prodigus. The Blade of Entitlement glistened in the light.

"Hello," said the boy without turning around. Prodigus didn't answer, but crept stealthily inward toward the center. "Fire is a mysterious force, is it not?" continued the boy. "It bears so much destruction; and yet, out of it eventually comes rebirth. Though it may disintegrate an entire forest, from the ashes comes new life, springing forth from their seeds after having waited so long in the soil for their liberation. In truth, fire does not destroy anything; it simply changes the form of the forms that it touches."

The man's fingers rippled along the sweaty hilt of the blade as he gripped it. Still, the boy did not turn. Prodigus stepped nervously forward, unsure of what to expect from what seemed like so easy an answer.

"So too do we find with the other forms of Disorder," said the boy. "They are inherently contrary to the plans of their inverse; but they push Order to change — to evolve — to continue to grow."

Prodigus was almost within reach of the boy, and the man took care to make few sudden movements. He wanted to end this swiftly and surely. The boy just continued his thought as he stared at the fire, perfectly complacent.

"Thus, the cycle continues in its way: building, and breaking, and building anew."

> No one force is right, nor is either force wrong
> They ebb and they flow, and the ocean rolls on
> While the fire yields ashes born out of the flesh
> Through the ashes is passed the essence redressed

The boy spoke softly, innocently, in juvenile rhyme — a whisper barely audible to Prodigus as he snuck inward to clutch his glorious destiny from the palm of the universe itself. The child still stared peacefully into the fire.

Prodigus pulled his arm back slowly, poising it for a single swift plunge, and drove the dagger deep into the boy's back. The blade pierced straight through his heart; the tip peered out from the front of his chest. Prodigus pushed his shoulders forward while pulling back upon the blade. His body slid lifelessly off the Blade of Entitlement and fell forward into the fire.

"You fool!" shouted a voice from high above.

Prodigus looked up to see a dark silhouette in the moonlight at the edge of the wall. He could not say to whom the voice belonged, but at this point he cared little: he had already succeeded in the dark task that would halt his unknown rival from ascending beyond the shackles of Limbus in his stead.

And as Prodigus looked upward, two other figures ran to the edge and joined the first. Without warning, the one in front leapt from the wall and soared down from the great height. The stranger crashed into the ground at the far end of the clearing, and the earth pulsed in a great wave that sped across the grove.

Prodigus was sent flying backwards as the surge passed beneath him; he shot upward through the air, landed with great force, and tumbled slowly to a stop. The blade flew from his hand upon striking the ground. Splayed out in the grass, Prodigus reached out discreetly to grab the dagger, and he slipped it slyly into his robes before rising.

As Prodigus came to his feet, Animulus stepped out into the light.

"I know what you are planning," he said, "for there is much I now see clearly. But you have failed, Prodigus. We have beaten you to the task before you even came to know what it would be."

"I take it you have rejoined your long-lost kin as a fully-fledged traitor of Inanimis," said Prodigus, buying time to discern what he could of these boastful words. He was self-obsessed and self-assured; but like his master, so too was he fearful and paranoid of any other who might dare to defy him.

Animulus did not respond; he simply held out a bright gem in his hand. It glowed with an insufferable brightness: a shade of irresistible red radiated throughout the grove, as dark as fresh blood and yet as bright as the sunset.

"You may have slain the boy," said Animulus, "but you will never find salvation without this."

Prodigus recoiled at the brightness, for the sight of it burned his eyes and instilled in him a trepidation he never knew was possible. Despite the unnerving sensation at the sight of the jewel, he was drawn by its allure all the same. He longed for it. He lusted for it. He would do anything to have it in his grasp. He despised and distrusted its bearer so greatly, but Prodigus believed him when he said that all his ambitions were in vain without it.

"You lie," said Prodigus, trying but failing to hide his intrigue.

"You may think what you wish," said Animulus. "But if you doubt me, it is only because you know nothing of this relic."

Animulus gazed into the gem in his outstretched hand, his thoughts drawing inward. Prodigus saw his chance to lessen the distance between them. He began to slowly meander closer, unassertive, both hands clearly visible as the dagger rested dutifully, concealed under his robes.

"This is the Heart of Praestes," said Animulus, lost deep in its light. "It belonged to the most powerful creature Limbus has ever known. Yet now... here it is, in my possession." His voice slowed as he spoke, genuinely struck in this instant by an abrupt realization of all he had gained.

Prodigus laughed loudly. He knew the legends concerning the mythical beast, but he cared little for mythology. He may have doubted the stone's origin, but that didn't detract from its appeal. Whatever it was, it unleashed a flood of the abundant greed brooding within him. He needed it, for it quite obviously possessed an incredible power that he didn't yet understand.

"The trinkets of your false idols are entirely inconsequential to me," he said, still moving steadily inward. With each step closer Prodigus came to it, the more the jewel enticed him. With each look he dared to cast at its aura, the more it clouded his capacity for rational thought.

"Only by unlocking its potential can one ever find transcendence," said Animulus, and he knew he spoke no lie. He knew as well that his wager was well warranted, and that his rival was consumed by an envy he could not defy. "It is a pity you spent your time toying with inane experiments and ill-fated excursions, when the answer you sought sits right here in my hand."

Prodigus continued advancing, and by the time Animulus was taunting him, he was but one quick motion away from possessing the thing he now desired above all else. He squinted in the brightness emanating from the stone, but Animulus kept his eyes fixed upon it, staring directly in its light and seeing nothing else.

"And a pity that, for so long, I had forgotten to search for it," said Animulus softly. His tone shifted from a boisterous taunt to the melancholic regret that so often comes with retrospection. All was silent.

Overpowered with lust, and with his enemy distracted, Prodigus saw his opportunity and seized it without reluctance or delay. Averting his eyes as much as he could from the blinding glow of the Heart of Praestes, he pulled the dagger from his robes and lunged forward at Animulus. The Blade of Entitlement again tasted the flesh of another: it plunged deep into the heart of the Scrutatorus and spilled the life out from within it.

Animulus staggered back. The gem slipped from his grip and fell to the ground. High atop the wall, both of the other Heretics grabbed their chests and staggered as well, step for step with their brother in the grove so far below. Animulus struggled for air, his lungs whistling as they came to terms with the gaping hole in his torso.

He looked down at his wound, placed his own hand on the treacherous hilt, and pulled the blade from his body. His brothers jerked accordingly as the dagger was removed from its position. They looked at each other one last time in love, and they smiled with a shrewd look of approval.

"I hope you find what we all need to find," said Animulus, barely able to speak through shallow breaths as the air escaped his lungs. They were the last words that Limbus would ever hear him utter.

He stumbled backward one last time and let the blade fall from his grip. It stabbed straight downward and stuck into the ground. And as Animulus collapsed, so did his brothers likewise fall, tumbling forward from the wall and plummeting to their doom. Thus were the Heretics slain in a single fell strike, and the Heart of Praestes surrendered to their foe.

Prodigus showed neither surprise nor remorse. He stepped calmly forward to where the jewel had come to rest and picked up his prize so that he might finally claim it.

Only by unlocking its potential can one ever hope to break the Veil, he repeated, recalling the words of Animulus as best he could – although they were not verbatim. Glancing down at the place where the blade had come to rest, he recalled also the words of the serpent. *With it might I find my destiny,* he repeated. He bent over to grab the dagger and wiped the blood from the blade with his cloak.

The Heart of Praestes had grown dim in the hands of its captor, and Prodigus peered into it deeply, in search of the source of the elusive light. Its absence only fueled his desire to discover the secrets hidden within. Unable to draw the light out, he sought to unleash it in the only way he knew how. He placed it on the boulder by the fire and lifted the dagger overhead, but he was interrupted yet again by another unexpected voice.

"Come quick!" shouted another obscure figure on the wall. "Sure enough – the traitor is below in the grove."

Fida turned away from the wall and rallied her peers behind herself. Dozens rushed to the edge; then hundreds; then more. The entire Council of Inanimis flocked to the walls at the grove's perimeter, and countless people of the city besides – the Trepidus and their followers on one side, the Interritus and their allies on the other.

Finding Modicus dead on the ground, the crowd began to unravel. Some wept, while others shouted for revenge; some implored their peers to be patient, while others urged them to take immediate action. The mayhem on the wall was broken by one voice that rose out above the rest.

"Silence!" it shouted. And as it commanded, so the people obeyed.

Davis stepped out from the trees at the edge of the grove. He looked up to the people of Limbus, rather than out at the villain before him. The echoes of his voice faded away, escaping the walls and drifting out across the land. When they vanished completely, there was not a sound that could be heard. There was nothing but stillness.

"I brought you all here so that we might find peace, not slip back into the turmoil that so easily consumes us." All were silent except for him, as they waited for this undeniable mystic to declare what he might. "Now," said Davis patiently, "Sobrius: step forward and present the will of the people."

Out of the crowd stepped the reinstated Council Chair. And arriving at the edge, he looked down to see his fallen kinsman below. He shed a tear for his passing; and for a time, he could not bring himself to move past it.

Prodigus, partly amazed by the great gathering of Inanimis, said nothing for now. He waited in silence – not out of respect, nor even for a desire to hear their accusations before discerning how he might refute them. Instead, he waited for them to present their case, so that he might raise all their hopes to the highest possible level before succeeding in his scheme before their very eyes.

"Prodigus of Inanimis," said Sobrius at last. "You are charged with High Treason by the people of the city. If you offer yourself willfully, you might find the punishment more merciful than that which you would have offered. How do you reply?"

Lifting his head to find Sobrius looking down on him, as it had ever felt to the man, Prodigus knew more disdain for him now than ever before – a feat he would have hardly thought possible. He laughed viciously, with a merciless hiss, sounding more like the serpent that encouraged the evil within him to grow than the human who possessed it in the first place.

"How do I reply?" scoffed Prodigus. "You have no grounds to accuse me of such an atrocity. How is it that the people of the city fell ill to your mutiny? How do they not see this ploy to obtain all the power for yourself?"

Prodigus felt no need to justify his deeds before fulfilling his plot; but in spite of this, his arrogance lobbied him to try, if only for the sport of it. He thought he could best them on both battlefields, and so would he achieve all the more honor for himself, ere the end of all things.

"We know all you have done," said Sobrius. "Once it was clear that your plan would lead to our mutual destruction, it was only a matter of time before your trusted accomplices became our willing informants. We know you planned all along to break the Veil. We know you forged the project data and destroyed the DMI office to eliminate the evidence. We know you wrongfully imprisoned two members of the Council, and that you planned to assassinate them after their detainment – a plan that was only foiled by their escape." He glanced at his fallen friend, and Sobrius faltered, fighting back against the breaking point. "And last: we know that you murdered Modicus on this very evening, for the moonlight still shines on his remains."

Prodigus feigned respect for the diligence of his nemesis, nodding his head as if impressed by the work they had put in to uncovering his plots. But being unable to refute their evidence would hardly diminish his intent.

"I see," he said pragmatically. "Then it will trouble you to know that your hero Modicus was no different than me in the end. If he had only been as resourceful as I am, I have no doubt it would be me lying dead in the moonlight. He would have taken for himself what we all would desire. As it happened, he only brought me the very key I needed to finish what I've started. Only one may enter through the door, and you are too late to stop me! I shall leave this place. I shall transcend to the Land Beyond, while all of you – and all of Limbus – are drowned in fire."

He looked again to the Heart of Praestes lying on the rock and lifted the dagger from his side. He turned his back to Sobrius and prepared to strike; but a different voice spoke his name, and commanded him to turn. It was a voice that had already spoken, and it was one whose willpower he could not resist. He turned around slowly, and unwillingly, straining his neck while wrestling against the pull of this voice from afar.

"Put down the dagger, Prodigus," said Davis. "It won't cost you anything but a small sliver of your ample pride."

This voice was one he had never heard before today, and yet it was familiar. And though it spoke with an authority he had never yet faced in Limbus, Prodigus would not give in freely or without a fight.

"And who are you, old fool?" he asked, turning to this new foe across the clearing. "You dare think yourself capable of contending with me?"

Davis simply laughed, but it filled all of Limbus with a deafening rumble which caused the earth itself to quake.

"You should know the name of Davis, for the serpent you serve no doubt feared it." He tapped his staff to the ground and Prodigus stumbled at the force it sent shaking through the grove. "With all of your tampering, you could not get the mountain to offer so much as a murmur; yet I am the one to whom the Great Volcano bows!"

He raised his hand through the air and a column of lava rose from the crater of Talionis. It extended hundreds of feet into the sky, but it neither spread nor fell, only paused for an instant at its apex. And as Davis cast his hand down again, the lava was thrust back into the crater.

In that same moment, at each of the outer stations of the DMI – the places closest to the mountain's nerves – the ground cracked, and lava exploded up into the air, forming pillars that gushed out like great fiery geysers. The columns filled the sky in all directions, merging with the raging Tempest and illuminating the entire atmosphere with a dreadful red that threatened to cast the whole world into ruin. The people on the walls averted their eyes in horror at the power of this apocalyptic sorcerer – one whom they had, for some reason, followed here to their own demise.

And in that moment, Davis was aware that he could break the earth itself in half if he so desired. He closed his eyes, and in the darkness saw a vision of the island of Amadea. He knew the tyrant who had ruled there in infamy, having conquered the world, for a time, until it was drowned in an inconceivable torrent. He hung his head, and the lava streaming forth from the ground fell back into its rightful abode.

"The world as we know it will come to an end if the Veil is broken, Prodigus," said Davis. "And still you would seek to enter through a door you cannot even open, let alone understand."

Never one to easily endure being humbled, Prodigus was nevertheless impressed by the inimitable display of power; but instead of instilling fear at the prospect of falling victim to it, the demonstration only instilled in him a greater desire to achieve it for himself.

"If it were not to be me, the privilege would only pass to someone else," he replied. To his credit, he believed it completely. "It might as well be me."

Davis sighed at his misunderstanding.

"In a sense, you are correct: only one may enter. But that does not mean that any one of us may enter."

Prodigus had now heard enough, for here was an explicit confession that Davis sought only to steal from him the privilege that he had earned for himself.

"Then you have revealed your true motives to us all!" shouted Prodigus. He circled to address the whole crowd and bellowed at them in derision. "You follow this man to help him impede me? And yet here has he made it clear that all he wants is to supplant me in my actions, so that he might reap the benefits for himself. He is no different than me – no different than your precious Modicus. You have just heard him yourself. And you would follow him when he would cast you to the fires all the same?"

Turning back to Davis, he grinned sadistically and spoke in a manner that would have made the Lord proud.

"You are right, Davis," he said. "I do know your name, for Imperator warned me of your intentions. The Lord told me also that you are weak, and unable to enter the doorway without the aid of another."

Prodigus stepped to the side and pointed to the fire, where the body of the child was searing into ashes in the hot coals.

"Alas," said Prodigus, "I have killed the Sage you sought, and you shall never have your precious salvation."

Davis hung his head in mourning at the sight of the child, but he soon lifted his eyes to Prodigus.

"Your iniquity never ceases to amaze me," said Davis. "But that is not the Sage of Salvation..." – and total silence fell.

"...I am."

Prodigus looked back toward the fire, but in that brief moment, the body of the boy had vanished. Disbelief quickly turned into desperation. Knowing there was no longer anything to stop his rival from transcending through the Veil in his stead, Prodigus turned back to the gem and held fast to his hope. The jewel offered him freedom, and his only remaining choice was to take it by force.

He stood over the Heart of Custos and raised the dagger high above his head a final time with both hands. He closed his eyes and envisioned all the glory in the universe. Soon it would bow before him – and only him. His hands started shaking nervously, and he hesitated, as if suddenly fearing what transcendence might mean.

"Only one may enter," repeated Davis, but this wayward part of him was not listening. "Only one; but as the one is Many, so are the many One."

The man's hands shook even more forcefully where they hovered while holding the dagger; but as of yet, he did not act.

"Please, Prodigus," said Davis. "Do not let your greed turn to spite."

The shaking spread to his whole arm, and soon his legs too began to tremble. There was only one way out for him now, and he would finally be the one to take it.

"Shall only one of us go," asked Davis, "or shall we all go as One?"

Prodigus didn't take the time to answer, for he couldn't believe it was possible. He drove his hands downward in a vindictive stab, and the blade shattered the Heart of the Guardian where it rested.

The people of the city could not see what happened next, for a light far brighter than they had ever seen exploded out from the center of the grove. It spanned the whole width of the clearing, and its height extended through the gap in the clouds, piercing the sky and only ending far beyond it, if ever ending at all.

It took many moments to fade, but when the light finally departed, there was nothing left except the Blade of Entitlement, sticking straight out of the boulder. And there it would stay, trapped in stone, until the unmaking of the world.

∞∞∞∞∞ ∞∞ ∞∞ ∞∞∞∞∞

7.11 \ The Founding of Concordis

∞∞∞∞∞ ∞∞ ∞∞ ∞∞∞∞∞

"I don't understand," said Fida. "Prodigus is gone and yet we're still here. Surely we can't both have won."

"The world did not end," said Davis, "because the Veil was not broken. There is but one way through the door, and he had not the key. But your intuition was not wrong, Fida. Had you, the people of Inanimis, not succeeded in averting his scheme, the world would have ended indeed. Or perhaps I should say: it would have started again. All that we now know would be lost – all our tremendous progress wasted."

"And what of Prodigus?" she asked.

"Destroyed by his own malice, like the one who helped it flourish."

"And the Heart of Praestes?" asked Sobrius. "What of it? How did the brothers know it would serve as our salvation?"

"They sought long for the Guardian," said Davis. "And they came to know it well, once they found it in the end. The Scrutatorus did not know exactly how the Heart would bring about this end, but they had faith in its source. One way or another, it would have healed Prodigus of his affliction. Sadly, he chose the path that led to their shared annihilation."

"But how?" asked Fida. "How could a simple stone possess such power?"

"Do you not know?" said Davis, but kindly. "What Prodigus came to be is not unique to him. He had no greater capacity for selfishness than any of us, and he knew it; but that truth blinded him, for we are more than our capacities. For now, we are sentient creatures, and we may choose to act on our aptitudes or not. Prodigus chose one extreme, but it is not the only path. As for power, the stone is but a symbol – it has no power of its own. But a symbol might in time become a potent talisman of the force behind it. And in unleashing the force of his antithesis, his own force was negated.

"Yet as important as the Heart proved to be, it was not the only thing the brothers gained in Immolatio," said Davis. "In truth, it was not even the purpose of their visit. To their surprise, they found it there, high up on the cliff, barely visible in the sand, resting where a great wave had once raised it from the depths of the sea. They suspected it might help resolve the immediate threat at hand, but they knew that such a threat was merely a symptom of an underlying illness. The true purpose of their journey was to find the wisdom necessary to address the problem at its root."

Davis pulled a set of scrolls from his robes and handed them to Sobrius.

"The Guardian is known by many names," he continued. "It is Custos, overseer of Amadea; it is Vilicus, Praestes, and Ostiarius; it is Coerator, Satelles, and Claustritumus. It is the keeper of the Way, and it was the Way that it sought to bestow upon the brothers, and indeed upon us all."

And with these words, Davis nodded to the Council Chair.

320

Sobrius unfurled the first scroll and read it aloud for all to hear.

The Seven Tenets of the Collective Community

    1. Division of Labor and Contribution of Shared Goods
    2. Appropriate Allocation of Compiled Group Resources
    3. Mechanisms for Peer Monitoring and Conflict Resolution
    4. Transparency in Deeds, Motives, and Conflicts of Interest
    5. Genuine Collective Consensus in the Making of Decisions
    6. Shared Rituals for the Reinforcement of Group Cohesion
    7. Encouragement of Diversity in Character and Thought

Sobrius unfurled the second scroll and again read the contents aloud.

The Seven Tenets of Existence in Nature

    1. Foresight for the Consequences of Actions for the Self and Others
    2. Grateful Reception and Humble Provision of Services to Nature
    3. Willingness to Change with the Changing of the World
    4. Acceptance of the Inseparability of Separate Entities
    5. Acceptance of the Permanent Impermanence
    6. Acceptance of the Illusion of Individuals
    7. Reverence for All Forms of Creation

"The Guardian was reluctant to offer its teachings in this manner," laughed Davis. "It had this to say as it handed them to the Scrutatorus."

    It is not usually necessary to express these ideas in such a form,
    but humans have an insatiable reverence for dogma and doctrine.

"I like to think of them more as a method for our success," said Davis. "May the Dual Seven Tenets lead us all to the glorious realm that some might envision only for themselves, but which none could ever achieve on their own."

Davis turned from Sobrius and stood on the wall between both factions of Inanimis. He spoke so that all could hear, in the voice that resonated through every facet of Limbus.

"Long have you sought to function well within your walls, and you have failed in as many ways as you have succeeded. Long have you also sought to function providently in the world outside those walls, and for every stride in which you made great progress, there remain two strides left to take.

"Let it never be forgotten that it was the ailments of Inanimis which almost brought an entire era of the world to its tragic end here today. And yet, so too was it the integrity of the same people that prevented this sad potential from becoming our reality."

Sobrius had been greatly moved by the contents of these teachings. He didn't understand their full depth – not yet – but he knew instinctively that these Tenets would serve as a scaffold on which they could forge a new era. And even in this bright and optimistic hour, his thoughts still dwelt with Modicus. It pained him immensely to know that his old friend had offered his life for the wellbeing of their city, a place he both loved and loathed so greatly. But it was for this reason that Sobrius knew that his sacrifice could not be in vain. Inspired as well by the words of Davis, the Council Chair stepped forward to address the people of the world in much the same way.

"Too long have we been divided as a people, arguing blindly among ourselves while the proper course of action passes us by. Let the city no longer consist of Interritus and Trepidus. From this day forth, each Councilor, and indeed each citizen, is to use their own good judgement and the mind granted uniquely to them, to chart our way forward in good faith, together as one people. Nay, we shall not comprise separate halves of the city of Inanimis; let us instead be united as the people of Concordis!"

The crowd erupted in a cheer, and for now, at least, they had harmony.

"And too long have we put our own interests first," he continued, "and so far above the interests of us all. Let us no longer consider only what we may do to further our own gains; let us consider how our individual gains may be furthered by first aiding each other.

"And lastly, for far too long we have cared far too little for the way in which we exist in our world. Too long have we denied the consequences of our actions, while the effects of our deeds run unchecked, but not unpunished. Let us work together, as we have never done before, to serve not only ourselves and each other, but the good of all of Limbus – for what is good for the whole will aid all of its parts."

Davis smiled, for he remembered hearing words of that sort before; and he was glad that, through it all, they had made an impression. He looked at these people on the wall around him, unified in purpose at last. And despite knowing their failings, a hope grew within him. Each still inevitably possessed all the flaws with which the individual is prone to be afflicted; but perhaps in working together under a novel framework, the flaws of the few might not be allowed to run rampant, to the detriment of the many.

Even after all these trials and tribulations, the true work was only just beginning. In this moment, however, Davis suspected that there was little more he could do. It would take the hands of time and the conviction of the people of Concordis to live up to their name. More importantly, he had a nagging sensation that he had somewhere to be.

Davis closed his eyes, and when he opened them again, he was sitting on a large rock by the sea, at the edge of a bay, far in the north of Limbus. There was still a doorway to enter; and it was true that, despite all his great strengths, he needed the help of another.

EPILOGUE \ PERIGEE

The fish in the pool below turned about gracefully in the same principal pattern, circling in the motion of an endless figure-eight. An entire age of the world had taken place, flashing before the man's eyes in the span of a single day. The fish moved slowly, like the building of a wave before breaking at the crest.

On this day, however, like no other day before, the crest broke.

Davis leapt down from the rock and reached his hands into the pool. He scooped the fish up, lifted it out of the water, and placed it on the far side of the bare rock isolating it from the rest of the ocean.

The fish swam off in the direction of the sunset far away, a single small creature in an Infinite Sea. As it vanished out of sight, Davis heard the voice of the Guardian resounding in his head.

Soon this time will pass, and then we'll have peace at last...

We will surely miss you, though we know we are with you
Wherever we may go – wherever the wind may blow
Wait for us down below, and soon, we all too will go
To give back what we've grasped, and then we'll have peace at last

It seems our cruel fate, but it is ours nonetheless
From a different view, we couldn't have been more blessed
So, take comfort with our soul out on the breeze
Deep down in the roots; up in the rustling leaves

Soon this time will pass, and then we'll have peace at last
When you have asked each last question that you could ask
Lay down in this warm grass, and let go of what you've grasped
Then all this time will have passed, and then we'll find peace at last...

The voice eventually faded away as it repeated the melodic words –
– arriving at the beginning each time that it came to the end.

Davis climbed the beach and headed toward the rolling hills covered in beautiful purple flowers. He suspected that the door to Amadea might have finally been opened. As he stepped up to the grass at the edge of the beach, he looked out over the field and reflected on the sheer number of blossoms.

The flowers fluttered before him in the breeze, and they filled the entire valley. They climbed up the long slope, all the way to the forest far to the east; and to both the north and south, they stretched as far as he could see.

And yet, here at the westernmost edge of the field, there was a small depression in the sandy substrate, and it had not yet given rise to a flower. No doubt coming from far away in the depths of the unbounded ocean, he again heard the gentle voice of the Guardian in his mind.

"Small drops of water in the river know not that all their disparate forms in truth form one cohesive body," said the voice. "They know not the nature of the bonds that bind them to their kindred. And still, they cling tightly to each other as they make their way downstream.

"In spite of their efforts, and in part due to them, some are pushed or pulled away from one another, sundered into separate channels as the river breaks upon the delta. They have no sense of the ocean that awaits them as they tumble blindly along; and yet, despite all of its divisions, this broken river will find its way to the sea.

"So it is that you have come to the end of your journey, and it is time for you to leave this realm. Step down into the earth and find a place you have never been before — or rather, a form in which you have yet to be expressed — and while it is ever-changing and forever-anew, it may seem like home indeed."

And now it was evident that the ground before Davis had opened wide to embrace him, and he trusted where it led. He kneeled first to the grass, then calmly crawled into the hollow and placed his back against the earth.

The sun continued its serene decline in the western sky, and the gentle breeze began to build. The soft, sandy soil slowly stirred in the mounting wind, and grains gradually collected in the cracks between parts of his body.

When the last sand stopped its tumbling and came to a leisurely rest atop the mound, a small green shoot emerged from the center. A sole bud formed at the apex of the stem, and when it had grown to its full height, the petals unfolded to reveal a stunning purple flower.

Its name was *Amadea.*

The sun sank behind the horizon for one final farewell, and swimming straight toward that astral body — should any have been there to witness it — was the faint silhouette of a singular fish. Its tail undulated from side to side, until it crossed over the furthest horizon and was never seen again.

And then, there was not a soul left in Limbus, for they had all departed together. The strong found the weak; the bold found the meek; the selfish found the selfless; the darkness met the light. Together they all mingled — all the forces of the world — surging and receding, until they slowly disappeared and there was nothing left at all.

Davis opened his eyes for the final moment of existence as he knew it. Without any effort of his own, they were locked into those of his beloved wife Constance. She was staring through the glass pane on the surgical bay door, grieving and sobbing in sorrow. Doctors wriggled their hands around his mangled arteries, shouting this or that at each other in a panic to save his fleeting, fleeing life.

Davis didn't understand a single word they were saying, for there was only one left he even knew. It was a far cry from the last thought he'd experienced in his previous few moments of consciousness, as he sped down the hospital hallway, reveling in the hatred he felt for his fellow victim.

He struggled through the agony smothering every other one of his worldly sensations, and uttered the last thing he would ever say. Staring at Constance, he knew this sole remaining word was the only one he needed – for her, and for everyone else to whom he far too seldom spoke it.

He wheezed this last fateful gasp, a single wispy lament as the air in his lungs escaped him, and the life left his body to start cooling on the table. There was an eerie silence in the room, and eventually the doctors stopped fidgeting altogether.

"Time of Death – 7:07 AM," said the doctor. She turned to take off her gloves and tossed them lightly in the trash. "I'm sorry," she said to Constance as she walked out of the surgical bay with her head held low. "There was nothing else I could do."

THE LESSER IS SHED...

An Independent Author's Humble Request

I am a proud member of the Alliance of Independent Authors (ALLi), a professional organization for the advancement of ethical independent publishing. Please support authors by purchasing products directly from their website, not distributing or using pirated (stolen) materials, and helping to otherwise combat unfair and unethical publishing practices.

I wrote this book with no intention of ever selling it. I simply needed to write it, as a means of curating my reflections on life, death, society, and evolution. But now that it's written, I just want people to enjoy it – to think about the ideas within, and to talk about them with friend and foe alike.

But as an independent publisher, the odds are stacked against me in that endeavor. "Indie" authors certainly need to write books that are worth reading in order to be successful; but we also need our readers to be our champions if they deem that to be so. Thus, if you enjoyed this book, I ask only that you please provide a fair online review wherever you purchased it, and recommend it to friends, family – perhaps even your nemeses.

And to everyone who made it all this way to the "back matter..."

Honestly – from the bottom of my heart – Thank You.

About the Art

The cover is a highly zoomed-in plot of the Mandelbrot Set (a fractal). The spiral tree in the back matter is called a Glynn fractal, which appear under specific parameters of the Julia Set. Both were plotted with code written by Christopher Williams (http://usefuljs.net/fractals) and then digitally modified. The section dividers depict a Barnsley Fern, plotted (in R) and then digitally modified. All the artistic and design elements were created by the author.

Acknowledgements

Thanks to Julie Chouinard, Jon and Beata Chouinard, Glenn and Peggy Chouinard, Phil Schapker, Barbara and John Donovan, Jeff Lewis, Matt Hess, and many others for their love, support, feedback, and/or for patiently tolerating my obsession with this project over the last eight years. In particular, my brothers Jon and Phil bore the brunt of my rambling and provided a great deal of helpful input. Julie Chouinard deserves the most praise of all, for her incredible understanding as I toiled away on this passion through so many years. Beyond that, I want to thank all the countless, nameless people who gave me what I have – and helped me grow.

A few lines of a song by John Lennon and Paul McCartney appear on page 196 under an explicit "Fair Use" claim. It's called "All You Need Is Love."

And it's true.

ABOUT THE AUTHOR

Adam James Chouinard is a person, teacher, scientist, musician, author, and independent publisher based in Eugene, Oregon. Adam earned a B.S. in Marine & Freshwater Biology and M.S. in Zoology from the University of New Hampshire, as well as a Ph.D. in Zoology from Oregon State University. He currently teaches biology, animal behavior, evolution, and more at his alma mater. In his parallel life, Adam founded Proavia Press as an outlet for exploring Big Questions through the synthesis of Scientific Inquiry and Artistic Expression.

There is meaning in the madness. Our job is to find it.
Let's connect at proaviapress.com

AUTHOR'S NOTE

As a biologist, I am fascinated with what it means to be alive, and what those insights mean for our lives, every single day. But there are many ways of knowing, and just as many ways of being. Despite some of the narrative elements, this modern mythology does not pretend to ascribe "The Way." Rather than presume to have all the answers, this story is meant solely as a tool for us to keep asking some of the questions that (I think) matter most.

Who are we? Why are we here?

What does it mean to be alive? And to die?

What is an individual? A society? What could they be?

How can we ensure that cooperation triumphs over conflict?

How should we engage with the broader world around us?

Where do we come from? And where are we going?

What is the fabled Meaning of Life?

I think I finally found mine.

What's yours?

www.ingramcontent.com/pod-product-compliance
Lightning Source LLC
Chambersburg PA
CBHW071754110726
47908CB00006B/1804